Casual Executions

Assassination in Arizona

William Heuisler

Dear Linda & Jim
Two of my dearest friends
You'd better like this Book!
Love, Bill

ISBN: 1-4392-1464-6
ISBN-13: 9781439214640
Visit www.booksurge.com to order additional copies.

Author Bio:

The author, former Marine, ex-Tucson cop, Director of an Arizona Investigative Agency and chief investigator for the Governor of Arizona in the late '80s, investigated certain political aspects of the Don Bolles murder, worked briefly for Viola Faber's family on their mother's hit and run and has been involved in the rescue of racing Greyhounds for twenty years.

Nor ever be ashamed
So we be named,
Press men,
Slaves of the lamp,
Servants of light.

– *Sir Edwin Arnold*

This novel is dedicated to *Arizona Republic* reporter,
Don Bolles,
who was killed in a car bombing, June 2nd, 1976.

PROLOGUE

THE BEAST

Viola Faber should have been more careful crossing the street.

As she stepped off the curb onto the crosswalk in front of the supermarket her mind was on her daughter. Grace was coming over for dinner to celebrate her week-old promotion to Editorial at the *Arizona Register.* Viola was so proud; the *Register* was the biggest newspaper in Arizona. *So much to do before she arrives!*

The old lady hoisted the bag of groceries higher and hurried to cross the six lanes of busy Speedway Boulevard. The bag was heavy, but she did *not* approve of the way some of her bridge-club friends casually appropriated convenient shopping carts. Borrowing, they said. Well, theft was theft, no matter the reason. Viola Faber had never *borrowed* anything in all of her sixty-eight years. She grunted annoyance and hustled toward the center island, and toward her tidy apartment in the gated retirement village a short, familiar block away. She began to relax a little as she passed the front of a car that had stopped in the second lane.

One lane before the safety island. One more and I can rest, she thought.

The small woman stayed between the lines and braved the sea of cars.

Speedway was busy eastbound out of the city in the late afternoon, everyone heading home in a hurry. Most traffic stopped for her. Pedestrians were a pain, but had right of way in Arizona, especially when they were inside painted crosswalks.

Someone honked at the delay.

She pressed her lips together and shook her head at the rudeness so rampant in society nowadays. *The nerve of some people!*

The large, dark sedan hissed through traffic like a sleek thoroughbred, gliding effortlessly around other less elegant breeds and increasing speed as it swerved to break from the pack. The huge engine rumbled, sucked hot air and sighed raw power to the few pedestrians who glanced up from their lonely sidewalks in the gust of its passing. Chrome winked the setting sun, waxed fenders glistened muscle and tinted windows glowered cool privacy. At last, open road beckoned through a clump of slower cars. It was time to break free. The great beast rejoiced and veered to the open lane. The metal heart hammered. Faster! Faster!

One car followed. The second driver weaved through traffic and stayed a few cars back as ordered. The job had been boring, but, as the first car sped up, things became interesting. Through a gap in traffic he spotted a small woman crossing the street half a block ahead, hurrying toward the center island. Cars were stopping, but he figured the driver ahead hadn't seen her yet. A close call was coming. He smiled.

Finally the first driver saw her, but too late, too close. Tires snarled; the low-slung hood dipped, swung desperately to the side. Too late. Shiny metal slammed into the old woman. Hard chrome bent soft, old knees and tossed Viola Faber high into the warm Tucson evening and across oncoming traffic. The limp body in print dress, flowered hat and sensible shoes careened slowly through the air. Groceries sprayed three lanes and the safe center-island: milk, lettuce, eggs, bread, two boneless, skinless chicken breasts, a bottle of California wine and a pint of peach yogurt for dessert - Grace's favorite since she'd been a weight-conscious teen. The eggs splashed white and yellow on the asphalt and the brown paper bag dragged playfully across two lanes to flatten with a soft pop under a swerving taxi. Viola Faber pinwheeled a sloppy, diagonal arc forty feet over dozens of blindly rushing cars and long seconds dragged.

Her body finally thudded against the side-panel of a crowded bus stop. Thin old blood streaked dark tentacles down dirty Plexiglas.

People screamed.

The big dark sedan paused a few moments. The driver's door opened, but slammed shut again after a loud torrent of curses, as though the driver was angry - confused, couldn't see a body - and didn't fully realize what had happened.

Or perhaps the driver experienced a sudden, cautious afterthought.

Horns blatted annoyance at the slowdown, but traffic flowed a careless river. Hardly any drivers noticed. One pickup truck ran over the wine in a wet explosion. Other cars swerved to avoid scattered food and, except for the cars behind the suddenly stopped sedan, no one seemed to hesitate very long.

Finally the big car moved, smashed the loaf of bread under broad, black treads, picked up speed and disappeared in dinnertime traffic. Some drivers shook their heads at the slight delay and complained about glass and debris in the street as they fiddled with their radios and thought of their destinations. The people at the bus stop were confused. Some wept. Others walked away from the ugliness, and yet only a few seemed to realize what had caused the bloody corpse to fall from the sky. In fact, most of the possible witnesses weren't sure what they'd seen, or they just decided not to get involved...except for the second driver.

He couldn't believe his good fortune and laughed and laughed until he was miles away. The unlucky old woman had apparently been an unexpected gift of fate for him and his powerful boss.

But how could he possibly know the future?

CHAPTER ONE

THE REPORTERS

"You've got two days. Don't emphasize the tax increase or mention those rabble-rousing tax resistors," Ace Collins reminded Grace as she stood to leave his office. "We need *more* recreational facilities in Arizona, *more* attractive sports arenas. Tucson needs circuses, people having fun, making money...and voters want Government benefits. But some short-sighted fools don't want to pay for them." He stood, popped a Sen-sen in his mouth, crushed his notes in a white-knuckled fist and glared at his new editorial writer.

"Yes sir." Grace Faber smiled brightly at his angry green eyes and picked up her notes and papers. "I'll write the editorial just the way you want me to."

She turned and walked quickly to the door, trying not to let her hips swing too much under her recently tightened skirt. A woman in a man's world, she wanted him to see her as a professional and not merely as a young female. She knew her firm, shapely hips were her best feature; and the skirt hadn't shrunk - she'd widened. She'd overeaten during the emergency vacation she'd taken to bury her mother. The last two weeks had been a miserable siege of stormy tears and of anxious friends bearing gifts. Her clothes had contracted noticeably around her petite figure as she experienced how funerals and wakes generate torrents of fattening food.

"Oh, by the way," his harsh voice called as she opened the door, "I forgot to tell you. My condolences on the death of your mother."

Grace Faber turned, a pleased smile lifted her thin face to near beauty, but the editor didn't notice. Seated again, audibly crunching more Sen-sen, he'd resumed a frowning study of wire service tear sheets that crowded his wide, oak desk. The gruff, weeks-late message of sympathy had been dutifully delivered and carelessly forgotten in the same distracted moment.

No one greeted her as she passed through the newsroom. Grace was becoming accustomed to cool distance since her promotion; sequestration was the price one paid to be close to greatness she'd decided. She moved through the crowded room and sat at her plain, gray desk to prepare for her biggest task of the week: the Sunday Editorial of the *Arizona Register*. Her desk was crowded but neat; one of the privileged few abutting the wall. The rest were lined in an uneven square in the center of the huge room with wide aisles dividing wall desks from hoi polloi. She hadn't liked separation at first, but the added space allowed her to deal in relative privacy with the conflicting emotions of grief from the senseless death of her mother and the giddy thrill of her new, important job on the editorial staff.

She was overwhelmingly sad at her loss, but sensed mind-filling salvation in the drumbeat of weighty ideas and the prickly challenge of pleasing her new boss. She knew she deserved the job. She'd been with the *Register* eleven years since graduating *Cum laude* from journalism school at the University of Arizona. Her first job had been writing advertising copy. Four years later, Grace was editing and rewriting other people's copy from City Desk and a year after that she slid to a niche of her own covering community events for the Sunday Social Section. Grace had covered political weddings, celebrity-sprinkled mall openings and local art shows. Boring, but she made contacts, and her work was evidently noticed.

When the position in Editorial opened she jumped at the chance to work close to one of the most powerful men in Arizona. A dozen more senior people applied, but she got the job. She knew she'd won the position because of her intellect, her college record and her excellent performance on the job, but she also privately acknowledged the newspaper had needed to salt the all-male editorial board with a woman, and a trim, business-like, single woman at that.

Whatever, she sighed. It was good to be near the top - to be near Ace Collins, friend and confidant of important people. The editor was known to be a frequent hunting buddy of Attorney General Corbin; fellow-reporters had told her Mister Collins frequently entertained Senators and Congressmen at his home and was supposedly an acquaintance and supporter of one-time Presidential candidate and Arizona's legendary ex-Senator, Harris Lillienthal. Grace knew working with Ace Collins was her ticket to fame, her opportunity to pull herself from the inchoate mass of 9 to 5 wretches who thought the newspaper was just a job.

Drones, she thought.

The newsroom buzzed disorderly industry. A restless throng of hunched, introverted people tapped liquid finger-clicks and stared at the underwater green of computer screens. And they *were* incompetent drones. The coverage of her mother's hit and run death had occupied only one short column in the *Register*. She realized she was much too close to the matter, but when an old woman is run down on a main street of a busy city during rush hour and the police can't come up with an arrest for more than a week, there should be follow-up articles and, in her opinion, outraged editorials by the foremost newspaper in the state.

When she had complained of apparent police incompetence and the lack of comment by the paper, Editor Collins had cautioned her to wait. "These things take time," he'd said in the tolerant tone people usually reserve for children, the elderly and the grief-ridden. Time? Grace respected her boss, but she knew from watchful experience that time was the mortal enemy of most investigations.

Work! She spread her notes and began Sunday's editorial.

Grace Faber's keen mind connected nimble fingers with growing blocks of text on her green computer screen; she settled into the familiar rhythm and forgot the death of her mother for over an hour. Phrases like "paying one's fair share" and "government's necessary place in the private economy" attached themselves like lucid beads to short, plausible, declarative reasons to spend the necessary public money, finance the future and build a grand, new sports arena in growing, dynamic Tucson, Arizona. The bond election for the South Side Sports Arena was set for the same day as the off-year City election on the fourth of November, four weeks away.

• • •

She knew the bond question would be a close call. City Council races weren't much of a contest in this largely Democrat city, but raising taxes was a hot-button issue for the mostly blue-collar mix of ethnic Hispanic and red-neck miners and construction workers who comprised so much of the Tucson electorate. And there *was* organized opposition to the new arena: Citizens for Tax Relief, an anti-tax group led by a charismatic rabble-rouser named Mitch Young. Private polls showed the people were skeptical about a publicly funded arena. Grace knew the *Arizona Register* had to make the difference. The time-proven method was broadly written editorials weeks before voting day and another, more focused, editorial the Sunday before the election. Grace counseled voters to act in the interests of the community rather than listen to selfish naysayers. She ignored the increase in property taxes and didn't mention the anti-tax group. The *Register's* Sunday editorial was solidly in favor of passage for the fifty-million-dollar Sports Arena Bond Election.

She finished six column inches by five thirty. The newsroom had nearly emptied. She squinted through her glasses at the glass-fronted editor's office; Ace Collins had left for the day. She'd hand-carry her editorial to him in the morning before the staff meeting.

• • •

Her work was done. Now to the gloomier part of her life, her mother's unsolved hit-and-run. She'd recently been visiting a long-time friend on the police beat after work. He was a young reporter named Clyde Ralston who was paid to hang around the police station on South Stone Avenue and gather crime statistics.

Clyde considered himself an old-fashioned, crime-busting investigative reporter who got no respect from his bosses. He loved the police beat, had been there for years, working lots of unpaid-overtime in search of special, front-page headlines. His life revolved around investigations, scoops, exclusives... and maybe a Pulitzer some day. Grace knew his motivation wasn't only ego. Clyde believed in Truth, Justice and the American Way - a dogged investigator who'd broken some good stories. She also knew he was getting frustrated with his own newspaper.

Recently, he had told her the *Arizona Register* evidently thought he was *too* dogged. Clyde's current quest had to do with mob influence in dog tracks and he'd done an article on possible Mafia connections in Arizona tracks, but the young reporter couldn't get the *Register* to allow him time to follow up the story. Clyde said he wanted a special assignment, but Ace Collins said the budget wouldn't allow any specialization. So, for the time being, Clyde sifted through hundreds of police reports in a bathroom-sized office down the hall from the police station lobby to file mostly boring lists of burglary, robbery, assault and traffic statistics. Most police reports were copied by records and delivered to him around five o' clock each day, insuring Clyde's work would reach city desk *after* deadline for the day. His stories were a day-late and often dull, but he believed the work was important and an irreplaceable source of information about his favorite subject: crime in Arizona.

Grace drove her new Saab across town, picking up burgers, fries and cokes. She arrived at the gray-concrete, monument-style police station as the last orange glow of day silhouetted the jagged Tucson Mountains. An evening breeze swirled down the street and ruffled her long, red hair. She shivered in her light blouse and decided to bring a coat to work from now on. Desert evenings were deceptive in October as the warmth of the weakening sun fled quickly from early darkness. She had always loved autumn in Arizona until her mother's accident.

• • •

The reporter was deeply involved in the six-inch stack of police reports for the day. Head in hand, bent over a desk, he didn't hear her come in the room.

"Hey Clyde," she greeted his thick, black hair.

Clyde Ralston looked up and blinked distracted annoyance through large, horn-rimmed glasses while his eyes tried to focus. He wasn't used to being interrupted, but his darkly, handsome face split to a wide, toothy smile when he recognized the slender woman with the grease-stained bag of junk food. "Hey Grace," he greeted her in a deep, second-generation, Mississippi drawl. "What y'all got there, my dinner?"

"You got it, Clyde, three major food-groups, hamburgers, fries and cokes."

The husky, broad-shouldered young black man towered over the slight redheaded woman as he stood and reached for the food. "Thanks. I didn't get lunch today. Gang Unit made a big automatic weapons bust around noon and I filed an *outstanding* exclusive by three. The story ain't Mafia, politics and race-track-money, but it'll have to do. Local boys with some big ol' M-16s and Uzis."

Grace took off her glasses, pinched the bridge of her nose and shook her head. "Guns," she groaned. "They ought to melt them all down and build school buses with the steel. There is simply *no* earthly reason for private citizens to own guns." She sat in the only other chair in the room and watched Clyde take huge bites and swallow cheek-bulging mouthfuls without chewing more than once or twice. She enjoyed watching the big, young man devour his food. He took so much pleasure - eating as a sensual, almost sexual, experience - it had to be a *man* thing. Reminded her of her ex-husband. Living alone again after her three-year disaster of a marriage, she missed watching a man eat. Grace didn't enjoy eating very much and mostly made do with salads and pasta. The three burgers and two large fries were meant to please Clyde. The second fries and one of the burgers was for her, but often she purposely forgot to eat. Not a bribe, she laughed to herself, just a friendly gesture. She watched him unwrap the second and bite off a hunk.

He pointed the ragged burger at her. "You're a typical damn liberal. If y'all didn't live with packs of Dobermans in country clubs behind eight foot walls you'd see why some of us lesser folks," he bowed over the hamburger, "need guns to protect our hovels and hog jowls." Clyde chuckled around another bite and Grace snorted at the hog jowl reference. Clyde had a Masters degree in English from the University of Arizona and a degree in Journalism from Mississippi State. He was a happily married man who lived in a medium sized ranch-style house on the middle-class East side of Tucson with a pretty wife and two little girls. He'd probably never seen a hog jowl, but she knew he relished spoofing their ethnic and political differences.

The two had been friends for years at the newspaper, but had become much closer during the past weeks as she visited his cramped office each evening for information. Both reporters enjoyed discussions like this, even though their beliefs and reportorial priorities sometimes clashed. Light talk made Grace forget her grief and Clyde liked matching wits with a bright, if somewhat dogmatic, liberal.

"So, you got another exclusive, huh?" she prodded.

He answered around a mouthful of French fries. "Yeah, but this story'll be lucky to make the back page of the local section. Nobody got killed and the kids were all juvies. Seems like I'll never be allowed to go after the big ones."

"Be patient, Clyde, and keep plugging away," Grace said. "Hard work is always rewarded. Look what happened to me."

"Yeah? Well this ol' boy's gettin' mighty damn tired pickin' cotton for y'all folks up there in the fancy offices," he drawled, shaking his head in half serious resignation and wiping crumbs off his plaid shirt. His eyes returned automatically to the stacks of reports on his desk, but then he looked sadly down at the floor and began to talk about his favorite new obsession. "They found another heap of dead greyhounds in the desert near Broken Arrow Ranch yesterday," he muttered. "Twenty of 'em. Each one executed by a gunshot to the head. All piled up in a ravine near a ranch road with their ears cut off, just like last time."

"God, Clyde, with their ears cut off?" Grace repeated. "How horrible! What do you mean, 'like last time'?"

"This is the second time they've found heaps of dead Greyhounds in the desert near that damned Broken Arrow Ranch in the last year."

"Why would someone do that? Why kill and mutilate dogs?" she asked.

"They're not just dogs, they're racing greyhounds. They don't win enough races, they get old or hurt and some breeders and dog owners dispose of the poor animals like they were garbage."

"Racing? How come you're so sure they're *racing* greyhounds?"

Clyde looked up at Grace with a quizzical smile twisting his full lips. He wanted to be sure she wasn't kidding. "Hell, Grace, I've explained all this before."

"No you haven't. And I haven't seen dead Greyhounds reported anywhere."

"Right Grace, and if it *ain't* in the paper it *ain't* news," he recited his favorite dictum. "Y'all must've been too busy with your own troubles to read my stories about poor, dumb, dead animals." The smile softened, became gentle and understanding as he continued. "Breeders and dog owners tattoo racing greyhounds in their ears when they're just puppies so the race tracks can identify each dog. Tattooing ears is standard procedure. They use a litter number and the dog's date of birth. Makes an indelible mark and stops anyone from puttin' ringers in the races."

"Tattoos? In the poor puppy's ears? That's barbaric," Grace said and shook her head in contempt. "Then dog owners kill them when they get sick or old and remove the dog's ears to hide their identity, right?"

Clyde nodded agreement. "The best way to get rid of the unfortunate dogs without being identified as the owner and gettin' all the bad publicity is to cut the tattooed ears off after they shoot 'em. Business as usual. Feedin' useless animals costs money. We don't know *exactly* who the bastards are, but the locations tell us something." He leaned back, stretched his thick, muscular arms up high and stared at the ceiling. The chair swayed over on two legs and crackled like popcorn under his 250-pound frame. "You'd think big outfits like Broken Arrow Ranch and the Emprise Corporation could buy a nice little farm or something. Put those old dogs out to pasture with some of the millions of skimmed dollars the mob's runnin' through their race-tracks."

"The mob, Clyde?" Grace leaned forward and touched Clyde's knee. "I know it's awful, but you just said *dog-breeders* do these things. What does shooting greyhounds have to do with the mob?"

His chair banged down on all fours and he glared a quick flash of anger. "Damn Grace! You haven't been payin' attention! The pile of dead dogs was found in a ravine on the southern edge of Broken Arrow Ranch."

"Yeah, so?"

Clyde held his hands out in despair. "Broken Arrow Ranch is owned by two partners who run stables of greyhounds, Robert Lillienthal and Gus Greenbaum." He rattled off the well-known Arizona names as though they proved an argument.

Grace was still lost. "So?"

"Jeez Grace." Clyde shook his head in defeat. "I wrote a story about this. Robert Lillienthal is Senator Harris Lillienthal's brother. Greenbaum is a partner in the Emprise Racing Corporation with Bruno Malatesta. That's *Don* Bruno of the Chicago Malatestas." He slumped forward and fingered the stack of reports.

Grace still didn't understand why dogs being killed near a well-connected ranch was so significant, and she sensed Clyde was eager to get back to his police reports. She changed the subject. "About mother's hit and run, any word from traffic investigation? Could you find anything out about the missing supplements in mother's accident? Have they found anything, or anyone?"

Clyde glanced at the door and lowered his voice, "Sergeant Sparks told me they couldn't release supplements to the press. He said I had a damn nerve to ask."

"Oh come on! He knows you don't want the report, just the information."

"We *all* know that." Clyde licked his fingers, wiped them on his levis. "I figure he's hidin' the fact they don't have shit for information. Feels incompetent."

"Well he's not going to get away with stonewalling." Grace stood and smoothed her skirt. "They must have suspects, license plates or something. I'll come back tomorrow afternoon and talk to him. My mother's dead. Someone must pay. He'll have to talk to *me*." Grace glared at the pea-green wall.

"Don't have to wait 'til tomorrow," Clyde said quickly and chuckled. "The incompetent sergeant just went upstairs. Heard him come in the back entrance, rush past my door and hurry upstairs just before you arrived. Go get him!"

"What? Oh great. " Grace patted Clyde's beefy shoulder absently. "Thanks for the tip Clyde, thanks a lot!" She left the room before he could answer.

Clyde Ralston listened to her heels click across the tile lobby and pound up rubber-treaded stairs. "Good luck little lady," he whispered. Then he looked around in mock apprehension, picked up her abandoned hamburger and munched.

• • •

The long, bare hallway felt like a trap: naked tan walls, indirect florescent lights hidden in the low ceiling, sixty feet of wall-to-wall commercial-gray carpet and all the doorways closed. At the end was a black steel, fire-door. There was no people-noise. For a brief moment Grace had claustrophobic visions of small, Kafkaesque interrogation rooms and listened for the exhausted whimper of tormented prisoners. She lost her righteous anger and decided to leave.

"Can I help you," a high-pitched male voice asked from just behind her.

"Oh! You startled me." Grace turned quickly to the just-opened door.

A skinny, high-cheek-boned man stood in a doorway. No uniform. He wore rumpled tan slacks and a white shirt that hung limply down thin, pale arms.

Even though he looked like an undernourished accountant she decided he *must* be a cop, but her lungs pumped fear as she struggled to recover composure.

Small muddy-colored eyes dropped from her face to her laboring chest. "Yes? What do you want?" he squeaked without a trace of a smile.

"I'm...I'm with the *Register,*" Grace said and reached out a hand to be shaken. "Looking for traffic investigations, a Sergeant Sparks." She smiled and answered her own question. "You must be Sergeant Sparks. Nice to meet you."

His hand returned pressure, but his eyes still crawled on her blouse.

Grace moved toward him as though he had already invited her into the office.

His little eyes darted up to her face. He seemed startled she was so pushy and dropped her hand. The eyes returned to her chest and noticed she was much closer. He stepped back from the doorway. "Yes, I'm Sergeant Sparks. What can I do for you, Miss?"

Grace slipped past him and began to sit in the first chair in front of a paper-filled desk when she noticed another man, big in a blue uniform, full of authority. He rose from a chair against the wall and brushed by Grace without acknowledging her presence. She smelled after-shave, talc and starch. Grace sat down, gathered her wits and wondered. She'd seen *him* before, the Chief of Police. With the iron-gray hair, thick neck and bulky, broad-shouldered body, he fit the obviously tailored uniform with two gold stars on each collar like someone from Hollywood casting. As he passed the Sergeant he growled something that sounded like, "Handle this mess."

Grace settled in the chair and spoke without missing a beat. "Nice to meet you, Sergeant. I'm Grace Faber, next-of-kin to Viola Faber. Remember her?"

He flinched. She'd caught him by surprise. "Next of...? You said reporter. You're the woman's *daughter* too?" Confusion flowed down Sparks' bony face from fluttering eyes to a thin lower lip twisting in the grip of yellow, corn-teeth. His high forehead glistened sudden sweat and he turned to close the door so he could gather himself.

Sometimes the method worked. Sometimes it paid a reporter to be pushy. Grace made a living observing people. She was sure this Sparks was full of guilty knowledge. The reactions had taken a fraction of a second, but she knew.

He turned back to face her. His face had calmed to a level cop-stare.

She was ready, Psychology IA. "We have information...," and she stopped.

"This is not the place," he filled the silence. "Regulations prohibit...." he began to recite the police-procedure creed drilled into all police bureaucrats.

"...but she died almost two weeks ago," Grace interrupted. She tilted her head and turned her face up to him in a deceivingly vulnerable posture. "And my mother was run down in front of dozens of people." Grace lowered her voice, allowed a curdle of pain. "*Someone* saw her die," she said. "We've received information you are hiding...a person. We want to know why you haven't arrested him yet?"

"He is *not* a suspect! Your information is incorrect and I *demand* to know the source..." his shrill voice dwindled as he saw her face tighten to a nasty smile. Sergeant Sparks realized he'd been snookered.

Grace stood. "Who is he, Sergeant Sparks?" She spat the words in the little man's face. "Who is this scum who ran down an old woman and drove away."

"Get out!" His face swelled. Blotches of red colored his pale cheeks.

"Not until you tell me you're making an arrest…and soon!"

"I can't tell you a damn thing." He pointed out the door. "Get out! This is an ongoing investigation and we haven't developed enough information to present to the County Attorney." His eyes were fixed on hers now, no more bosom peeking. "You may be next-of-kin, but you are *not* a policeman or an officer of the court. You are breaking the law even *being* here on the second floor without a pass."

"I am a taxpayer. I bought this building and I pay your salary," Grace fumed. And I do work for the *Register*. If you don't come up with an arrest soon there will be an editorial demanding to know why not!" She stormed out of the room into the hall. As she made the turn she glanced back into the policeman's office.

Sergeant Sparks had snatched up his phone like a lifeline. He leaned over the desk, fumbled with the square, black receiver and frantically punched buttons. When he saw her watching he kicked the door shut.

Grace stopped at Clyde Ralston's little office on her way out of the police building. "Guess what, Clyde." she muttered angrily.

Clyde squinted near-sightedly up through his glasses, shifting gears again.

When he didn't answer right away she continued. "I caught him in his office, and they *do* have a suspect who they say is *not* a suspect!" Grace put her hands on her hips and stamped her foot. "They won't tell me who it is."

"Of course not," Clyde said and smiled at her anger. "That's the reason they do those supplementary reports along with the regular police incident report. So they don't have to show the press what they're doing."

"I threatened them with an editorial."

"Uh oh," Clyde winced behind the horn-rims, "Ace won't like that."

"You don't think they'll tell him, do you?"

His dark face creased with concern. "An editorial? They damn sure will."

"But I'm her daughter, for God's sake! I think they *know* who killed her."

"All the more reason." He chuckled. "Hey calm down. He prob'ly won't fire you. He'll be afraid to sack his new, token minority. And at least they're working on the case." Clyde hesitated a moment, put down a paper and gave her full attention. "Grace, you just said, '*they*'. Who'all else was up there when you busted in?"

She grimaced and raised her eyebrows. "The Chief, I'm pretty sure…big, gray-haired with two stars like he was a Major General," she joked.

"You threatened Chief Hobbs? That's big time. Could be *real* trouble."

"Yeah, maybe, but I didn't actually threaten the Chief. He'd already left the office when I mentioned an editorial, but I don't care. I'm gonna light an editorial fire under these guys if they don't get a move on."

• • •

Next morning Grace sensed something smoldering when she knocked on the editor's open door and he made her wait while he finished reading. She stood in the doorway and glanced nervously around at the plaque and picture-laden walls of the spacious office. Along with Ace Collins' college degrees and U.S. Air Force citations of discharge, promotion and bravery were certificates of appreciation from every fraternal and political organization in Arizona. Grace was particularly impressed by three framed photos of the athletic, darkly handsome young Ace Collins when he'd been in the Air Force - in two he wore pilot's coveralls and in one a dress uniform adorned with pilot's wings and rows of colorful ribbons.

Minutes later he scribbled something on a typewritten page and looked up. "Yes, Grace. Come in and leave the door open."

She marched to his desk. "I have the editorial, Mr. Collins."

"Yes, yes, give it here." He reached and took the sheet of paper from her fingers with an audible snap. The licorice-smell of Sen-sen wafted across her face. "Sit down," he indicated a chair. "There is something else we must discuss."

"If this is about Sergeant Sparks..." she began.

"Miss Faber, you've overstepped your authority," Ace Collins broke in before she'd finished. He had aged favorably from his Air Force days to a tall, beefy man with the square, well-barbered face of conspicuous success. Grace watched the anger expand. His voice was held low and his thick, hairy hands rested calmly on the paperwork, but under the full head of iron-gray hair, his face had turned the color of raw beef. He held the anger in check, but it was frighteningly obvious to Grace as he leaned forward over his desk. "Chief Hobbs called me at my home last night. He was very disturbed that I had threatened one of his police investigators with an unfavorable editorial."

"He said *you* threatened?" Grace protested. "I never used your name."

"That may be so, Miss Faber, but the impression was deliberately left."

Grace felt tears filling her eyes and hated the weakness. "Mister Collins, please understand. No matter what the Chief said, I never meant to involve you." Her soft voice pinched out to silence.

Ace Collins saw the tears. His instinct was to fire this young upstart on the spot, crush her like he'd crushed so many others who'd caused him problems, but he knew he couldn't do that. Ditching his new editorial writer now would draw too much attention to the *real* problem. *Scare the little bitch*, he thought. The Editor of the *Arizona Register* sat back in his chair and tented his fingers under his chin. He stared at the young woman for long moments, letting the venom he felt in his heart invade his thick gaze. At first Grace didn't meet his eyes. A minute passed in slow silence. The newsroom hummed with industry behind her through the opened door.

More time passed. Soon she had no choice but to meet his level stare.

He impaled her eyes with sharp, terrible hatred and held her frightened gaze as though he was preparing to uncoil and strike. Grace gasped in fear and the tears ran freely down her pale cheeks. She was frightened, but worse, she realized she'd probably lost her wonderful new job. The young woman sobbed quietly, pinned by the fierce green eyes, speechless with despair.

Ace was enjoying himself. He enjoyed making employees squirm, particularly the women. He imagined this slim young thing crouched at the foot of his bed, face smeared with blood and tears, swollen lips begging him not to hit her, but really wanting him to use her smooth, young body again and again. He blinked at the irony. No! Those days were over. He couldn't even bed his scrawny wife any more - as if he'd want to. His body had finally failed him at fifty. Doctors said he consumed too much alcohol. He sneered at the quacks and blinked again.

Grace saw the blinks. Reprieve? "Please Mister Collins, give me another chance," her voice quavered. "This is my first month in editorial. I haven't learned the ropes." She realized how she must sound, what her mother would think. Never lose your dignity was always the rule. Buck up! She took a deep breath, gathered strength and sat up straight. "This will never happen again. I promise you."

Ace sighed. Almost as good as sex used to be, or that first exhilarating drink in the morning. She was thoroughly cowed, but the game had lost its sting. The meddling little twit! He couldn't fire her, but something else would come along. He twisted his mouth in a crooked grimace he meant to be fatherly and forgiving. "I understand," he murmured just loud enough for her to hear. "You are a young girl who has lost her mother. I will give you another chance on two conditions." He paused and raised carefully trimmed gray eyebrows in expectation.

"Yes sir?" Grace took the cue. "What are those?"

Ace Collins raised one finger. "First, you will *not* meddle in police matters again unless I expressly order you to." He paused again.

"Yes." Grace nodded assent. "And the other?"

The editor leaned toward Grace again, this time in an attempt at comradely confidence. "Second, for the sake of your professional reputation, we will keep this matter from the rest of the staff. This foolish indiscretion will be strictly between us." He abruptly clamped his lips together in a grimace meant to illustrate the point.

"Oh, thank you, Mister Collins. You won't be sorry."

He sat back and dismissed her with a wave of his hand and began to read her draft of the Sunday editorial.

• • •

Later that evening, as she lay steaming in a fragrant tub with a glass of pale, gold chardonnay, Grace Faber had a chance to reflect on her near miss and seeming good fortune. She'd been reprimanded, but that was all. In the daily staff meeting later that morning Ace Collins had complimented her fine writing and advised the others her editorial would run on Sunday. As far as her work was concerned, all seemed well for Grace, but the whole matter bothered her in ways she'd not had time to examine. She sipped the wine and considered.

Mister Collins had been considerate in not exposing her sin to the others. Doing her a favor, wasn't he? Those icy eyes, that hateful stare. Doing her a favor? She'd never seen such raw anger and malice in her thirty-two years. She recalled her abject fear and helpless tears with guilty shame. Just like a woman, Grace mocked herself. Oh well, he *was* a powerful man, supposedly a war hero. She remembered the office photographs. He'd been a decorated fighter pilot in Viet Nam according to Clyde. She'd embarrassed the powerful man and he'd checked his righteous wrath. Grace guessed his restraint was admirable. Editor Collins was obviously a man of control, dignity and character. She was lucky to work for him. Wasn't she?

Grace picked up the big, soft sponge and squeezed lilac-smelling, bubbly foam over her heat-reddened shoulders and breasts. She looked down. Tea-cup-sized, she mused, but shapely. Her ex had loved to kiss them and suck their child-like nipples until they were raw and tingly. He'd been a problem to live with, but she missed his sexual attentions. Her fingers stroked and lifted one, cuddled the soft weight. They were very sensitive now that her period was due. She sipped the cool wine and thought of the few men she had known in her life. Then she thought of her friend, Clyde, and realized she wouldn't be seeing him any more. She *had* promised her boss to stay away from all police matters without his permission. A little arbitrary, but her promise obviously included the police station.

"Darn it!" she whispered. Seeing Clyde had been a way to let her hair down and relax while she tried to unravel her tragedy. She'd miss him. Disappointment turned to concern when she thought of her dead mother and the prospect of patiently sitting around waiting for news from the flawed police investigation. "Darn!" She said the word aloud this time, drained the wine and reached for a towel. There was no way she could wait for that skinny Sparks character to do his job. But how could she disobey her boss without him knowing? Wine-shiny lips stretched to a self-mocking smile as she remembered her Agatha Christie books. Hercule Poirot? James Bond would be nicer. She wrapped the big, fluffy towel around her slender body and stepped from the tub.

A private investigator seemed the perfect answer.

CHAPTER TWO

A FAVOR

Midnight was near. Mack was fighting for self-preservation and losing.

"Cormac, you are the only one who can," Chickie whispered and bit his ear.

"What about Vinnie," he protested. She was the only person who ever called him Cormac. Chickie Malatesta resembled other women the way oaks resemble daisies. Six foot, 180-pound-statuesque with deep-set eyes, high cheekbones and a craggy jaw, she wasn't quite beautiful, but had an incredible figure and loved to share. He'd been secretly dating the wonderfully large woman for years, off and on. She'd caught him tailing her *Capo Mafiosi* father eight years before when he was an undercover cop in the Organized Crime Detail and told him to take her to bed and expose her or she would expose *him*. Unhappily married and attracted to her lavish body, Mack had shrugged off scruples and taken the plunge. The risky relationship had long outlasted his train-wreck marriage, but now there were new complications. Chickie had recently acquired an infamous new suitor named Vinnie the Monster Romano who was an enforcer for Chickie's father.

"Vinnie will never know you helped me," she said.

Chickie Malatesta was fortyish, spoiled and deeply frustrated. Her problems were more complicated than a raging id, a hesitant lover and a jealous suitor. Her biggest problem for most of her life had been an obsessively overprotective father. Most men didn't *dare* take her out. She suspected that was what her daddy wanted, as though Don Bruno wanted his daughter all to himself. He said he wanted her to marry, but she knew her father did not want her to have a serious relationship with another man. In spite of her father Chickie had dated many men. All had been in vain until Mack. She knew Cormac Robertson had the strength and the connections to take her away from her father. Chickie planned to run away with him...someday.

Mack didn't know about her long-term plans. To him she was just a fun-loving, sexy girlfriend with a very dangerous father who supposedly hated cops. He enjoyed the risky sex with no strings and didn't think about the future. Thoughts of marriage to Chickie Malatesta never entered his mind. Cormac Robertson was six-three and carried 220 moderately conditioned, pounds. Chickie was his female match. For years Mack and Chickie had connected every few weeks and they thought they'd been very careful to keep her protective father - and now the notoriously jealous Vinnie - from knowing about their liaisons. Mack enjoyed the danger. He'd never regretted knowing Chickie Malatesta until tonight. He tried to change her mind. "But your dad will damn sure wonder why an ex-cop's involved."

Chickie handed Mack the rum bottle and hugged him. "He won't notice who helps the lawyer. This is my third DUI," she whispered to his neck. "Daddy warned me last time. He said they'll put me in a padded cell. That it would serve me right."

Mack knew he shouldn't risk *this* favor. They were in the cab of Mack's white Ford pickup truck in the nearly empty parking lot of a pretentious east side-Tucson singles bar called the Ivanhoe. He couldn't see her big brown eyes in the humid darkness, but he smelled hot sweat under rich perfume, felt the pressure of firm breasts, heard her heavy breathing and wanted her. Chickie Malatesta softened him up with lingering kisses and dug at his crotch like a potato farmer. He held her away after a long, rum-spiced kiss. "What do you want me to do?" he gasped, already knowing what she would say.

"Help my lawyer. He says they've got me cold, sugar. You still have friends on the police department and you're a hot-shot private investigator."

"Your lawyer wants you to hire *me*?" Mack said and sipped from the bottle.

"Yeah. Well, kinda." Chickie's plump, wet, lower lip pooched out.

"But this is all your idea, right?' he smiled ruefully into the darkness. "You want me to work a case against my old buddies on the force and try to help the daughter of a Mafia boss out of a drunk-driving charge? Chickie, you know I'd lose every contact I have on the department."

For a moment she eyed him speculatively over a regally arched nose. Then she pulled her tee-shirt over her head and arched her back. Football-sized breasts bobbled free and musky perfume washed over his face. Mack lowered his head, began to forget caution, and tangled his nose in the thick chain of Chickie's big, golden cross. Two inches long and a quarter-inch thick, the ornament probably weighed eight ounces; she always wore it, said it was a gift from her Daddy. The cross helped Mack remember the risk.

"But your father will want to know why you've come to *me*," he groaned.

"Sugar, if you don't help me, he's gonna cut me off. No car or freedom means no Cormac. And they could keep me for months in some Betty Ford hospital."

Mack thought that was probably just what she needed, what they both needed, but avoided saying it. "Chickie, it's just a damned DUI... mmph," the words were smothered in a determined kiss. She opened his buckle and unzipped his fly. He tried to grab her hand, but she reached in and gripped him in her fist.

"Damn it Chickie," Mack complained, "somebody could've followed you."

"Nobody knows I'm here," she growled into his mouth.

He set the half-empty Bacardi bottle on the floor and filled his hands with firm, sweaty softness.

She worked him free of his underwear and pulled him out.

Cool air hit his sweaty skin. He suddenly felt self-conscious and pulled back from her kisses to look out through the half-fogged window at the cool October night. He wiped a hole with his palm and scanned the dimly lit asphalt. "What about Vinnie?" he asked. "Or my old buddies on the Organized Crime Task Force? Didn't you tell me Vinnie and the police follow you everywhere you go?"

"Screw Vinnie and screw the cops," Chickie Malatesta grumbled. "My girlfriend's boyfriend gave me a ride here from the east-side mall in *his* car. We watched very carefully. No cars followed us here. Shut up and kiss me."

He held her shoulders. "Chickie, working for you will kill my reputation."

She laughed and kissed him energetically, tried to swallow his face and nearly succeeded. Her lips slid wet velvet across his cheek and Mack gasped as her tongue fluttered in his ear. Hot breath thundered live steam through his head and he shivered. Now both her hands stroked and pulled at him. Chickie lowered her head.

He groaned in joyous despair. Reputation? What a joke.

• • •

Cormac Robertson had the slightly shabby reputation of an ex-cop who'd left the department in mid-career and become a private investigator. People assume ex-cop- P.I.s have shady pasts. Partly true. Mack was an ex-marine, ex-mercenary, ex-cop in his mid forties who'd made a mess of his life. He'd ruined his police career after the boozy disintegration of a bad marriage by drinking even more heavily. Soon he was placed under intense Internal-Affairs scrutiny. Drinking and pain provoked each other. Work suffered and IAD made reports. Mack felt the shoe-fly eyes and became filled with disgust for a police bureaucracy that ignored a good arrest record and wanted to punish stress-ridden cops instead of counseling them. Angry retirement soon followed and he fell into P.I. work by default. Cop experience had prepared him perfectly to work for the other side.

Three defense law firms in Tucson contacted him within months after he left the department. They offered the smudged ex-cop plenty of work and guaranteed yearly retainers. Defense work - cutting criminals loose? Not really. Investigators for defense attorneys spend most of their time covering their lawyer's ass. Most defendants are slam-dunk, scum bags begging for jail and a big part of defense P.I. work is uncovering a defendant's lies before he gets into court and embarrasses the defense lawyer. Some cops resented Mack, but most realized the situation and confided privately they'd rather have a straight shooter like him on the other side than some sleaze who'd lie on the stand. They also said half-jokingly that, if Mack could break their case, the bust was probably bad police-work to begin with.

In this particular instance Mack knew, if he helped the daughter of a Mafia Don beat a DUI charge, even his best friends in the department would disapprove.

Chickie Malatesta decided he was ready, lifted her skirt, climbed on Mack's lap and bounced up and down, chafing, bending, smothering him with her largess and grunting in greedy delight.

Mack gasped pain and pleasure into her deep cleavage and the gold cross hammered his forehead. Lustful Chickie weighed him down like a ton. Strong hands twisted his shoulders, slid up to his neck and nearly tore off his head. Grunts and groans became yelps of delight. The big woman crushed him into the seat, firm breasts stifled him breathless, pain wracked his body, but thirty seconds later he was already holding himself back.

She bounced higher and harder, grinding him into the vinyl seat.

Mack felt the big Ford pickup rock and shift as if busting all its springs.

Hold back! Think of something else. Sure! God, the ecstasy! Danger too. Damn, what if I slip out and she slams down? Could it break?

Mixed emotions. He didn't care. Hot Damn! Mayhem or orgasm, which would come first?

Chickie thundered on. Yelps became wolf-howls. Springs rasped. The truck bounced. Finally, a male voice screamed pain and release and then two voices mingled in unrestrained joy.

Silence. The hot truck-cab filled with soft endearments and heavy breathing.

"Nice work, baby," Chickie gasped. She yanked the tee shirt down over her sweat-slick torso and turned on the dome light to comb tousled hair and repair her make-up. "You're not gonna let your lover woman go to jail, are you?"

Mack just wanted to snooze. Exhaustion had pulled the life from his muscles, but relief made him smile weakly into the sudden glare. He'd survived another coupling with the lusty titan. "No," he murmured. "Have your lawyer call me first thing tomorrow. Get me the police reports. I'll see what I can do."

Mack thought he heard a noise outside. He squinted in the dome light and glanced at the fogged windows. He suddenly felt like a target. "Turn the damn light off!"

"Relax, sugar, nobody's out there." Chickie fluffed her shoulder-length, blond hair and yanked ineffectually at the short skirt. She turned to Mack and smiled. "And you don't have to wait for police reports. Got them right here. "She reached into her saddle-bag purse and pulled out a thin sheaf of paper. "You can read them in bed. I made an appointment with my lawyer for the morning."

"Pretty damn sure of yourself," Mack grumbled, "now turn off the light."

Chickie smiled again and shut off the light. "You just let everything rest a while, sugar." She leaned, gently tucked him in and zipped up his fly. "Now take me home. We'll read all these silly police reports and rest up for tomorrow at the lawyer's office."

"Take you home?" Mack yelped. "You think I'm crazy? If your dad decided not to kill me, that psycho, Romano, would." He shook his head and pointed at the front door of the bar. "You'd better get a ride home the way you got here, with your girlfriend's boyfriend."

Chickie's voice purred in Mack's ear. "They've gone home long ago. Don't worry, I wouldn't risk your life, sugar. I don't live in the main house any more. I'm a big girl now. I live in daddy's old gatehouse down next to the main road."

"Gatehouse? Aren't there lots of armed guards?"

"No, silly," Chickie giggled. Warm breath tickled Mack's ear. "You've been watching too many *Godfather* movies. My father's retired. There are only two family men with daddy any more, and they're more like servants than bodyguards. The gatehouse where I'm living is on the edge of Speedway Boulevard, three miles from the main ranch and far away from

Vinnie or Daddy and his two men." She licked his ear and her hand dropped to stroke his sore crotch. "For some reason lately daddy's been giving me lots of extra freedom. We'll have total privacy at my place. Now drive me home."

Sure. Total privacy. Mack rolled down the window and looked around the dimly lit parking lot. Something had spooked him. A noise? Furtive movement? He didn't usually ignore instinct, but he was tired. He sighed and turned the key.

Chickie put her head on his shoulder and rested contentedly.

Mack drove east while his mind tried to rationalize his recklessness. And he had plenty of time to think. Grace Ranch, the Malatesta home since the late sixties, sprawled at the base of the Rincon Mountains on Tucson's far east side at the edge of the National Forest. The trip was well over twenty miles; thirty minutes past the built-up edges of the city over dark, nearly deserted roads cutting across the high desert through tangled scrub and tall Saguaro toward the mountains. The Rincons shadowed the valley and blacked out the lowest stars. And they were oddly menacing. Not jagged and lifting to poke the sky, but rounded, mile-high lumps of stone silhouetted low against the east like crouching thugs. Dark on dark, night hidden inside night, driving toward the Rincon Mountains at night gave Mack the feeling he was driving off the edge of the earth.

Every now and then a stoplight broke the dark monotony and the two or three cars in Mack's traffic-clump stayed together between stops, taking comfort in their combined headlights. He watched his mirrors as usual, but didn't notice the dark sedan until he impatiently accelerated the pick-up through a yellow light and saw a car behind him run the red. "Chickie, Look! See that dark-colored car behind us?"

"Huh?" She sat up and turned to look.

The other car seemed to be overtaking them.

Mack pressed the gas. The speedometer climbed, forty-five, fifty, too fast. Desert whizzed by. They flew through the night, but the other car was gaining. He eased his 45 Colt Commander from the door pocket. Worn grips snuggled in his hand. He'd carried the gun for years. A lightweight, titanium version of the government 1911 model that fired the same 45-caliber round, the pistol had been his off-duty weapon as a cop. He was deadly accurate at any reasonable distance.

Headlights filled his rear-view mirror. Sixty. Sixty-five. He drove with his left and held the big pistol across his chest waiting for the other car to catch up. If they want trouble, too damn bad for them, he thought. "Do you recognize the car?"

"Wait. Can't make anything out. Headlights blinding me," Chickie muttered. She didn't seem very alarmed, only annoyed at being awakened.

Seventy-five. Eighty. Too damned fast!

The road entered the low hills and shallow washes of the foothills. Tires yelped and snickered and grabbed. Springs creaked tension and squealed relief. The big, white pickup truck swooped to the tar and tiptoed up again like a drunken dancer. Crazy, Mack thought. Careening down a winding asphalt ribbon into terrible darkness at the steep edge of the headlights, he had trouble seeing ahead. Headlights blinded him. Mack batted the mirror aside. Relief. He glanced at the side-mirror. The car behind wasn't overtaking, just holding about six car-lengths.

Eighty-five miles an hour! Ahead, a long, sweeping curve disappeared into a dip. The big truck slammed down into a sand-smeared depression, slipped on the loose dirt, jinked sideways and lost balance. Rubber screamed, but the tires bit into asphalt and the pickup righted itself. They lunged out of the ravine swaying on the suspension, just barely under control.

Chickie fell against the passenger door and bounced back against Mack's shoulder, arms and legs flailing in the small cab. "Slow this truck the hell down!' she screamed. "You're gonna kill us!"

Another curve was coming. Mack eased up on the accelerator. The other car slowed also. Probably playing games. Chickie was right. This *was* stupid. Maybe he was overreacting to some teenagers on a joyride. Stupid. He'd let his nerves put them both in danger. Mack let the truck slow down to sixty, and then fifty.

The other car kept its distance.

Mack opened his window and glanced around at darkness beyond shifting headlight shadows. No lights or humans for miles. They were out in the middle of the high desert under the deep, cold gloom of the Rincons. Must be getting close to the Malatesta ranch gate, he thought. Speedometer read forty-five. Comfortable.

"Think a minute Chickie," Mack shouted over the wind-noise. Does your Goddamned boyfriend have a dark sedan like that?"

"I've told you, he's not my Goddamn boyfriend!" she snapped back. "And there's no way he could have followed me."

"Not your boyfriend, huh? Well it looks like we've got trouble anyhow."

Mack hefted the pistol, looked ahead into darkness. He thought he could see a twinkle of house lights on a high spot in the darkness ahead. The gatehouse?

Another straightaway. The car behind speeded up, pulled out to pass.

"Here they come," he hissed. "Get down!"

"Maybe it's my father," Chickie yelped. "Oh God, Mack, don't shoot my daddy." But she put her head down on Mack's thigh.

"A little late for caution," Mack said, taking slack in the trigger.

The big dark sedan roared up alongside and stayed even with the truck for a moment. A late model Lincoln was looking him over, windows closed, tinted dark. Mack thought he glimpsed a pale face in the driver's seat. A white man, but nothing distinct. Couldn't see anything to shoot...yet.

The big car added speed and began to glide past the pick-up truck.

Mack relaxed a little, took the muzzle of the automatic pistol from the window ledge. "Just checking us out I guess."

As the rear passenger window of the large Lincoln pulled even with Mack the engine roared and the big car began to pull away.

"I guess he's leaving," Mack yelled.

Mack relaxed his grip on the gun, held the pick-up to the right edge of the road and waited for the lighted license plate to come into view. Foolish mistake.

The big sedan slowed again. A rear window slid open. A gun barrel!

"BOOM!" A funnel of fire swept the front of the truck, pellets raked the hood and rattled like hail on the windshield. Star-cracks appeared like magic.

Shotgun! Mack's nerves screamed. He hunched down on top of Chickie's head and sighted the 45 over the window ledge.

Hold on their open window. Movement. Squeeze the trigger. Now!

But the pick-up's right front tire slipped off the asphalt into soft, uneven sand. The steering wheel shuddered. They slewed to the right. Mack bounced to the roof. Chickie's head slammed into the bottom of the steering wheel. She screamed in terror. Mack swore and grabbed the wheel with both hands. The 45 clattered against black plastic, pointed uselessly at the roof. Helpless, Mack thought. Gonna get my careless, damn head blown off! The truck jounced to a stop. Blood pounded, adrenalin squirted panic. Chickie sobbed on Mack's lap. He leveled the gun, looked for a target. Split-second images raged.

The dark blue - or black - sedan seemed to crouch down on the road and gather itself for a sprint. Mack heard rubber squeal as it accelerated. Just as the pale-colored license plate came into Mack's view - *MNG...* - the lights went out, headlights and taillights. A rush of gaseous wind buffeted his truck and the big, dark vehicle disappeared down the black straightaway like a night mirage.

And then everything was dark. The shotgun blast had taken out both their headlights. Couldn't see the other car any more. Couldn't see the road, only branches hanging over the cab. They had stopped under a large, old mesquite tree.

Now what? Would they come back to finish the job? Or was the shooting just a warning?

No headlights in the middle of nowhere. Was that shot meant to kill or just disable them in the desert? Mack had strong opinions, but couldn't be sure.

Chickie raised up from his lap, sniffed back tears and peeked through the star-spangled windshield into the desert night. "God that was close."

"Dunno about close if they *meant* to shoot out my lights." Their breathing rasped and stormed together. The engine hummed and jiggled.

Chickie sat up straight, swore about a broken nail.

"Shhh!" he hissed in her ear. "Listen. They might still be out there."

Engine noise covered the sounds of the desert night through the open window. To survive they had to hear. Mack turned off the key, pulled the door handle, hesitated. "Down on the floor!" he whispered. "Safer down there."

Chickie tucked her generous body down under the dash without a word.

The door opened wider. Bright light flickered on. Shit! He'd forgotten the dome light! A target at the pistol range, his skin prickled, waiting for the bullet. *Move! Now!* "Stay here!" he whispered and pushed the door half open, rolled out of the truck and fell to the ground in a heap, punching all the wind from his lungs. Damn! He kicked the door closed and waited to breathe. Mack sucked air and lay still a moment, 45 out, finger tight on the trigger, waiting for the pain to stop.

Listen to the night, dummy, he thought in disgust.

Mack opened his senses and concentrated on the dark world around him. Hot metal ticked in the engine, slow playful wind-eddies whispered secrets in the mesquite. Crisp, dried-seed smells of Fall floated like kitchen-spices, sharp sage and nutty mesquite mingled with the warm-pepper bite of sand and alkali. He crawled farther from the truck and waited. A lizard or snake slithered from his elbow to a crackle of leaves and a bird repeated soft questions fifty feet away.

He waited for more, the purr of an engine, a scuffle of shoes, the harsh, eager whispers of man-hunters, or even his shot-up radiator dripping in the sand.

Nothing, no trace of human sound, and they'd evidently missed his radiator.

He visualized the pale license again. *MNG* and a blank. Vinnie Romano? Mack began to test alternatives. Kids on a joyride? With a shotgun? Not likely. The license plate had been light colored. Not Arizona, maybe California or Kansas, but probably Illinois, his mind insisted. They'd followed Mack's truck for miles. Who would waste a shotgun load on headlights? The shooter had been in the *back* seat. Not spur-of-the-moment, no accident. They'd shot high enough not to disable the tires or radiator and wreck the truck in a ditch. Had to be a warning.

Mack ran an enemies list through his mind: Criminals? Cops? Or Vinnie? What difference? This hadn't been a hit. He put away the 45, stood and walked over to the truck. "That was just a warning, Chickie," he leaned in the open window. "They could've just as easily blown my head off, but I figure they didn't want to risk hurting you."

"A warning! You mean from Vinnie?" She sat up, looked around and fluffed her hair, recovering quickly now that the danger seemed over. "But I told you, there's no way Vinnie could've followed me. My girlfriend and I snuck out her back door and walked to the mall to meet her boyfriend. He gave us a ride to the bar in his car. Nobody followed us. We watched carefully."

"Could this boyfriend have talked to Vinnie, or your father?"

"No way. He's legit as hell. The guy doesn't even know who I am."

"Well he's one of the few," Mack wisecracked. If it wasn't Vinnie, he was stumped. He had enemies, but the ones with the stones to use a shotgun wouldn't have aimed at the headlights. "Who knew you were meeting me at the Ivanhoe?"

"Nobody. Look, I told you this already" Chickie said. "My girlfriend didn't even know where we were going until they dropped me off. And *you* didn't even know where to meet until I called you from the bar phone."

Mack gave up. "Okay. Doesn't matter, but we've got to wait out here for daylight. I can't drive you home without headlights."

"No. We can walk home from here," Chickie said and climbed out of the truck. "We're almost at the ranch, probably no farther than a half-mile."

Mack flinched away from the dome-light and slammed the door shut. "Okay Chickie, I'll walk you home."

They walked a mile into the tumbled foothills. The small gatehouse stood next to the ranch road fifty feet back from the main road in a brushy clearing at the lonely mountain-end of Speedway Boulevard. The stone, one-story, red-tile-roofed building looked like an old carriage-house with a square, two-story tower at one end. The place reminded Mack of fieldstone outbuildings on big estates he'd seen as a boy growing up in the suburbs of Philadelphia.

"No lights," he observed as they approached the steel-strapped door.

Chickie turned. He saw her eyes glint in the star-tempered darkness. "How many times do I have to tell you, I live here alone in complete privacy."

"Yeah, well tell that to your father's bodyguards, or to Vinnie." Mack waved at the dim, gravel road winding uphill toward the main part of the ranch. "He could've driven by here an hour ago, laughing like hell and reloading his shotgun."

Chickie jingled her keys a while and then opened the big door.

"Well he's not here now. Come on up, sugar." She grabbed his hand and pressed it against a breast - firm, but soft as hot silk under the flimsy tee shirt. "Sleep in my bed for once. I'm a little shook up."

Mack was feeling jumpy again. "You just don't get it, do you?" he said. "Somebody warned me tonight...maybe warned us *both* to stop what we were doing. Next time he might try to kill me with that damned shotgun."

"Damn it Mack," Chickie pulled on his hand. "It must be nearly two a.m.. We have an important appointment in the morning. My bedroom's in the tower, you'll be safe there.

Come on, we'll read the arrest report, fool around and then rest up for that lawyer."

Mack touched the big pistol tucked in his belt. Protection. He was tired and tempted, but he thought to pause for one last, important question. "Does Vinnie Romano have a key to this place?"

"Well, yeah. He works for my father." She shrugged. "He checks the place out when I'm not here. I don't like it much, but daddy insists."

Mack turned away and began to walk back toward the main road.

Chickie stamped her foot on the step. "Oh come on, Mack! Sleep with me."

"No thanks, Chickie, I'll walk back to my truck and drive to my studio at first light." He waved over his shoulder without turning. "Won't get much sleep, but it's safer that way. See you tomorrow."

CHAPTER THREE

LOOPHOLE

Bernie Frank was a mob lawyer, fortyish, fat and blue-jowled. He patted his bald head with a monogrammed handkerchief and stared at the rumpled P.I.. His hairy wrist dangled thick, gold jewelry out a starched french cuff and he wore the thousand-dollar silk suit as though born to it. He seemed sure of his position in life and acted like he didn't have to sweat little people like private investigators.

Chickie Malatesta sat silently and watched her lawyer glare at Mack.

Mack hadn't shaved, smelled of alcohol, wore no tie and looked as if he'd slept in his wrinkled khaki pants and worn sport-jacket. "That's all," he motioned at the woman. "Chickie there just wants me to make magic with the cops."

The lawyer sighed resignedly. He'd go along with a client's whim...for now. As long as the *main* client stayed happy Bernie's life remained serene and profitable. Most of his work was small stuff like bailing wise-guys out of jail and delaying any "business-related" trials as long as possible - first-year law school stuff. But this was the boss's daughter. *This* case could hurt him if he didn't handle it just right. Most people believe lawyers can make magic for enough money.

Bernie had bailed Chickie out of jail that two-week-ago morning.

When he drove her home that dawn, Don Bruno had him summoned to the ranch house, to his large, richly furnished dining room for a cup of espresso.

"Driving and drinking is messy business," the boss had hissed softly across the huge mahogany table. "Do your best for my Chickie. Get my baby a deal. Maybe a few weeks in some hospital." The old man slurped noisily, coughed and sighed. His sparse, gray hair was mussed; the bony, sharp-featured face seemed pale and tired, but the bottomless Sicilian eyes had measured Bernie without emotion.

Bernie had nodded and gulped his coffee without a word, anxious to leave.

Hiring a P.I. wasn't Bernie's idea, but Chickie wanted him, said he was good. Good at what? Bernie noticed the loving way she looked at him and wondered if Don Bruno knew about this. If Vinnie Romano knew! He'd heard things about Mack Robertson, a rummy, but tough and smart. Chickie said the ex-cop could pull strings with police and save her from the hoosegow. Bernie grinned. He'd better hurry and pull those strings before Vinnie found out. The boss wouldn't care much as long as Chickie got off, but they didn't call Vinnie a monster for nothing. If this Mack guy hung around long enough the monster would know about it. Bernie wouldn't dare hide it, especially if the schmuck testified in open court and Miss Chickie ate him up with her big, brown eyes. Bernie took another look at Mack. Good looking in a slovenly way, but he could be a dead man who didn't know it yet.

"Just do what you can," Bernie soothed. "Cover the basics."

"Basics?" Mack scoffed. "The cops evidently covered the basics." He strolled across the large office, his shoes chuffing through extra-thick shag. Like walking in gorilla fur, Mack thought. He was tired. After walking Chickie to her house he'd returned to his blinded truck, waited for false dawn - about five o' clock - and rushed back to his studio-loft for three hour's sleep. He'd arrived at the tenth-floor lawyer's office looking like a ten-day drunk. Screw it, he thought, she wanted me involved. "Looks like a dead bang case, Chickie." He looked down at the seated woman. "There's nothing much I can do."

"But I wasn't drunk," Chickie protested. "The police set me up,"

She looked hopefully at Mack and tugged at the skirt riding up her tan thighs. She was obviously uncomfortable in a chrome-leather sling-chair that looked like an instrument of torture. Mack couldn't help admiring her through his hangover. Usually she dressed in tight skirts and revealing tops with her blond hair worn loose around her shoulders or pulled back in a flouncy pony-tail. Today the big woman had tried to look like a businesswoman, or a lawyer's wife. Gold gleamed at her wrists and around her neck. She wore a loosely tailored, gray linen, sleeveless sheath that de-emphasized her lush curves. Blond curls piled high in frosted gold feathers added inches to her height. She looked impressive.

Mack imagined her naked, blinked it away. She'd dressed for the occasion and almost made the luxurious office look good. A typical lawyer's office, the room was designed to boost a distended ego and impress gullible clients with price if not taste. Bernie had clashed thick, gray shag rug with chrome-leather furniture, cherry-wood-paneled walls and a pale yellow, pressed-tin ceiling. Mack decided he didn't like Bernie, but sort of envied the rug. Be better than owning a pet, he thought. Must've cost more than a car, though. He forced his mind back to the problem.

"Set you up, Chickie?" Mack asked. "This is supposedly your *third* DUI bust. How in hell do you figure they set you up?"

Chickie bristled like a big cat, leaned forward and nearly fell out of her chair, but Bernie Frank held up a short, stubby finger to stop her.

"Let me, Miss Malatesta." He settled back in his chair and pushed his fists under his soft chin as though he were a professor. "Two weeks ago, at six in the evening, agents of the Organized Crime Task Force report they followed Chickie Malatesta from her home at the entrance of Malatesta Ranch to a bar called the Happy Frog on the east side of Tucson. They set up inside-outside surveillance and watched her drink rum and cokes for three hours until she left the bar and began to drive home. They followed; decided she was driving erratically and had consumed enough alcohol to be legally drunk. They pulled her over and radioed a city screen-unit to meet them and make the arrest and do the paperwork." The plump lawyer raised his hands, palms-up. "She only blew a .08, but she allegedly used extensive profanity, kicked one city cop in the shin and is described in a supplementary report as 'extremely combative and disorderly'." He pointed at the offending report on his large, pond-shaped, glass desk. "We're lucky they didn't charge her with resisting arrest and assault on a police officer."

"The task force didn't take part in the actual arrest?" Mack asked.

"They stopped me," Chickie answered. "Damn unmarked cars. Two of them, forced me off the road, but they left when the other cops..."

"Yes, yes," Bernie interrupted. He smiled and held up his hand to prevent any more outbursts. "They radioed the city and followed Chickie's Cadillac for six miles before they forced her over. The city cops caught up and made the actual arrest. All legal. The O.C.T.F guys filed their cover-reports in two full supplement sheets using the case number on the city arrest report. They apparently didn't want their part in this matter to make the papers. Drunk driving arrests are evidently beneath them, but they're using this incident to embarrass Mister Malatesta."

"They had cops bust me three times before," Chickie broke in. "Twice for DUI and once for soliciting prostitution. Hah!" She puffed out her generous bosom and poked it with a long, red fingernail. "Can you imagine me soliciting?"

Bernie and Mack looked at her chest and shook their heads in unison.

"So." Mack ran fingers through disorderly reddish-brown hair and began to add everything up for himself. "They've got official witnesses to the drinking and the driving. There's an iffy Breathalyzer test on record and a messy arrest to top it all off." Mack smiled apologetically at Chickie. "Doesn't sound promising, babe."

"But Mack you've got to do something!" Chickie's eyes misted and she fumbled a handkerchief to dab carefully at their unmascaraed corners. "Can't you talk to someone? Don't you have friends on the force who will do you a favor?"

Mack glanced at Bernie and wished he'd stayed in his nice soft bed. "Chickie, the system doesn't work that way. They've already written the citation and filed the paperwork." He shrugged. "There's no way they would tear all the reports up and forget it, even if I were Chief Hobbs himself."

Chickie was crushed. Tears glistened. Her lower lip quivered and she grabbed in her purse for another handkerchief. "Oh Mack, I was counting on you. You mean there's nothing you can do? They'll put me in jail forever." The last word was a plaintive wail and she buried her face in the new, dry handkerchief.

Mack glanced at Bernie again and caught the tail end of a satisfied smirk. The prick was enjoying Chickie's disillusionment. The hotshot P.I. can't save the damsel in distress. Anger overwhelmed caution. This damn sure wasn't over yet. "When's the court date?" he asked the smug lawyer.

"Tuesday, October 12th, eight days from now." Bernie pronounced the words slowly like a sentence of death and Chickie's sobs increased in volume.

"Don't give up yet." Mack leaned and patted Chickie's tan shoulder. "I'll check around, talk to some people and see what I can do." He made a quick exit. Cormac Robertson, Private Eye, wanted to have a stiff drink, go to bed and sleep 'til dinnertime. He wasn't sure he could help Chickie, but left without a backward glance as though he knew what he was doing.

"That's the last we'll see of *him*," Bernie said with a satisfied smile.

• • •

"You're defending this broad?" the burly cop sputtered. He didn't bother removing his reflector-style dark glasses even though they had just been seated in a booth at Denny's restaurant. Whitman, the uniform nametag read - the name was one of those on the DUI report.

"Well, she's my client, yeah," Mack said a little defensively.

"Don't you know who she is?"

"Look, just because she's Bruno Malatesta's daughter doesn't mean she's a gangster, does it?"

"They're all thieving, murdering scum in my book," the policeman muttered.

Mack tried to smile. "Listen, I understand how you feel, but can you tell me a little bit about the arrest? Just for the record."

"Okay, what do you want to know?"

"Was she driving erratically?" Mack asked.

"Yeah, all over the road," Whitman said. "Lucky she didn't kill some..."

"Where was this?" Mack interrupted the comment. Tape was running.

"What do you mean?"

"I mean, where were you when you first saw her driving erratically?"

"Well, I didn't *actually* see her driving," Whitman said. "The other officers on the scene were the ones who observed the driving. I just heard their accounts."

"You arrested her, didn't you?" Mack said quietly, trying to remain calm.

Officer Whitman was becoming impatient also. "You read the reports, didn't you? The Organized Crime squad stopped her and made the bust, we just did the DUI paperwork and transported their prisoner."

"One other thing, "Mack continued quickly. "The location wasn't very clear. The report mentions a three-mile pursuit to Speedway and Houghton road, but never mentions exactly where you guys took over. Where *exactly* was the bust?"

"Exactly? Let's see, she was sitting in her white Cadillac." The cop's lips pressed together with suppressed anger. Or was the reaction simply confusion?

"Right," Mack prompted. "Where was the Cadillac?"

"Where was the Caddy....hmmm. I'll have to check on that and get back to you." The young officer forced a professional smile that reeked of dislike.

Mack wondered if he might have found a weak spot. "I've been recording this conversation. You don't mind do you?" He pulled out his pocket-sized tape recorder and continued without waiting for an answer. "When you called in you gave a location, remember? Come on, the bust wasn't that long ago, just two weeks."

"A tape recorder?" the policeman repeated. "Listen Robertson, you can record anything you want, but I've had enough." Officer Whitman spoke in a low menacing rasp. "My Sergeant says he's an old friend of yours. He asked me to give you five minutes and answer some of your questions, but I don't think he realized who you were working for." Leather creaked, heavy boots clumped under the table and the angry cop slid out of the booth. "Just how much is the Mafia paying you?"

"I'm doing this for free. She's a friend." Mack didn't mind the Mafia remark. The crack just gave the cop away, showed his inappropriate anger. But at what?

Nowhere on the reports - original arrest reports or the supplements - was the *exact* location of the arrest mentioned. They all said Speedway and Houghton. He figured he'd stumbled onto something. Mack had to find out exactly what. Maybe he'd show the snotty Bernie Frank how to make some magic after all.

• • •

Mack Robertson wasted the next five days receiving cold shoulders from Whitman's squad sergeant, Organized Crime Task Force investigators and the office of traffic investigations. His Squad Sergeant buddy shrugged him off, said he disapproved of Mack's client and told him not to interfere with his squad any more. A surly O.C.T.F. Sergeant made him wait two hours for a careful statement of police information policy, and no new information. Traffic investigations was a last resort, but no better. Sergeant Sparks refused to discuss the matter, told Mack to read the reports and referred him back to the Organized Crime people.

"I was there yesterday," Mack muttered angrily.

"Well go back there, it's their bust." The skinny, plainclothes sergeant sneered calmly up at the ex-cop-troublemaker and then slowly, pointedly resumed his paperwork.

"Beat cops made the actual arrest," Mack pointed out.

Sparks ignored the statement, didn't bother to look up.

Mack knew this was the traditional bureaucratic flim-flam: keep sending the poor, dumb sucker to another desk. He stood awkwardly at the second-floor office door. No one had invited him in and he held his trip-wire temper in careful check. There were other ways to skin this cat, weren't there? There had to be another way to get the information. Maybe a beer would help.

Back in his downtown office- home-photo-gallery just before sunset, Mack took a cold beer from the refrigerator under the loft in back, sprawled on his imitation leather couch, chugalugged half the bottle and went back over the police paperwork sheet by sheet. Same thing over and over. Traffic citation, arrest report, alcohol report, property voucher and booking sheet. They all gave the location of the arrest as 1100 North Houghton road. Mack knew 1100 North was the corner of Speedway and Houghton, right on the edge of the city. In fact Houghton *was* Tucson's east-side city limit. Everything east of that intersection was in the County. On which side of the street did they stop her? How to find out without depending on the police? Wait a moment! He remembered the car. What the hell did they do with the car after the arrest? They wouldn't just leave a late-model caddy at a dark intersection in the middle of the night and they damn sure hadn't called her father to come pick it up.

Mack finished the beer, opened another and shuffled papers. On the bottom section of the face-sheet of the arrest report: Disposition of Vehicle. A towing company was listed under suspect vehicle in the arrest report, Peterson's towing on South Park Avenue.

Two days later he found the tow-truck driver and convinced him to write out and record a statement.

• • •

Bernie Frank didn't stand up when he saw the P.I..

Mack strolled unannounced past the secretary onto the shag rug and handed the lawyer a legal-sized sheet of paper and two small tape cassettes. "She's clear. Turns out they busted her in the County," he announced. "Just out of the city limits. City cops had no jurisdiction to make the arrest."

Bernie was awash in mixed emotions. This would help his client's daughter, but he was more than irritated with Mack's last-minute interference. The high-priced lawyer didn't bother to hide his annoyance with the shabby, run-down P.I. "You gave this case up as a 'dead cinch' a week ago in my office," he said. "And you wait until the afternoon of the day before trial to bring me *this*?"

"I just found the tow-truck driver yesterday." Mack was too self-satisfied to be annoyed with the lawyer. He'd found a way to save Chickie from the D.U.I. and maintain a low profile in the case. He'd expected the lawyer to be pleased, but he should've known better. Sounded like the fat bastard was guarding his turf. "That's his signed, witnessed statement and I taped the whole thing while he was talking."

"Okay, okay," Bernie said and waved the paper in the air as though the statement was worthless. He'd spotted a flaw and quickly recovered his poise. "So we say the bust *was* in the County. They'll just claim the doctrine of hot pursuit. They'll say they observed a crime and pursued her out of the city limits."

"The beat cops didn't observe shit," Mack corrected. "When the first city officer came on the scene to arrest her she was sitting in her car by the side of the road on the northeast corner of Speedway and Houghton in the damn County."

Bernie picked up a thin case folder and opened it. "Doesn't say *that* anywhere in the paperwork." He fanned out reports like a winning hand.

"No, they didn't write it down on purpose." Mack lowered himself carefully into a flimsy, leather chair-sling and felt the chrome bend. "But when the arresting officer - Whitman's his name - gets on the stand, try to pin him down on location." Mack shrugged and grinned. "When Whitman gets vague, you show the judge the tow-truck driver's statement where he picked up the Cadillac. The judge hears the cop covering up and sees the arrest was out of the City, he'll cut Chickie loose."

Bernie was in a quandary. Mack was right, but that didn't help Bernie. He wanted to get Malatesta's daughter off without giving away credit. He thought about the problem while pretending to read the tow-truck driver's badly scrawled statement. Bernie's eyes rested on a grease smudge at the bottom of the paper. Don Bruno would be grateful, but not to Bernie. Suddenly he saw a way to burnish his image. He was known for his ability to settle things out of court. "Why don't I call the judge? I'll advise him the case is out of the city's jurisdiction, he'll call the city prosecutor and we can settle the whole thing tomorrow morning without a trial."

Mack knew what the lawyer was doing, but he also knew there would be a problem with any deal. The P.I. knew the prosecutors better than the mob lawyer. "Wait a minute." He raised a cautioning finger, annoying the fat lawyer even more. "If you do that they *won't* deal. You'll just warn the bastards, give them a chance to refile in the County and rearrest Chickie on a complaint from the Task Force guys. The City Attorney will drop the complaint and the County Attorney will refile the thing in Justice Court, bring in the O.C.T.F. officers to testify and *they'll* nail her."

Bernie realized his mistake. "Right, but...," he began to change the subject, but Mack continued his lecture on the law in Tucson, Arizona.

"...we should go to trial and convince the judge to throw the complaint out of *City* court. The prosecutor could still refile, but that wouldn't look good. Refiling in the county would look like a petty vendetta and you could argue double jeopardy."

Bernie snorted disgust with the armchair advice. His neck swelled even more over his shirt collar and he began to sweat in the air-conditioned office. He'd taken enough amateur crap, but didn't say a word, not right away. Bernie was both a slick lawyer and a professional coward. His furious mind began to devise a roundabout way to punish this rummy, P.I. for his chutzpa. He realized the answer almost immediately. He didn't like losing credit for legal maneuvers, but would suffer the loss to convince someone else to punish Mack Robertson. The embryonic plan was almost perfect. He'd been concerned about sharing credit with this insolent fool. Better he should give *all* the credit to the ex-cop. Bernie decided to praise Mack Robertson to Mister Malatesta, bring him to the attention of the boss and, of course, bring his zealous efforts on Chickie's behalf to the tender notice ofVinnie Romano. Bernie clenched a fist under the desk and swallowed his anger. First a smile to confuse. "Ah Mister Robertson, you are a very thorough investigator." He stretched the smile until expensively capped teeth showed to the gums. "And of course you're correct. You have an excellent knowledge of the legal system."

Mack puffed a little even though he doubted Bernie's sincerity. "Thank you Bernie, I try," he said.

"You're right about this case of course," Bernie continued his plan. "We must bring it into City Court and..." The lawyer paused, pretending to remember something. "By the way, that cop, Whitman? You've been *so* thorough. You taped that conversation with him? He turned the statement into a question.

"Sure," Mack said and pointed to the cassettes on the desk. "He admitted he saw no erratic driving. He even gave me his permission to tape, after the fact."

"Well you'll have to testify in court, you know." Bernie slowly, gently built the trap. "This is a technicality, but I can't possibly introduce taped conversations in evidence at this late date without your court testimony as foundation."

Mack had hoped the signed, witnessed tow-truck driver's statement would be enough to impeach Whitmore's fudging on the car location. He didn't want to be called on the stand by a mob defense lawyer. "Come on, Bernie, you don't need the tape, just use the statement. The judge'll see the bust was out of city jurisdiction."

The lawyer savored the moment. "Sorry, Mister Robertson, I know this is a hassle, but we want to be sure and save miss Malatesta from jail, don't we?"

Mack was nervous, but quickly resigned himself. "Yeah, I guess you're right." And then he had a cautious afterthought. "For the record, I'm *your* investigator, right? Chickie and I are friends, but you don't have to advise Mister Malatesta that she wanted you to hire me, right?"

"Of course not," Bernie said and glowed with anticipation. His next question was very carefully phrased. "By the way, how much did Chickie say I would pay you to help her?"

"I don't know." Mack glanced at the lawyer's complacent face. He could use the money, but wanted to show the fat prick some class. "Chickie's an old friend. My work's on the house." Mack walked out of the office feeling righteous as hell.

After a count of three, Bernie Frank picked up his phone and hit the speed-dialer. "Vinnie? It's me, Bernie Frank. Yeah. Good news for you and the boss." Bernie nodded his head and smiled at the harsh voice of Vinnie Romano. "This P.I. named Mack Robertson did a lot of work for Miss Malatesta..." Bernie's grin spread his cheeks to sweaty parentheses around the beautiful teeth. "What? Oh yeah, I said Robertson. You know him?" He paused and held the phone away from his ear while Vinnie shouted a few words. "Well he's gonna get Chickie off of this DUI rap. *And* he's doing it for free. What? Yeah, for free! Listen, Vinnie, no offense, but I think this Robertson guy thinks she's gonna be real grateful." There was another outburst and then Bernie smiled into a dead phone.

That afternoon he notified every reporter he knew about Chickie's trial.

• • •

"All rise! The Court of the Honorable Judge Courtney Kane is now in session." The elderly judge breezed in like a man in a hurry and motioned with one hand for everyone to be seated. Mack had arrived early and was seated in the first row behind the railing just in back of Chickie and Bernie at the defense table.

"Is the City ready...."

Officer Whitman testified about erratic driving, alcohol on breath, abusive language and Breathalyzer tests. He fuzzed the details of location as expected.

Mack waited for Bernie's cross-examination.

Bernie hardly looked up from his papers, "No questions, your Honor."

No questions? Mack began to worry.

The other city arresting officer testified. No mention was made of the exact location. Bernie *still* had no questions. The prosecution rested.

Bernie Frank stood, straightened his suit-front, arranged his French-cuffs, smiled at the judge and called Mack Robertson as his first witness.

Mack passed the defense table on the way to the witness stand. He winked at Chickie, glanced at the fat lawyer and did a double take. There was no serious mien, no reassuring smile; only mirthful triumph lit the lawyer's small, brown eyes. Mack knew something bad was happening. He stepped into the witness box, turned to face the half-full courtroom and had raised his hand for the swearing-in, before he noticed two television cameras and more than a dozen reporters with notebooks crowding into the room. Mack realized he'd been forced to center stage, been suckered. Bernie had made *him* the defense case and even called the press!

Television lights glared. Pens scratched busily.

"I understand you have information about a City jurisdictional problem that could help Miss Malatesta," Bernie Frank began quietly.

Mack nodded, but before he could respond, Bernie continued. "Why don't you tell us all about the Tucson Police Officers' mistake in your own words."

Mack hesitated a moment, shrugged and told the court about the tape of Officer Whitman and the statement he had taken from the tow-truck driver.

The City Attorney was stunned. He listened a moment and tried to interrupt with an objection that was rejected by Judge Kane. Finally, unable to control himself, he jumped from his seat and waved a paper in the air. "I object! I thoroughly object to this irregularity!" he fumed. "We were not made aware of this evidence, and furthermore, this witness was not on the defense witness list. Your Honor, please, please, you cannot allow this travesty!"

Bernie Frank turned calmly to face the judge. "Your Honor, we *had* no witness list. Mister Robertson volunteered this signed statement and tape-recorded information only yesterday evening. There was no time to notify the court that its jurisdiction was in question."

The judge was fully aware of the busy pens and television cameras. He had realized from the prosecutor's first word of objection he couldn't get away with suppressing jurisdictional evidence on a lawyer's technicality. "I have already said I will allow the testimony," he said. His gavel rapped everyone to silence. "Mister Frank, I don't like this, but if you have a motion to dismiss, I will entertain it."

The prosecutor was apoplectic, would not wait for the motion, could not bear the final insult. "The City moves to drop the charge," he said and sat down.

Judge Kane cut Chickie loose, issued a warning to the prosecutor not to waste his time in the future and left the courtroom. Bernie followed the judge.

Television cameras moved closer, lights blazing like small suns. Some members of the press rushed to leave while others waited to watch the TV talking heads try for interviews. The chagrined cops and the angry, flustered prosecutor brushed quickly through the crowd of questions and left without another word to anyone. Reporters turned to Mack; TV lights washed the witness chair.

Chickie Malatesta jumped up from the defense table and ran to hug her hero. She squeezed him to a gasp and kissed him full on the mouth. "Oh Mack you did it!" she squealed. "Daddy will be so happy." He stood, fending her off, but she kissed him again, molding her big body to his, really turning on the heat.

"Chickie, be careful, damn it!" Mack sputtered. This was exactly what he'd feared most. "Your father will see that kiss on the evening news." He held the happy woman away and turned to face the thrusting microphones and dangerous questions. Before he could respond to a shouted question about ex-cops turning on their buddies, he thought he glimpsed a burly man with a smooth, unnaturally pale bullet-head shoving rudely through the crowd near the door. Vinnie Romano?

Mack had never actually seen him. He'd seen mug shots and rare pictures in newspapers and he had read a file and rap sheet years before in Organized Crime files. He remembered shots of a young wise guy with a half-smile, hard eyes and lots of thick, dark hair combed into a pompadour. He'd been handsome back then, smirking and mocking the official camera, but looks were deceiving and Vinnie was reputed to be a psychopath, a vicious demolition, torch-man for the Chicago mob. Vinnie Romano was called monster because it was said he enjoyed the burnings and always hung around fire and explosion scenes to experience the results of his work. They said he loved the screams. Mack remembered Police Psychiatrist notes in the Romano file had remarked how abnormal, solitary and often-sadistic sexual gratification was frequently associated with pyromania.

Mack had recently asked around - cops talk about mobsters. According to the cop grapevine, about a year ago, Vinnie had become trapped in one of his own fires at a mob-owned laundry. He'd evidently stayed around for enjoyment and waited too long. Something exploded and the Mafia torch man had been splashed with flaming cleaning-fluid, suffering chemical burns over half his body. Word was he'd barely survived and had come west to heal. Little had been heard of him since he'd arrived in Arizona except that he was supposedly ashamed of his new hairless appearance and kept pretty much in seclusion. He'd stayed out of trouble in Tucson and was supposedly expecting extradition papers from Illinois on the arson, but he wasn't hiding and he wasn't hard to pick from a crowd. According to cop-gossip, his new "trademark" was ugly white scar tissue covering his completely baldhead.

Had the monster seen Mack testify for Chickie...and her gratitude?

CHAPTER FOUR

CONDOTTA

"This man has tried to help," Bruno Malatesta interrupted the angry young man. "He has performed a service to her. Is his reward to be death?"

"This *espumar* has put his hands on your daughter, Don Bruno," the curiously liquid voice gurgled. Vinnie Romano forced himself to speak calmly. He did not wish to seem disrespectful to his powerful patron. "He uses her. I have seen it. He kissed her in public." Vinnie's short powerful fingers grasped the air. A gold I.D. bracelet dangled from a blotchy, hairless wrist.

Don Bruno Malatesta leaned back and swept his eyes over the rows of hand-hewn 4x8 Alaskan Fir beams bracing the porch poof. He swallowed anger and sighed pleasure in the rustic workmanship. Never allow your true feelings to govern, he carefully reminded himself. "I will not risk our new project to satisfy your anger," he said and carefully kept his eyes on the roof beams. He had paid the workmen a year of their salary in 1965 for the six months they had spent building his ranch house.

"This is more than my anger," Vinnie hissed. "The kiss was an insult to you."

Don Bruno remained silent. He finally was able to calm his irritation with this difficult, but useful young man by contemplating his profitable retirement.

While still a strong man in his mid-fifties, Bruno Malatesta had finessed a risky war for leadership in Chicago by taking early retirement from the family's businesses in the Midwest and moving to a warm climate to live out the second half of his life. The retiring Don, his ailing wife and their outsized young daughter had been accompanied by only two of his most trusted soldiers; there was no need for protection in the neutral deserts of Arizona. Thirty years passed in quiet bliss and scattered sorrows. His wife had died and his daughter was ungrateful for his love, but other parts of the retirement had been interesting. Don Bruno had dabbled in the legitimate world of bars, restaurants, hotels, dog tracks and wet his beak in the deep pool of Arizona land speculation. Opportunities fell in his lap, local politicians, merchants and other men of influence used him as a secret bank; he had extracted promises of future cooperation and percentages of their businesses in return. All legal, friendly and quiet as befitted a retired Man of Honor.

A smile lifted the grim lines of the old man's face as he considered his good fortune. When he had moved to Tucson, Las Vegas was a faint glimmer in the New York family's eye, a resort in the desert that provided a neutral playground for the *amici*. But over the years Meyer Lanski's gamble had paid off beyond even that clever man's wildest dreams. The glimmer became a molten glare, a volcano of money enriching everyone with the foresight to invest in the desolate sands of Nevada. Meyer shared the good fortune with his dangerous partners and their relatives. Casinos bloomed like weeds in the parched desert. Soon Las Vegas gambling money enriched all the families. But the money also became a matter of intense interest to Government tax collectors. The Governments in Nevada and Washington D.C. wanted a cut - demanded nearly half the golden flow. This was unreasonable, an insult. A scheme was devised to reduce the tribute by skimming off a percentage of the profits before they were officially counted. What then? What to do with those many millions of skimmed dollars that supposedly did not exist?

How to turn black money into white profits?

Don Bruno nodded knowingly at his dark-lacquered roof-beams.

Banks could not hide money from a suspicious government that probed and examined them like an old cuckold with a young wife, but the families remembered their honored patriarch living out his years in the warm Arizona sun. Don Bruno Malatesta was less than an hour from the casinos in a light plane - and only five or so hours by car - from growing piles of black money. He was most happy to help. He'd developed friendly associations in Arizona. Companies that handled cash in large amounts were formed with influential Arizonans. Politicians were reminded of past, and possible future, favors. Friendly laws were passed. Dominant members of the community were enlisted for seemingly innocent investments and public opinion was massaged. Almost overnight Don Bruno became the Magician in the West. Black money was brought to Arizona and washed white again.

For years the Don had lived a peaceful existence on his ranch and watched the river of skimmed Las Vegas money disappear into the Arizona entertainment empire of hotels, bars, restaurants, Indian bingo parlors, horse and dog tracks. Then an embarrassing problem had arisen. Lately the skimmed gambling money had become a flood - too much coming in. The mob needed bigger laundries, bigger circuses. The answer? Sports arenas. With profitable concessions, expensive tickets, corporate boxes and off-track betting connections, Sports arenas were quite simply bigger versions of bars, tracks and bingo parlors.

They were incredibly expensive to build, however.

Don Bruno's friends in business, media and politics came up with the obvious answer: taxpayers could be persuaded to buy their *own* circuses through bond elections. Once the arenas were built, there were connected companies - like Don Bruno's Emprise Corporation - that would lease the cash-heavy operations and concessions. So lately, taxpayer-funded coliseums became the newest rage in Arizona, darlings of connected politicians, playthings of the moneyed elite.

There were problems. Dangerous local opposition - an anti-tax group - had formed against the approaching Sports Arena bond election and a young reporter was digging alarmingly near the truth. To make things worse, the editor of the influential newspaper, a long-time associate, was drinking too much and falling apart. Don Bruno had asked for help. The families sent Vinnie Romano.

"Eh? A kiss?" Bruno finally said. "I know kisses. Whaddyou mean, a kiss?"

"You know what I mean, a man-woman kiss." Vinnie half-whispered, "Open mouth and in public like he was her damned husband."

Bruno dropped his gaze to the bald young man. "They was just celebrating." *This crazy man really wants my Chickie*, he thought.

Bruno knew the man thought of himself as ugly now. Vinnie was unsure, even furtive when the Don's daughter was present. Once a confident young man with thick hair, Vinnie Romano had changed. His features were presentable, but strangely smooth and regular. The burning had taken Vinnie's hair, eyebrows, natural facial skin and most of all, his pride. The reconstructed features were taut and without texture - skin stretched across facial bones like a pale mask. Not ugly, as Vinnie apparently believed, but odd. Boiling fluid had also burned his lungs and taken most of his voice. Bruno had heard the story many times: An explosion - something had gone wrong with the torch job. Other men saw Vinnie running from the building, a screaming ghost of blue flame. A sudden downpour had doused the flames, but sirens wailed, coming close. They said Vinnie had crumpled to the street, smoking like a charred log in the rain. They left him for dead. The cops found a burned man with an I.D. bracelet sunk into fire-blistered flesh. They put him in an ambulance and wrote him off as a dying suspect.

Vinnie spent more than six months in the burn ward where they saved his life and rebuilt his face with skin grafts. He found what was left of his voice in the fifth month and, when the Cook County Prosecutor began to show an interest in the healing suspect, the bosses decided to ship Vinnie to their old, retired friend in Tucson who needed help with *special* problems.

The younger man bowed his head. "Don Bruno I have spoken to you about your daughter." Vinnie's voice clogged and gurgled in his seared throat. "I wish to make her my wife if she will have such a man as me. This is a matter of honor."

"Enough!" Bruno Malatesta's voice boomed, then dropped to a whisper. "You will not argue with me, Vincenzo. You are here for business. When the work is done we will see about my daughter, as I promised."

Bruno considered the problem of Vinnie and Chickie. His daughter had made the mistake of showing kindness to Vinnie when he arrived from Chicago. Vinnie had evidently taken her kindness to mean much more. Chickie had been frightened. She'd asked her father's permission to move from the main ranch to the gatehouse to escape the strangely needy man's attentions. Bruno had been in a quandary; he had to heed his daughter's wishes, but needed Vinnie's talents for a while. He'd decided to satisfy both situations at once. Don Bruno mentioned certain problems he was having with Chickie and asked Vinnie to watch her - *without her knowing* - and he told Vinnie about a *special* system he had arranged. He then confided to Chickie that Vinnie would be keeping his distance for a while. Vinnie wasn't wholly satisfied, neither was Chickie, but the matter was settled temporarily.

And his daughter had become a delicate problem long before Vinnie.

Bruno intended to deceive them both and suggest compliance, but he was very aware his daughter had long been escaping his control...and with a cop. Don Bruno always planned everything very carefully. He knew decisions in life and business should be allowed to grow in their own time, but sometimes a nudge was required. He'd seen pictures of the kiss on the news - that same big, ex-cop hugging and kissing his little girl. Nothing to dwell on, *yet*. But the kisses only confirmed the ex-cop had more than unusual influence on his daughter. After the anger built and then subsided again like his evening indigestion, he decided he would use this Robertson person in spite of Vinnie Romano. "I want to talk to Cormac Robertson," he said. "You deal with your problems when I have finished my business with him."

• • •

"I saw you on television," Grace Faber said as she walked up to the table and held out a small, well-manicured hand. She was his noon appointment.

"Not much of a recommendation," Mack grumbled and stood to shake her hand. This prospective client sounded very young and naive. Television? He figured this wouldn't be a serious job, probably wanted him to follow her hubby.

"On the contrary." Her voice became very businesslike. "Your exposure of the clumsy police attempt to entrap Miss Malatesta impressed me greatly."

"Well, well, *entrap*, huh?" Mack realized the small redhead might be knowledgeable after all. "What can I do for you, Mrs....? Mack asked with a smile.

She decided not to answer the rudely implied question. Pleasantries would not be necessary. Initial impressions at first meetings were normally crucial to Grace as a journalist and interviewer, but in this case, she did not intend to interview or examine Cormac Robertson. She was only hiring his apparent courage and honesty. She sat down and unfolded her napkin without answering.

He drank deeply from his beer bottle and watched her decide what to say. Evidently Grace Faber was a cold, deliberate woman. She pretended to look out the window at the shimmering fountain in the tree-shaded courtyard that formed the centerpiece of the downtown Tucson restaurant, but her gray eyes were cloaked in thought behind their glasses and didn't seem to notice the beauty.

She was very conscious of his probing gaze, his rough, gritty presence. Her attention turned to the screen of remembered observations. Grace had watched him on the news and studied the photograph of the courtroom kiss that accompanied the *Register* story the next day. The newspaper had run a long article about the high-principled ex-cop who had turned on his police brothers and exposed an attempt to frame the sexy daughter of a Mafia Don. He sounded like the hero in a bad novel.

Trouble was, Cormac Robertson didn't look the part.

He looked big and tough, but rumpled and terribly weary. Lines traversed his clean-shaven face. Crow's feet etched the outer corners of cold gray-blue eyes, a once-chiseled nose had been broken once or twice and deep, crooked scars dented one cheek and the left side of his forehead below thick reddish-brown hair. The only softness in Robertson's face was the mouth, the strangely sensual lips that curved in knowing smiles when they weren't wrapped around a beer bottle. Hard to tell with some men, but he looked a badly abused forty-five. The right age, but definitely not her type. As they'd shaken hands she'd noticed he examined her as though she were the daily special at a slave auction, only glancing at her face, but fully inspecting her body. He was jaded to a sneer, a sexist and obviously a drunk like her father. She also couldn't forget the sloppy, kissy-kissy scene with the big, brassy Mafia woman in the front of the courtroom on the six o' clock news.

She turned from the window and looked into his cold eyes. I'm not going to date him, she reminded herself, just hire him to light a fire under the police. "I want to hire you to find out who ran down and killed my mother." she said.

"Ran down...your mother?" the sardonic smile vanished. He suddenly looked concerned. "You mean a hit and run?"

"Yes. Whoever did it didn't bother to stop." Her voice quivered a bit.

"The police aren't working the case?"

Grace felt increasingly uncomfortable discussing her crushing tragedy over starched tablecloths, menus and silverware with busy waiters nearby. "Not to my satisfaction. Look, I don't want to discuss this here. Could we go to your office?"

Mack's office was a desk, couch and chair crowded under his sleeping loft in the back of his photographic studio. He always met clients in restaurants. "I'm sorry, but my office doubles as a kitchen and bedroom." He smiled again and finished the beer. "We have enough privacy here and we *do* need to eat."

She sighed, nodded and sipped ice water from her frosted goblet.

Grace Faber smelled good. Gardenia. Probably White Shoulders, he thought. Mack's sense of smell was very highly developed and increased his enjoyment of food and women, allowing him to experience aspects of life others couldn't know. He breathed her in and smiled at a curlicue of nervous sweat. But other than her smell and the thick auburn hair pulsing almost gold in the sunlight, Mack thought she was plain as hell. The rest of her looked like somebody's kid sister. A small, pursed mouth, thin nose and weak, gray eyes under Ben Franklin spectacles fit the bony, triangular face of a Dickens waif. A fox-face of care and caution, and hardly any figure was visible under the blue blazer and tan slacks. Not much to look at. Apparently unpleasant as well. "Want a drink?" he asked.

"No, thank you." She pressed her thin lips even thinner. Her disapproval of his having two beers at a business meeting was plain. "But you go ahead and have another. Becks isn't it?" She poked at the still-frosted empty.

"Yeah, Becks." He raised his hand and beckoned the waiter.

They ordered and ate without much conversation. He devoured a blood-rare New York steak, baked potato, some boiled julienne vegetables and drank two more beers while she picked at a spinach salad with feta cheese and mushrooms.

He drained the fourth beer and leaned forward. "What makes you think the police aren't doing their job?" he asked.

She described what she knew of her mother's death and related her fruitful, but nearly disastrous bluff with Sergeant Sparks. "They know *something*, but my boss, Ace Collins at the *Register,* is furious. He told me to stay away from the police."

Her voice faded and she mashed bits of pale goat-cheese under her fork.

Mack was stunned. "Well I'll be Goddamned!" *Aloof, self-important, he should have known.* "You're a reporter!" The word came out like a curse.

Grace glanced up at the big man and met his hostile stare. "Yes. Why do you care what I do for a living?"

"The Fourth Estate, bastion of freedom, coming to *me* for help," he mocked and shook his head. "I guess I can handle the shock, but this will be a first."

Grace was ready to give up, just get up from her chair and leave without another word, but she didn't want to stiff him for the check - a matter of pride. She decided to tough the awkward situation out. "What's wrong with reporters?"

"Buncha self-righteous, liberal, finger-pointers with no concept of the real world." He said and pointed his finger at the redhead, "If you people had any..."

"How dare you!" Grace exploded and tossed her glasses on the table. "If not for the press you would be a subject of the British Crown, slavery would be a cottage industry in the South and Spiro Agnew would be a respected ex-president!" Grace was in full gallop at the end. She delivered the last few words with vigorous flourishes of her cheese-laden fork.

Vinaigrette-moistened Feta sprayed across Mack's scarred forehead, leaving white, lumpy drops drooling into his eyebrows.

She gasped, paused a moment to watch. "Take *that* you swine," she muttered.

He began to wipe his face and smile at the same time.

Grace was appalled at her lapse in manners, but couldn't cover the giggles quaking her petite belly. Tears flowed down her cheeks. She bent over and erupted in laughter. She knew she sounded like a lowing cow, but couldn't stop.

He was surprised at her un-ladylike guffaws. They were contagious. He joined her and in moments the two were lost in loud, raucous laughter.

Later over coffee she explained in more detail and Mack said he would investigate the hit and run. Grace Faber agreed to pay him fifty dollars an hour and listened as he told of *his* experience with Sergeant Sparks at Traffic Investigations. Their differences were quickly forgotten and they became cautious friends before the bill arrived. She referred to the incident as their Feta *accompli*.

• • •

The whispered voice on the phone was hard to understand. "Mister Malatesta says he...owes...a favor. He wants to see you tonight."

"Who is this?" Mack figured it out as he asked. Vinnie!

The whispered voice rose to a sudden angry husk. "Don't matter who *this* is. *You* just listen. Drive out Speedway to the gatehouse at Malatesta Ranch and somebody'll meet ya." Heavy mucous-laden breath blustered over the line. "You unnerstan' me? Six o' clock tonight. You be there."

• • •

A cool fall sunset splashed the Rincons in purple. Light died slowly and shadows crawled up the massive slopes, leaving night in the valleys. Mack reached the end of Speedway at ten after six. There was a familiar-looking dark sedan waiting at the entrance. No lights were on in the gatehouse. He wondered if Chickie was home and thought of her big, sleek body. He shook off the warm thoughts and finished the fourth beer of the six-pack he'd brought along for company. Two gray-haired bouncer-types got out of the car. One walked toward Mack's pickup, he was older, sixtyish, but big like a retired defensive lineman or ex-heavyweight boxer.

"Come wit' us," he said as Mack rolled down his window.

A small relief settled in. This didn't look like a beating or a hit. He left the 45 and beer in his truck and, resisting the impulse to check the license plate, got in the back seat of their car. Relax, he told himself, he'd done the Don a favor and Chickie had said there were only the two bodyguards. They were both in the front seat. Mack *was* still worried about Vinnie Romano, but now he was more curious than anything else. This trip was probably not dangerous. If Bruno wanted him dead he would have been dead on the road the other night. Vinnie had said Mister Malatesta owed a favor. What could he have in mind? Money?

The house was an inn-sized two-story, red wood A-frame with a dark shingled roof and eight or nine windows lighted in front over the curved driveway. Mack saw carved Bavarian-style wooden balconies under glowing second-floor windows. He figured the place must have twenty rooms. The two elderly goons left him at the front step as a huge, iron-strapped door groaned open slowly.

"Welcome to my house," Bruno Malatesta said in a thin voice. He was slight and bent with more than eighty years and Mack began to doubt the myths, but the old man glanced up, met his gaze and sly energy flashed like a spear. Fierce old eyes seemed to read his inner thoughts and the Don smiled knowingly before motioning Mack down a paneled passageway leading to a lobby-sized hall with hand-hewn furniture scattered in conversation clumps. A fireplace large enough to roast a whole steer yawned at the far end of the room.

Mack looked around carefully. He expected to see Vinnie the Monster lurking somewhere with murder in his eyes, but there was no one in the big room. Half way to the fireplace a table was set with coffee and a bottle of Anisette.

The old man turned. "I wish to show my appreciation for the service you have done my family," he said in a soothing voice.

Mack decided to be as honest as was prudent. "I did it for friendship. Your daughter, Chickie and I have become very good friends in the past few years and I thought she was getting a bum rap from the police. I would have done the same for *any* of my friends, Mister Malatesta."

"I will not insult you by offering money," Don Bruno continued as though Mack had not spoken. "My lawyer tells me you would not accept payment from him, but that you did us this service out of...ah, love for my daughter."

"Perhaps that is too strong a word, Mister Malatesta," Mack protested.

"Yes, yes." He lowered himself into a leather couch and motioned for Mack to sit across the table. "I am aware of your *friendship*. I do not approve." The voice hardened, the old eyes flashed fire. "But that is not why you are here." He busied himself pouring a cup of black coffee that smelled both syrupy and harsh like Cuban or Turkish. The old man poured an inch of Anisette into a glass, sipped one and then the other, smacking his lips and closing his eyes as strong tastes jolted and stimulated an aging palate. When he noticed Mack hadn't moved, he waved impatiently. "Take it! Take it!' he said, voice breaking to a dry cough, "Haugh! And we will discuss my daughter, Chickie. Haugh! How to make her well again."

"Make her well?" Mack repeated. "Is Chickie sick?"

"You should recognize her sickness." Bruno swallowed with obvious difficulty. "I mean no insult, but I understand you have had, ah, problems with strong drink in your past."

"Yeah, that's true," Mack said. He could have said the problems weren't really over, but decided not to.

"So you see," Bruno continued. "Your saving my daughter from the courts will have a mixed result." He held a blue-veined hand in front of his face, pushed the fingers to the thumb and gestured up and down. "She is free from the heavy hand of the law, but she will not get the weeks of rest and treatment she needs to flush the alcohol from her poor, tired system. They say fifteen to twenty days in a clinic would be sufficient. You save her from prison and condemn her to a life of degradation." The wizened old man shook his head in puzzlement and sorrow. He seemed lost in the large, leather couch; Bruno Malatesta didn't look like a feared and deadly Mafiosi chieftain, Mack thought. Instead he looked like an aged father, tired and dejected and worried about his free-spirited daughter.

"Your lawyer never said detoxification treatment was an option," Mack said. "*She* mentioned it, but I thought for sure she'd go to jail after her third DUI."

Bruno Malatesta leaned forward and refilled his Anisette glass and one for Mack. "You know what is *condotta*?" he asked.

Mack hesitated. "Well, I think *condotta* means contract, Mister Malatesta."

"Yeah, *condotta*, contract. Because you have involved yourself so deeply in my family's misfortune...because you have done only part of a service to me, I wish to make *condotta*." Don Bruno fixed his piercing eyes on Mack. "You will talk my Chickie into entering the Western Care detoxification clinic for three weeks."

"What? What makes you think she'll listen to me?"

"I did not ask you to interfere." The voice cut the air like a razor. "But since you have decided to do me a favor, I contract with you to finish the job."

Mack was getting angry. "And if I fail?" he asked with some defiance.

"You will visit her and encourage her." Don Bruno ignored Mack's question. "When she has been at the treatment center for two weeks, I will pay you five thousand dollars, and I will pay another five thousand after the third week. That is my contract with you." The old man sat back, pleased with himself and his deceptively simple *condotta* with the greedy, and very gullible, ex-cop.

• • •

The driveway was long and dark, at least a two-mile walk through waist-high bush and prickly pear and groups of trees that blocked the stars. No moon. A soft wind shifted dry mesquite and acacia as though snakes slithered through the crisp air. The night was typical for the high desert, full of sound and movement and smells. Mack breathed the wet-green of a broken branch, a twist of alkali raised by his shoe and the dry must of empty seed pods under the trees. Small animals shifted in the bushes near the narrow road, moving away from his shuffling feet.

Don Bruno had dismissed him without ceremony after their discussion. The two goons in the car had evidently left. Damned inconsiderate, Mack thought as he trudged along the crumbled tire-ruts. Oh well, a little walk wouldn't hurt him and it had been a good night's business. Ten thousand dollars was good money for three weeks babysitting a good-looking woman. So why did the contract bother him?

Mack saw the gatehouse. Lights out. Ten o' clock or so.

"Who's knocking? Who is it?" her voice hissed through the thick door.

"It's me," Mack stage-whispered.

"Go away!"

"Damn it Chickie, open up!" Mack's voice rose to full volume. "It's me, Mack Robertson."

The door opened. Darkness. Something pale moved. "God Mack, I thought it was that monster again." She hugged him and pulled him inside. The door closed and they kissed in the dark hallway.

Mack leaned away from her mouth. "What do you mean? Was he here?"

"Oh, hell yes, he sneaks in here all the time."

"Does he bother you? Molest you?"

Her body shook against him. He thought she was sobbing, but her voice bubbled with amusement. "No, no, he's too shy for that. He sneaks in when I'm not here. I think he likes to sit in my walk-in closet and play with my clothes."

"Your clothes? What the hell do you mean?"

Chickie tugged impatiently on his arm, led him up a circular flight of stairs to a room at the top of the tower. "This is my bedroom," she said and switched on a light. She was fully dressed in Levis and a man's wrinkled shirt. Her hair was mussed and flattened on one side as though she'd slept on it. Chickie looked tired and sober.

"He sneaks in and plays with your clothes?" Mack repeated. "How do you know?"

Chickie turned and sat on her muslin-canopied, king-sized bed. Her fingers first toyed with a plain white cotton nightdress folded on the turned-down covers and then gestured across the bedroom to a large walk-in closet. "Oh they're all mussed up when I come home. I guess he tries them on and then puts them back, but I know he's handled them because I can smell him on them." She shuddered with disgust, "And he brings my vanity stool in there with him." She pointed down at the rug. "The stool-legs leave deep marks on the rug in there."

Mack walked to the large closet and gazed along rows of lingerie, dresses, blouses, slacks, sweaters and coats. He reached up and tugged the long chain attached to a bare-bulb fixture in the middle of the closet ceiling. The aisle rug showed four deep indentations that seemed to match the legs of the pink-pillowed stool in front of the vanity against the wall near her bed. He imagined the baldhead bowed under the bare bulb in the midst of all the delicate clothing, thick fingers caressing soft cloth. Mack felt a crawling sensation on the back of his neck. "Why are you still dressed?" he asked. "You look as though you've been sleeping."

She smiled and combed her fingers through the flattened hair. "Does it show?" Chickie posed a moment at the edge of her bed, arms up, back arched, breasts straining the white shirt, but then she sighed and dropped the pose. "I'm afraid to get undressed any more. Daddy says he told him to stay away, but I'm afraid Vinnie's gonna get brave some night and come in when I'm asleep."

Mack reached up and tugged the closet light off. He wanted to get out of there, wanted to get Chickie away. He knew how to accomplish that now. "Chickie, I think I have a temporary solution to your problem." He sat next to her and held her hand. "Tonight I made a contract with your father."

Fear drew lines at the corners of her eyes. "Contract? What do you mean?"

Mack explained the contract to convince her to enter the treatment center and the two five-thousand-dollar fees he would be paid after the second and third weeks. "An odd arrangement, but he probably figures the third week will be the hardest and I'll need the added incentive. This way you can get away from Vinnie."

"But a treatment center is a *hospital*, Mack," Chickie objected. "I'm not sick and I damn sure don't intend to quit drinking." Her lower lip pouted determination.

Mack picked up the white cotton nightgown and held it up. See-through and low-cut with little buttons down the front, he imagined her shrugging the cloth from her shoulders, but banished the thought. "Look, tell you what, I'll split the money with you, five thousand apiece. You'll only be there a few weeks and I'll come visit you. Plenty of good food and you can sleep in this sexy nightgown again."

She considered. The idea *did* solve the Vinnie problem. And the money would be a windfall; for years her daddy had never given her enough allowance money to move away from him. Five thousand would get her a place of her own. "We share the money and you come visit me often?"

He nodded. "Fifty-fifty and I'll be there a couple of times each week. I think Western Care has visiting hours between four and six."

"But the place isn't a *real* hospital, right?"

"Western Care is a place where rich people dry out or kick drug habits," he answered. "You'll meet some of the best people in Tucson there."

"But what about a drink now and then?"

"Honey, for five thousand dollars you can last a few weeks without rum and coke. Besides, if the craving gets *real* bad I'll smuggle something in."

A smile lifted the corners of her generous mouth. "Sounds like fun. Sign me in this Western Care place tomorrow morning."

"Good. I'll stay here and keep watch until morning," Mack said and sighed with relief. "Maybe you can get some sleep if I'm here."

Chickie's smile broadened. She began to unbutton her shirt. "Sugar, sleep is the last thing on my mind right now."

CHAPTER FIVE

THE WITNESS

Hit and run investigations are a bitch if they aren't followed-up right away. Witnesses tend to drift, lose memory, and those who weren't contacted at the accident usually avoid follow-up investigators out of guilt for not coming forward at the scene. Mack knew he couldn't go to the police for help after their Malatesta embarrassment. He would investigate the hard way: read the paperwork and walk the streets. He did what he always did when he began cases, opened a beer and sprawled on the couch with the paperwork Grace had given him. First thing, he noticed there was damn little paper for a pedestrian fatality on a main street during rush hour. There were accident reports with scale drawings and measurements, ambulance reports, hospital emergency room sign-offs, and a coroner's finding of death from massive trauma, but only two witness statements from people who apparently saw very little, if any, of the accident. And there was not one supplementary report attached or referenced. Odd.

Three more beers and he glanced at the clock. Time to visit Chickie at Western Care. She'd been there two days and was probably getting restless.

Western Care was a medical facility that reminded Mack of a high-priced resort. The redbrick, two-story building spread an elongated *W* across a shallow, desert valley with swimming pools and tennis courts tucked under huge picture windows. Riding stables and jogging tracks were a short stroll away, and everything was surrounded by an extravagantly green eighteen-hole golf course.

Chickie was in her room reading the latest James Lee Burke novel, *Burning Angel.* Appropriate, Mack thought. She had placed her chair in the middle of a huge splash of October sunlight that streamed through the double window. Long legs dangled over the arm of an overstuffed chair. No clothing was visible.

"Damn, Chickie, aren't you afraid somebody'll walk in like I just did?"

"Hi, Cormac!" The tanned woman swung her legs around and sat erect in the big chair. She wasn't naked after all. She wore a red, thong-style bikini that covered the vee of her groin and the tips of her breasts. She held out her arms. "Come over here and kiss me, sugar."

Mack locked the door and joined her in the chair. After a few slippery minutes bending, twisting and swearing, she hauled him over to her bed.

Twenty minutes later someone tried the door and knocked.

"Okay," Chickie called. "Come back in ten minutes." She gathered her wisps of bathing suit and slapped Mack on the stomach. "Time to get up."

"Who the hell is that?" he grumbled. "You got a boyfriend here already?"

"Hell no." She stood over him and stretched. "Most of the patients are too strung out or shaky to be interested in me." Chickie ran tentative fingers down her flat stomach, testing for flaws. "Some of the doctors act like they want to give me a pelvic exam though." She strutted toward the bathroom and Mack watched the taut globes of her buttocks flex and shift a soft tango.

He began to stir again. Could his tired body...?

She disappeared. Mack looked at his watch. Five forty five. Time to go to work anyhow. He hauled on his clothes and left as a young, bespectacled oriental man arrived and began to explain to a showered Chickie how she could achieve greater mental health and physical flexibility through the discipline of *Tai Chi.*

• • •

Mack parked his shot-up truck - with expensive new headlights - in the supermarket parking lot and looked around. This was the accident scene and the right time: Speedway Boulevard at rush hour. Grace Faber's mother was hit around six; the police report said the call came in at 6:08 p.m. The supermarket was in the middle of an aging commercial block and the fatal crosswalk led from the market parking lot across six lanes of traffic. A raised center-median-safety-island divided east and west-bound cars. Viola Faber hadn't quite made it to the safety island.

He paused and considered the traffic. Once a sleepy cow town, Tucson had grown like cancer from 1970 to 1994. The population had exploded to half a million people mostly from the East, who brought their ambitions, winter-relatives and cars. Now the city filled the valley, mountain to mountain, with quarter-mile grids of intersecting 45-mile-an-hour highways. Cars were king, horses were rare and pedestrians were something to steer around. The West had become civilized.

Viola Faber had lived halfway between crumbling old, downtown Tucson and the busy foothill suburbs. Mack listened to the hum and screech of vehicles, smelled hot rubber and catalytic converters and shook his head at progress. He wondered what this woman, born before supermarkets and television, had thought of the modern cacophony. She was of his mother's generation, scarred by the Great Depression's financial ruin, shocked by Pearl Harbor and stoically enduring three wars and years of nuclear menace. He felt sorry for her and wanted to punish whoever had broken her frail body and left it like trash beside the road.

A hit and run on a crowded street in fading daylight? How hard could it be? He wondered why the police hadn't broken the case yet. Hit and run accidents were like most unplanned, violent crimes. They were abrupt, sloppy, sometimes in front of hundreds of eyes, and with an easily identifiable suspect: a car with a license plate. The secret, as in most investigations, was canvassing the neighborhood and asking questions. With all the traffic streaming by and rows of businesses lining the street, somebody must have seen the old lady get hit.

Mack walked to the first shop on the long sidewalk, a liquor store.

He worked the street until dark and came back the next day - different day, different people would be at work. Once or twice an odd feeling tingled, like he was being watched. He ignored it. Two days working both sides of the street and he began again. There were the liquor store, the shoe store, Circle K, coin shop, hairdresser, antique store, a blue-collar bar called Pat's, Zip's Video and a T.V. repair shop. All were concerned, interested and sympathetic, but no one had seen anything useful the day Viola Faber died. A bus stop near the corner half a block away filled and emptied customers dozens of times during the hours Mack walked, but most bus travelers hadn't been there that evening or were too authority-shy to do more than smile at his official-looking identification and shake their heads at questions. Crossing the street near the bus stop Mack felt the prickly feelings again. He looked up quickly, spotted a big, dark car cruising slowly along the curb-lane on the other side of Speedway down the block near a self-service gas station. The car moved away. He saw it again later, a block in the other direction. "Okay, Vinnie," he whispered and adjusted the Colt Commander in his belt under the jacket. Still, Mack felt a little nervous as he searched a wider circle around the accident scene.

The attendant's booth in the self-serve station faced parallel to Speedway. The chance of a witness was poor, but he tried and the young Pakistani woman who'd been working that night remembered only sirens and an ambulance. He turned away determined to overcome despondency with hard work. There was a post office sub-station fifty yards across an empty parking lot from the gas station.

He was halfway across the concrete when the dark sedan careened into the gas station and swerved toward Mack. Nowhere to run! His eyes filled with the chrome grill. The engine roared, tires squealed. Ten yards away, lurching closer. Mack swore at his stupidity. Out in the open with no cover. Closest thing was the gas-pump island. Six pumps. Gasoline. Worst place to be in a crash, or when shooting starts, so Mack dodged toward the station booth. He saw the Pakistani woman through the glass, her mouth a wide, round scream.

Rubber screeched. The sedan swerved, cut him off. Shiny skin showed briefly through the driver's window as the car careened close. Too close to avoid!

Mack dove under the bucking bumper and rolled past the near tire. Thump! He clipped his head on the chrome. A tire bit his shoe, but missed him. The car turned. Coming again! He rolled toward the gas pumps and crawled up the cement step into a tangle of pump hoses and slops of gasoline and wrapped his body around the base of a pump. *Now, if the son of a bitch wants to kill me, we'll both light up!*

But scuddering tires and roaring engine sounded farther away. He had a moment to fumble out the 45 and look for a target. The dark sedan had turned, hauled a wide loop around the booth and stopped fifty feet away. Deciding?

"Come on you sick bastard, let's both burn!" Mack bellowed and snapped off a shot that missed high. He couldn't see the driver or a front plate, but he knew.

The engine yammered impatience, screamed higher. The car jerked into rubber-melting motion and fishtailed wildly, trailing black smoke to a bouncing turn out of the station and into traffic before Mack could shoot again.

He got up and left before the cops arrived. There was nothing they could do.

• • •

Back to work the next day and Mack decided to cover postal employees. The sub-station Post Master seemed surprised anyone was still working the case.

"I spoke with police weeks ago. Darn shame, these old people," he shook his head in sorrow. "We've lost three in that very crosswalk since I've been here."

"All of them elderly?" Mack asked.

The gray-haired man pulled his postal-blue sweater around bony shoulders and shivered in the stale-smelling air-conditioning. "Elderly? Oh yes, there's a retirement village down Flower Street, you know." He pointed vaguely to his left. "The high point of their day is picking up the mail from the kids and grandkids."

"Picking up the mail? Doesn't the Post Office deliver?"

The old Post Master stiffened. "Of course we do!" he snapped. "But for the past dozen years or so these old people have been hearing all those terrible stories about mail and benefit checks being stolen from mailboxes." He sniffed and glanced out the glass inner doors to the large, marble lobby. "They rent Post Office boxes for safety. People from the retirement village empty their boxes every day after the four o' clock mail-drop." He seemed disturbed by the irregularity of it all.

Mack asked the obvious. "They come here after four? So people could have been picking up their mail at six when Mrs. Faber was killed down the street?"

"Well, I guess..."

"The hit and run was two weeks ago last Monday," Mack pressed. "Try and remember if you saw anyone here that evening."

The old man hesitated. "Exactly what time was she killed?" he asked.

"Just after six p.m.."

The Post Master looked relieved and slightly smug. "We close our windows at four thirty and everyone has left by five o'clock sharp because of union overtime regulations. I'm always gone by five forty after I lock the hallway doors. Obviously, I could not have seen *anyone* in the lobby at six."

Mack turned away; didn't bother to thank him for his time.

• • •

She looked depressed before he was half way through his report.

"So that's it, Grace," Mack finished. "No leads yet, but I'm still looking." He didn't mention the gas station trouble.Vinnie Romano had nothing to do with her.

"And you've spent how many hours?" She looked tired and the day had just begun at 7:15 in the morning. He'd called the night before, given her partial information and she'd asked to meet at Denny's before work the next morning.

"Only about ten," Mack lied. "Not enough to really make a dent in the case."

"Well I didn't sleep much last night after you called. I'm not sure how long I can afford to keep you working." Her eyes filled, she fumbled her glasses off and dabbed with a napkin.

He looked away and sipped his coffee to give her time to compose herself. He thought she looked better today. No make up. Naturally red lips, thin, but nicely shaped and her eyes were large and slightly tilted without the distortion of glasses. So young looking, and he thought she was even thinner than last time; the silk blouse hung loosely from thin shoulders and hid all but a hint of her figure. He sighed. Mack had always been a sucker for a woman with tears in her eyes, no matter how plain. He smelled the gardenia again. Something made him decide to be noble. "Look, Miss Faber, let's not worry about money. I've kinda taken an interest in your mother's death and..."

"No, I won't hear of it...I insist," she interrupted and then stopped. Anger or embarrassment had reddened her face. She was almost pretty.

He stared at her blushing cheeks and waited for the rest.

"I insist you keep a strict accounting of your time," she continued. Her eyes lowered under his scrutiny. She slipped her glasses on. "I will not accept charity, and that's final." Her head bobbed once after the last word. Her ears were burning. *The nerve of this man!* She thought. *And how very nice of him.*

"Well okay," he said, "but there is *another* way you can help."

Her eyes met his, searching for condescension or worse and remembering the televised kiss. "I don't know," she asked. "What *exactly* did you have in mind?"

Mack smiled and shook his head at the sexual implication. "The police only listed two useless witnesses on the face sheet. No other names or statements. That time of day, there *had* to be more witnesses. Either they're not working the case or they're hiding something." He held her gaze and frowned at the thought. "Could you get some reporter friend of yours at work to check police records or casually ask around for names? I need *names*. We need witnesses."

Grace glanced at her watch. "I'm going to be late if I don't leave, but I know just the man: Clyde Ralston. I'll call today and ask him. I'm not supposed to be involved in police matters so maybe we three can meet somewhere after work."

Mack nodded. "I'll call you at the paper this afternoon."

She slid from the booth and hurried towards the restaurant door. His eyes followed her hips. They were round and tight, not as thin as he'd thought. Nice legs too. He tore his eyes away and concentrated on the case.

Something had been tickling the back of his mind since he spoke with the Post Master. He went back over the conversation. Some of the elderly people from the retirement village had worked out a daily routine. They waited for the four o' clock mail drop and then went to check their boxes. No help. Viola Faber was hit at six, an hour after the Post Office closed. None of her neighbors would be out that late unless they were across the street shopping. No way to check that without asking each one, knocking on every door. Mack was resigning himself to going door to door in the retirement village - two hundred or so condos - when he realized *exactly* what had been said the day before. The postmaster had said they close *the windows* at five o' clock! He'd said he locks the *hallway* doors and he'd insisted there was no way he could have seen anyone in the *lobby* after he left. Not much help, but a damn strange way of saying it unless...unless the lobby was open after he left. The post office probably never closed the lobby. But so what?

He smiled at his hopes and ordered more coffee.

• • •

The lobby had remained open after five. This was the eighth elderly person and he'd nearly decided to quit for the day. Mack was supposed to meet Grace Faber and the police reporter at a bar called the Shanty at seven thirty. There was barely time to go home for a hot shower after this hopelessly failed long-shot.

He held out his identification like a peace offering. "Sorry to bother you. I'm investigating a hit and run death down the street in the supermarket crosswalk about twenty days ago. Her name was Viola Faber. I'm looking for a witness."

She smiled and nodded - a strange reaction, no surprise, confusion or fear. "How did you know?" the old woman wagged a bony finger. "You police are amazing. Franklin just told me about laughing potato-head the other day."

Potato head? Mack figured she was senile and only continued the questions to be polite. He was used to being taken for a cop so he ignored the woman's mistake. "Yes Ma'am we try. Who is Franklin and exactly what did he tell you about... about laughing potato-head?"

She was a flirt, flapping her eyes and smirking as though he'd asked for a kiss. "Well officer, this is probably none of your business, but Franklin is my boyfriend. He's married you know, lives out on the east side, can't stay out at night and takes the bus so she won't know. I walk him to the bus before supper every Monday and Friday evening at five fifty or so. We meet at the recreation center."

"Thank you very much Ma'am." Mack decided to get away from the talkative old woman as gracefully as possible. "Sorry to have bothered you."

"Franklin says he saw a peculiar-looking man who laughed at the accident."

"He *saw* the accident?" Mack repeated. "Where can I find this Franklin?"

She wagged the finger again, "Oh no, I can't give you his address. Franklin is terrified of his wife, he would think I'd betrayed him."

"Look Ma'am this is a *dead* woman we're talking about," Mack said.

"I won't give you Franklin's address," she said, "but his phone number is 294-8342. Call after ten a.m., his wife plays tennis on Saturday morning."

• • •

He'd stopped at the library and was late for the meeting.

The Shanty was an up-scale college tavern with clean, new pool tables and dozens of expensive, imported beers. Mack sniffed the familiar, friendly fragrances of wet yeast, cigarette smoke and perspiration. Grubby in Levis and baggy sport jacket, he regretted not taking a shower, but there hadn't been time. The bar was crammed with earnest young anglers in tank tops seeking smooth-skinned dreams or relief from academic tension. Bright-eyed girls with long, loose hair and sleek, muscular boys sullen with angst rubbed shoulders, guzzled beer and tried to act cool while eyeing each other in search of not-too-complex connections.

Grace waved to him from a table on the enclosed patio past the crowded bar and beyond the pool tables. As Mack drew near, a huge young black man stood to greet him with a wide smile of welcome.

"Hey, Mack." He held out a hand the size of a menu. "Grace tol' me all about you. Nice to meet you. The name's Clyde Ralston."

Mack felt small. The kid's shoulders blocked out half the patio and Clyde's Adam's apple bobbed at eye level. He put his hand into a warm mass of meat and muscular fingers, tried to get a grip on something before his hand was broken, but

Clyde didn't show off. He exerted a little pressure to show respect and let Mack's hand drop.

"Nice to meet you," Mack said and smiled up into friendly brown eyes behind thick, horn-rimmed glasses. "Kinda big for a reporter, aren't you?"

"See, I told you." Grace's soft voice barely rode over bar-noise. "Always the cynic with a world-weary attitude."

"Yeah, Grace, you told me." Clyde grinned at Mack and folded himself down into a chair. "But you didn't mention his movie-star looks and yuppy wardrobe."

Mack hid a smile by turning toward the bar and motioning to a fat lady in an apron nearby. He called for a Becks and swirled a finger at their table for another round. The fat lady nodded and disappeared among smooth, young shoulders.

Grace motioned him to sit. "We've been talking shop," she said, loud enough to clear the noise. "Clyde wants help digging around the racetrack for a story about politics and dead greyhounds the *Register* won't let him follow-up, and you need cop-information. Maybe you two can help each other. By the way, what kept you?"

"I'm late because I stopped at the library to cross-check a phone number," Mack said. "I found a shaky lead. Some woman says she has a friend named Franklin Blaine who *might* have seen another person who witnessed your mother's death." Explaining the lead made him realize how thin the information really was.

Grace leaned forward with interest, the thin face no longer as tired and drawn as that morning at Denny's. She took off her glasses and squinted anxiously across the table. "Might have seen a witness?" she repeated. "Good. Who was it? What did Franklin Blaine say?"

"Can't call him until tomorrow morning." He held up his hand to stop the question. "The guy's married and having a long-time affair with a woman at the retirement village. *She* doesn't want me to embarrass him in front of his wife."

"But you should call *now*, this is my mother we're..." Grace began to protest.

"Cool it, Grace," Clyde interrupted. "Sounds like Mack's handlin' it right. You know a pissed-off witness is worse than no witness at all. Better to cooperate with the woman and wait 'til tomorrow to question the witness to the witness."

Grace stared down at the table, not fully convinced.

Mack appreciated Clyde's intervention. The drinks arrived. Mack quickly drank half of his beer, wiped his mouth and sat back. "Don't get your hopes up too high, Grace," he said. "The old woman sounded a little confused. She mentioned somebody she called potato head." Mack sighed and turned to Clyde. "But it's all we've got unless *you* can get us something."

Clyde chuckled and pointed at Grace. "She'll explain the problem getting information out of the cop shop, but I'll try again to get some names for y'all."

Grace gazed admiringly at Clyde. "If anybody can, Clyde's the one. He's the best darned investigative reporter we have at the paper."

"Yeah," Clyde growled. "I'm doin' just great. Stacks of dead racing dogs near a mobbed-up ranch, tons of Vegas money goin' through unregulated dog tracks and the same damn people pushing politicians for *more* ways to launder money through new sports arenas. I got a story workin' here, but nobody pays attention."

Talk was drowned. The juke box began to play Pink Floyd's *Money* at high decibels and they watched the crowd of college students shift and mingle. There were clumps of laughing, peeking girls and groups of back-slapping boys talking sports, but most of the crowd was engaged in meeting and shouting at the opposite sex. One or two loners sat on the edge of the ritual and drank and watched.

Pink Floyd finished his multi-million dollar complaint about money and began a strident lament about fascist teachers. Mack listened to the plaintive whines and frenzied guitars for another ten minutes and eventually the music stopped.

Clyde filled the vacuum. "By the way Grace, since I'm speakin' of sports arenas, there was a bad fire last night. One guy's dead. It's probably arson, but no matter what it was, it'll be a big help to Ace Collins' new pet editorial issue, I expect."

"A fire? Sports arena? Where? Who died?" Grace reacted like a reporter. Mack expected her to pull out a notepad and scribble.

Clyde leaned forward. The table began to tilt, but he didn't notice. "An anti-tax group's headquarters in the back of a print shop down on South Stone Avenue was gutted around midnight. A guy named Mitch Young got burnt to a crisp."

"Mitch Young was killed?" Mack asked, hoping he'd heard wrong..

"Yeah. His print shop burned down and they were sure the body was him. This afternoon the coroner made positive identification from dental records."

"Damn! I've known him for twenty years. A real dedicated guy." Mack bowed his head. "Mitch ran a small printing company. Got tired of high taxes and jumped into conservative politics in the late '70s. Remember? His group put a Proposition 13-style tax-cut on the 1980 ballot. A good man. Arson you say?"

"Yeah." Clyde bared his teeth in a pained grimace. "Report said there was a strong gasoline smell. They found Mister Young's charred body in his bathroom. The coroner says pieces of glass were imbedded in what was left of his face and upper body." Clyde took off his glasses and began cleaning them with a beer-wet bar napkin. The dark, expressive face drooped in sorrowful empathy.

Mack realized the young man was visualizing the crime scene and having trouble controlling his emotions. Tough to be a softhearted reporter, he guessed.

"That 'pet issue' crack was a pretty rotten, Clyde," Grace said, enunciating her words too clearly over the background noise. Her face was ruddy with anger.

"Well you and Ace *did* do one of those 'bonds are wonderful' editorials about the bond election coming up." Clyde met her hot gaze and didn't flinch.

Mack had the impression the two reporters argued politics often.

"That editorial was my boss's opinion, simply interpretive journalism." She swallowed hard and looked down at her beer. "You don't think the fire had anything to do with the sports arena bond election do you?"

"The fire totally consumed the print shop, " Clyde said. "Flames destroyed the anti-tax-group headquarters in back and burned boxes of anti-bond-literature the group evidently planned to mail out this weekend. Arson investigators say they found scorched anti-bond election letters scattered all around the fire scene."

"The fire could've been a coincidence," Grace insisted.

"Right Grace," Clyde snorted. "A coupla weeks before a big bond-election a large mailer tellin' voters to vote *no* gets burned up and the leader of the anti-bond group gets fried in his own bathroom. A damn strange coincidence." He paused and thought about it, "And ain't the bathroom a damn strange place to die?"

"Mister Collins *did* allude to Mister Young," Grace admitted, "but he told me not to mention any tax resistance in the editorial."

"And, if it ain't in the paper..." Clyde began.

"...it ain't news!' they both finished together and smiled across the table.

"Poor Mitch," Mack muttered and stood up to leave. Beer tasted sour and cigarette smoke was suddenly nauseating. "Please ask about witnesses," he reminded Clyde, "and I'll be happy to try and help with your race track story."

Grace was pleased the two had connected and she was oddly optimistic about the hit and run investigation. "Call me when you talk to Blaine," she said.

• • •

Franklin Blaine didn't want to talk about the hit and run.

Mack figured he'd seen too much prime-time TV. Evidently, he had lots of money and was full of that fanciful, surface-smug that people with money seem to develop. A ten-fifteen phone call on Saturday morning and he stonewalled like a con. Mack had cross-referenced Franklin's name, address and wife's name from the Cole's Directory reverse-listing of phone numbers at the library. He mentioned the Franklin address and threatened to question Franklin's wife at dinner that night.

Franklin quickly caved. "Well in that case I will tell you on the phone, but do *not* record my statement. Under no circumstances will I agree to testify in a court of law." He combined careful enunciation and glib delivery like a television preacher.

Mack tried to remain pleasant. "That's just fine, Mister Blaine. Court won't be necessary if you cooperate fully. We probably won't need to question you in person if you can give us a full description of this man over the phone."

Franklin hesitated, thought about it. "Wait just a minute here. In all my long years of experience, police have *never* questioned witnesses on the phone."

Mack thought that sounded like a hang-up in about a second. He let anger crawl down the line. "Listen, you two-timing bastard, I'm *not* a cop. I'm a private investigator working for the dead woman. If you don't describe laughing boy you'll wish you'd died too."

"Oh, my lord, are you threatening me?"

"You bet your womanizing ass!" Mack felt like a bully, but it worked.

"No, please don't hurt me!' Blaine's voice broke to a sob. "Hurting me will not be necessary. Just promise you won't tell my wife about this."

"Talk to me!"

"Okay! I was sitting at the bus stop, a dirty place. Sheila waved goodby from across the street and I began to look for the six-ten to Wilmot Road."

"Right, go on." Mack wanted to get to the point, but realized the man was relaxing and reliving so he let him ramble along.

"Cars, cars, but no bus," Franklin continued. "I tried to rest and meditate. Next thing I know there's a horrible howl of tires and a soggy thump. I guess I knew what'd happened, but there was nothing to see, only a few cars in a cluster. Then the body hit the plexiglass next to me. Blood was dripping. I was in shock; all I could do was stare at the blood. Then I heard laughing and looked around. He was sitting two cars behind what I realized later was the accident. He had opened his window. His reaction is hard to describe. He was looking at the woman's body and laughing as though the whole thing was a small, private joke. It was ghastly!" Franklin Blaine stopped speaking. His breath whispered across the mouth-piece.

"Go on Mister Blaine, Mack urged. "What did he look like?"

"Dreadful. Bald with a stiff pale face like the Phantom of The Opera. He frightened me. I didn't mention it to anyone for weeks, but I had to tell *someone* to keep my sanity. I joked with Sheila that he looked like a potato-head, but that was a joke. His head *did* look like a potato, but a boiled potato, a boiled white potato."

Mack felt excitement sizzle through his veins. "Did you talk to the police?"

"Of course not. I was frightened my wife would find out where I was. And besides, the man who was laughing didn't actually run into the woman. I think he was behind the car that must've hit her."

"Right. And could you see that car, the one you think might have hit her?"

"No, not really. My view was mostly blocked by another car and I was paralyzed with shock."

"Mostly blocked?" Mack urged. "Could you see anything?"

"I have an impression of a dark-colored fender, but that's all," he sounded apologetic. "I was spellbound by that dreadful laughing person."

"Did you notice laughing boy's car. Were you able to get *his* plate number?"

"No, I was too upset, but it wasn't Arizona. It was a lighter-colored license. God! That horrible laughing will haunt my nights until I die."

"A lighter-colored license?" Mack repeated. "What do you mean?"

"I mean light like California or Kansas or Illinois," Blaine said.

CHAPTER SIX

SMALL LIES

Grace wanted to go right to the police. "They can find this potato-head," she declared. "He obviously knows something about my mother's killer. He'll have to tell them what he saw, or who."

"Wrong, Grace," Mack said. "Blaine won't cooperate and I'm pretty sure I already know who potato-head is. He won't talk with the police either."

"Who is he?"

"Most likely a recently injured torch named Vinnie Romano from the Accardo-Giancana family in Chicago." Mack sipped coffee from a dainty cup and took a bite of a steaming blueberry muffin Grace had bragged was 'fresh-baked'. "Word is, he got burned doing an insurance job in Chicago last year and showed up in Tucson to heal, dodge subpoenas and work for Chickie Malatesta's father."

Grace looked up from her coffee, a little shocked by Mack's easy knowledge of Mafia gangsters and unsettled by the woman's name. "Chickie?" she said. "She's your girlfriend, isn't she?" Grace remembered again those television images of Mack hugging and kissing the voluptuous, middle-aged blond.

"Not exactly, but we've been bosom buddies for a few years," Mack joked.

Grace Faber was confused and disturbed by conflicting feelings. This was the first time a man had been in her living room since her divorce and she'd enjoyed fussing over him. When he'd called that morning with news of the witness, she'd invited him over for coffee and rushed a batch of blueberry muffins into the oven. Grace was beginning to appreciate the rumpled detective in spite of her initial reservations and his bad opinion of journalists. He was nice looking in a rugged way, but she realized what she liked most about Cormac Robertson was another version of the things she disliked. He was a gruff man who suffered from, and luxuriated in, a complete lack of subtlety. Scars and insight; perhaps hard knocks had calloused Mack Robertson to other people's feelings and sensibilities, but, compared to some of the self-consciously transparent men of the eighties and nineties, Mack stimulated her the way a cold shower refreshed. Grace smiled to herself. For some reason she wanted to show off homemaker skills to this man.

"How do you like the coffee?" she asked to cover her inattention.

"Good coffee." Mack grinned and looked around. "Nice home."

Grace Faber lived in a ranch-style home in a slightly frayed middle-income, University-area neighborhood, slowly changing from owner-occupied residential to student-housing rental. The two-bedroom house had a small fenced-in front yard and a big back yard next to a detached garage - too big for a single woman and property values were dropping. Grace was looking for a buyer. Problem was, real-estate agents brought prospects on Saturdays, Sundays and holidays. With the death of her mother, the new position at the *Register* and home-show-time on weekends, Grace was worn out, frazzled and stranded home most Saturdays. Mack couldn't have picked a better day for a breakthrough.

Enough chat, her reporter's mind insisted. She was intrigued by Mack's information, but disturbed by his reaction to her suggestion about the police. "A Mafia arsonist? You mean you're not going to turn him in?" she asked.

"I didn't say that," Mack answered. "But we don't want to screw up a lead."

"What do you mean?"

Mack sat back and surveyed the very feminine room while he thought.

Potpourri room freshener, lemon Pledge and blueberry muffins combined to a nearly unbearable domestic perfume. The place made Mack feel married again. The living room was filled with vases, colorful Mexican dolls, bursting magazine racks and brightly upholstered furniture. A large bookcase held text-books, paperbacks and a multi-book Encyclopedia; the walls were covered with prints, knick-knacks, ceramic animals and astrological signs. Even the coffee table was Early American butler-style with fold-up sides. Sensory overload distracted him.

He closed his eyes and concentrated on the bizarre implications of Vinnie Romano being at the scene of Viola Faber's death. "Blaine saw what I think was a burn-scarred man who'd just undergone plastic surgery sitting in a car with light-colored plates," he muttered. "The man was probably Vinnie Romano and I figure he wasn't there by accident." Mack raised one finger to forestall her questions. "He thought the tragedy was funny, or very convenient. Could he have been watching your mother? Could your mother have met anyone in organized crime? Did she gamble or play numbers? Was she recently on a jury at a criminal trial?"

Grace flinched, but realized Mack's train of thought and knew he had to get the questions out of the way. "No, of course not," she said quickly.

"So we can infer Vinnie's either a bloodthirsty maniac or he knew the person in the hit and run vehicle and thought the situation was somehow amusing."

Grace sipped her coffee. "Or maybe he's a bodyguard," she said, "part of an entourage. Could he have been following his boss, Bruno Malatesta?" She watched Mack's eyes. "Or Bruno's daughter."

Mack nodded thoughtfully, unconscious of the scrutiny. "That's possible, but Chickie drives a white Caddy. Franklin Blaine was definite the H and R vehicle was dark." He looked up. "You know, you're right! The hit and run driver *could* have been Don Bruno." Mack thought about his *condotta* and smiled at the irony.

"Okay," Grace said in a tight, angry voice. "We've got a Mafia Don with lots of expensive lawyers. *That* could be why the cops are going so slowly. A big-time gangster ran down my mother and they can't make an airtight case, but how do *we* prove it? Why not turn Blaine in to the cops?" Grace was trembling. She offered Mack another muffin and poured more coffee. Some dribbled into the saucer.

Mack watched her pour, shook his head. "Because he won't talk to them. He's afraid his wife will find out about the other woman he was meeting."

"He told *you*," Grace pointed out.

"Yeah, but I threatened him. Police can't do that."

"Why not? He witnessed a crime in progress. They can threaten to take him downtown."

"No, they can't. He did *not* witness a crime in progress. He only witnessed a man laughing at a crime-scene. There's a big difference."

Grace was becoming angry and depressed. "So what do we do?"

Mack had an inspiration. A sudden notion erupted full-blown that would bring Vinnie police attention, maybe keep the crazy bastard away from Mack, and possibly force someone's hand in the hit and run. He leaned forward. "I can't let this information go to waste. Monday I'll go to the police with the hit and run witness identification. If they throw me out, I'll take the story to your newspaper."

"You?" Grace was stunned. "I don't understand."

"Well, you can't go to the police. You're in trouble with your boss at the *Register* already. My name is mud with the police and I figure they'll laugh me out of the station, but if I do it right, your newspaper might just be interested."

"If you can't use Franklin Blaine, then what can you tell them?"

"I'll tell them about a Mafia torch laughing at an old woman's death."

"But you just said Blaine won't back you up," Grace objected. "He'll refuse to tell them and that'll be the end of it. No reporter or detective, not even an old cop-friend of yours, would accept a second-hand witness. They'd look foolish."

"You don't understand. "I'll say *I* was the witness; got stuck in a traffic jam, heard this guy laughing, looked at him and noticed part of an Illinois license plate. I'll say I didn't realize there was a hit and run until I read the paper and met you."

Grace stared. Disbelief widened her smoke-colored eyes behind the glasses. "Have you lost your mind? You'd lie? And what Illinois plate do you mean?"

"*MNG* something " Mack answered, remembering the night and the shotgun. "I saw the license plate a few weeks ago. I'm sure the number is Romano's or one of Malatesta's men. Police'll probably verify the plate through Illinois Motor Vehicle."

"And if they laugh at you like you expect they will?"

"That's why you're paying me. We need to get publicity, smoke a killer out. If the cops laugh, somebody at the *Register* might be outraged, or at least interested in the reasons the police don't care about some gangster named Vinnie, the Monster laughing like hell after his boss runs over an old lady."

• • •

Cold anger, averted eyes met Mack; he felt like a criminal. After they recognized the tall ex-cop, none of the desk officers would acknowledge him or meet his gaze. And one of them had even been a squad mate.

"Witness to a hit and run?" another, younger officer repeated.

Mack simply nodded and didn't bother with nuances.

"That'll be traffic investigation." The officer phoned someone, said a few quiet words and paused a moment before he looked up and smirked unpleasantly at Mack. "Yeah, he's standing right here." After another muttered sentence he hung up, motioned to the stairs in the back of the lobby. "Go on up."

Mack walked across the lobby, conscious of the eyes on his wrinkled jacket.

• • •

"So, because Vinnie Romano was laughing at a hit and run on Speedway you figure his boss is the perp?" Sergeant Sparks asked sarcastically. He leaned his skinny shoulders back in the high-backed, reclining desk-chair and laced fingers behind his head. Small, yellow teeth peeked through a sneer.

"You guys got a better suspect? Mack asked. "I understand you've been looking at someone." He leaned back in his uncomfortably straight, office-chair and crossed one leg over the other as though completely at ease.

Sparks reacted as if he'd been jabbed with a pin. "No we haven't! If we *had* a good suspect, he'd be in front of a grand jury."

"Well I'm handing you a good suspect, Sergeant," Mack said reasonably. "Go pick up this psycho button-man and ask him to squeal on his boss." Mack pictured the confrontation and smiled at the slender Sergeant.

Sparks bristled at the smile. The traitor ex-cop who'd ruined the police case against the Malatesta woman was toying with him. He fumed helplessly and tried to hold his temper. He knew as well as Mack Robertson that a Mafioso like Vinnie the Monster wouldn't say anything to police, but would request a lawyer and walk in an hour. More importantly, Sergeant Sparks already knew without a doubt that Mack's information was worthless - in fact it was dangerous - but he couldn't reveal why.

"Turning on your old employer?" Sparks tried to turn the tables on the smug P.I., "Mafia's not paying you enough?"

Mack decided it was time to end the game. He uncrossed his legs and stood. "Look, if you don't want to handle this I'll go question the Mafia bastard myself."

"You will not!" Sparks yelped. "This is a police matter and you will *not* interfere with my investigation." The small eyes narrowed to slits. "Or must we file criminal charges against you for interfering with an investigation and spreading misinformation about a case? I could get your P.I. license pulled."

Mack allowed a small frown to pinch his eyes and clumsily rubbed a hand across his mouth as though covering an unbidden smile. He held the pose a moment and waited for Sparks to play out his part in the farce.

"So! That's it." The traffic sergeant stood and pointed across the desk, "You're determined to interfere, to confuse us." He paused a moment, stuck the pointed finger against his own head and drew the intended conclusion. "You embarrassed us with the Malatesta woman and now you've dreamed up an impossible witness to embarrass us again." He clenched his bony fist and shook it in Mack's face. "Get out of here before I arrest you. You're a disgrace to law enforcement...I can't believe you ever wore a badge."

Mack frowned. "Does this mean you won't question Vinnie the Monster?"

"This means we're *not* doing what some down-at-the-heels private dick-head wants us to do. Now get out of here!"

• • •

The *Arizona Register* was well guarded against possible local unrest and, of course, foreign terrorists. Mack parked in the street and walked to the gate.

An extremely fat guard sitting in front of closed-circuit camera screens in a glass guardhouse looked up from a girly magazine and regarded Mack with half-hearted suspicion. "Help ya?" he said.

"I need to see a reporter who covers hit and run traffic deaths," Mack said.

"You got an appointment?"

"Appointment?" Mack couldn't believe his ears. "What the hell do I need an appointment for?"

The guard grimaced in annoyance, hitched his heavy body around on the stool and let his hand drop to the mace canister on his belt. "Look buddy we're runnin' an important business here. You can't just walk in and wander around."

Mack's mood was turning nasty. He held out his empty hands. "Look, no weapons," he said. "I just wanna talk to a reporter."

"What the hell. You a wise-guy or somethin'?" the guard snapped.

"Yeah, I guess you could say that," Mack admitted. "But I want to see somebody. I've got a very important piece of information about a murder."

"Then why don't you take it to the police?" The guard glanced down at his skin book. He obviously wanted the interruption to go away.

Mack decided he'd wasted enough time. He was going to walk past the booth, but suddenly remembered Grace worked for one of the bosses of the paper. "Look you officious jerk," he leaned down and snarled into the small window-grill. "If you want to keep your job, you'd better tell Ace Collins I've got information that puts Vinnie the Monster Romano at the scene of the Viola Faber hit and run. And also tell him the police won't even question the bastard."

"Mister Collins!" the guard gasped. "Why didn't you say so?"

Mack looked at the building while the guard phoned in. There was a lot to see. The place was a fortress, probably built in the unruly seventies. He concluded the press had inherited paranoia along with their other prerogatives. The impressive *Arizona Register* building was an acre-sized, three-story concrete bunker surrounded by spiked iron fences. There were no windows on the first floor and all vegetation was cleared from around the base of the building. Mack noticed the second-story windows had beveled casements, slanting down and to the sides for what he decided was a wider, deadlier field of fire.

• • •

Ace Collins motioned the investigator into his glass-walled office without standing. His heart had lurched when the guard announced a man who wanted to give the newspaper information on the Viola Faber hit and run and had asked for him specifically. He indicated a chair. "This is a little irregular," he said scowling pointedly down at his paperwork. "I *am* a very busy man."

Mack had heard a lot about Collins even before he met Grace. The editor was someone he resented by definition. He looked down at the squarely built, gray-haired man in the striped shirt with the blue collar and searched his memory. A political type - mover and shaker in Tucson - Collins supposedly possessed prestigious, ivy-league degrees and an enviable war record. He owned a 400,000-dollar home in the foothills, was twice past president of Rotary, served on the boards of two banks and one major utility company and obviously wore his pride proudly. Editor Collins was frequently reported as a behind-the-scenes advisor to national political candidates. He socialized with Senators and Congressmen, was regularly seen at state dinners with the Governor of Arizona and was known to have solid connections with the President of the United States.

This casually arrogant man was rumored to trade lots of favorable press to anointed candidates for influence on selected issues and favors for other friends. The way Mack heard it, this good-old-boy club elected and appointed each other to positions of mutual benefit from which they passed around inside information and government contracts, further empowering the powerful. And the newspaper was in a peculiarly crucial position to skew issues and favor candidates. Name recognition equals political contributions and Mack knew the best-known politician who spent the most money received the most votes from a poorly informed electorate.

Collins had all the advantages. Mack's innate sense of fairness was particularly disturbed that a lousy newspaper editor was frequently appointed to influential Gubernatorial commissions that made water, land-use and fiscal-policy decisions affecting the life-styles, homes and businesses of all the people of Arizona. Over the years Mack had never once seen a middle-class guy on an influential commission and he'd never once seen an influential commission that wasn't eager as hell to spend public money on projects the public didn't realize they needed. But Mack was also philosophical. He guessed the pattern was the same everywhere and couldn't help wondering at the general failure of the system.

Mack ignored the indicated chair in front of the editor's desk and sat in a large, brass-studded settee that formed part of a conversation grouping on the other side of the spacious office. He calmed the anger, made himself comfortable and breathed in a masculine mix of rich cologne and old leather. He thought he caught a hint of Sen-sen and wondered if Collins was a secret drinker. Still ignoring the editor, the investigator leaned back in the soft cushions and allowed his eyes to wander the photos, plaques, and awards covering most of the office walls. Ace seemed particularly proud of his Air Force days. There were half a dozen pictures of fighter planes, two photos showing a younger Collins in pilot coveralls and one in a dress uniform loaded with two rows of combat ribbons and pilot's wings.

"Viet Nam?" Mack asked.

"Yes. I was a fighter pilot. Phantoms," Ace Collins said with obvious pride. "Were you there?"

Mack nodded. "For a while. In a Special Operations Group. Slash and burn stuff called Operation Phoenix." He indicated a photo of young Ace Collins standing at an airfield in coveralls with a Phantom jet in the background. "Nothing as glamorous as you guys."

"Glamorous?" Ace objected. "There's very little glamor in air combat. Just ask my good friend, Senator John McGraw, if being shot down and held prisoner in solitary confinement for six years was glamorous."

"That's true. Six years. Hard to believe anybody could stand that."

"A brave man," the editor agreed. "Our new American heroes are prisoners of war and astronauts - those who can endure. If you're interested in Senator McGraw, there's a fighter pilot's reunion next month at the El Conquistador Hotel. Senator McGraw will be one of the speakers on the Viet Nam War. I will be the other."

Mack wasn't really interested in listening to war stories - had enough of his own. The screams and smells and stark terror often visited on hot, sweaty nights, but he decided to humor the newspaperman. After all, he needed his help.

"You're speaking on Viet Nam?" He looked over and met the editor's flinty stare. "Yes, I'd like to hear that. How can I get a ticket...ah, an invitation?"

"My secretary will arrange that on your way out." Ace Collins recovered his brusque manner. "Now what did you want to tell me about this hit and run?"

Mack stood and walked to the front of the editor's desk. He put on an earnest face and spread his hands in explanation. "Mister Collins, I've heard about your reputation for honesty and courage," he lied. "I figured you for a last resort."

"What do you mean?" Ace Collins was relieved and puzzled.

Mack gestured toward a large window. "The police are stuck on this hit and run investigation. I gave them a witness, but they don't want to question him."

"They don't?" The editor thought a moment, didn't want to seem too anxious. "The guard said something about a monster, a Vinnie Romano, being a witness."

"Yeah," Mack agreed. "I saw him there, laughing like hell, a car or two behind the accident. I've seen his mug shots and rap sheet; Vinnie's called Monster because he's crazy, a mob enforcer. Heard of him?"

"Vaguely. We don't have much Mafia activity in Tucson." Ace's heart began to race again. *Now for the big question.* "What do you think he saw?"

"That's the point. I don't know what he saw. Nobody's questioned him."

Collins wanted a drink very badly. *Later. Calm down!* "You're telling me the police know about a witness to this terrible event and haven't yet questioned him?" He clenched his fists, clamping down on the creeping need.

"It's not quite that simple, but yeah," Mack answered.

"Why not?" Ace popped a Sen-sen and forced his breathing to an even pace. "What do you mean by, 'not that simple'?"

Mack shrugged and grinned self-consciously. "Well, *I'm* evidently the problem with the police traffic investigators. To mix up a few metaphors, I bloodied their noses three weeks ago in the Chickie Malatesta DUI trial, and they think I'm blowing smoke up their ass on this monster thing."

Ace Collins was always impatient when the common-man tried out pseudo-intellectual claptrap on the professionals. *Mix up metaphors my ass!* His head throbbed; he tried to cover his feelings, but suddenly realized a newsman in this situation *should* be impatient. Impatience would be a normal reaction. He reverted to reality and allowed himself to show anger. "You are wasting my time," Ace growled. "Cut the crap and get to the point Mister...er, Robertson. If the police don't take you seriously, why should I?"

"Because a woman died," Mack reminded him calmly. "You're a journalist. Don't you care if a Mafia Don ran down an old woman on the street?"

"Mafia Don?" The editor said and began to relax, to breathe normally. Hot rage for vodka cooled and eased to a slow, thin flicker. The man was a confused fool. This would be pleasant sport after all. Ace Collins bit down an urge to laugh. "A Mafia Don?" he repeated. "But you said he was an enforcer, and just a witness."

"Right. But I figure there were *two* of them at the scene. Vinnie Romano was probably in the car behind his boss when Bruno Malatesta ran down Viola Faber."

"Why? What makes you think Bruno Malatesta ran down the old woman?" The editor was relieved to be able to act like a reporter.

"Because of two things." Mack held up two fingers. "First, Vinnie was behind the hit and run vehicle and thought the whole thing was funny. Second, it explains why the cops are acting snake-bit. Why they're so damned hesitant to release the name of a suspect until they nail down a case."

"But he could've been behind a total stranger," the editor objected weakly.

"Okay, if it was a stranger, why was Vinnie laughing so hard?"

Collins just shrugged. His mind was racing. This was becoming very complicated. Additional questions died in the middle of a new thought, a brilliant idea. "You're absolutely correct, Mister Robertson." Ace's voice was smooth and commanding, like a combat veteran's should be. "This possibility is too important to leave untested. I'm going to put you in touch with one of my best reporters." He tossed two more Sen-sen into his mouth with an audible popping sound. "Give him the information. He'll investigate this Mafia gangster."

Mack had a fleeting premonition. "Who is this reporter?"

"My police-beat reporter, a young man named Clyde Ralston."

"I'll go see him first thing tomorrow." Mack said and hid his smile.

Ace Collins reached for his phone. " I'll have him drive in right now."

"Sorry, but I can't. It's five o' clock. I've got an appointment with a sick friend. I'll look up Clyde Ralston tomorrow."

• • •

Chickie was frightened. "Mack, Vinnie's found me!" She hauled him in her room and slammed the door. Her face was pale, streaked with tears and her hands gripped his arms like vise-grips. "He beat up my masseur in the parking lot last Saturday and he was evidently in my room last night."

"He's found you?" Mack repeated. "Are you sure he was here?"

"I *know* he was here," she said. "My clothes are a mess and Johan, the masseur described the man who beat him. We've got to do something. I can't stand this much longer, he's stalking me, and now he's watching me sleep at night."

"Tell your father," Mack suggested the obvious. "He'll call Vinnie off."

"No he won't, he doesn't understand. I've talked with him about Vinnie for months. Daddy just smiles and tells me to be nice to him and play along for a little while longer." She shrugged and looked off to the side, embarrassed by her thoughts. "He doesn't know what Vinnie's like. I can't tell my father I'm afraid of Vinnie...that I think he's sick. Daddy says Vinnie's shy and harmless."

Mack figured the old Don had told Vinnie to keep an eye on her, but he couldn't very well say that. Chickie thought she was here to get *away* from the monster. "How the hell did he find you? Did he follow you from somewhere?"

Chickie looked hurt. "Of course not. I've stayed right here at Western Care for the past twelve days. I was enjoying the rest, and I need that damned money."

"Look Chickie, you can last another few days." He stepped back, looked her up and down. "You're looking good, haven't had a drink in twelve days and you've gotten a lot of rest. Vinnie can't really hurt you here and the stay is worth five thousand dollars. You can hack a week more for five grand, can't you?"

Chickie *had* changed. Tan, sleek and sober, she was toned up, looking years younger. Her blond hair was pulled back and tied with yarn. She wore a sweaty-smelling tank top and no-nonsense, loose-fitting blue shorts. She didn't bother with sexy or coquettish, but pushed Mack into the big chair, bent over him and spoke in a low, urgent voice. "Look, Mack, the problem is not just the masseur; Vinnie's apparently threatened two or three others. Some patients are talking about the bald man they see hanging around. My Japanese therapist quit and a cowboy down at the stables who took me for an afternoon horse-ride has disappeared." She lowered her voice some more. "The workers are tired of trouble. They know who I am and they're ready to call the police. I have to leave *now!*"

Mack shrugged helplessly, "Well, I guess that's the end. Your father *should* be mailing the first five grand to me in a couple more days, but if you go home now, a few days early for even the first payment, we can probably kiss *all* that nice money good by."

"Yeah, I know," she said. "So I have a better idea." Chickie stood straight and chewed on a long, expensive fingernail. The fear and vexation on her face became an unfocused, speculative squint into middle-space. For a brief moment Chickie Malatesta's high-cheek boned face looked a little like her father's.

Mack sensed trouble. "What idea?" he asked. "Vinnie's found your hiding place and you're leaving. Bruno will be very disappointed. We've lost five thousand each because you can't hold on a few more days. Now you think you have a *better* idea?"

"Yes. Come get me tomorrow, real early in the morning. I'll stay with *you* for a week or so."

"With me? No!" Mack was appalled at the recklessness of the idea.

She smiled at his wide eyes and opened mouth. "My plan's not as crazy as you think," she said. "Vinnie's the key. Apparently, he sneaks in after midnight and only stays about an hour until the nurse comes in for my two a.m. pill. If we leave early that next morning, he won't know I've left for another whole day. Once he discovers I'm gone, he can't very well tell my father he's driven me from my room by sneaking in at night. He'll probably spend a day looking for me around the clinic and then he'll hunt all over town at the bars I used to like. Meantime, daddy sends you both payments and I'll show up at daddy's ranch in ten days, sober and healthy, and pretend nothing happened." She gave him an arch look that dared argument.

"What about the nurses and hospital staff?" he asked. "They'll tell your father you left before your treatment was over."

"No they won't." She leaned down and whispered in his ear. "They'll be glad to be rid of me and I have an appointment with the director tomorrow. He's a nice, harmless old man who's been badly neglected by his wife. We play checkers in his office and we've become good friends. We meet again tomorrow after dinner in his office for a game and a friendly chat. I'm going to make a bargain with him." She winked. "Sort of a doctor-patient confidence: they get rid of a problem, but say nothing about it and his hospital doesn't need to return part of their fee."

"Chickie, isn't it foolish to trust someone like that?"

"No, Mack, the fee is a lot of money. More importantly, I can't stand it here much longer." Her voice rose. "I need peace of mind, some sleep and a drink!"

Mack didn't understand the urgency. "What's so bad? Talk to this hospital-director friend. Tell him to have people guard your room. Stay here. Tough it out."

Chickie was close to tears. "Oh Mack, I can't. I don't know if I could stand another week and Vinnie would damn sure hurt a guard. You don't understand. Vinnie comes in here, opens my closet and my suitcases and handles my underwear and all my clothing. He doesn't know I can smell him. It's a foul, hot stench. I'm scared to death. I can't stay here much longer." She collapsed into his lap sobbing.

"Okay, Chickie," he murmured. "I'll be here at your window at three in the morning tomorrow night." Mack kissed her cheek, stroked the back of her neck and wondered how bad it could get.

CHAPTER SEVEN

THE MONEY LAUNDRY

"Them are called brindle," Louis Carfagno said and indicated the tall dog's brown and black markings. The five-year-old gray-black, tiger-striped Greyhound was named Great Alliance. He limped a bit as the old trainer led him out of his kennel, but seemed to ignore the cast on his paw as if he knew what the white plaster meant and hoped the bad omen would disappear. "This un's a champion racer," Louis continued. "He's a three-year moneymaker who broke his right-front paw during the last turn in Saturday's sixth race. Won the race on three legs, but his racing career's prob'ly over."

Mack, Clyde and Louis stood in front of a kennel in a pre-fab metal building the size of a World War Two airplane hanger. The forty-foot high, steel-girdered roof was crammed with ribbed duct-tubes leading to humming swamp coolers and the cement floor was lined with three rows of barred, concrete kennels. Nothing soft here, everything was industrial-clean in the dog track holding area. The place reminded Mack of a big, damp jail. Wet lime and strong disinfectant swirled in the already too-warm early afternoon and the building was full of small movement.

Two teenage boys hosed down a cage at the opposite end, forty yards away and dozens of nervous dogs stirred behind their bars. The dogs paced and panted, strangely quiet. Professionals. Greyhounds are fearsome looking, deep-chested animals, easily three feet tall. Whip-thin legs swell to bulging shoulders and ham-sized haunches; slender tails curve loose S-shapes from high-arched hindquarters. Despite the swamp-coolers, their narrow heads split wide, baring white teeth in wet grins and long, pink tongues dripped cloudy saliva in the close heat.

"Most of these dogs are friendly, right, Louis?" Clyde asked nervously.

"Yep, they're all friendly," the old man said. He led the big racing dog right up to Clyde and Mack. "This un's on probation now."

Mack looked into Great Alliance's large, almond eyes for signs of aggression and saw only intelligence and aloof disinterest in the brown depths. Friendly? He reached and scratched behind one droopy, triangular ear and noticed the blue tattoo on the pink skin inside. His fingers grazed the muscular shoulder and he was amazed at the fine, soft coat and skin. Rubber-tough bulges rippled as the dog decided to move a bit closer. The long head tilted toward his hand and deep, serious eyes regarded Mack with fierce estimation. *Deciding where to bite?* Mack removed a nervous hand. But Great Alliance gave his fingers a quick, wet lick and a nose-nudge for more petting. Mack obliged.

"Figured I'd show you the situation," Clyde said, smiling at the investigator. "I'll give you the tour, take you to the clubhouse and later you can tell me about this monster guy with the weird sense of humor."

Mack photographed the reporter and the trainer standing beside the injured dog. "That's quite a beautiful dog," he said. "What happens if he doesn't heal?"

"Yeah, Louis," Clyde urged. "If a dog can't race, tell Mack what happens."

Louis Carfagno was gray-haired, sun-weathered and painfully arthritic. His curved back leaned to the side and his fingers resembled big, broken pretzels. He glanced furtively around and reached a deformed hand to the tall champion. "Costs ten bucks a week to keep a dog," he muttered and rumpled Great Alliance's tattooed ear. The thick, knobby fingers were clumsy, but gentle and loving. "They put 'em down. This 'un's extra special. He's won so many races they're givin' him a fightin' chance. I got two weeks to heal 'im up to par. If he don't, they put him down."

"What? A champion, and they can't afford to feed him?" Mack asked.

"Nope, 'fraid Al's a gonner if'n he can't run a quarter mile in twenty seconds."

"See, Mack, they run fifty-thousand dollar races and get a sixty-thousand-person gate each weekend, but can't afford to feed a damn dog," Clyde lamented.

"But aren't these dogs still worth money as breeders?" Mack asked.

Louis shook his head. "Breeders? Hell no, not if they're partial to injuries. There's plenty of dogs and we get damn little money to feed and board 'em."

Clyde walked toward the door. "Come on, Mack, time for people food."

Mack gave the lean, muscular greyhound another pat, nodded to the old trainer and they left and headed toward a structure Clyde called the clubhouse.

The large building looked like an enclosed football grandstand with bleachers at the bottom, restaurants half way up and glass-fronted suites at the top level.

"More than twenty years in Tucson and I've never been here before," Mack remarked as they walked toward the clubhouse around the edge of the fenced-in track. He pointed almost straight up, fifty feet above the restaurant level to the very top of the amphitheater. "What are those glass boxes, Clyde?"

"Those are the VIP boxes," the reporter said as they maneuvered past a clean-up crew and started up the stairs. "They're leased by the season so businesses and corporations can entertain clients and lobby politicians."

"What businesses? What clients?"

"Valley National Bank, Del West Corporation, Diamond Bell Ranch, Broken Arrow Ranch, Santa Cruz River Project..."

"Wait a minute!" Mack interrupted. "Santa Cruz River Project is a regulated utility, the electric company for the whole County. They're not supposed to entertain clients or lobby politicians with our rate money!"

Clyde laughed as he climbed. "Hah! That's what you think. Public utilities are really private companies licensed, franchised and regulated by the politicians. They can't donate to campaigns, but they can damn sure wine and dine people."

Mack shook his head at his naiveté and stood aside as four workers in coveralls from a local meat packer grunted down the stairs carrying a large, empty meat cooler. Cold ammonia drifted in bitter, white fumes from lumps of dry ice in the bloody water at the bottom. Mack thought of angry animal ghosts. "What's all this activity during the day," he asked. "I thought the dog races were later?"

Clyde Ralston paused on the stairs, turned and rested a heavy, dark hand on Mack's shoulder. "Dog racing ain't what this place is all about, Mack."

Mack thought he'd heard wrong. "But this is a dog track."

The broad, brown face split around square teeth, a chuckle bubbled and Clyde enjoyed the joke for a few moments before patting Mack's shoulder. "Hey man, look around. This big ol' place ain't about racing, or dogs. This is about money." He waved his arm around. "Sky-boxes, imported booze,

Wisconsin beef, Cuban cigars and there's even women for sale along with all the beer, hot dogs, ice cream and popcorn. This place is all about, cash and *concessions*, Mack."

Mack shook his head in wonderment. "I've put twenty-five years in Tucson as a cop and investigator. How come I've never heard about any of this?"

"Hey, Mack," Clyde laughed through his words, "you're beginnin' to understand. If something ain't in the newspaper then it *damn* sure can't be news."

The two men sat at a table near the stairs in an open-sided restaurant.

There were thick rugs, starched tablecloths, fresh flowers and heavy silverware along with a good view of the track. A beefy ex-boxer-looking white uniformed waiter sized them up and brought menus. Mack set his camera on the table, ordered two Becks and sat back to look around at dozens of service people preparing food, chopping ice, filling coolers and setting places at the fifty or so tables. There were maybe twenty other customers scattered around. Most were shirt and tie types at tables toying with food and studying racing forms, but Mack saw a few rowdier men in levis, pearl-button shirts and cowboy hats crowded at the end of a long mahogany bar. They shouted bets, exchanged handfuls of bills and slammed down beers while watching a closed-circuit boxing match on an enormous wide-screen TV. "This place is ritzy as hell for a race track that can't feed an injured dog," he remarked as he watched the waiter point them out to one of the bartenders.

Clyde emptied his water goblet, ice and all, in a gulp. "Aaah, hits the spot." He leaned forward. The table tilted and Mack grabbed for his water. "Look, Mack," the big reporter said patiently. "Think of the track this way, the dogs are just an excuse. If there ain't dogs, there's quarter-horses, Indian bingo, football, basketball or race cars. The *real* purpose for these places is to get the suckers off the street and throwing their money around. In a loose atmosphere of fun and gambling there's always lots of unregulated, untraceable money changing hands."

"Right," Mack nodded. "Gambling against house-odds, the suckers eventually lose and the house always wins, but that doesn't explain..."

"Hold it right there!" Clyde broke in. "Y'all sound like my editor, Mister Ace Collins. Neither of you understand this stuff. You're still talking 'bout small-time money. Gambling and house-odds ain't what this track is all about any more."

Mack frowned in confusion, and at being compared to Collins. "But you said this story of yours was about money."

They both stopped talking while a bar waitress brought them two frost-dripping glass mugs and dark green bottles of Becks. As she left, the waiter reappeared and took their orders for buffalo wings, French fries, more beers and two large cheeseburgers apiece. This time Clyde ordered for both of them.

"This lunch is on the newspaper, Mister Private Eye." He grinned and rubbed his belly. "I can use your investigative experience, your past Organized Crime Task Force connections and your camera work on this caper. The paper's buying, but if y'all can't finish those cheeseburgers, I'll clean up for both of us." His eyes glowed good humor behind the thick lenses and his teeth gleamed like Chiclets.

Mack was about to refuse the free lunch on principle until he noticed what pleasure the young man was taking in the ritual. He smiled back and held out his hand. "Thanks, Mister Reporter," he responded and they shook hands, grinning like fools. "I'll help you solve this caper and then we can shoot the dirty hoodlums, romance the gorgeous dames and drink cheap whiskey straight from the bottle in my desk drawer." They laughed and clinked beer mugs.

Serious talk returned while they waited for the wings, fries and burgers.

"My story *is* about money, Mack, black money." Clyde continued as though there'd been no interruption. "Arizona's right next to Las Vegas. Vegas casinos can take in one, two million dollars over a big weekend. It's a river of coins, ones, fives, tens, twenties, fifties and hundreds. Most big casinos usually average a quarter million cash even on slow week nights, but that's not what they show Uncle Sam." He paused to tilt his head back and drain his beer. "After all the Mafia movies like *Godfather* and *Casino,* everybody in the country knows the *real* money in casinos is the profits they skim *before* the money gets counted and reported to the I.R.S. Everybody knows, but nobody stops to think what the wise guys do with all this unreported cash." Clyde threw up his hands and beseeched the ceiling. "*Nobody* realizes the mob disposes of tons of coins and millions in small bills each year. Question is, how?" He glared the question through his thick glasses.

Mack said the obvious. "They launder the money."

"Right!" Clyde shouted and slapped the table, bouncing their glasses. "But to *launder* money means you've got to make cash appear to come from a legal source."

And Mack finally understood. "I get it," he exclaimed. "The crime families who control the Vegas casinos have a skimmed river of illegal coins, fives, tens and twenties to convert back to legal money." Mack pointed at the track betting windows below. "They need legal, mob-controlled, unregulated places in nearby states that handle lots of small bills. They provide operating funds, pay off races for friends, bribe politicians, stock vending machines and buy all that untraceable food and liquor for restaurants, bars and concessions with all that skimmed money. That way they turn illegal money into legal profits."

"Exactly," Clyde agreed. "They used to buy restaurants, bars and vending companies - businesses that handle cash. But in the late seventies the casinos began raking in too much cash and the boys needed bigger laundries." Clyde swept his hands around, indicating the dining room and racetrack. "Voila, my man! Emprise Corporation was brought in to promote gambling and sporting facilities in Arizona! Arizona has three horse tracks, six dog tracks, four Indian bingo halls, and *now* they want to build city-franchised sports arenas in Phoenix and Tucson. Remember, race tracks, Indian casinos and, of course, sports arenas, are *all* natural laundries."

The food arrived. The beefy waiter set up a tray near the table and brought each item to them with a theatrical flourish. Mack noticed he seemed particularly solicitous of Clyde and decided the waiter was discriminating in reverse. The food was Mack's style: chicken wings dripping cayenne, crunchy fries and thick, medium-rare cheese-burgers bedded on fresh tomatoes and crisp lettuce - the meat protruding a half inch wider than the bun. The two hungry men wolfed the wings like quick candy and then began the serious eating. Talking ceased for a while.

"So you decided to write about mob laundries," Mack mumbled through a half-full mouth. "What got you started? And what happened to your stories?"

Clyde finished the last bite of his second burger and eyed Mack's plate. When Mack picked up his second burger, Clyde sighed disappointment, ate his last French fry and picked at the chicken bones piled on his plate. He kept his head down and spoke quietly. "Everything started for me when they found dead greyhounds with their ears cut off. That really bothered me. I decided to find out why *anybody* would do somethin' so mean and bizarre. After doin' some research, I wrote an article about dog track owners, particularly the Emprise Company of Chicago, and the way they treat dogs. But the important thing was, I made a big deal about the dogs bein' shot at Greenbaum and Lillienthal's Broken Arrow Ranch!" He emphasized the famous names and looked at Mack with goggle-eyed amazement. "And you know what? Some of the strangest guys suddenly started talking to me. Guys with grudges against the big boys - and also some others at the track who resented the way the dogs were treated...guys like old Louie."

Mack nodded sympathetically. "Taking a chance, an old cripple like that."

"Yeah, but he loves those dogs. I didn't name him. Couldn't name any of the workers, but they weren't my best source anyhow." Clyde slid forward, lowered his voice. "I talked to some of the wise-guys who always hang around. Asked about the track owners. Lower-level mobsters like to name-drop, makes them seem like big shots. Names came up like Moe Dalitz, Bruno Malatesta, Anthony Zerilli, Pete Licavoli, Joe Bonnanno, Joe Tocco, Gus Greenbaum and Robert Lillienthal. The last two were most important to me because of the Broken Arrow connection."

"Lillienthal, the ex-Senator's brother," Mack added to show he knew.

"Right," Clyde nodded. "So I wanted to do another piece, naming names, but the story didn't ring true. Dog tracks seemed such penny-ante stuff for these big-time players. I decided to talk to some of the actual people. I went out to Malatesta's Ranch to see Bruno Malatesta and to Joe Bonnanno's house on Elm Street." Clyde raised a finger for emphasis. "*And* I went to City Hall and the State building and brought up Emprise Company's convenient ownership of race tracks *and* Vegas casinos. *That's* supposed to be against the rules! The good ol' boys at City Hall laughed at me. Bruno Malatesta and Joe Banannas were polite, but asked me to leave. Some threatened." He chuckled. "Hell, they threw me off Broken Arrow Ranch. A few guys talked enough for me to know that dog tracks and dead dogs on Greenbaum's and Lillienthal's Broken Arrow Ranch weren't half the damn story."

Mack waited for more, but the reporter took off his glasses and gazed at the pile of bones with a sorrow too intense for vanished chicken and cayenne pepper.

"Yeah, then what?" Mack urged.

"I put it all together and wrote the last story. They spiked the damn thing."

"Spiked? What the hell does *that* mean?"

"Spiked means the editor decided not to print the work I submitted," Clyde said with a sigh.

"Why not?"

"Because Collins said the story was mostly speculation and involved too many confidential informants to be straight news. And he could be right."

Mack was stunned at the last wishy-washy remark. He'd just watched a bright, tough reporter turn to a sack of self-doubting mush. "That's bullshit!" he snapped. "Most of what you guys do at *The Register* - and every other newspaper for that matter - is half-baked speculation. Damn near every story I read quotes highly-placed or unnamed sources."

"That's true Mack, but I was tossin' around some powerful names. And the truth is, I *don't* have proof. Not yet." Clyde reached over and gripped Mack's arm. "But I think it's possible to prove something by ***who*** is involved and what's ***not*** there. So, what do you think? Will you help me research some of these names and give me some independent, photographic proof there's money-laundering goin' on at this dog-killin' track so's I can force Ace Collins to print my story?"

"I'll do what I can to help you, Clyde," Mack promised. Then he told the reporter about the crazed Mafia enforcer and how he'd been present at Viola Faber's hit and run. He told about the man's pale, stiff, bald-headed appearance and the Illinois plate, MNG something. He didn't mention the real witness, Franklin Blaine.

Clyde nodded. "Yeah, I got a message from Mister Collins to check with y'all on a witness to Grace's mother's hit and run." Clyde was suddenly thoughtful. He replaced the thick, horned-rimmed glasses and scratched his head. "An out of town enforcer? A pyro, you say? You know Mack, that anti-bond guy, Mitch Young? His death was a professional torch job. There *could* be a connection."

"You really think they'd kill somebody for a sports arena?" Mack asked. He recalled the reporter's story. "A new laundry? And Malatesta has a piece of this dog track through Emprise? Damn! Vinnie Romano could also be a prime suspect for torching Mitch Young and his anti sports-arena headquarters."

Clyde shook his head. "But there's no way we can prove that."

"Maybe not, " Mack said. "But if you do a news story on a Mafia enforcer simply *witnessing* the hit and run death of an old woman, the story will force the cops to do something." Mack raised a cautionary finger. "If we're right about the Sports Arena connection, the mob just might try to shut you up real quick."

Clyde grinned without humor. "I'll do the story. That's my job."

The waiter offered dessert, but the two men weren't in the mood. Clyde handed over a credit card and they waited and watched as the amphitheater began to fill up for the early afternoon dog races.

• • •

The armored car sparked the profound question.

After Clyde signed the credit card receipt they wandered down the stairs toward the lower lobby and the betting windows. They were just in time to see a large vehicle pull up the driveway next to the track and around the side of the clubhouse. The square, gray armored car parked next to a door that obviously led into the rear of the betting-window area.

"Is that how the skimmed money gets here?" Mack asked.

"Good question," Clyde said and checked his watch. Three o'clock. He'd been waiting for this, the reason he'd brought Mack on Tuesday. "But the Mafia can't use armored cars to bring their skim-money from Vegas. Armored cars take money to and from regulated banks and businesses. They have to keep records. That armored car isn't bringin' any money here at all. They're only takin' money out. Come on!"

They hurried down the last of the stairs, past the betting windows and out onto a small driveway between the end of the clubhouse and the fence around the track. The truck was parked ten feet away, back door wide open.

"See, damn it?" Clyde huffed. He was out of breath from the quickstep.

"Yeah, I see. What do you mean?"

Clyde looked down at Mack as though he was the stupidest human being alive. "Just take your damn pictures and hurry! They won't be long."

Mack focused the camera, snapped one shot.

"No, no, inside the damn truck!" Clyde was nearly screaming in frustration.

And then Mack realized. The big armored truck was empty - *money all going out and none coming in.* Bingo! He shot a half a roll of film, opening the aperture each shot, adjusting to the dim light inside the truck. He moved closer for a better angle, zoomed in.

Clyde grabbed his arm. "Come on man, somebody comin'. Lets boogie!"

A skinny armored-car guard staggered out the door from the clubhouse with two bulging gray sacks suspended from each arm. "What the hell!" He dropped the bags and unsnapped the holster at his hip. "Hey Joe, get out here in a hurry!" he called over his shoulder. The guard was very nervous, maybe thought he was in the middle of a robbery. He drew his gun. "Freeze you bastards!" he yelled, but his voice broke into falsetto on the last word.

Mack grinned. "Hey, relax, we're tourists." He let the camera dangle from its strap and held out empty hands. "Just taking pictures. Watch where you point that."

The guard's hand was shaking, the gun muzzle wandering inches in every direction; "I'll point my gun where I want. Now you get...get..." he stopped because he obviously didn't know what to tell them to do.

Mack glanced at Clyde's worried face and began to laugh and talk at the same time. "Don't worry, he's not going to shoot. Let's go!" He grabbed Clyde's hand and pulled him into motion. They ran down the driveway past the truck.

No shots were fired.

"Damn, man," Clyde puffed. "I thought he was goin' to shoot our asses."

"Sheeit, Clyde, he couldn't hit the sky."

They laughed uproariously like a couple of kids while they trotted around the end of the building in the direction of the parking lot that covered a city block in front of the racetrack. Neither man was fast. Three or four minutes later they jogged around the long side of the amphitheater and past the main entrance to the large, asphalt parking area.

"Oh shit," Clyde said. "My car!"

They stopped running and watched three burly men in suits smashing the windshield of Clyde's little Nissan Sentra with baseball bats.

The men bashed and battered, finally punching through the shatterproof film, bashing again and pulling Clyde's press placard out. One of them whooped in triumph and brandished the card in the direction of the clubhouse.

Mack didn't think they'd seen him and Clyde yet. They'd driven separately to the track. Mack's truck was several rows beyond Clyde's and still looked undamaged from a distance. Maybe they didn't know about the P.I. "Come on Clyde," he hissed. "Forget the damn car. We'll make a run for my truck over there."

The parking lot was only a quarter full, but the cars were all bunched close to the entrance. The two big men bent down and ran hunched-over behind rows of parked cars, trying to get around the three men waiting at Clyde's Nissan only four aisles away. Both were breathing hard after sneaking past three cars. They ducked down, dodged across an aisle, hid behind a van and scurried across another aisle. Wait, peek and run again. Almost there! Sunlight had softened the asphalt and their shoes didn't scuffle. Mack's Colt Commander was in the truck's door pouch. Once he had that 45 in his hand the damned baseball bats were moot as dinosaurs.

Crouch and run! There were two more rows of cars.

"There them bastids go!" a gruff voice shouted.

"Let's get the nosy sonsa' bitches!" another joined in.

So much for sneaking away. Time to fight.

Mack stood and watched the three men in suits and ties running easily and confidently down the nearest aisle between them and his truck, bats carried like rifles. The first was thirty feet away. Hefty shoulders, dark hair, he looked Italian.

Clyde stood, pocketed his glasses and lifted his fists. "Mack, we're in for it."

"Yeah, buddy, arms up, go in low and bull under their damn bats."

Clyde glanced quickly at the older man. "What? You act like you've done this stuff before!"

"Once or twice," Mack said and tried to figure out how to avoid a beating. He knew with their size they each had a chance against *one* guy with a bat, but the third man could stand back while they grappled with his buddies and bash in the backs of their heads. They had to take the first guy out fast. Mack looked around for a weapon. There was nothing but locked cars and asphalt.

First guy was closer now, slowing down to a walk, slapping the bat in his meaty palm. Confident and smiling – *smack, smack*. The other two saw him slow down and they dropped to a walk too. The parking lot was deserted. Easy pickings. No sweat. They spread out to come at the two men from different directions.

Mack watched the first one. He could hear his labored breathing; see the tight grin and the scar tissue above small, dark eyes. The guy was enjoying the beating before it happened. Then the broad face twisted to fighting rage, sucked hot oxygen. "Hey you fuckin' nigger, we saw you eatin' lunch. You been snoopin' around the dogs again? We read your last story in the paper. This time we're gonna teach you to mind your own business!"

"You calling me a fuckin' nigger?" Mack snarled. "I resent that!"

Clyde chuckled. "You're enjoying this too much, Mack. We're gonna get a whippin'. What the hell do you know 'bout this humbug shit that I don't?"

"Clyde, my young friend, the only thing I know is, you never show fear. That only encourages the bastards. Back your large ass in here with me."

Mack and Clyde moved together, back to back, between two cars - a late model shiny and an old clunker. Mack lowered the camera to the ground and slid it under the clunker with his foot.

The first guy was coming around the car like he was gonna hit a home run. "Fuckin' reporters," he growled at Mack and shuffled forward slowly. "You been messin' with the wrong people. I'm gonna scramble me some stoolie brains."

The clunker! A two-foot-long radio antenna stuck up at a slight angle from its faded fender. Mack snapped it off and lunged like a fencer at the bat-man's eye.

Surprise made it possible. The man didn't expect an attack. His eyes widened just long enough for Mack to sink an inch of antenna into the left one.

"Aaargh!" The thug dropped the bat and fell to his knees. "Aaaah, shit!' he screamed again and tried to pull the rusty steel out of his eye.

Mack kicked him in the head. He fell over backwards and lay still with the antenna swaying out of his face. One down. Time to kick ass! "Okay Clyde, follow me!" Mack picked up the first guy's bat and ran for the closest of the other two suits. "My turn, you bastards!" he shouted and waved the bat over his head like a battle-axe.

But the second hood stood his ground, set himself and took a full swing.

The bat caught Mack hard on the shoulder. He reeled against a car, knocked half-senseless, shoulder screaming bright pain. Then he heard the other one moving in from the side and Mack decided he was gonna get a serious beating.

Clyde bored in low, full speed, caught one at the waist and slammed him into a car hard enough to drop them both gasping to the tar, with Clyde on top.

Mack was recovering from the stunning shoulder blow, but pretended he was badly hurt, leaning against a car, bat down, moaning like a hypochondriac.

The last hood moved in quick to finish Mack off. "Gonna break your fuckin' head!" he yelled, and lifted his bat high over his head for a skull crusher.

The move was almost too easy. Mack waited for the last moment and swung his baseball bat up in a hard tee shot between the hood's spread legs. The hardwood bat lifted the man six inches off the ground and bit so deep he couldn't scream. Head-breaker grunted and crumpled to the asphalt, holding his smashed crotch.

• • •

"Now do you understand, sir?" Clyde beseeched Ace Collins. "We've got photographs of the empty armored truck. The thugs mentioned my story about the track, busted up my car, gloated over my vehicle press placard and assaulted us with bats to get revenge. All that should be enough to run with."

Ace Collins was sick. Raw nausea pulsed his gut. Gray spots danced.

The two battered ruffians had burst into his office just as he was about to have his four o' clock pick-me-up. He'd had the bottle part way out of the drawer when they banged on his office door. He'd handled the hit and run well; now more complications. Sometimes he wished he could get away from all the deceit and pretense and just go relax somewhere and laugh about his past. Fat chance.

"You left these men bleeding in the parking lot?" Ace asked.

"They attacked us with baseball bats, poor bastards." Clyde grinned at Mack.

"Someone will notify the police." The editor tried to insert some sanity.

Mack was sitting in the same soft leather settee as before, nursing his sore shoulder. He reached into his pocket and held three pieces of paper up to Clyde. "These guys won't be calling the law," he said. "They're out-of-state hoods. Looked Italian. Two of these phony I.D.s say they're James Brown and David Jones from Chicago. The third is a Nevada driver's license in the name of Samoots Amatuna." Mack glanced at Clyde. "He's the one with the bad eye."

"The point is, Mister Collins," Clyde continued. "They wrecked my car and threatened to beat me because I wrote the dog track story for *The Register*."

Ace Collins sighed. He knew he had to get this over with. The cool, sweet song of alcohol shivered promises to his scalding veins, teased his desolate mind. Not now! I *can't* deal with this now. "We're going to run a hit and run piece soon. Now what is this *other* story you want to write?" the editor asked very quietly.

Clyde raised his fist and towered over the editor's desk like an angry dark colossus. "I want to tell the disgusting story of dead greyhounds shot for lack of ten dollars worth of food in a sport facility that easily grosses fifty thousand a week! And then I want to ask why an Atlas Armored truck comes once each week to pick up money. And why the trucks are always completely empty when they arrive."

"Of course they're going to be empty," the editor protested. "They're *picking up* the weeks receipts, aren't they?"

"Like I told you, Mister Collins," Clyde explained. "Armored cars usually deliver small change and pick up big bills at the same time. I've checked around town and Atlas Armored is the only company they use at the track. I interviewed their dispatcher. She says they only make that trip *once* a week on Tuesday and..."

"Yes, yes," Ace Collins was suffering. "So what? Get to the point."

"The point is, all businesses need small change. No armored car ever brings small change, or *any* cash to that race track. Nobody ever seems to bring *any* large amounts of money to the track, at least, not by any normal carrier," Clyde said.

"So what?" Collins repeated. "This is hardly conclusive of anything."

"So the race track pays all its employees and suppliers in cash. Every week people come and cash their company paychecks, or bring their fifties and hundreds to make bets, buy booze, food and cigarettes. The track uses vast amounts of small change. They need ones, fives, tens and even quarters." Clyde spread his hands wide. "Ask yourself, where does the track get its small change? I'm willing to bet they get it by private carload from the slots and gaming tables at Las Vegas!"

Ace Collins was stumped. But now he understood other things. "How long will you need to write this?" He had to delay *this* story.

"We need some research, but I have the story almost written. Maybe two or three days." Clyde was happy. A smile stretched the words to a down-home drawl.

"We'll need to do a special layout, pictures and all." The editor pretended to think out loud. "Sunday a week would be the best time. I could refer to your article and the awful conditions at the dog track in my weekly editorial..."

"This ain't about conditions, Mister Collins," Clyde interrupted. "And we can't wait that long! The Sports Arena bond election is next week. Remember the fire at the headquarters of the anti-tax group? There might be a connection. The Sports arena concessions could be set up to launder Vegas mob money as well."

"What!" Ace Collins stood. His chair scooted back with a clatter. "A crummy story about small change and a bunch of dead dogs has nothing to do with our new sports arena!" He shook his finger in the air. "Pay no more attention to this so-called laundering scheme you've dreamed up and get out of my office!"

Clyde rocked back on his heels. He was about to argue, but decided he'd said enough for now. Mack got up slowly and both men walked to the office door, conscious of angry green eyes boring holes in their backs.

"Ralston, have that dog and small-change story ready for the end of next week." Collins ordered. When they'd left he opened his desk drawer with palsied fingers and poured two crystal inches into a coffee cup. He drank swiftly and sighed with relief. Alcohol eased his anguish…and his guilt. After a long minute savoring clean, cool energy sliding through his veins he picked up the phone.

CHAPTER EIGHT

A LIGHT BULB

Her window was stuck. They made a terrible racket before they finally got the heavy casement-style, crank window open far enough to accommodate Chickie Malatesta's large body and her three bulging suitcases.

"Thought you'd never get here," she whispered. "He was here again around midnight." Mack felt her shiver. "This time I only pretended to be asleep."

"What did he do?"

"What he probably always does, opened my suitcases, played with my clothing and stood in the shadows watching me sleep, always breathing like a thunderstorm. He stayed an hour or so and then left as quiet as he came."

"Well, I'll be glad to get you away," Mack said.

"Thanks, sugar," she squeezed his waist. "I appreciate all your trouble."

They hustled through night shadows under thick trees and bushes along the side of the building and headed toward a dim corner of the parking lot where Mack had parked his truck. Four a.m., the weak part of the night. The moon had set. He peered from the bushes, looking for watchers before breaking cover. Nothing.

"What's the matter? Think he hangs around here all night?" Chickie asked.

"Anything's possible with Vinnie," Mack grunted and pulled her toward his truck, waiting for a shout or a shuffle of pursuing feet, but too sore and tired to care.

They made it to the truck, threw her bags in the back, piled in, and Mack drove slowly out of the complex with his lights out.

• • •

Bachelors are never really prepared for female guests. He awoke at noon on Wednesday. When he sat up he stared in amazement. Every available level space in his office below the loft was covered with half-empty luggage, woman's clothing, make-up bags, parts of a hair-curling kit and damp towels. Mack wondered how one person could ever use all that stuff. Must've taken all morning just to spread it out, he thought. He considered climbing down the ladder from his loft and groaned. The shoulder felt like a bone bruise and he knew he was in for weeks of pain, but he also understood the injury could've been much worse. "Mornin' Chickie."

"You finally awake, sugar?" Chickie pranced out of the bathroom naked. Her big, conical breasts and ample buttocks bounced and shivered joyously as she puttered at the stove. "Stay up there and rest. You deserve it." She stood on tiptoes and handed him up a cup of coffee. Then she began to dress.

"Where the hell are you going?" he asked. "You're supposed to be hiding."

She wiggled into shorts, slid feet into sandals and stretched her arms into a sleeveless, cotton blouse, enjoying his eyes and posing. "My girlfriend's picking me up. We're going shopping at the wholesale outlets up in Casa Grande." She frowned down at a lump in the shirt and pulled her gold cross and chain out of the tight blouse, dropping it so it bounced on her chest.

"That's better." She arched her back. Nipples poked small, dark fingers in the thin cloth. "I'll be back for dinner."

Mack was exasperated by the risk. "You can't do that! Vinnie could be looking for you! What if somebody who knows your father sees you shopping?"

"Listen sugar." Her expression turned serious. "Casa Grande is sixty miles up the interstate in the middle of nowhere. I'll be safer up there than I would be here."

A horn honked. She picked up her purse and left the studio.

• • •

Two hours later a beefy older man Mack recognized as the bigger of Bruno Malatesta's two bodyguards arrived in front of the studio in a dark Lincoln. Mack spotted him through the front window and figured their breach of contract had been discovered already. Damn! This Chickie thing just kept getting worse and worse! All this aggravation for a friend...for sex! He cursed his perpetual bondage to an over-active libido and slid the 45 into the back of the waistband of his Levis. He opened the door with a good head of anger and a half-assed explanation already in his throat. "Yeah? I've kinda been expecting you guys," he said. "What can I do for you?"

"This is from the boss," the man said in a prize-fighter's growl. "He says you done good so far and you gonna get a bonus when his daughter gets out of the clinic next week." He lifted a blue cloth overnight bag and held it out to Mack.

And Mack realized they didn't know.

He shifted his body so the man wouldn't see the feminine disarray in the back of the studio. His hand reached for the bag before he told it to. "Well thanks," he said. "Tell Mister Malatesta I appreciate his keeping our contract."

"Yeah," The tough-looking old man examined Mack for a nervous moment as though searching for good qualities, or a place to punch. Then he shrugged and swaggered back to his car. Mack recognized the sedan - Illinois plate, *MNG-410*.

Mack hefted the bag, felt the shift of paper and quickly closed the door. As he walked to the desk in the rear he opened the bag and reached in. It was a bank-robber's dream, three inches deep and a foot by two feet of fives and tens and twenties, old money, soft and slippery with years of time and thousands of fingers. Mack was a little disappointed, expecting neatly wrapped bundles of hundreds, but money was money, right? He thought of Las Vegas skim money and wondered if this was a small part. Maybe. But was the contracted money all there?

Forty-five minutes later he'd counted the money - five thousand dollars in old, small bills. He pulled out a few hundred, packed the rest in a pillowcase and back in the overnight bag. Mack paused as he began to put the bag in the closet. A lot of money; paranoia struck like a fever. He held the bag and stood in the middle of his small living space. Where the hell could he hide money? The studio was guarded with plate-glass windows and flimsy old doors with beveled key-latches - a burglar's dream. He'd never worried about security before. Hell, he didn't often have this much cash at one time. Finally he decided the pickup truck was safer than the studio. Mack crammed the cash-stuffed overnight bag down behind the bench-seat in the truck-cab and parked the pickup in front of the studio.

He finally relaxed enough to look around at all the female chaos and was thankful the bodyguard hadn't wanted to come inside. She'd only been there a day! Frilly blouses draped counter-tops, stockings dangled from doorknobs and make-up accouterments covered his sink drain-board. Mack breathed the powdery, feminine smells. They made him think of his young client.

He called her at work. "Clyde's doing the story on our witness," he began. "What...? Yes he is, and Mister Collins gave him permission and sent me to him."

Grace was obviously feeling conflicting emotions. She asked when the story would be running and then asked if Clyde was putting himself in any danger.

"I'm meeting him later to go over the details," he answered. "The hit and run story should run this coming week. We're aware of the danger and Clyde's promised to be careful. He's a big boy. Yes, I'll be keeping an eye out for him also."

Mack wanted to meet with her, but couldn't think of a good enough reason.

"I'll call you when I know more," he said.

• • •

"Come to our house for dinner, Mack." Clyde's voice sounded even deeper on the phone. "I told my wife about our escapade yesterday and she can't wait to thank you for saving her handsome hubby's large beautiful ass from a beating. You can meet my little daughters too."

"You finish the Viola Faber story yet?"

His laugh gurgled. "Yeah, I wrote your damn story, but I'm way behind on police paperwork. We can do a final check of the Faber hit and run after dinner."

"That'll be great, Clyde, but I've got a woman-friend staying with me and I can't leave her alone." Mack was sure Chickie'd be back in time. She'd said dinner.

"Bring her along," Clyde said without hesitation. "Any woman friend of yours can damn sure meet my family."

Yeah, sure, Clyde, Mack thought to himself, *wait 'til your family gets a load of Chickie Malatesta.*

Chickie returned from Casa Grande at dark just as Mack was preparing to call Clyde and cancel. There was no time for her to wash up and change her clothes for dinner.

He told her about the money delivery.

"He was here?" she asked in a little-girl voice as though she'd never expected it. "Here at your place? My God, I expected him to *mail* you a check."

"Yeah. Well, one of his men handed me a bag. Let's go, we're late."

So Chickie arrived for dinner at the Ralston's in her short shorts and tight, sleeveless tee shirt with long, blond hair loose and wild around her shoulders and the gold cross bouncing on her chest. Mack wore jeans and his tweed sport jacket.

At first handshake Clyde seemed taken aback by Chickie's size and bold, sexy appearance, but Janice took charge and whisked the large blond over to the little girls on the couch where the two very dissimilar women began that cooing noise females make around children. Opposites, Mack thought. Blond Chickie stretched her clothes and seemed to fill the room. Janice wore an understated rust-colored scarf around short, tightly curled, black hair and an ankle-length dress of soft, beige cotton that only hinted at her small, sleek figure.

But Janice Ralston was a match for Clyde, as small, cinnamon-beautiful as he was big and darkly handsome. Their daughters, two-year Sylvia and baby Martha, took their parents' classic features to soft unfinished promise like small impressionist paintings. Huge hazel eyes, cupid-mouths in heart-shaped faces and braided hair tied in multi-colored ribbons reminded Mack of small, brown angels.

Clyde and Mack decided to get drinks before sitting down, but stopped and lingered in the hallway like two schoolboys, Mack ogling the large, bosomy blond and Clyde caught in the dream-come-true of his little family.

My family, Clyde thought. *Come a long way from the Delta, Grandpop.*

His parents were very proud of him and so was his grandfather. Mom and dad were teachers at Mississippi State and his grandfather still lived on the land *his* father had worked as a depression-era sharecropper. The old man talked about the day in 1949 when he and his father had borrowed the money and bought their own farm from the land his family had worked for so long. Clyde loved the old man. When he went south for visits he'd spend special time on the farm listening to the family patriarch talk of hopes for the future and his past struggles. Joyous about the coming years and proud of the ones gone away, grandpop said they were both life lessons, but Clyde noticed his Grandpop always spoke of the future first. "Clyde, you a good boy," he'd always say. "Gonna be the best they is, just like your momma and poppa...and me o' course." And the old man would chuckle.

Then he'd tell of the old years, the hard years of his youth.

"Them years was rough," he'd say. "We worked the land, sent young 'uns to school and fed the family on cotton money, but Tildy always put some aside." Tildy was Clyde's grandmother, Matilda. She'd died years before when Clyde was in school, but she died in her marriage bed just five miles away from the house of her birth. Clyde knew his grandparents had saved every cent and gone hungry themselves to put his father through school. His father had done the rest. He'd worked hard, scrimped, saved and won a scholarship to the State University where he'd found his wife, his life's work and, eventually, a family. Clyde thanked God every day for his parents and grandparents, he knew he was the result of their years of sacrifice and hard work. He felt the pull of the past, of the Mississippi farm and the debt he owed. He smiled down at his two daughters, proud of his home and his accomplishments, but he always reminded himself to look to the future first, just like his grandfather.

While Clyde gazed lovingly at his little family Janice looked up. Their eyes met. Mack felt the warm exchange and envied them. Then the reporter turned to his guest, grinned triumphantly and hustled Mack into the kitchen to check food and find beer. The two men filled the kitchen. Clyde ordered Mack to grab two beers from the large side-by-side refrigerator and busied himself in the double stainless-steel sink, cleaning boiled shrimp in one and rinsing in the other.

"Janice loves them shrimp," Clyde drawled. "But I always gotta clean 'em."

"You live pretty good for a damn reporter," Mack remarked and gave Clyde a beer.

Clyde grunted amused agreement deep in his chest. "Yeah, I get all that graft money." He turned, pointing a dripping shrimp at Mack. "But you know I *have* put in a hell of a lot of overtime lately on this dog track thing."

"All your work's finally gonna pay off," Mack reassured. "You're gonna get your dog track story printed the way you want despite that overblown asshole, Collins. Hell, after what happened at the track, he *can't* ignore you any more."

They chatted. Clyde discovered Mack and he had a lot in common. They both loved blues, classical music, Mel Gibson-Danny Glover movies and the old time Pittsburgh Steelers. When Clyde had finished cleaning thirty or forty shrimp, and they'd shared a few more beers, the two men had thoroughly discussed everything from Muddy Waters and Brahms to *Lethal Weapon II*, Mean Joe Greene, Dwight White and Jack Lambert. They loved them all.

More beer and everything was funny as hell. They joined the women in the living room and Clyde kissed Janice before announcing a grand tour of their house. Janice smiled lovingly and decided dinner was ready. Little Martha was asleep on Chickie's lap and Mack noticed the blond wasn't drinking.

Clyde showed his home with broad, proud flourishes. Master bedroom with an ornate wrought-iron king-sized bed, bathroom off the hall next to another, smaller bedroom filled with muppets posters, stuffed animals, a bunk bed and a crib with a little Bo Peep mobile suspended above. Again Mack envied the young man his family bliss. Part of him wanted to try again...someday.

Dinner was done in segments. First shrimp. Everyone had a taste and then the two youngest were taken, complaining bitterly, to the kitchen to be fed by Janice and then to bed. By the time Janice returned there were six empty Becks on the table, only three shrimp left and Mack and Clyde were discussing making a beer run.

Mack expected some trouble about all the beer, but Janice smiled warmly at Clyde and wagged her finger, "no more beer until dinner." She kissed her husband and sat on his spacious lap.

"There's hardly any shrimp left," Clyde said around a mouthful. "Sorry honey. We would've saved you more, but you were gone so long."

"Clyde baby, you *know* I don't like sea food. You pretend to get all this fancy stuff for me, but I know better. You buy me delicacies and then eat them yourself." She glanced at her guests with an amused frown. "Come on, Clyde, we'd better get some food in these people." She pulled him to the kitchen.

Dinner was roast pork, mashed sweet potatoes and peas. Janice presided over her odd guests and effusive husband with good humor. The graceful woman had gently put Chickie Malatesta at ease, dealt calmly with hungry, irritable children, handled a beery, rambunctious husband and fixed a fine meal - all this in a few hours. Mack admired her grace and her hypnotic beauty. Large gray-flecked hazel eyes flashed intelligence and warmth, but he sensed the misted windows revealed only hints of private moods and deep emotions. Over homemade peach cobbler Clyde proudly announced Janice had been all-state track champion at Mississippi. State. As she served her guests Mack noticed five years of marriage and two children didn't show on her figure.

After dinner Mack read Clyde's story of the hit and run and the search for the scarred, cold-hearted Mafia witness who obviously thought more of his boss's reputation than a human life. Clyde gave a description of the hit and run, a short biography of Viola Faber and then detailed the criminal career of Vincent Romano. Great contrast: angry, gut boiling and poignant at the same time.

"Good stuff, Clyde." Mack set the sheet of paper down. "When will the *Register* run this?"

"Since I have Ace Collins' blessing, they'll run this story as soon as I file. The sad tale of Viola Faber will hit the streets this weekend at the latest."

Mack shook his head and smiled. "And if it ain't in the news..." he didn't have to finish Clyde's favorite saying. "You're right, Clyde. The power of the press is truly amazing when a story helps the good guys." He tapped the paper. "You know this article implicates Bruno Malatesta without using his name?"

The reporter nodded proudly. "Slick, huh?"

"You know that could make you a target, don't you?"

"They would *never* harm a newspaper reporter. They know better."

"Very few reporters single-handedly try to nail a mob boss," Mack reminded him. "This article might force the cops to question Vinnie the monster and to investigate Bruno Malatesta for manslaughter."

Clyde Ralston eased back on the sofa and slid an arm around his wife. He grinned like he'd won a Pulitzer Prize. "Good. That means I'm doing my job."

• • •

Ten o' clock. Tired from too much beer and a satisfying meal, Mack drove slowly toward downtown Tucson and his studio. Chickie dozed until her head fell back and she snorted. She slid over and put her head on Mack's shoulder. "Nice people," she murmured. "She's a classy lady. First black people I ever got to know close-up. They seem just like a regular family."

Mack smiled. He'd forgotten Clyde and his family were called black.

"Cormac?"

"What Chickie?"

"You ever think about getting married again?"

"Once in a while," he said. "But I have a few beers and the craving goes away." He glanced at her face, lighted softly in the dash lights. "Why? Got something in mind?" He was joking, yet felt terribly sad. Mack knew he couldn't marry Chickie Malatesta. And it wasn't just because of her father. He recognized the double standard, but after years pondering their unique situation, he knew memories of her sexual promiscuity would linger in his mind and intrude at the wrong times. And besides, most important, he didn't think he loved her enough.

• • •

Vinnie sat in the dark car shivering with anticipation. This was the best and the worst time. An enemy was about to die screaming. He loved that, but hated the waiting. Too bad he couldn't watch one of his babies deliver its intense gift. But wait! Maybe he could hide in the alley and watch the man die through the little bathroom window. He grasped the door handle and began to lift when caution stopped him. What if the madonna-stealing bastard came in the back door? That would give it away. The back door was the weak spot. He smiled. This had been one of his easier jobs. The spring bolt had yielded quickly to his screwdriver. Jimmy marks would show in the daylight, but by then the whole building would be black rubble. Too bad for those people living in the apartments upstairs, just more screams. Been waiting a long time too, he thought. The private Investigator usually came home earlier than this. Maybe he'd gone with her to Phoenix after all. No. He'd seen the tall bastard take the satchel of money after she'd left that morning.

Wait for him all night. Wait until he screams.

The white truck came up the street and pulled into the parking lot next to the studio. Lights washed the three parked cars. He ducked down and peeked carefully over the dash. Two people climbed from the pickup and wandered to the front door of the studio, arms around each other's waist. They looked tired and full of soft thoughts about sheets and pillows and warm dreams.

Two people! *One of them a woman, her hair shiny in the pale moonlight.*

No! She couldn't be there! *Chickie had driven to Phoenix that morning. The radio-receiver said so!* He opened the car door, scrambled out, but they were inside before he could warn her.

• • •

Mack unlocked the door, reached in and flicked on the studio lights. He looked around carefully before telling Chickie to enter. He'd not felt the following eyes as strongly since the missed attack at the gas station, but he figured caution was always best when a Mafia enforcer has a grudge. He slid the Colt Commander back in his belt and walked through the studio toward the kitchen under the loft. "Did you lock the door?" he asked as he felt her come up behind him.

"Of course, sugar, don't worry," Chickie brushed past him, stripped the tee shirt over her head and tossed it toward an opened suitcase. "Really need to get some sleep, but I gotta pee first." She opened the bathroom door, let her shorts drop to the floor and went in.

Mack heard a shuffling sound, turned and saw the front door knob moving.

An excited voice called something he couldn't decipher. A drunk? Vinnie? He reached for his pistol. Stopped cold. A breathy nip of gasoline floated in the studio air. Thoughts rioted. An instant of paralysis and he remembered: *Mitch Young was burned in his* ***bathroom****!* Mack turned to warn her, "Chickie don't...!"

"POP!"

A flash of light became a furnace roar filled with human screams.

"Aaaahhhgggh!" Sounds slashed the night, "Aaaaahhhghhhggg!" - sounds all drowned in fused flesh. The screams soared long moments high above the light and smoke like maddened spirits, but then they perished under the burning. The screams bubbled down to dull, deep moans.

Mack ran toward the flickering roar. Stood a second at the door.

The small room was blazing inferno. The walls were alive with white and yellow fingers. Sooty smoke rode flame spikes down to the long, writhing lump of seething heat and pulsing light that was Chickie Malatesta.

Mack ripped the shower curtain from its bar and dove on the burning woman. He gritted his teeth against the searing sting, felt his hair lift to heat and blaze away like paper. He covered her. The plastic curtain melted apart in his hands and stuck to him in rags of flame. Mack sobbed with effort, pulled her to him and crushed the hot tongues with his body. But fire still roared around them, gaining strength from the new fuel.

Despair emptied him. They were both going to die.

No! Through the boiling air he glimpsed the cool porcelain of the square, white toilet tank. He reached and yanked with all the mad strength left in him. The tank moved, shifted from the wall. He pulled again. The tank gave way, crashed to the floor and enveloped the two bodies in a waterfall of cool water. More water shot in a furious stream from the broken pipe into Mack's sobbing face.

• • •

Burn pain is bone deep, but Mack decided pain was better than dying.

He was a wreck. He'd lost half his hair, his eyebrows and a layer of skin, but they said his face would heal to bad sunburn in a few weeks. The problem was with his hands; he wore inch-deep, fluffy white gloves of taped gauze over gray ointment that smelled like peppermint and cooled his scalded nerve endings.

"You're lucky," the doctor said. "Another minute in those flames, you'd have lost your fingers. You have second and third degree burns, but your hands should heal with a little time."

A little time! Mack thought of Chickie and her screams. His vision blurred. Vengeance called, but he knew without his hands he was nearly helpless.

"How long, doc?" Mack's sore throat produced hoarse croaks. He held up thick, white mittens. "How long before I take these off?"

The thin doctor sighed with impatience and ran slow hands over her tired, distracted face. "You're lucky to be alive Mister Robertson. You've received a bad sunburn and some blisters. You can go home tomorrow, but you won't be picking your nose for weeks." She shook her head at macho men and left him to the police.

The old arson detective's name was Wes Anderson. He'd served a year past twenty-five, working to increase his pension percentage. They'd known each other for years, but never become friends because of a difference in style, and the fact that Wes had declared himself born again in 1975 and never tired of discussing religion. "Thank the Good Lord you've been given another chance," he whispered urgently. "I hope you make good use of it and mend your ways."

The other detective, younger and slightly embarrassed, moved over to the edge of the bed and pulled out his notebook. "You got any idea who did this?"

"A mob enforcer's followed me for three weeks," Mack's rough voice husked. "A torch from Chicago named Vinnie Romano."

The two detectives exchanged glances. "What makes you say that?" the young one asked. "Did you see him?"

"If I had, he'd be dead," Mack grunted and cleared his throat. "I reported him to Sergeant Sparks last Monday. If *that* skinny prick had done his job, Chickie would be alive today! Ask Sergeant Sparks about Vinnie Romano."

"The dead woman wore a gold cross around her neck," the young one continued as though Mack hadn't spoken. "The gold partially melted in the fire. We found a small, powerful, directional transmitter imbedded in the cross." He looked up, pen poised. "Why do you think Miss Malatesta would wear a transmitter?"

That explains how they found her all the time. Daddy's gift had been an electronic leash. Her trip to Casa Grande had thrown Vinnie off. The radio signal went north and faded.

Vinnie decided she'd gone to Phoenix. Good time for a hit. The torch probably didn't notice the signal had returned when he'd tried to light up Mack. "The nasty bastard burned his sweetheart by accident. Poor Chickie."

"Chickie?" Wes repeated the name and nodded solemnly like a confessor. "The dead woman, of course," he murmured. "By 'nasty bastard' I assume you mean Romano. Or do you mean her father, the Mafia boss, Bruno Malatesta?" He nodded again. "Quite a bunch, aren't they, those Italians?"

Mack knew the drill. Cops go for reactions. They goad people to admissions and never allow a witness the satisfaction of an answer to a question or any confirmation of statements. That could spoil later testimony in court. There was an i.v. needle in his arm and he was covered in salve and gauze like a mummy, but he struggled to sit up. "She couldn't change who her father was!' he croaked like a frog. "That poor woman didn't deserve to die like that. Nobody does." Mack ran out of breath and realized how weak he was. "Get the hell out of here and go arrest Vinnie the monster." He finished in a whisper and rested for just a moment.

• • •

When he awoke the cops were gone. But the hospital room was crowded.

Grace Faber and Clyde Ralston waited next to his bed, looking even more uncomfortable than he was. Grace saw his eyes open. She reached to touch him.

"Mister Robertson, I'm so sorry about Miss Malatesta," she whispered. Most people whisper in hospitals, Mack thought aimlessly, respect for the dying or the dead, like a morgue or a mortuary. Chickie's screams filled his head.

"...hell you doin'?" he asked. The noise sounded like a creaking door.

Clyde was concerned and agitated. He bent over and blocked all the light. "I'm sorry about Chickie," he said softly. "I know how you felt about her. I'm glad *you're* gonna be okay, though, and I've got some news for you."

Mack cleared his throat and winced at the sensitive tissue. "You don't have *any* idea how I felt about Chickie," he said in a near-normal voice. "I'm not even sure how I felt. Hello, Grace, thanks for coming. What's the news, Clyde?"

"They printed my hit and run story today," he said around a grin.

Mack smiled weakly at Grace and nodded. "Well we damn sure did it."

Grace looked troubled. She knew their victory was hollow, built on a lie. "I checked the wire this morning," she said. "Bruno Malatesta's lawyer has issued a statement denying everything. He says Mister Malatesta can prove where he was on the day of the accident and that Mister Malatesta has let Mister Romano use his car on occasion, but takes no responsibility for its whereabouts on the day in question. He says his *former* employee is out of his control and may have been driven insane by past injuries. Attorney Franks says his client disavows responsibility for the actions of Vinnie Romano and will sue the police for harassment and the *Register* for libel if they bother him or print any more false allegations about him."

"Talk about *chutzpah*," Mack said. "That'll scare Sparks and the Chief."

"Yes," Grace agreed. "And notice he called Vinnie insane. But still, I take some small comfort that the punishment Mister Malatesta received for killing my mother was of biblical proportions. To lose a daughter like that and to have to blame yourself for her horrible death is far worse than any prison."

"Yeah, right," Mack muttered impatiently. "*If* he blames himself. He said Vinnie Romano had been driven insane. Almost two days have gone by. Have the police arrested Vinnie yet? Do they even have him *charged* with Chickie's death?"

"Word at the station is he's disappeared," Clyde answered.

"Bet he left the state," Grace added and looked for somewhere to sit.

Mack patted the bed and nodded. She blushed, carefully arranged her skirt and sat down near his ankles. Clyde took the only chair in the room.

Ten more minutes went by in small talk before Mack remembered he didn't have clothing or shaving gear - as if he could bear to shave. "I'll be getting out of here soon and I don't have anything to wear. Clyde, could you bring me some clothes and my shaving gear from the studio?"

Their faces fell with bad news. Grace was closest. She leaned, touched his raw cheek and flinched from the ointment. "Mack, you can't live in your studio for a while. The rugs are sopping wet, most of your belongings and photographs are covered in soot, the place reeks of smoke and the bathroom is in ruins."

Mack was stunned. He'd forgotten what happens when they put out a house fire, even a small house fire, And the photographs - water, smoke, ruins. His studio, his work, his home was uninhabitable. All he had left was a shot-up pickup truck and a heart full of unfocused guilt. "God damn, what a mess," he sighed. "Chickie's dead, I'm all crippled up and everything's gone to shit. I should've been more careful."

"Her death was not your fault, Mack," Clyde said. "But you damn sure found out who killed Grace's mother and helped me on the track story."

"Clyde, how cruel!" Grace protested. "This man has just lost his woman and his home. He doesn't care about my problems or your dog track."

Mack eyed Grace carefully. He appreciated her sentiments, but decided not to wallow in her peculiar compassion. He waved his white mittens at her. "None of that really matters now," his voice was stronger with anger. "Somehow I want to find that murdering son of a bitch, Romano!" Mack thought a second and shook his head at Grace. "I think he's still around. That firetrap was aimed at me, and he'll blame me for Chickie's death. I don't think he'd leave the state. He'll want revenge."

Grace chewed on a knuckle. "And you're hurt. We must protect you from him. Anybody can come in this hospital... and we still don't know how he killed Miss Malatesta...we don't know how the fire started."

"I wouldn't worry about that ugly bastard sneaking in here," Mack said. "He doesn't exactly blend in and face-to-face hits aren't his style. By the way, I'm pretty sure he started the fire by booby-trapping the light switch."

"Yeah," Clyde said. "I went to the scene and watched the arson crew. They were paying special attention to the ceiling light socket in your bathroom. They were taking out the remains of the bulb-neck and putting the pieces in a bag."

"Yeah, the light is the trigger," Mack nodded. "Remember Ken Young? Both Chickie and Mitch Young died in bathrooms. Vinnie does something to the lights."

"Doesn't matter, Mack, you can rest easy," Clyde said. "The police are after Vinnie and, worse for him, Bruno Malatesta is damn sure looking for him. The Don's gonna put the insane guy in his grave for killin' his daughter." He grinned down at the detective. "Anyway, I'm sure Vinnie's long gone from Tucson."

CHAPTER NINE

WRECKAGE

The remote-controlled airplane swooped high over the desert like a sparrow catching gnats in the sun. It dove and soared with fluid grace, but the turns were awkward and an observer would have called the pilot a novice. Farther and farther the plane flew. A hundred yards away the turns became sloppy and the slender shape jinked clumsily and fell into near spinouts.

Losing control - too much distance. Now he knew how far the signal reached.

Vinnie moved the black control lever sharply. Morning wind lifted the plane to a near stall and it looped once before plunging back toward earth, soaring closer, winging over and crashing into the sand at the bottom of the dry wash.

Shiny, bone-tight fingers plucked the plane from the sand and broke the fuselage in half. They took the receiver module out, detached the tiny control wires, tossed the wreckage back to the sand and put receiver and shiny, black control box in a small tote-bag. Vinnie felt reborn. No more fire.

Fire had betrayed him again.

Like that time in Chicago....

• • •

Out of the darkness pain was worse. Vinnie couldn't close his eyes for a while. Madonnas bathed the dry itch every fifteen minutes until they sewed on new eyelids and gave him darkness again. Darkness and pain were all he possessed for a while. One or the other.

They kept him naked. Covered his body in a tent and bathed him in stinging tubs of brine. They began to cut the charred flesh on the third day, pulling pain from his head and shoulders. He moved his head to see them work, but his neck crackled and they put him in a leather vise. Pain reassured him. Doctors gave him different pain as the days oozed. They cut his cool thighs to red torment and put the cold wet on his face and arms. His bandaged arms and hands wanted to move to the soft, white madonnas, but the new, sore skin was stiff and jellied like cold bacon.

When they were sure he was born again they took away the pain.

He was a slow, confused prisoner of Demerol for long whirling days and nights. His world was water, sponges and the white tent around his raw body. The madonnas talked to him, but his words were gurgles. He couldn't move and couldn't talk to the women. His muzzled mind seethed all the while his flesh was healing.

In the beginning his genitals were swollen, but they recovered after weeks of slow drifting. Soon Doctors removed the catheter. His urine flowed normally, but he was concerned about his manhood. Had the burning taken his manhood? There had to be hope, but there was no way to know because of his bandaged hands and because the madonnas treated him as though he was a pillow or a tray of food, moving, pushing and turning him without acknowledging his searching eyes or testing his humanity. Time crawled. Doctors, orderlies and madonnas continued to treat him as an inconvenient stranger. He wondered, trapped in silence.

But one day a madonna met his eyes and swam inside. She was young. A plain, heavy-set girl, full of compassion, intrigued by the science-fiction scene of a larvae-like human with raw, red flesh and hot, brown eyes. In nineteen lonely years she'd never attracted a steady boyfriend. She gloried in her new opportunity for a captive male audience. The injured man in the tent was obviously young and his seared body was nonetheless well formed. The situation repelled and fascinated her.

Her name was Dora. Days went by. Ugliness faded to friendship in her mind. She began to spend off-duty, evening hours with Vinnie Romano, taking fulsome delight in long, rambling conversations of heart-felt opinions and bright questions answered only by eye-blinks and liquid gasps. One night she heard him using the bedpan. As usual, she emptied the pan and cleaned him. This time she held him in her pudgy hands, glanced at his blinking eyes and squeezed and stroked him. Long moments passed. Nothing happened. "What a shame." She murmured and dropped him, pretending not to care. She stayed a while longer, turned out the light and left.

No, not this, his darkness blossomed pain again. But maybe failure was temporary. He grasped the hope and shut out despair. Vinnie Romano still looked the same in his mirror-mind: a faintly scornful lady-killer whose dark eyes flashed adventure from a chiseled Roman face. He wanted to run a comb through thick hair and laugh at this plain excuse for a woman, but instead he clutched at her image. She was all that was left for a while. Dora and hope filled his days.

Dora gave Vinnie her company often through the next months, celebrating her benevolence. He held onto hope. She welcomed feelings of kindness and smiled at the gasps of frustration from the massively sutured man in the burn tent.

Vinnie healed. Yearning bloomed again. Maybe. One night Vinnie's seared vocal cords gave more than gasps. "Love you," gurgled up his throat.

Dora was appalled. The passive patient wanted more of her. Words gave him identity. The wreckage on the bed was real with a past and future. A future he evidently wanted to share. She ran from the dim room down the bright hallway.

"Love you," Vinnie pleaded.

But he never saw Dora again. Eight months later he found another madonna in Tucson. Now she was dead and Bruno Malatesta had disowned him. Vinnie's smoothly pale mouth twisted to self-pity and he rubbed his scarred head to rid it of memories. He would keep his word: one more job for the Don and then vengeance.

• • •

Like a stretching exercise, arms up high, Mack turned, bent, angled and spread his raw body in the hot pulsing water, always making sure to keep his thickly bandaged hands above the spray. He had to shower two or three times a day in Grace Faber's bathroom. With only relatively minor injuries, Mack had stayed in the hospital just a day and a half and had needed a temporary bed.

Clyde had offered his children's room. "Hell, Mack, you can sleep in Sylvia's bunk bed and the girls can move in the big bed with me and Janice." The reporter had grinned while imagining his crowded family.

"I have an extra bedroom," Grace had declared. "Mack will stay with me."

Of course he'd protested, but there really weren't many other alternatives for a homeless man unable to drive his truck or even feed himself.

Mack had been in her home about eighteen hours so far, showering frequently, wearing her robes and slurping soup from bowls on the table. He'd never before understood how important hands were. Going to the bathroom for instance. Each time Mack relieved himself he felt that he needed to shower. Handling soap was another impossibility and he felt dirtier as the hours went by.

After his latest shower they met in the hall. "When the doctor released you yesterday afternoon I don't recall her telling you to take all those showers." She said seeming genuinely puzzled.

He was embarrassed. "After the toilet, I can't use my hands very well. I feel better after the water washes me off."

She understood his discomfort and felt terrible. Should she offer to help? The thought was interesting. Her imagination filled with his nudity. She blushed and smiled. "Oh God, what was I thinking about? Maybe we should have a nurse come in for a few days. It never even occurred to me that you..."

"No nurse will be necessary." Mack held up his bandaged hands. "In another couple of days I'll take these damn bandages off and be out of your hair."

Grace tugged her robe together and considered the big man dripping in her hallway - burned-out hair, blistered face and forehead, bandages, a wreck. She glanced at the hairy legs and knobby knees fully visible under the short, terry cloth robe and decided she *could* enjoy his disorderly presence if he was cleaned up. And he badly needed a shave. The three-day beard sprouting through his burn-reddened skin made him look like a bum. She thought of her mother's disapproval of the few men in her life. What would she think now? In robes! She hid another smile. And they had to spend more days together. "What makes you think I want you out of my hair?" she said. "You exposed my mother's killer and suffered greatly for it." She tilted her hips, let her arms fall loosely to her sides and looked him up and down. "I'm very grateful. Next time you decide to bathe I'll be happy to help you."

Mack was still in pain, felt dirty and knew he must smell ripe. He noticed how young and vulnerable she looked without make-up, wrapped in the short, terry-cloth robe, and how clean she smelled. He was full of Chickie's death, but his willful eyes followed her shapely legs when she turned and walked away.

After lunch she was reading and sunbathing in her back yard in a form-fitting one-piece bathing suit. Mack wanted to join her, but the sight of the smooth, slender body on the chaise made him decide he couldn't stand his itchy beard and sticky odor. He wanted to shave his raw face and decided to take Grace up on her offer of help. He took another body-bending shower, filled the tub with hot water and used his foot to suds up a good foam before he sat in the water and called her.

The bath was very pleasant. She carefully shaved his tender face, scrubbed his back and chest and began to wash his hair. While she soaped his hair, he looked down the soft, shallow valley of her bathing suit at small, pale globes flexing and shifting and marveled at their delicious shape. Like ripe peaches, he thought, and felt himself becoming aroused. She caught him looking and sloshed rinse water in his face. His bandaged hands moved to her shoulders, but he winced at the searing pain and lay back. Her strong, brisk hands slicked coconut-smelling conditioner through his hair and he watched her thin lips purse in concentration close above his face. For a while he forgot his injuries and the numbing loss of Chickie.

Grace read his mind all the way. She was amused by his examination of her breasts and had seen his penis stir and thicken through the cloudy water. She wondered what it would be like. It was nice to be admired again, but she couldn't forget the dead Malatesta woman and the sloppy television kiss. She scooped water in his hair and washed her mind of temptation. After rinsing the conditioner she stood and toweled herself off and became aware of his eyes again. Grace blushed, tugged at her bathing suit and turned away. "That will be all for now. You look presentable enough. I'll go fix supper. Put on your robe and come talk to me in the kitchen." She walked from the bathroom full of confused feelings.

• • •

The phone rang hours later and he reached to answer it before remembering no one knew he was there. He was slumped on the living-room couch in his robe. Hell, couldn't pick the damn thing up anyway.

Didn't matter, Grace came from washing the dishes. "Probably the real estate agent," Grace said and reached across him for the phone. Her loose blouse brushed his burned face and he smelled gardenia again.

"Hello? Clyde! Why are you calling me on a Friday night? What? Who called? You're downtown? Yes, sure." She frowned and held the phone for Mack. "He's downtown. Says Romano called him and wants to deal," she whispered.

Mack held the phone between bandaged hands. "Hey Clyde, what the hell do you mean....?" He was interrupted by the excited reporter and listened for almost a minute. "That's crazy!" Mack finally said. "There's nothing Romano could trade for manslaughter. The track story? Yeah? Is there?" He nodded slowly as Clyde Ralston's voice continued to explain the situation.

"What's he saying?" Grace hissed.

Mack shushed her. "Clyde, if he has information on Lillienthal, he should deal direct with police." Mack waited for another sentence. "He won't huh? Doesn't trust 'em. We'll be there in twenty minutes. Don't meet him alone, he's a murderer!"

Grace could hear Clyde's deep voice shouting through the phone receiver.

Mack's bandaged hands fumbled with the phone. He shook his head before shouting, "Now? Then why did you call us?

Insurance! But Clyde, you can't!" Another pause. Suddenly Mack's shoulders relaxed. He sat back with the phone cradled in his gauze mittens. "Okay, meet him in the restaurant. But call us from the lobby as soon as you're finished. What...? No we won't call the police, not yet." Mack let the phone slide to his lap and looked helplessly at Grace.

"What's he going to do?" she asked.

"He's meeting Vinnie Romano in ten minutes at the Clarendon House Hotel. Romano wants Clyde to broker a plea-bargain tonight with the County Attorney for a manslaughter deal on Chickie's murder. He says Romano will trade photocopies of documents tying Arizona politicians to Emprise Corporation and Vegas money-laundering operations. Clyde says Vinnie mentioned Senator Lillienthal's brother."

Grace grabbed the phone and began dialing. "We've got to call the police!"

Mack mashed his bandages down on the disconnect. "Clyde would never forgive you. He says Vinnie's watching the place and says if he sees cops, no deal."

"We should be with him. He can't trust Romano." She chewed her knuckles.

"Meeting's in ten minutes. We would take twenty minutes to get there."

"Oh Mack *why* is he taking this chance?" Tears welled in Grace's eyes.

"Grace, *you* of all people should understand. Clyde's a first-rate reporter. He has no choice. This information could be dynamite. If Romano can connect money laundering to the Senator's brother, the scandal could be the biggest story of Clyde's career." Mack struggled to stand. "Help me get dressed, we should head downtown anyway, just in case."

• • •

Vinnie watched the Nissan Sentra pull in the dimly lit parking lot and park in a group of cars near the entrance to the hotel. The large man struggled out of his little car like a dark snail emerging from a shell and hurried into the lobby with a spiral notebook fluttering in his hand.

Vinnie smiled and hefted his bundle. He kept to the shadows and hurried around to the edge of the parking lot closest to the Nissan and crouched in some bushes. Two cars away, maybe twenty-five feet he estimated, and dropped to his belly. He crawled under the nearest car, pushing his bundle before him. Slid under the next car, and finally under the Nissan. After a moment's work with the bundle of dynamite and two twists of wire on the front axle, he connected a shiny metal box to an electric detonator and pushed the detonator into the soft end of one of the three sticks of dynamite. The duty he owed his uncle was almost done. He crawled back to the bushes and hurried to an outdoor phone booth.

• • •

The phone rang while Grace was starting the truck.

"Oh God, it might be him," she said. They hurried back inside.

"Told you not to worry," Clyde's voice greeted. "Vinnie called me at the hotel desk and postponed our meeting."

"Oh Clyde that's great, so you're okay." Grace breathed a sigh of relief.

He snorted a derisive laugh. "I'm standin' all alone in the hotel lobby. Y'all can relax. He said he's gonna call me later tonight at home and give me most of the information by phone. He says it's real hot stuff...big names and all. You'll probably read all about it in the *Register* on Sunday. See ya, Grace."

• • •

Saturday morning. Early sunlight flowed through the curtains and bathed the back bedroom in golden warmth. Mack was feeling better, the pain had faded and his skin heat was lower than the day before. He'd been able to sleep most of the night without the shivering sweats that supposedly accompany bad burns.

He heard the front door open and then a cry of pain.

"Grace?" he called. "Grace, what's wrong?" No answer. He struggled out of bed and ran to the hallway. She wasn't there. "Grace?" *Could it be Vinnie Romano? What if he'd hurt her?* He glanced at his bandaged hands. No weapon. Didn't matter. Not any more! He growled deep in his throat and rushed down the hall to the front door. He'd tear the bastard's throat out with his teeth!

There was no one but Grace. She sat on the front step, breathing in hiccups, her mouth writhing in mute anguish, tears streaming down her cheeks.

"What happened?" Mack leaned down to her. "Are you hurt?" He checked the front of her robe, her pale, twisted face. She seemed unhurt. He stepped out into the yard and looked around. No one was there. "Grace, what's wrong?" Then he noticed the newspaper on the step and saw the heavy, horrible headline.

Arizona Register reporter bombed in car

Clyde Ralston suffers multiple injuries in car bombing.

Mack ran to the phone.

• • •

The hospital was full of the calamity. Hallways were crowded with reporters, police, well-wishers and the wide-eyed creeps who always circle public tragedies. Clyde was supposedly on the third floor. The floor was sealed.

Grace used her press card, but a brusque, serious uniformed cop at the end of the third floor hall stopped them. Over his shoulder they could see a quiet huddle of people thirty feet away. Mack saw Janice. He raised his bandaged hand to call or wave or comfort, he wasn't sure. She saw the movement and looked up. Their eyes met. Hers widened with recognition, but clenched immediately with terrible pain. She slowly shook her head and turned away.

"Okay folks, back on the elevator," the cop said. You got no business here."

Grace held up her card, was about to object.

"Nothing we can do here anyway," Mack mumbled. "Let's go downstairs."

Mack saw Karl Jenkins doing paper work at a desk in the hospital lobby. Karl and Mack had been squad mates for two years and were still good friends. He led Grace to the police detective.

Karl felt their eyes and looked up. "Hey, buddy." He smiled and stood, running nicotine-stained fingers over his carefully combed blond hair. "I heard you were mixed up in this." Then he noticed Grace and zeroed in on her thick, auburn hair. Women were his downfall. Of medium height and squarely built, Karl had the bright, blue eyes and taut good looks of a thirty-year-old, and the social life of an alley cat. But he was a damn good detective. He looked closer and saw her tension. "Do you know Ralston? Are you related to...?" He realized his blunder and looked the question at Mack.

Mack introduced them without mentioning her job. "We've been involved in this mess a while, Karl. Grace is a good friend of the reporter." Mack paused. "Hell, we're *both* his friends. We came to be with him and see how he's doing."

"Friends huh?" Karl repeated and motioned them outside away from the crowds milling near the door. "Damn zoo since the paper hit the streets," he muttered while lighting up a Marlboro. "Can't figure how they knew; we didn't release the hospital or the extent of injuries. There's *gotta* be a leak somewhere."

"We tried three hospitals before this one. Are you working this, Karl?"

The detective blew a cloud of smoke off to the side, scratched one finger through his immaculate hair and considered the question a second too long. He glanced at Mack and the message passed. Mack knew detectives on cases like this liked to stay anonymous to the press as long as possible. Karl Jennings had been around Tucson twenty years and had finally placed Grace Faber's face as that of a reporter. That put him in a tight box with an old friend. This case was too delicate, too political. "Mack, we can talk later," he said quietly and began to move away.

Grace put one small hand on his arm and stopped him. "Please," she held her voice low and tears brimmed in her eyes. "This is *not* newspaper business, detective, he is a dear man and a close friend. Tell us how bad it is. Do they know whether he will live?"

Mack stepped forward and reached for Karl with a bandaged hand. "Word of honor, buddy, this is very personal. Not a whisper to anybody, I promise."

Karl considered the small redhead a moment, then he looked at Mack's bandaged hands, reddened face and fire-scorched hair. "You been through a helluva week haven't you?" He offered Mack a cigarette.

"I've had better weeks," Mack said and refused the cigarette with a head shake.

"Well my friend, this isn't going to help." Karl looked around and lowered his voice. "I'm only working the hospital paperwork. Jack Weaver and Andy Watzek caught the case, so anything official will have to come through them."

Mack nodded he understood the importance of covering Karl's ass.

"As for your friend upstairs, Ma'am." Karl lifted his eyes to the building. "He made a sort-of death-bed statement about twelve hours ago, but he's a tough kid. He's still hangin' on."

"Oh thank God," Grace murmured.

Karl shook his head and spoke through a gust of smoke. "No ma'am, it ain't like that. He's lost most of both legs and one arm. The explosion should've killed him outright, but he's a pretty big guy. I don't think his being alive is a blessing. His injuries are real bad. He's been in a coma on life support since last night."

"The bombing was around 8:30 last night at the Clarendon House, right?" Mack asked. "I called Homicide this morning when I read the paper. I told them about his phone calls and the aborted meeting with Vinnie Romano at the hotel."

"Yeah we know about the supposed meeting," Karl said. "His wife told us about the phone call: a typical mob set-up. The bomb went off under Ralston's car as he was pulling out of the Clarendon House parking lot. They found pieces of a remote-control receiver in the wreckage. The blast nearly broke the car in half. Rescue got there in about four minutes. He was in bad shape, but conscious. They said his last coherent statement was, 'They got me; Mafia, Emprise, Romano'."

Mack hung his head. "Vinnie Romano's a vicious psychopath. I tried to warn Clyde, but he said the mob would never hurt a reporter."

Karl tossed his cigarette and patted Mack's shoulder gently. "That's what reporters always say, buddy. Listen, I know I don't have to tell you this, but you *should* have called us last night."

Mack closed his eyes and shook his head. "I know, Karl."

• • •

Bruno Malatesta buried his daughter that day.

Chickie would have laughed. The afternoon ceremony was turned into a free-for-all farce when the two old button-men began to rough up a few pushy reporters and break television cameras. Breaking cameras and pushing reporters is evidently an unpardonable sin to TV news directors and they reran the scuffle two or three times that night. Mack watched the riotous coverage on both the early and late news. Bruno was only a gray glimpse in the background of one lingering pan before the fights broke out. The old man had evidently stayed in his car, window open to the priest's eulogy. His thin, stricken face was half-lost in the hard shadows from TV lights. Later, his lawyer, Bernie Frank, held a press conference. He protested the press presence at the funeral and reissued prior written statements of his client's refusal to take responsibility for any alleged acts of a guest. He admitted a Mister Romano may have used Mister Malatesta's home and car at some time in the past, but again threatened libel and slander suits if any of the outrageous allegations against the grieving Bruno Malatesta were repeated in print or TV news.

• • •

After a week passed there wasn't much left of young Clyde Ralston.

Right leg, left leg, right arm, one by one his mutilated limbs were amputated during the hundreds of numbingly heroic hours he persisted in surviving. Doctors said he should've died instantly from such an explosion. The dynamite bundle had blasted a two-foot hole in the steel underbelly of his Nissan Sentra, pulverizing his legs, blasting him from the car and propelling hunks of metal to the top of the four-story hotel. Still, he fought for life.

But the *Register* covered the bombing of their reporter in very selective detail. The articles carefully identified the *alleged* killer and reran Clyde's angry hit and run story that they briskly assumed had triggered the violent act. The big hole in the press coverage became evident as dreary days passed and the reporter clung to life. While Mack and Grace kept a distant death-watch, Mack began to think Clyde's sacrifice may have been in vain. The slant of all the TV, radio and print was that Clyde had been bombed because he implicated a Mafia enforcer in a hit and run. Emprise and the connection to Romano's boss was mentioned, but never explored. "Police say there's no evidence that would link anyone else..."

Mack marveled at the power of a libel threat to effectively muzzle the press. As days passed he wondered if even the *appearance* of justice would be served. No arrests were made in the first week. However, in the bright light of unprecedented nationwide publicity at the killing of a reporter, the police put forth a massive effort to locate Vinnie Romano. Malatesta Ranch was systematically searched. The first day they found his clothes and some personal possessions in a guest room, but no other traces of Vinnie the monster were discovered. Every shift worked hours of overtime. A ten-block area around the Clarendon House Hotel was canvassed, house-to-house in vain and a volunteer mounted Sheriff's posse on horseback scoured the foothills and the wild mountain reaches of the Malatesta Ranch. They didn't spend much time in the wilderness. No one expected a city-boy Mafiosi could survive in the boonies for long and, after a few days, they figured he was long gone from Arizona anyway. Mack wondered if the madman had finally left the state.

He hoped not; his hands were healing.

On Tuesday the fifty million dollar sports arena bond election passed by less than two thousand votes in an abysmally low voter-turnout. Mack realized the election and the expensive result wasn't very important to the stunned community.

Without Clyde's story to warn them, why should it be? But next day the City Clerk announced bids for construction were being accepted and that concessions in the new facility would eventually be franchised to a local business conglomerate which included on its board of directors some of Tucson's most respected citizens.

• • •

Those next days passed in a dirty blur of torment and disappointment.

Mack and Grace were never able to see Clyde. He was in the intensive care unit. They were allowed to the third floor that next Monday.

Janice was slumped semi-conscious on a green sofa in the Intensive Care lobby. Mack was shocked at the change in the once confident, vibrant woman. Her amber skin had drained to gray, her large eyes were sunk into bleak circles of bone and her hair was fallen to a loose tangle. She looked dully up at them. No recognition fired the hazel eyes, but she knew them. Her eyes returned to ICU, to the deadly door. Her voice rasped down the worn path of anguish. "They've taken my fine, big man and chopped away at him until there's only his brave spirit layin' on that awful bed. I'm sure he can't let go because he knows the newspaper betrayed him."

"The newspaper betrayed him?" Grace repeated. "What do you mean?"

Janice raised her head and glared at the reporter. "I mean they never ran his story last Sunday! That editor of his came here Tuesday and I asked him about it. He said the bombing knocked quite a few stories out of the Sunday newspaper."

"You mean they've spiked his dog track story again?" Grace asked.

Janice nodded and stared blindly at the door to ICU.

"Why, for God's sake?"

"That Mister Collins said he would need another reporter to recheck details, talk to witnesses and do a rewrite before the *Register* could run Clyde's story."

"Why the hell is all that necessary?" Mack asked.

"That sanctimonious man stood right where you two are standin' and told me my husband's article couldn't run as written because Clyde was witness to most of the interviews and he *certainly* couldn't answer questions or do follow-ups."

Grace was shocked. Her little world was coming apart. Her mother was dead, Clyde horribly injured, and now the newspaper - the rock of her certainty and core of her comfortable beliefs - was failing her friend. "Janice, that's terrible. They can't do that!" She held the woman's hand and pondered their mutual loss, and the bond that never had been. They'd met often at newspaper functions, but had never become close. She mourned the friendship never born and tried to understand this newest, and somehow darkest, development in their overwhelming tragedy. "I promise you, Janice, Clyde's story will not be spiked!" Tears for her friend ran freely again, "I will speak to Mister Collins. He *must* listen to reason!"

Janice just nodded and closed her eyes.

• • •

Clyde breathed his last the second Wednesday after the bombing.

The young reporter had struggled eleven incredible days the way he'd struggled all his career. No half-measures, no surrender. There was no quiet, easy death for Clyde Ralston.

• • •

There was no wake. The funeral was closed-casket. The event was attended by hundreds of reporters from across the nation. Police treated the funeral as one of their own and turned out from every department in Arizona in full dress and tough, somber demeanor. The political and business aristocracy was there, shaking each others' hands and frowning importantly for television cameras. Mack and Grace sat in the back row and watched Janice try to pretend to her smiling, curious little girls that the ceremony around that long, shiny closed box up on the altar wasn't the end of her world.

After most pews had filled and people settled to whispered waiting, a bent old man in a mis-matched suit of gray coat and wrinkled brown trousers rose from amongst Clyde's family and shuffled into the aisle. Under the sparse mat of tightly curled white hair the skin of his face and neck was dark and creased like weathered, sweat-cured wood. He didn't go up to the coffin, but leaned on the end of the pew and spoke to the gathering in a deep, rich voice that carried all the way to the back.

Mack realized it was Clyde's grandfather.

The old man glanced around and showed white teeth in a hesitant smile. "I'm speakin' for the family. You nice folks come to see Clyde off. We 'preciate that. Clyde surely 'preciates it. He was a good boy. I knew he was meant to shine when he was growin' up - always curious, always wantin' to know about the way things work. I'd set him on my knee and try to explain things." The old man turned and looked at the shiny coffin, bowed his head. "I told the boy to look to the future. Told him the sky's the limit in these wondrous times. And he came here." The grizzled head raised again to the crowded church. Mack thought he saw moisture gleam on the leathery cheeks. "I told him the sky's the limit and he came here to Arizona. This is a hard new land, full of wind and rough brass. Ain't no soft edges here...no slow water nor easy-goin people. This dry, brown land ain't right for a delta boy and I guess he angered some folks. Well, Clyde's reached the sky now. His future's with these little girls, Janice and Martha here...and with the Lord. After this here ceremony's over I'm takin' Clyde and the rest of my family back down home to Mississippi where they belong." The old man nodded once and sat down.

Others spoke. Friends of Clyde reminisced softly and fondly. Mack noticed the words most mentioned were determination, courage and a warm sense of humor. Tears flowed, wistful smiles were shared. Grace was white-faced and dry-eyed in shock. Mack wept into his hands and tried not to make any noise. At the end of all the goodbyes and well-wishing, in a bizarrely eccentric touch of bad taste, Ace Collins showed up in his beribboned Air Force Reserve full-dress uniform and began a clumsy, obviously hastily-written, eulogy.

Mack hauled Grace out in the middle of the editor's fifth sentence.

CHAPTER TEN

CLOSE-CALLS

Vinnie heard voices and scrambled back into the bushes. It was the investigator with *another* woman - a redhead. He lay in the bushes at the edge of the church parking lot with his bundle of dynamite and watched them drive away in the white pickup. Sunlight hurt his eyes and stung his delicate skin. Vinnie crawled back to his car. Too late; couldn't even follow them, but he'd find the thief again. He'd continue watching the studio. This time revenge had been very close.

Vinnie Romano had known the funeral would attract cops, but he knew the madonna stealer would attend also. He hadn't been able to find the investigator since he'd booby-trapped his bathroom. He'd staked out the gutted studio, but the P.I. hadn't been there for weeks. This chance had to be taken. Vengeance was all that was left. Driving through Tucson traffic that sunny day had been a hell of jangled nerves and uniforms. Sure enough, cops had been everywhere - cops in different uniforms, in different cars. Could they be still searching for him? Impossible. How could they know? Then he realized most weren't *local* police. They weren't hunting him. They'd all come for the stupid reporter's funeral.

Bombings are more difficult to set up in daylight. He'd located the white pickup truck, parked as close as he could in a spot near the landscaped edge of the parking lot and waited for the crowd to enter the church. The pickup had been three lanes away and closer to the church door. People kept arriving. Each time he was about to crawl under the cars another group arrived. Finally there was silence. Everyone was inside. Vinnie eased out of his car and slid under the first car and the second. One car to go. He began to enjoy thoughts of the blast and the blood, and yes, the fire. But at the last moment another car had pulled into the parking lot, cruised slowly as though looking for a spot, or maybe searching for him! He belly-crawled back into the bushes and peeked out to see a tall, gray-haired man in a blue uniform full of ribbons and medals get out of a big black sedan and march to the church door. He'd recognized the man and thought how far they'd both come in a month. Minutes later, before Vinnie could move from the bushes, the P.I. and his new woman had come out of the church and driven away. He'd missed again.

The frustrated mafiosi drove slowly through the back streets toward the east side of Tucson and his refuge. Calm darkness was where he belonged, was what he craved. Cars swarmed, people smiled at each other and moved their mouths. The sunlight blinded him. He needed to hide a short while and gather himself.

His car pulled to a curb.

The cathedral drew him to its cool, arched mouth. White towers flashed high in the bright sunlight and broad steps led to incense-laden memories of youth. He looked around quickly and hurried to the darkness. Reverences of childhood comforted. Shadows welcomed. He paused in the vestibule and stared down years. Rows of low, wooden pews lined the dwindling aisle and pulled his vision to the white, marble altar. Footsteps and recollections echoed as he moved past smoky rows of votive candles burning tall holes in the gloom and making somber statues dance in their shadows. Puttering wax smelled warm and soft, even to his seared senses. Vinnie knelt and remembered family Sundays back east. He recalled the hurried mornings: empty stomachs, scarves and warm hats, his mother's worried urgencies and father's stern impatience. He and his brothers and sisters - so close and careless in the knowledge life would always be the way it was and *they* would always be the way they were - standing, kneeling, mumbling tattered words of Latin, smelling incense and feeling the soft, powdery edge of his mother's worn missal. Vinnie Romano longed for the dry host, the long walk back to his pew full of enormous relief at another redemption. Never again. He had already died once, tasted awful despair, and died again. He was beyond them now, and beyond redemption. He had finally traded all the hope and all the memories for the pleasure of his rage.

Rage was all he had. There was not even his family any more.

After all the years in the same house, family and name, his brothers had abandoned him at the burning Chicago laundry. They'd left him to die that horrible time when he'd needed them, left him for the police and the scalpel. After all the anguish, the soaking, cutting and darkness, when it was known he would survive, no one had visited or sent mail. Not even his mother had come to his lonely hospital room. He'd heard nurses whisper there were no visitors because everyone was afraid of the District Attorney, but *he* knew it was because he'd become so ugly.

Footsteps slid over tile. Vinnie glanced up. A priest was coming down a side aisle. White face and Roman collar blazed in the shadows. "Can I help you my son?" the smooth voice murmured. "I heard your weeping. What is troubling you?"

Vinnie ducked his head away from the approaching priest. He couldn't afford to be recognized. Time to leave. His description had been widely circulated. Vinnie stood and hurried to the vestibule. Before he left he leaned to a holy-water font and reached to dip a reverent finger. Like an apparition in a dream, a face appeared in the still water. Yellow candlelight licked shiny skin and deep hollows in a round, hairless head. "Ghaa!" Vinnie recoiled in horror from the vision. Surely even God would despise such a creature. He lurched away from the holy water and fled out into the glare.

The priest had nearly caught up with the bald man in the vestibule. He glimpsed pale skin. A fetid stench trailed the hurrying man like a cloak. "Wait," he called, "God can help!"

"No one will help me!" Vinnie howled and ran down the broad stairs.

The priest noticed the despairing voice was loose and garbled as though from a damaged throat. He wondered if the man needed a doctor and began to follow, but remembered the pallid face he'd glimpsed in the dim light, and the awful smell. He paused and made the sign of the cross. "God help us all," he muttered.

• • •

Vinnie needed to get back. Began to drive too fast, reckless in grief.

It had been a mistake. The cathedral was a trap of childhood, of false hope. There was no redemption. Memories were more painful than the present, and the future was a hole. There was no point fooling himself, he had nothing but his revenge. The car slowed down on its own. Vinnie wrapped his lower face in a scarf, and began looking down and away from people at stoplights. He turned onto the less-traveled streets of residential neighborhoods and went back to his cave the long way, out of the city on residential streets into the dirt roads of the foothills and down the mountain road that ended in a deep canyon behind the Malatesta Ranch. He covered the car with mesquite branches like before and walked the mile or so to his sanctuary - a deep, hollowed-out space between two large, brush-choked rocks. Later, in the early twilight, after he'd listened and watched for hours, he snuck through the half-mile of desert to the back of the gatehouse. After eating from one of the cans in the kitchen pantry he went up to her room. Shuddering with anticipation, he took the small stool and sat in the middle of her things, touched her clothing, smelled her perfume and brought her back.

• • •

Two weeks after the funeral there was little reason for Mack to stay. His hands had healed. The landlord and insurance company had cooperated in cleaning and repairing his studio. The place probably wasn't back the way it had been, but he figured he could bathe and sleep there. There was no reason to stay in Grace's house, but he knew she hadn't survived yet, knew he shouldn't leave her alone.

He hadn't mentioned leaving. They hadn't discussed much of anything. They had eaten and slept like two strangers in a rooming house, hardly speaking and avoiding painful words when they did. He learned to deal with his pain and guilt rather quickly while he healed, but Grace didn't cry anymore, didn't smile and spent her days as though sleepwalking. One day, a week after the funeral, she had gone to work promising to speak with Ace Collins about Clyde's article. That night she had come home and gone to her bed without a word. They hadn't spoken since.

The front door opened and closed; it was time for a confrontation.

"Hi Grace," he said as he met her in the hall. She looked worn, no makeup and a little disheveled. Not the Grace he had met just a month before. "You need a drink and we need to talk."

"You can drink for both of us," she muttered and brushed by.

He reached out and grabbed her shoulder. "Wait a minute. Don't walk away from me, from our problems."

Her face became angry, then sullen. "From what? There are no problems any more. There's no anything any more."

Mack guessed what had happened at the paper. Grace had gone into the editor's office without knowing the full story - neither he nor Clyde had ever bothered to fully explain the racetrack laundering scam to her. She'd surely demanded Clyde's article be printed and, of course, Collins had confused the issue. "That's the way the bastards always get you, Grace," he said. "They always say you don't know what you're talking about."

She looked curiously at him. "Who does?" she asked. "What do you mean?" But she didn't pull away.

He decided his guess had been accurate. "Ace Collins. What did he say to you last week about Clyde's story?"

Her gray eyes shifted uneasily under the glasses as though she were ashamed of what she was about to say. "He said I was interfering in matters that were none of my business. When I insisted, he said Clyde's story was only about mistreated dogs and small change, unimportant things that obviously had nothing to do with his murder." Grace paused thoughtfully and nodded her head. "And Clyde *had* been talking about dead greyhounds and small-time crooks at the racetrack for over a year. I remember he'd even written a story about them, and nothing much ever came of it. Clyde always told me he needed more proof. Well maybe there never *was* proof! Maybe there never *was* an important story."

"There was a story," Mack said. "I photographed evidence of a good story."

Grace was hoping she was wrong. "Mister Collins also said there were many reckless allegations about important men in the story, but very little proof."

He gently touched her cheek. "Grace, there was enough proof for lots of questions to be asked. And that's what I thought newspapers were supposed to do. Clyde was a damned good reporter, and an intelligent young man."

She took off her glasses. "I know. I know." She began to cry. "But what if he was killed because you lied to him about seeing the witness to my mother's death?"

"So *that's* what's wrong." Mack said and led the sobbing woman to a chair in the living room. "My lie about Vinnie. Do you think Clyde's death was my fault?"

She shook her head. "Not just you. I was part of the lie also."

Mack knew he had to convince her quickly or lose her forever. He allowed some of his anger and frustration to escape in a loud burst. "Remember Clyde's last words: Mafia, Emprise and Romano?" he shouted. "Goddammit, Grace, two of Clyde's last words were Mafia and Emprise! What about the Mafia? What makes Emprise so special? Do you think a notorious Mafia hit man just wandered into Arizona by accident? And after the way Chickie died in my bathroom, do you *really* think Mitch Young was burned to death in *his* bathroom by accident?"

Her tear-filled eyes lifted and blinked confusion. "No."

"Well then stop this bullshit about a hit and run witness," Mack growled. "Your mother's accident was tragic, but not worth killing a reporter for."

"If that's true," Grace murmured, "then why is he dead?"

"Did Clyde explain the millions involved in this race track laundering scheme," Mack asked softly. "Did he say it *could* involve passage of the new Tucson sports arena and maybe some of the most powerful men in Arizona?"

Grace nodded. "Of course. Clyde's been talking about that for months."

"Well his newspaper should be pointing *those* facts out to the public instead of covering them up and confusing the issue." Mack went into the kitchen, opened two beers, handed her one and drank deeply from the other - his first in days.

"I don't drink beer," Grace said.

"Shut up and drink." Mack gasped from the cold. "It'll help you think."

Mafia, Emprise and Romano. Grace remembered the words like the Lord's Prayer. *Emprise! Mack was right. Facts* ***were*** *missing. The newspaper was missing them.* "Romano and Mafia could obviously mean Vinnie," she reasoned out loud, "but what is this Emprise all about? Why hasn't Emprise been written about?"

"Clyde told me about Emprise," Mack said. "Emprise is a Chicago company that owns Las Vegas casinos and a percentage of six Arizona dog tracks. He asked me to help gather evidence that Emprise was laundering money skimmed from their casinos." Mack finished his beer and stared at the bottle. "We took pictures of an empty armored car to prove the Tucson dog track wasn't getting any operating money from the local banks. So where was the money coming from? Clyde figured *that* was enough circumstantial evidence to run a story and ask some questions."

"Millions of dollars? Emprise? Mafia money?" Grace whispered. "Sounds like a movie, but why would a newspaper editor...?" she drank some more beer.

"Yeah, why?" Mack agreed.

Grace Faber was afraid to ask herself the next question. Her whole life had been built around the premise that certain public institutions, like government and the press, were basically good and necessary. Of course there were bad people in both, but the *Arizona Register*? That was almost unthinkable. She tried to recall every word in that last conversation with her editor, how he had belittled her dead friend's story, how he'd passed over her objections with tolerant smiles. Why didn't he see the sinister design as clearly as Mack did, as *she* was beginning to? Weren't Clyde's last words clear enough? *Mafia, Emprise and Romano*. Grace drank another big gulp of bitter beer. The liquid was very cold and hurt her teeth. She shivered and drank some more. Then she pointed the bottle at Mack. "But that means Mister Collins is suppressing information on the death of an *Arizona Register* reporter! Why would any newspaper editor do that?"

"Maybe for big, complicated reasons," he said. "For starters, Emprise is co-owned by Gus Greenbaum and Bruno Malatesta."

"Yes. Clyde mentioned them. So?" she encouraged.

"Gus Greenbaum also owns a big piece of Broken Arrow Ranch and at least three of our local greyhound breeding stables. Bruno Malatesta has very old, very close connections to the Giancana-Accardo Mafia family in Chicago."

Grace leaned forward. "You're saying Ace Collins is ignoring Emprise because he's afraid of the Chicago Mafia?"

"No. His reasons are probably more subtle than that." Mack was thinking as he spoke. "More likely he's hesitant to involve someone more important in Arizona than Gus Greenbaum, Bruno Malatesta or Tony Accardo. Ace Collins surely knows Greenbaum's partner at the Ranch. He could be protecting Robert Lillienthal."

"Oh come on," Grace scoffed. "Protecting whom? I've heard stories about Robert Lillienthal, but it's ridiculous to say he wields that kind of clout."

"Look, Grace, Arizona's still a frontier state. Mafia or not, the pioneer families run things. Nothing gets done without an okay from the good-old-boys."

Grace had been a reporter in Arizona for years. She knew quite a bit about Ex-Senator Harris Lillienthal and his younger brother Robert. They were part of the hierarchy of wealthy Arizonans she had frequently run across while working the social section before her promotion. Great grandsons of a pioneer merchant, they were born to the family business. Harris Lillienthal had once been a Republican candidate for President and had been involved in politics for thirty years, but Robert Lillienthal had concentrated on business. Along with farming and ranching interests, he was a director of Arizona's largest bank, was reported to hold majority stock in Hobo Joe's restaurants - a chain of fast-food franchises - and was owner of a trendy and successful downtown Phoenix beef and ale pub called Robert's Club.

"He's supposed to run a fast track," she said, shaking her head in disbelief. "Some unsavory friends, gambling and lots of women, but the brother of a U.S. Senator mixed up in cover-ups and murder? My God, Mack, that's incredible."

Mack nodded. "Yes, that's certainly hard to believe, but it explains a lot."

Grace blinked in angry disbelief. "Okay! Let's say you're right. What possible pressure could even such powerful men as the Lillienthal brothers have put on the editor of Arizona's largest newspaper to keep Emprise out of the news?"

"I don't know what leverage the Lillienthals have," Mack said. "Maybe they know the publisher. Or the country club set might just be sticking together."

"I don't necessarily believe all this," Grace said as she stared out the front window. "But if Emprise *was* Clyde's story, and if the *Register* refuses to print the story because of the big, powerful names involved, what can we do about it?"

"I've been thinking about that for the last two weeks," he said.

She didn't say anything, made an odd noise. He thought she was coughing, but he looked more closely and saw the first smile he'd seen in many days, a teary grimace, and her slender body was shaking with both mirth and pain.

Mack watched her a while and grew impatient. "Grace? Grace, stop it! What could possibly be funny about all this?"

She sniffed back tears, chuckled, took off her glasses again and wiped her eyes, "Oh, Mack, do you know what I was thinking?"

He shook his head.

"I was going to suggest we take our suspicions to the police."

• • •

Next day Grace got a message at work to call a number.

"Yeah, whaddya want?" The too-loud, graveled voice filled her earpiece, it sounded old with an eastern accent.

"My name is Grace Faber. I have a message to call this number." The thought flashed, *could this have something to do with the killing?*

"Yeah," the voice groaned, now low and monotone. "I was sorry to hear about that kid, Clyde. He was a nice young man. Bad way to go and all that."

Grace began to relax. This probably wasn't Vinnie Romano. "Yes, thank you. He was a good friend. What's your name? What can I do for you?"

"Listen, you know a tall guy with a scar on his cheek?" The voice ignored the questions. "Clyde introduced me to him."

She guessed he meant Mack. "Yes, I think so." No harm telling him that.

"Yeah, well tell him Louie wants to see him tonight after the track closes."

"Louie?" she repeated. "What's this about, Louie?"

"Tell the guy with the scar to meet me tonight just before midnight."

She could tell he was hanging up. "Wait!" she yelled into the phone. People at nearby desks looked up at her outburst. "Where should he meet you?"

The phone clanked against something, hanging up? But the voice came back. "He knows where we are. Tell him they're killin' Great Alliance tonight."

• • •

Darker than a grave, he thought. Near midnight. Wonder if it's a trap?

Mack and Grace had driven lights-out for a block and parked near a big square trash dumpster on a street at the far end of the track. He wanted to get near the track's kennel building and look around without committing himself. The large metal building showed no lights or movement. Mack checked his 45, opened the windows and listened. A puff of breeze ruffled papers in the dumpster. A plane roared off the runway four miles south and busy traffic whispered from blocks away. Conflicting smells of dry dust and rancid grease floated from the trash.

He checked his watch. Eleven forty five.

They sat for ten more minutes. Nothing moved. Time to check, to look for Louis Carfagno and his greyhounds. "Wait here," he whispered. "If you hear shots don't do anything, just start the engine and wait here for me. Understand?"

"Mack, I *should* come with you. Besides I'm scared to wait here alone."

"Damn it Grace!" The whisper became a growl. "The only reason I let you come along was because you said you'd do what I told you."

"Oh, all right!" He felt her bounce on the seat with anger.

He unscrewed the dome light before opening the door and was half way out when he had a sudden urge to make a statement in case he never get another chance. Mack slid back into the truck, pulled her to him and kissed her lips.

He was gone before she could react. Grace smiled and then frowned into the night.

They evidently left the track lights on all night. Big, bright blooms of light around the oval track cast everything else into sharp darkness. Keeping to deeper shadows and stopping often to watch and listen, Mack walked slowly toward the black shape of the kennel building. No people, no guards, no movement. But what was there to guard? Dogs. Guards would be *inside* the building.

He opened a sliding metal door a few inches, peeked inside and realized no one would hear him no matter what noise he made. Swamp coolers thumped, whirred and buzzed overhead. Nobody was near the door. Where was Louis? Was this a trap? One small overhead lamp cast a twenty-foot yellow circle near the door. The center of the huge expanse was crowded darkness filled with low square shapes of concrete and steel bars. He remembered the smells: disinfectant, wet concrete and pungent body heat. Shadows shifting in shadow told him of pacing dogs, but there was no larger movement, no pacing humans, no Louis Carfagno.

After standing completely still inside the partly opened door for at least five minutes Mack didn't see or hear anyone. He decided something was wrong, pulled out the 45 and began to edge his way around the inside of the barn-like building toward where he remembered Great Alliance's kennel was located. He kept a hand out to feel the wall as he moved down the side of the building, looking down each long concrete row as he moved closer to the center. He wondered if Vinnie Romano was waiting somewhere in the darkness.

A rounded shadow moved near a kennel door.

Mack pointed the 45, took slack in the trigger and guessed. "Louis?"

"Yeah, it's me," a ragged voice answered. "You got here too late." The old man was slumped on the floor at the end of Great Alliance's row. "Too late."

"What the hell do you mean, too late?" Mack whispered.

"They took 'em about a half hour ago, sixteen of 'em and Great Alliance." The old man held his voice so low Mack could barely hear him.

"Took them where?" Mack asked.

"Back to the ranch in an old horse van."

Mack held the pistol ready and walked part way down the long row. He looked carefully into the dark, empty cages and peered off into the gloom for movement. No dogs at all on this row and the building seemed empty of people.

"No guards, Louis?"

"Nah," the old man sighed, "I'm the guard tonight. They leave me here when they go to kill dogs. They know I won't do nothin' to hurt a dog and them three'll get the dogs done quick enough without me."

"Three men?" Mack repeated. "You mean they need three guys to kill a bunch of helpless dogs?"

"They like shootin' dogs, dammit," the old man wheezed. "Makes them feel powerful to execute a bunch of poor ol' dumb animals. And I tol' you to be here before midnight; what took you so long?" He struggled to get to his feet.

Mack grabbed the old man's arm and hauled him up. "Never mind that!" he said impatiently. "You say they're going to kill that racing dog, Great Alliance? Where? Where the hell have they gone?"

"Out to that ranch, that Broken Arrow ranch."

Mack's memory went back to that afternoon with Clyde, to the tall regal champion he'd petted and photographed. That dog was going to die tonight! He pulled the crippled old man toward the door to the big building

"This ranch, how far is it?" Mack asked.

"Twenty miles thataway," Louis said. He pointed a vague finger at the north wall of the large building. "Off the Florence Highway near the big Central Arizona Project ditch."

"How long ago did they leave?" Mack hurried the old man toward the door.

Louis Carfagno limped as fast as he could. "Told you. Half an hour ago."

• • •

They hurtled too fast through their short, brilliant hole in the night. Fifty miles an hour on dirt, bouncing and skidding down a dusty ranch road. Headlights sliced across scrub and cactus at the edge of the road. Beyond that, Mack glimpsed cleared fields and darkness. Barely under control, the pickup swerved in and out of ruts and erosion holes as Mack yanked and pulled at the steering wheel. The three people bounced wildly back and forth on the bench seat and up high enough to hit the roof. Mack had broken all the speed laws and busted three red lights getting out of the city. He'd only slowed to fifty when they'd finally turned onto a dirt road.

"You sure this is the way?" Mack yelled as the truck skidded into a wide desert clearing where two deep-rutted ranch roads crossed.

"Yeah, right here! Right, I said!" Louis thrust his arm to the right and swiped Grace in the face, knocking her glasses askew. "Sorry Ma'am! Almost there; maybe two miles more."

"What if they see us?" Grace fumbled her glasses up and stared ahead.

"We can't let them see us too soon." Mack said.

He killed the headlights, wrestled the truck onto the right-hand road and allowed the pickup to slow down to thirty - driving blind down a rutted ranch road. Tires followed the ruts until Mack's eyes became more accustomed to the phantom shapes of the starlit desert. Slower, but it was still too fast for Mack's reflexes to correct to the images flashing under the hood. The truck plowed on, slamming through the night. Ghostly gray and dead black, a pale world sprang from ink twenty feet ahead, prickly pear and mesquite, tall scarecrows of saguaro. Shapes flashed into view and disappeared past swift windows before he could react.

Mack slowed more for safety. Then he thought of the dying dogs and disregarded his instincts. He pressed the accelerator down as though he was stamping on his fear. The engine howled. Springs bounced and jangled. The high desert night rushed by the pickup truck in splintered seconds.

They were headed north through the wide, rolling expanse of Avra Valley toward low rugged mountains called Tortolitas. Mack knew the mountains were there, only a dozen or so miles ahead. They rose on the northern horizon during the bent heat of day like a tumble of arrowheads, but they were invisible now.

Three shots cracked the night. Echoes rolled across the desert.

Sounded close, maybe a few hundred yards! Mack listened for screams or yelps from the dogs. Should they stop and sneak up on foot? But dogs were dying.

Three more shots, much closer. Mack still couldn't see anything ahead.

"The hell with this," Mack growled. "We're going in *now*, bright and noisy!" He flicked on the headlights and gunned the engine. The truck speeded up to thirty, forty miles an hour and bored a big, bright cave in the darkness.

A white shape glimmered just inside the headlight cone, fifty yards ahead. The long rounded cage of a horse van took shape. Something moved - a white shirt. "Crack!" the air ripped apart near Mack's ear. A starred hole appeared in the windshield. "Boom! Boom!" More shots. A headlight sprinkled its glass. Grace screamed and scrambled to hide beneath the dash. Louis Carfagno didn't duck, he seemed paralyzed. The pickup crashed through ruts and roared closer to the van.

"Boom!" Another starry hole appeared. The back window disintegrated, spraying their shoulders with bright chunks of glass. Mack knew they were sitting ducks in the truck. He pointed the surviving headlight at the big white van and slammed on the brakes. "Get out now! Hug the ground and stay behind the truck!" he yelled. The truck shuddered to a halt. He popped open the door and dove out, rolling as he hit and grabbing for the 45. He rolled twenty feet from the pickup and lay prone in the dirt with the automatic extended straight out toward the van. Mack took a classic fist-cupped shooting position and squinted through settling dust.

Motion! A white face and blue denim was under the van. Mack sighted low and brought the blade sight down into the rear-sight slot. Carefully. Squeeze.

"Boom!" Another shot spanged off the truck. Mack flinched, lost the target and relaxed tension on the trigger as he brought the muzzle back. Blue denim was gone - nothing to shoot at. *Three guys* Louis had said. If they were smart they'd be moving into the desert to come at him from the sides. The brilliant cone of the pickup's one headlight swirled gnats and desert moths. The large horse-van shone bright white. A dog howled. Mack saw movement inside the white cages, heard frightened mewling and frantic claws tearing at metal. More howls. Dogs were reacting to the gunshots. Some were still alive! He listened for heavier movement and hoped Grace and Louis had gotten behind the truck.

Seconds dragged. Dust tickled his nose and he sniffed back a sneeze.

Another howl. Something moved at the near end of the van. Mack shifted the pistol. A figure moved into the light and pointed a pistol at the pickup. Mack put the front sight on a blue denim belly below a raised arm and took trigger slack.

Blue denim shot out the last headlight. "Boom!" Night closed down again.

Night-blind, Mack clenched his eyes shut and held the vision on his retina. He sighted just below the remembered shoulders. Center, squeeze. "Boom!" The 45 jumped in his fists, slamming his wrist back. A splintered scream and the sloppy sound of a body falling brought a smile. *One down, two to go*, he held his eyes closed and rolled. Two shots smacked the dirt where he'd been. Close, but the shots gave him a fix on at least one of them still near the van. He opened an eye and saw low fire-flicker in a ravine behind the horse van. The fire had been invisible in head light glare, but now served as wavering backdrop for the long silhouette of the van.

A shadow moved low to the ground like a crawling bush.

Mack sighted low and fired.

The shadow scrambled back behind the long vehicle. A miss. Damn! Mack remembered to roll again, but waited a second too long.

"Boom!" The sound came after a searing sting down his leg. He was hit! Not too bad, he could still roll away. His fingers probed a long shallow furrow in his calf. The bastard had almost nailed him. Had to be high where he could see the whole area around the pickup. Had to be inside the van! Mack knew he couldn't shoot at movement; he'd hit a dog.

Two or three dogs were howling now. It was time for a trick, a diversion. Mack decided to scream. "Aaarrggghh!" he allowed the shriek to subside to a groan and rolled another ten feet or so, and another. Then he lay quiet with the 45 extended and waited for his vision to open up in the dark.

"Mack, are you hurt?" Grace's voice pealed through the night and he heard feet sliding through the dust near the truck. She was running toward his scream, ruining his plan and putting herself in danger. No shots traced her noise. He knew they were waiting for a better target. "Mack? Where are you?" she called.

He heard shushing feet scrape to a halt and imagined her looking around. Should he call her? No. They'd both get shot. Mack ignored her and rolled farther away from the pickup. He felt the ground sloping down and realized he was sliding into a ravine. Rough dirt crumbled. He slid three feet into a shallow, dry wash that ran in the direction of the van. Yes. Fire-flicker made shadows dance behind the shape of the horse-van. He peeked above the ravine edge. Couldn't see the pickup or Grace. Mack crawled down the ravine toward the dancing glow.

"Mack, where are you?" Grace's plaintive voice pierced the night.

Frightened dogs answered her. Long yelping wails pleaded for an end to fear.

The shape of the van cut the night sky. Mack crawled close enough to the fire to see a spraddled, leggy heap of dead greyhounds piled in the bottom of the ravine, partially buried by a cave-in of the ravine-edge. This time they'd decided to bury the evidence. *After the Clyde Ralston story*, Mack thought as he climbed out of the dry wash and crept closer to the back of the horse-van.

A foot scraped metal. Someone cursed.

Mack froze in the open, washed in treacherous firelight, blind to the deadly shadows. He hunched down waiting for the dull shock of a bullet.

A whispered question hissed. An answer came from somewhere to his left.

"Mack where are you?" Grace called again from out in the open.

"Go get her!" a whisper from the van ordered sharply.

They hadn't seen him. Mack moved toward the voice, not worrying about the noise. He knew where they were. Up to the van, onto the fender! Metal squealed. Point the pistol. There, a slim shape! Too slim, a greyhound. Where was the dog-killing son of a bitch?

"What the hell?" a voice asked. To his right a bulky shadow moved, turned.

Mack snapped off a shot without aiming, "Boom" and heard the bullet strike meat. The shadow folded to the steel floor with a grunt. Probably gut-shot and out of it for good. Mack jumped down from the fender and dropped to the ground. He hugged dirt and waited, expecting shots from his left. Nothing.

Dogs scrambled against their cages, but they were shocked silent now from the close shot and the smell of human blood and offal.

Then there was a scuffle of feet in the desert. Grace screamed.

"Okay, you fuck," a rough voice snarled in the darkness. "I've got the broad. Back over towards that fire and drop your gun or I'll blow her brains in the dirt."

"Right," Mack said, still on the ground. "Don't shoot her. I'm giving up." He tucked the 45 in the back of his belt and stood up, partially covered by the van. He knew he was half-silhouetted against the small fire in the ravine so he moved his right arm in a tossing motion and kicked the dirt a moment later, simulating the sound of a fallen pistol. "There, I've thrown away my gun, you can relax." He stayed near the van so the man holding Grace would have to move much closer for a clear shot.

Scuffling sounds moved closer. Then two shapes appeared fifteen feet away. Grace was sobbing. She stumbled and nearly fell when she saw Mack. A big guy with a bandaged eye held her across the chest and tried to aim his gun over her right shoulder. One-eye. Mack recognized him from the dog track parking lot. A head, arm and shoulder were exposed as he struggled with the woman.

"Oh Mack, you're not hurt." Grace stumbled again spoiling one-eye's aim.

"So, It's you!" He recognized Mack. "I'm gonna enjoy blowin' *you* away, you stinkin' *scungil*." The heavy-set thug got a firmer grip on the woman and tried again for steady aim over her shoulder.

Mack moved out from the protection of the van, closer to the wobbling gun. He knew he had to take the chance before the hood got any closer. He pulled the 45 out of the back of his pants, turned sideways to avoid the shot he knew was coming and leveled his pistol at a spot six inches above Grace Faber's right shoulder.

"Mack, no! Grace screamed and threw up her hands to ward off the bullet.

"Boom!" Mack snapped off the shot as the front sight centered.

One-eye cranked one off by reflex. The wind tickled Mack's cheek.

Grace dropped to the ground in shock. The thug sprawled out behind her, his arms reaching for heaven. The 45 round had blown his neck apart and punched him to the ground. He probably bled to death before his feet stopped twitching.

It took a half hour to calm the surviving dogs and coax them into the back of the pickup with Louis Carfagno. Eight dogs were left. Great Alliance was one of them. Still favoring his front leg a little, but minus the cast, the big champion finally settled in the back of the truck next to the trainer's bent body and accepted pats and scratches as though he was doing the old man a favor.

Grace still sat in the dirt staring at her feet as though the world had ended.

"Good ol' boy, you are," the old man crooned to Great Alliance. "We sure saved your bony ass in the nick of time."

"The bastards killed nine dogs," Mack said quietly.

"Yeah." The old man took off his cap, wiped his forehead and shook his head. "They kill 'em out here cause they're registered wit' the racing commission. Greenbaum thinks he'll lose his racing ticket if the commission finds out he kills any more money-losers without some kind of permit."

"So we turn him in and he loses his racing ticket," Mack suggested.

The trainer stopped petting Great Alliance and frowned up at the stars. "You think they gonna care more about dead dogs or dead men?" he asked.

Mack realized his stupidity. He closed the tailgate behind the dogs and the old man and walked around to help the shaken woman. She sat bent over, hands splayed in the dirt like she was drunk or injured.

He knelt and hugged her shoulders. "Well, Grace, we saved eight of them."

"But you killed those men," she mumbled and stared at him as though he was a stranger.

CHAPTER ELEVEN

ILLUSIONS

By next morning the eight greyhounds had become accustomed to Grace Faber's garage and fenced-in yard. Louis Carfagno had slept in the garage with his survivors. He was sitting in a patch of sunlight in the back yard with his arm around one. "This 'un is Serengeti Fancy," he ruffled a reddish brindle's droopy ears. "She's taken a shine to Great Alliance, but he pretend he don't see her."

The red brindle female was smaller than Great Alliance by six inches, but had more pronounced markings on her lean muscular body. Bold, black facial bands striped her muzzle and outlined her large, intelligent eyes, reminding Mack of pictures he'd seen of Queen Nefertiti. She stayed close to the big male, occasionally licking his muzzle and bumping him coquettishly. He tolerated her.

"Coffee's ready," Grace called from the kitchen.

Mack took the nearest steaming cup on the counter and nodded his thanks. She wouldn't meet his eyes. Grace had been pensive and silent all morning. None of them had gotten much sleep, but she was clearly troubled by dueling emotions.

She'd slept with Mack for the first time the night before.

When they'd arrived at the house in the shot-up pickup the sky was gray with false dawn and everyone was exhausted.

They'd pulled the truck into the garage, put rugs out for the dogs, given Louis a pillow and a blanket and headed for their beds. A little later Mack felt the covers lift from his body and Grace slide in beside him. She muttered something about not being able to sleep and quickly fell asleep, arms around his chest, breath purring softly against his neck.

Mack was sore from still-healing burns and the new leg wound. He was weak from blood-loss and weary of long adrenalin-blistered hours, but suddenly wide-awake and very conscious of the warm female body pressed against him. He turned toward her and groaned as his blood-crusted leg brushed against her foot.

"Mmmph. What?" she mumbled.

"Grace, what are you doing here?"

But she only sighed against his shoulder and drifted off again.

Mack's free hand curved over a hip, slid across a thin nightgown and under her arm to cup a small, firm breast. Grace turned her body into his hand and snuggled closer. The nipple rose to his sensitive palm and, in spite of his fatigue and injury, Mack felt himself harden. He stroked her, kissed the slightly opened lips and thought of long, smooth legs. His hand moved lower, down to bare skin and began to slide soft material up her thighs.

She opened her eyes and looked blearily at him.

"Mack that was awful tonight, the dead dogs, the shooting and the killing."

His hand stopped moving. "Yeah, but we saved eight of them."

"Those men," she muttered. "I know the one said he was going to kill you, but did you *have* to kill them? Couldn't we have called the police?"

He remembered bullet holes in his windshield and tried to understand her inability to accept the killings. His hand moved up from her thigh to stroke her cheek. "We had no time. They would have killed us, you, me and Louis. They shot at us before they knew who we were. We had no choice, Grace, no choice at all."

"But did you have to kill them all?"

He lost patience. "Listen, Grace, the one who grabbed you is dead. I don't know about the other two." A cold smile stretched his mouth. "I think I hit the first guy in the chest and the second one in the gut. They both might have lived."

Her eyes opened wide with shock and sorrow. "No! Those men were only *wounded*? You left them out there in the desert to die?"

"What should I have done? Call an ambulance after I shot three men because they were killing some dogs? The cops wouldn't see things quite that clearly. With my reputation in this town, they'd call the shootings first degree murder."

Grace glared at him and turned away, jerking the covers with her.

He groaned at the dilemma, his injuries and his tired body. What the hell, he thought, she was too damn naive to understand. He sighed and snuggled against her warm hip. Sleep interrupted simmering thoughts.

He'd awakened to late morning sunlight glaring across his face and reached for her. No one was there. A breath of gardenia lingered in the folds of the pillow.

• • •

Louis Carfagno was nervous in the bright kitchen surrounded by frilly curtains, copper pots and baking smells. He tugged at his cap brim and then gripped his coffee cup in twisted, swollen fingers. He was anxious to return to his dogs.

"Need to buy 'em some food today," he said to no one in particular. "They ain't eaten decent in two or three days."

Grace pulled a baking-tray of steaming biscuits from the oven and turned to Louis with a frown. "Don't they feed these poor dogs at the kennel?"

"No ma'am they don't." Louis stared at the brown biscuits and shook his head. "Not if they're fixin' to kill 'em in a day or so."

Grace passed around plates, pastry and a butter dish and they spent the next few minutes eating and sipping coffee. Something occurred to her, she looked up and pointed a butter knife at the old man. "Would you let me quote you in a story for my newspaper, a story about greyhounds?" she asked.

Louis Carfagno thought a moment, removed his cap and wiped his sparse gray hair. He knew his life had changed forever when he decided to rescue the greyhounds. He would never work at another racetrack as soon as word got around. Dog tracks had been his life for forty years, both in Illinois and Arizona. The Malatesta family had given him work at their Hawthorne Kennel Club in Cicero because he was a distant relative of one of their Capos. He'd moved west to join Don Bruno in the seventies. And worse, Louis was sure he couldn't even keep the *dogs* in Arizona any more, their ear-tattoos would betray them. He hoped to find homes for the greyhounds with some trainer friends in North Carolina and Florida and then try for a job with an east coast breeder. He hadn't thought farther than that.

"Sure," he shrugged, "Whaddyou wanna know?"

Grace went out of the kitchen and came back with a small tape recorder. "I'm going to ask you about the dogs and the track owners, whatever you can tell me." She set the recorder on the counter and turned it on. "This is an interview with Mister Louis Carfagno who worked for the Emprise Company at dog racing tracks for many years..."

Mack reached over and turned the recorder off. "Wait a minute, Grace! Louis has done enough. A story in the paper could get him hurt, maybe killed, and besides he doesn't know anything that'll help us, he was just a dog trainer."

"I *want* to do a story on the dogs," Grace insisted. "He is a track employee."

"Was a lot more than a dog trainer," the old man grumbled. "I worked the starting gates in the seventies. Even worked the betting windows for a few years."

"Clyde already did a story on dogs," Mack reminded her, "and his efforts didn't impress Ace Collins. What makes you think you can do any better."

Grace glared. "We have to do something besides shoot people in the desert."

"Ace Collins?" Louis repeated. "You said *Ace Collins?*"

"Yeah," Mack nodded. "Ace Collins is Grace's boss at the *Arizona Register* newspaper. Why, Louis, you know him?"

The old man laughed softly and rubbed a splayed hand across his weathered face. "Damndest thing I ever heard." He looked sharply at Grace. "I called you at some newspaper...the one that young fella said he worked for. You say you *both* worked for this same Ace Collins at this same newspaper?"

Grace was puzzled. She nodded silently and stared at the dog trainer.

Louis Carfagno was both amused and frightened by this new information. He needed time to mull it over. He clumsily helped himself to another biscuit and then held his cup up so she could pour him more coffee. The old man took a bite, sipped at the hot coffee and sat back sideways so the chair would comfortably fit his curved back. "This Ace Collins is a real wing-ding. We know him at the track."

"A wing-ding?" Grace repeated. "What does that mean?"

"A high roller. He drinks heavy and bets stupid," Louis answered.

"Mister Collins bet at the dog tracks?" She couldn't believe her ears.

"Yep," the old trainer said. "Been a guest at the Broken Arrow box for years. Talk was, he dropped heavy dough up there wit' Greenbaum and the boys."

"And heavy drinking too?" Grace added.

Louis laughed. "Lotsa times he passed out in the Broken Arrow box." He swept an arm toward the ceiling. "Coupla the boys'd carry him down all them stairs to a car - big rich man, all limp, his hands draggin' in the spilt beer and butts. Quite a sight for them workers. Happened every month or so 'til sometime last year."

Mack's eyes searched for Grace's. "There's your connection," he said.

Grace tugged her robe tight around her shoulders and gripped it together under her chin as though she was suddenly cold. Her eyes fled Mack's gaze and suddenly returned. "Gambling debts and drunken friendships would not cause a newspaper editor to connive in covering-up the murder of a reporter. Even *you* must see that."

"Maybe not, but if he owes Malatesta and the boys at the track lots of gambling debts, that would damn sure give him a good reason to editorially favor a sports arena bond election that helps them!"

Grace stood very still as though listening to an inner voice. Her eyes lifted to the kitchen clock and she seemed to awaken from a trance. "Oh, my God, I have to get dressed. I have to be at work in thirty minutes!"

The old man finished off his biscuit and went out to his dogs.

Mack drank coffee and waited. He met her in the hall before she could leave and walked her to her car. At the car door he faced her. "We slept together last night," he said, "but nothing happened."

She avoided his eyes. "Mack, I can't talk about this now."

He shook his head and held her shoulders. "We have to talk. I'm healed now. I can move out of your house, but do you want me to?"

"Mack, I don't know what I want and this is *not* the time to have a talk." She removed his hands from her shoulders, but held on to one hand. "We both should stay here with Louis until he decides what to do with the dogs."

"Okay, that sounds good. I'll swing by the studio later, pick up my mail and see what clothes I can salvage, but we really should talk about what almost happened last night."

Grace pressed her lips together, her eyes blinked anger behind her glasses. "You stand for everything I abhor!" she snapped. "Violence represents all that is bad in our society. I'm grateful for your help, but afraid of your methods and I'm not sure *anything* will ever happen between us...and that is not what is important!" She paused and calmed herself. "Look, Mack, Louis' information on Ace Collins changes everything for both of us. We can't count on *anyone* else now, we must find the truth for ourselves! The police are obviously too incompetent or frightened of lawyers to do their job and now my own newspaper is becoming suspect. We can't just let the investigation into Clyde's murder end with Vinnie Romano's vengeance." She reached out and touched Mack's cheek with a soothing fingertip. "We'll work together, Mack. I'll check Mister Collins' background to find out what *more* he's hiding from the world and you must find out what the police are doing, if anything. Maybe you can steer that Karl friend of yours in the right direction."

"Okay Grace," Mack agreed quickly. He was relieved the anger had passed. "We'll work together with no promises made and no strings attached. I'll be happy to stay here with you and sleep in the guest room. Later this morning I'll buy dog food for the greyhounds, go have a long talk with Karl Jenkins and then check in at my studio." He tried to hold and kiss her, but she turned and he only managed to peck her on the cheek.

Louis said forty pounds of dog food would last them a day or two. Mack rebandaged his leg and went to buy the bag of food before calling Karl Jenkins.

• • •

They met for lunch at Pat's drive-in. Karl got in Mack's shot-up pickup and picked a piece of glass from the seat. "Those are bullet holes in your windshield, ol' buddy." He put a cautious finger on one. "Is this what you wanted to talk about?"

"Sort of," Mack said and unconsciously rubbed the bandage under his trouser leg. He'd decided to explain the whole mess for his old friend. "Did you get a report about dead greyhounds and shot-up thugs on the Broken Arrow Ranch last night?"

"No. You know that's Sheriff's Department jurisdiction," Karl said. He shook his head and smoothed back his sleek blond hair. "But we'd have heard. As far as I know there was nothing reported dead or shot on Broken Arrow Ranch last night. Why, what happened?"

"No report? I might've known," Mack said. "This is too involved to begin with last night's shooting. I'm gonna need your help so I'll start at the beginning."

Karl Jenkins lit a Marlboro and settled back in his seat. He'd been a cop too long to interrupt a talkative witness with unnecessary comments.

"I've been working the hit and run death of Grace Faber's mother and a high-end money laundering scheme at the dog track." Mack began. "Both cases came to involve the dead *Arizona Register* reporter and Vinnie Romano. Either one or both investigations might have gotten the reporter killed."

"You were working *two* cases with Clyde Ralston?" Karl repeated.

Mack nodded and looked out at the crowded drive-in parking lot. A stocky, but pretty, carhop in shorts and tee shirt appeared at the truck window.

"Four hot chili dogs and a pitcher of beer, Maggie," Karl ordered before Mack could speak. "I'm buying. Sounds like this story might be worth it."

Mack continued. "First, Karl, you should know there were also *two* Clyde Ralston newspaper stories, but the one about the money laundering never got printed." He told of his investigation into the unsolved hit and run and his fake identification of Vinnie Romano as a witness - explained lying to Sergeant Sparks and recruiting Clyde Ralston to expose Bruno Malatesta as the hit and run driver. He skimmed over the trip to the racetrack and Chickie's death in his studio and ended with the sequence of events the night of the bombing of Clyde Ralston's car. "Clyde's newspaper says he was killed because of the hit and run story he did for me on Vinnie, but I think it was because of the other investigation..."

The girl interrupted again. She attached a tray full of chili dogs and beer to Karl's window and gave him a knowing smile. Karl tossed his cigarette, handed her a twenty and patted her on a plump shoulder. Mack reached for the frosted pitcher and poured beer. They sucked down mugs of icy, foam-topped beer and unwrapped steaming hot dogs covered with mounds of Pat's spicy chili, known throughout southern Arizona as the best tasting in the world - if you survived the fiery burn.

"Know her?" Mack asked, pointing at the car-hop with his hot dog.

"Are you tellin' me you lied to both Sergeant Sparks *and* that reporter about seeing Vinnie Romano at the H and R scene?" Karl demanded through a mouthful. He dismissed the personal question like it hadn't been asked.

"You got it, Karl," Mack admitted. He put down his half-eaten chili dog and stared unseeing out the window, appetite forgotten. "The asshole who actually saw Romano at the H and R scene wouldn't cooperate. I *had* to do something."

Karl Jenkins put down his food and turned toward Mack with a dead-serious frown. "I don't want to overstate this, but it sounds like your lie about bein' a witness might've gotten that reporter killed?" Anger and exasperation had darkened his blue eyes.

Mack heard the anger and felt guilty and betrayed. "Karl, I don't think that's the way the deal went down. If that were true, he'd want to kill both of us, right?"

Karl thought a moment. "But someone *did* try to kill you in your studio and got Miss Malatesta by mistake. You said Vinnie Romano tried to kill you in your bathroom because he was jealous of you and Chickie Malatesta, but how do you know he wasn't tryin' to silence a phony-ass witness? And what the hell does a hit and run on Speedway Boulevard have to do with this money laundering you mentioned and some dead thugs and dogs on Broken Arrow Ranch?"

"Goddamnit, Karl, I'm getting to that!" Mack was tired and sore. There were things the policeman was forgetting. Mack turned and looked his angry friend in the eye. "You're right. I was stupid to lie about the hit and run, but you're forgetting Clyde Ralston's last words. He said, Mafia and Romano, but he also said Emprise. You know about Emprise don't you, Karl?"

"Yeah. Casinos, dog tracks and sport-franchise concessions, Emprise is supposed to be Vegas-based and probably mobbed-up. So this reporter's dying words meant he thought Vinnie worked for the dog track company, right?"

"No, that's *not* what he meant," Mack corrected. "He meant the Mafia and Romano killed him because he was going to expose a Vegas-dog-track-money- skimming scheme involving Emprise and some powerful Arizona politicians."

Karl smiled tolerantly and lit another cigarette. "Come on, ol' buddy, that's a stretch. We've all heard rumors about this shit before. They don't mean nothin' and some dog track scam's not worth killing a reporter for." He flicked the match out the window and blew a thin stream of smoke at the bullet-starred windshield.

Mack reined in his temper. "Okay. Let me explain what Clyde Ralston was working on..." He began to acquaint his old friend with million-dollar laundries and local politics. Chile dogs cooled to greasy, reddish paste while Mack painstakingly detailed the sports arena-Indian bingo-horse track-dog-track-laundry-strategy. He led Karl through the whole investigation, from dead racing dogs on the Greenbaum-Lillienthal Ranch, to one-way-empty armored car trips, the fight in the racetrack parking lot and the torching of Mitch Young before the sports arena bond election. Then he showed the detective his photos of the empty armored car.

Karl Jenkins nodded at the photos. "Fine. Makes sense in a circumstantial way, but this is *not* evidence. There's no way you could take this mess to court."

"Clyde didn't want to take it to court," Mack said. "He wanted to ask all the questions in print. He wanted the public to know there were dogs being killed for pennies while millions of illegal dollars were being laundered through the dog track. He wanted the public to know about the money scam *before* they voted on a new fifty-million dollar sports arena that would probably be used in the *same* way by the *same* damn people!" Mack was breathing hard - the last few words shouted across the small space. Anger buzzed behind his eyes and pounded his temples.

Karl knew his friend was no fool. The anger made him begin to believe. "Let me get this straight," he said quietly. "You think Clyde Ralston was killed because he was going to write the money story before the sports arena bond election?"

"Exactly." Mack chopped the smoke-filled air with his hand. "I figure Malatesta brought a hit man into Tucson to kill Mitch Young and stop the anti-tax campaign. The Clyde Ralston bombing was a spur of the moment addition."

The policeman shook his head in bewilderment and grimaced at the boiling thoughts his friend had conjured up, and at their implications. "Pheew, that *is* a helluva stretch," he said and blew smoke at the cab ceiling. "To actually murder a tax activist *and* a reporter; the mob doesn't like to hit reporters. What's so special?"

"Maybe I wasn't clear, Karl," Mack growled. "We're talking billions here. These people are skimming millions a year and laundering the money in Arizona dog tracks and sports facilities. This new sports arena will allow them to double or triple their laundry operation. We're talking about a multi-billion dollar money-cleaning operation after a few years. Do you think the Mafia would let a local tax protester and some unimportant police-beat reporter get in their way?"

Karl believed and sympathized, but he was a cop jaded to the corruptions of politicians and resigned to the imperfections of the system. He was impatient with crusaders and enjoyed arresting people, not writing newspaper stories about them. He wanted to bust Vinnie Romano and Bruno Malatesta if he could, but all the talk of laundered mafia money was a foolish pipe dream without hard evidence.

"So where's this all going?" he asked. "What do you want from me?"

Mack knew what his old friend was thinking. They had been through a few political firestorms together and neither had any illusions about justice. The difference between them was that Karl believed there was nothing he could do about some things except keep his head down and do his job. Mack knew there was *always* something you could do if you cared enough and had nothing to lose.

"I want to know why the police haven't even questioned Bruno Malatesta about the deaths of Viola Faber, Mitch Young and the bombing of Clyde Ralston."

Karl Jenkins tossed his cigarette butt, picked up his cold chili dog, sniffed at it and dropped it on the plate. "You ruined my lunch with your horror stories," he said and shrugged. "Homicide hasn't talked to ol' Bruno about the reporter because they've got nothing to connect him to the bombing except Vinnie, and they can't find Vinnie. Same thing's true about both torch jobs."

"What about the hit and run?" Mack prodded.

The detective grinned at his old friend. "You mean the one you lied about?" He didn't wait for an answer. "Bruno Malatesta wasn't a suspect for even two hours after you fingered him. He had an ironclad alibi. His lawyer said he was at Johnny Gibson's barber shop on Sixth Avenue getting his weekly trim and gossiping with old timers when Viola Faber was killed." Karl watched Mack's face sag in astonishment. He laughed and continued. "There must've been fifteen witnesses at that barber shop. Don Bruno was *definitely* not the driver at the Faber hit and run."

"Holy shit!" Mack exploded. "All this time I've been sure he was the driver. Now what? Why the hell didn't the police release this information to the press?"

"Well they can't. There is another, ah, suspect," Karl said slowly.

"Who damnit!"

"Nobody's supposed to know except Sergeant Sparks and Chief Hobbs, but it's somebody with enough clout to keep the lid on unless more witnesses show up."

"What does that mean?" Mack asked.

"That means the big boys are sitting on this one." Karl ran a hand over his hair and lowered his voice. "Word's out a witness to the H and R remembered a partial Arizona plate number and a half-assed vehicle description. Traffic investigations ran the partial through Motor Vehicle and came up with fifteen possibilities in southern Arizona. Sparks questioned every one of the possibilities and each one denied being on Speedway Boulevard that day."

Mack turned in his seat and faced his old squad mate. He knew Karl had more information, but that the detective was reluctant to share something this explosive, even to an ex-cop. "An Arizona plate? Come on, Karl," he said. "Whose plate? I know you well enough to be sure you have an idea." Mack reached over and touched his friend's shoulder. "I won't give up my source. Tell me."

"Okay, I'll tell you what I heard..." the detective hesitated. "But if you use this they'll know where you got the name and nail my hide to the wall. You've got to promise me you'll find other independent confirmation before you act on this."

"Karl, I promise you no one will put it together."

"Okay. The witness was pretty sure the car was a dark sedan. That matched three of the fifteen hits. The chief saw the names and put a lid on the investigation."

"Why? Do you know the three names?"

"I damn sure know one of them." Karl smiled at Mack. "I heard Sparks laughed at you when you made Bruno Malatesta as a suspect. He laughed because he already had *three* prime suspects and Bruno wasn't one of them."

"Stop the bullshit, Karl! Who is it?"

"One of the three names was Ace Collins of the *Arizona Register*."

CHAPTER TWELVE

THE HERO

Ace Collins closed his eyes as shuddering relief washed his raw nerves.

The pressure of events tormented him, made him need alcohol more often. Oh God, he groaned, when would the troubles stop? The problems had begun long ago when they'd learned his secret. Then the gambling, drinking, the debts to Don Bruno, that damned accident, and now the death of a foolish reporter. If just one piece of the awful structure came loose the avalanche would crush him. Last month had been the worst of his life; he needed liquor more than ever, but was determined to keep control. He wanted another drink, but restrained himself as he saw someone coming toward his office door. That damn Faber woman. He waved her in before she could knock. "Yes, what do you want?" he snarled.

Grace Faber flinched from his gruff voice, but she was determined. Over the past weeks her whole value system had been called into question. She had begun to doubt the justice system and, much worse, she was beginning to doubt the integrity of the *Arizona Register*. She'd planned this carefully and wanted to give Mister Collins the chance to prove himself before she would believe the worst. She swallowed her fear and met his fierce glare. "Mister Collins, I want your permission to complete Clyde Ralston's investigation into possible Mafia influence in the dog tracks, the Emprise Company and the promotion of the new sports arena."

Ace Collins was stunned. He had squelched this dangerous story twice. What did she know? He held his anger in check and probed for information. "Do you have any new facts or evidence," he asked. "I told the unfortunate Mister Ralston twice that the *Register* would *not* run allegations claiming prominent people and successful local companies were committing crimes without concrete, corroborating evidence. We are not some cheap scandal rag."

"I have nothing new, but Clyde said you *were* going to run his story," Grace objected. "He said his story would be running that next Sunday. That was the last thing he said to me the night he was killed." Tears filled her eyes at the mention of his last words. She removed her glasses to wipe her eyes and cursed her weakness.

The editor relaxed and savored her tears. They dampened his rage. He wished again for sobs and soft flesh and decided to be gentle until he fully crushed the revolt. "I know these past weeks have been difficult for you and I *am* taking that into consideration." He raised his hand and smiled when she involuntarily stepped back. "But I must warn you *not* to defy me. I have explained this before; Mister Ralston was mistaken. I *never* promised to run his story on that Sunday. You know yourself, Clyde's little project was never discussed at our staff meeting that Friday. He was a hard-working reporter, but a little reckless and overconfident. I can assure you there was never a firm decision to print his unsubstantiated allegations."

For a moment Grace was lost. Her confidence bled away. She wanted to flee from cruel reality, but realized running would be the worst thing she could do. She gritted her teeth and resolved to be strong for Clyde Ralston and for her dear mother. But what could she do? Why would the editor want to kill this particular inquiry, this particular story? She remembered what Louis Carfagno had said about gambling and drinking in the Broken Arrow skybox at the dog track. Louis had said the editor had often lost heavily. There had to be a connection! She could avenge her friend by exposing this tyrannical fraud, but to expose him she needed information. Grace reached across the desk and gripped the editor's hand. She did it instinctively - males never seemed to resent a woman's touch. "Mister Collins, I never meant to defy you." Her glasses fell to the carpet and she allowed tears to spill again. "I am honored to be working under you and I respect your decisions." She squeezed his hand. "Maybe Clyde *was* too impetuous and that's why he died."

In one flattering gesture she hoped to distract and bemuse him.

"Yes, well remember that in the future," he muttered. The editor was caught by surprise. Her hand was so soft, so moist. He wanted to bend the thin bones in his fist, but caught himself and reveled in her submission. The little twit had attempted to rebel and learned her lesson. There were a few sweet moments left, he thought, and decided to fire her as soon as the opportunity presented itself. Grace was in luck. Perhaps he wouldn't have been fooled if the heat wasn't coursing through his veins and his mind wasn't reeling from the last fateful month. For the time being, at least while she touched him, his rage and suspicion had receded.

"Please forgive me Mister Collins," she smiled weakly and released his hand. "I will never cause you any more problems." Grace didn't wait for an answer, but scooped up her glasses from the carpet and almost ran from his office.

Ace watched her trim legs scissor across the newsroom. A worm of suspicion wiggled. Should he make another phone call? Should he warn them of another problem? No. She had no new information and another incident would only call more attention to the *Register*. He leaned back and thought about a drink.

• • •

The Sports Arena had to be the connection. Why else would an editor be so careful about a potentially hot story? Grace knew she had to find a link between Ace Collins' business affairs and the racetrack or sports arena. Gambling debts and drinking weren't enough to explain his dereliction of duty. She decided to try the reference library, the personnel files and then the newspaper morgue.

She was surprised to discover his first name was really Ace - Ace McAllister Collins. *Who's Who* of Arizona listed him, but the national *Who's Who* did not. The newspaper morgue had articles mentioning he was a graduate of Princeton, an Air Force veteran of Viet Nam and had been editor of the *Arizona Register* for twelve years. His bio said Ace Collins was on the board of First Valley Bank and the Santa Cruz River Project. It mentioned he'd headed the local cancer drive for the last three years, was an active member of the Air Force Fighter Pilots Association and had twice been president of the Tucson Rotary club. Grace was mildly disappointed. Pretty average for a big-time editor, she thought, but what about the bank and the Utility Company? Could either of them profit from a sports arena?

Grace ran a check of known contributors to the sports arena bond election campaign and found three names of bank directors. Her heart beat a little faster until she realized the amounts of money were under $250.00, hardly enough to explain a cover-up of criminal activity. Discouragement set in when she realized the futility of her quest. If there was something to hide, the secret would surely be well hidden. She went back to her desk and tried to appear busy while her mind tested and rejected ideas. She noticed two pink message slips on her desk, both from Mack, wanting her to call home immediately. She shook her head in exasperation. There was too much to do, she couldn't be worrying about *him*.

But a smile accidently slipped onto her face as she thought of his hands on her body. Then she remembered the killings and his too casual acceptance of them. The warm thoughts disappeared in gray confusion and a new thought occurred. Why hadn't she read anything about the killings when she scanned the paper that morning? She went to a neighboring desk, borrowed a paper and searched the front page and the whole local section. Nothing. Maybe the bodies hadn't been found yet. She thought of buzzards and small, hungry animals and began to put the paper back when she noticed an item about local hotels preparing for the influx of veterans and their families that next weekend. A closer read told her the Air Force Fighter Pilots Association was having their yearly convention at the El Conquistador Hotel. She read the article more closely. Two speakers were being featured at the convention, Senator John McGraw and Ace Collins. The reporter said the *Register* editor made a point to speak at each of the yearly conventions. Farther down, the article remarked that ex-Senator Lillienthal, *a retired Air Force Major General*, was not attending due to schedule conflicts. The writer of the article noted the ex-Senator had *never* attended any of the recent Air Force Fighter Pilots conventions even though he had been a pilot himself. The piece attempted a light ending by speculating on the ex-Senator's desire to forget unpleasant memories of war. From the tone, Grace guessed the reporter probably wouldn't bother covering the dinner.

Thoughts of Clyde swam by. *If it ain't in the paper it ain't news*, he'd say.

Something was wrong. Grace's reporter instincts crackled like glass under her shoes. She wondered why the obvious question had never been asked. Could there be bad blood between the ex-pilots? Why? And what possible connection could this have to racetracks, sports arenas and the killing of a reporter? Since she'd run out of ideas, she called the ex-Senator's home in the Catalina foothills, introduced herself to a secretary and said she would like to arrange an interview.

After a delay of about two minutes Harris Lillienthal himself was on the line. "Yes? This is Harris Lillienthal," he said.

She'd never actually met him, but had grown up listening to his gruff voice on the news and felt like a fan meeting a celebrity. "Hello, Senator. This is Grace Faber, a reporter with the *Register*. I wondered if I could set up an appointment with you tomorrow or the next day."

"That would be just fine, Mrs. Faber," the low-pitched voice sounded friendly, but a little impatient. "But why don't we do the interview by phone."

Grace hesitated, she knew the difficulties of extracting information over the phone, and how many subjects simply said no and hung up, but she sensed the Senator's impatience and she wanted to get a quick answer. Perhaps she could put this loose end to rest and continue her paper-search into Ace Collins' background. She decided to get the question over with. "That's a good idea, Senator. I wanted to know why you're not attending the Air Force Pilots convention next weekend?"

"As I told another reporter from your newspaper last week, I have a previous engagement." He cleared his throat impatiently. "Why this interest in my affairs?"

Here goes, she thought. "Senator Lillienthal, I understand you are a retired Air Force General and have *never* attended these yearly conventions, even though they're often held here in Tucson." He began to interrupt, but she rushed on, "I wondered if there was a problem between you and my editor, Mister Collins?"

"What?" The rough voice took on an angry rasp. "What possible business could that be of...? Does Ace know you're calling me?"

"No, sir, he does not. I am calling without his knowledge. This is a matter of deepest importance about... Senator?" Grace realized the Senator had hung up on her. She tapped a fingernail on the desk and held the dead phone against her shoulder. There obviously *was* a problem between the Senator and the editor, but she wondered how it could have anything to do with racetracks. Maybe the Senator knew of the editor's gambling and drinking. Hmmm. A mechanical voice in her ear reminded her to hang up the phone. She wondered if the two men had served together. What were their units in Viet Nam? Normally a spat between two old veterans wasn't something she would have taken seriously, but for some reason her intuition told her *this* was more than just a disagreement. And this spat involved two people who, in one way or another, had been connected to Clyde Ralston's last story. What unit was Ace Collins in? How could she find out without alerting him?

She remembered the Air Force photos on the editor's wall. Some had labels.

The reporter glanced across the large room to her editor's office. He wasn't there. She checked her watch, three thirty, too early for him to leave. He was probably in the bathroom. Not much time, but she had to try. Grace stood, grabbed a handful of papers and walked quickly toward the editor's glass door. She pretended to be reading as she walked through the main newsroom.

No one paid any attention to her.

She paused at his door, knocked once and glanced at the hallway to the bathroom. Clear. Grace opened his door and moved quickly to the nearest wall. One photo showed the editor in his dress uniform splashed with colorful ribbons.

No label. She moved to the next - nothing but a picture of a jet fighter and a label that read *Phantom, Con Thien*. No help. She looked through the glass door. No one appeared to be looking at her. Next photo, no label, and the next, but over in the corner at the end of the couch was a smiling Ace Collins in blue coveralls with a helmet under his arm. She moved closer and squinted at the 8 x 10 photograph.

Yes! There was a long white label at the bottom-center of the picture frame. Numbers and names, did she have time? She jerked her eyes away from the picture and looked over her shoulder out the glass door...and saw him! He was halfway across the newsroom already! Too late to escape. She leaned close to the picture. *145th Fighter Wing, Con Thien, Viet Nam* burned itself into her memory. She quickly sat on the couch and lowered her gaze to the muddle of papers in her hand.

"What are you doing in my office?" He was surprised and cold, but casual.

Grace decided he didn't suspect anything. First thing in her mind was the convention. "I wondered if you would like an editorial this weekend on the Fighter Pilots convention?" she asked.

He turned and fixed her with concentrated attention. "You wondered," he mocked. A sneer dragged at one corner of his mouth, but he seemed to reconsider the thought and the woman on the couch. His eyes dropped to her stockinged knees tilting up from the deep couch, skirt pulled high under the papers on her lap. "Why would you wonder such a thing?" he asked. "For a newspaper to crow about its editor would be unseemly, don't you think?" Suspicion stirred, but demons drummed in his veins and churned the empty pit. This pitiful wanton craved his approval - his mercy. He wanted to beat tears from the pale face and open those thin knees, but those pleasures would never be his again. He turned away in renewed despair and dismissed the distraction. The time was near for his afternoon relief.

"Yes sir, sorry to have bothered you." she said and stood to leave.

Grace fled to her desk and wrote down the numbers and the words, *145, Con Thien*. She waited for her heart to slow and absently fingered the pink message slips. Almost time to go home. Davis Monthan Air Force Base was right here in Tucson. The search should be easy, but she couldn't afford another misstep. Maybe Mack would know the best way to trace an Air Force unit roster.

• • •

He forced himself to wait for night. The bundle was ready - three red sticks tied with baling wire and attached to a radio receiver wired to a detonator - enough to break a truck in half or fill a room with charred meat. Nothing would interrupt this time. Every day since his last attempt Vinnie had spent long, cramped hours in parking lots around the investigator's studio. Sometimes, he'd waited all day and half the night looking for the white pickup or a light in the window.

Finally his patience had paid off.

After two weeks the tall woman-stealer had driven into the parking lot next to his studio, spent half an hour and emerged with an armful of clothing and a suitcase. After the investigator loaded the truck, he carefully locked the studio door. Apparently he was moving. Vinnie stroked his deadly bundle and followed the white pickup home. The time had come, but he would prepare and wait until night.

• • •

She bunched her fists in her auburn hair and growled a soft scream. "He's a suspect? God, Mack, I'm so angry I could rip my hair out. You mean my editor could have run my mother down on the street, driven off and then sat in his office all those weeks, pretending to be a newsman? How could any man be so evil?"

Mack moved closer on the couch and put his arm around her shoulders. "I don't know, but remember we can't use this information right away. Karl Jenkins could get fired and nobody at the police station would back us up anyhow. A single witness-partial-plate hit of three names on some DMV list is not enough proof to arrest anybody. Somehow we have to find independent proof that Ace Collins was the hit and run driver before we can act." He smiled at her and tried to change her mood. "And don't rip your hair out, it's one of your best features."

Grace stabbed him with an angry glance that soon clouded with speculation. Hard anger eased to gentler thoughts as she realized the futility of unfocused anger and, at the same time, appreciated having the big, serious man with her, caring for her through the most awful crisis she could ever have imagined. "Okay. This is very difficult, but I understand the need for discretion," she said and snuggled closer, holding his upper arm and taking comfort in the thick muscle filling her hands. She wasn't sure how she felt about the battered investigator, but knew she needed him. She had one last question. "Now what do we do?"

Mack was grateful to be on familiar ground. "Now that we have a clear suspect the job's a little easier. I simply go back to the scene of the accident and do the interviews all over again." He held up his palm. "Only this time I'll show all those potential witnesses a picture of Ace Collins."

"Yes, but." Grace's comment was interrupted by a shout from the back yard.

"Hey!" Louis called. "I need some help here with these hungry animals." His gravelly voice broke into laughter.

The day had faded to cool twilight, sun down behind the mountains, but enough light to see eight large dogs mobbing Louis Carfagno as he tried to pour food from a forty-pound bag into three bowls. Three dogs were on their hind legs, paws on his curved back and bent shoulders, nudging and licking his face. The others were pushing and shoving to get near a bowl before their mates. Louis was laughing and staggering under the weight of the bag and the dogs. Dog food began spilling on the grass, but the happy dogs ignored the spilled morsels, more intent on process than results. Louis suddenly sat down hard in the middle of the pack of dogs and they climbed on his lap, knocked off his knit cap and nuzzled his gnarled face and grizzled hair in wild, joyous roughhouse. Mack noticed greyhounds weren't like most dogs. There wasn't a sound from any of them and they didn't snarl at each other or show any overt aggression other than bad manners.

Mack ran to help. As soon as he touched the bag his face was covered in gratitude and dog saliva. He recognized his eager attacker, the reddish brindle with one lop-ear, Serengeti Fancy. He rumpled her crooked ear. She grinned and slurped his nose again. "Didn't you feed them once this morning?" he asked the laughing trainer.

"Yep," Louis gasped and shoved a dog from his lap. "They ain't hungry, they're just happy to be out of them damn cages for once in their lives." He found his cap, put it on and looked up with an exhausted smile. "Hey, you don't think we could get about five more bowls, do ya?"

They sat on the back steps as the day coiled to night and watched the animals play musical bowls. As soon as one was situated in front of a full bowl he would spot another full bowl and shove toward that. Eight dogs shoved and crowded each other in complete silence. No snarling and very little eating was done.

"They don't need a lot of food, these greyhounds, you feed 'em once a day and water 'em good and they're happy." The old man spoke like a proud father.

"They're such nice dogs," Grace said. "So gentle, and yet they look fierce."

"Yep," Louis said. "Gentlest dogs in the world. Hunting dogs and fierce in the wild, but these 'uns been raised by humans from pups, handled all the time and always around other dogs." He hesitated a moment. "And there's another reason: Tracks don't like dogs that fight, so that's pretty well bred out of 'em or they don't live long."

Mack asked a question that had nagged at him since Clyde first told him about the dead greyhounds in the desert. "Louis, since these are such nice dogs, why don't the breeders and track owners put them out to stud or give their old animals to farms and ranches or to good families that want good dogs?"

The old man hoisted his bent body around and met Mack's eye in the fading light. "Why hell, son, don't you know? They might have pups. These dogs are the pick of *all* the litters. These 'uns are racers, moneymakers, and their pups would make money too, if'n they were allowed to have 'em. Only certain ones are bred and the breeders are damn jealous of their breeding stock." He tugged his cap and shook his head. "Hell, mosta them breeders'd rather shoot the good racing dogs than pay to neuter 'em or lose money to one of their pups three years from now."

"Louis, that's awful," Grace said. "How many of these dogs are killed every year, do you think?"

"Waal lemme see, about a thousand pups get born every year and only a few hundred of them ever race. Only about a hundred win big money."

"You mean they're killing hundreds of greyhounds every year just to prevent them from having pups and to guarantee exclusive racers to these dog tracks?"

"That's about the size of it miss," the old man said.

The evening was nearly full dark when Mack felt a wet muzzle under his hand. It was Great Alliance. The big dog wanted some attention. Mack petted and stroked his fine soft fur and repeated stupid questions the way people do. "You're a good boy aren't you? Come on, boy, don't you want to sit? Come on, *sit*!" he urged.

"You can forget that," Louis said. "Greyhounds ain't built to sit. They either lie down or stand. Ain't no in between." He seemed to enjoy giving lessons about his favorite subject. "They was bred in Egypt by kings to run down lions in the desert. Big silent runners, they was, and two of 'em could pull down a lion. But sit? No siree. 'Nother thing, did you know these dogs won't climb stairs? They never learn in them kennels. You gotta teach 'em step by step if'n you want a house dog."

"That's amazing," Grace said. "Speaking of house dogs, have you decided what you're going to do with them, now that you've saved their lives?"

"Got me some friends in North Carolina and Florida who'd just love to get their hands on some good ol' dogs like these. They'll treat 'em real nice and let 'em live out their lives in peace..." he chuckled at his thoughts. "They'll welcome a few litters from the bitches too, no mistake. I got some money saved up. Think I'll get me an old van and fill it with blankets. Then me and the hounds'll take us a trip east in a day or so."

Mack felt Great Alliance move from under his hand and watched the tall shape disappear into the shadows of the back yard. He could see vague movement and hear soft grunts and rustlings as the eight dogs settled down for the night. "Should we turn on the back light," he asked.

"Naw, they're used to sleepin' in the dark and exercisin' in the light."

"They need much exercise?" Grace asked.

"Greyhounds are sprint dogs," the old trainer explained. "They can get a full workout in a thirty-foot dog run or even a small yard like this 'un. Mack could hear the grin in his words. "You folks just wait 'til they get used to this place. They'll be runnin' back and forth and bounding around like a herd o' young deer."

"Yes, but you're taking them away soon," Grace said a little wistfully.

"Got to, ma'am." Louis nodded agreement. "There ain't nothin' in Arizona for us no more. Me and the dogs gonna start a new life somewhere we's appreciated."

"That's kind of the way I feel," Grace muttered.

The three sat in silence. The big city hissed and groaned around their dark, quiet envelope of privacy. Nearby, a train blared deep warnings and clattered its loose path; a siren in the distance answered another bleak tragedy and a lonely plane flew far ahead of its roar in the star-blasted darkness miles above. There were houses full of people fifty feet away and streams of cars roared from traffic lights beyond the next roof. A university, an airport, an Air Force Base and the twenty-sixth largest city in the United States splashed light and flung people in busy swirls, but for a few brief moments, three humans and eight dogs breathed the cool night, listened to the struggle and savored their small, fragile island of peace.

Grace stood and rested her hand on Mack's shoulder. "Mister Carfagno, I insist you sleep in my spare bedroom tonight," she said to the old trainer. "I will not be able to sleep, thinking of you on a blanket in my garage."

Louis Carfagno was used to sleeping on a single-spring iron bunk behind the kennels with a clean shirt and boots for a pillow. He considered crisp sheets and a soft mattress and grinned. The half-acre yard was fenced with five-foot chain-link and the gates were all latched shut. No dogs would stray tonight. "Well that's real nice." he said. "Guess these dogs'll be okay out here in this nice yard of yours."

• • •

Her slender body bloomed pearly white in the star-glow. He sat on the bed and kissed her flat stomach.

She bunched her fists in his hair. "Oh, Mack, is this right? Should we?"

He tongued her navel. His hands cupped firm globes of buttocks, fingers exploring their hot crevice. His mouth marked crisp hair and softness, moved up to warm gardenia, supple weight and nipples clenched like raisins.

She hissed at the pull of his teeth and tugged him over on her bed.

No time to explore or wait for smooth sweetness. The need was immediate. All the danger, grief and fear demanded hot solace. Two souls empty of the past and unsure of the future plunged hungry mouths together, seeking and raging to burn brighter than life. "Oh, God! Now!" Storms roared through their shuddering bodies, faster and faster, scalding their minds and leaving them gasping.

Mack hadn't felt such overwhelming intensity since the shock of his first bold fumbles in adolescence. He wondered if he was in love, tried to speak his thoughts and failed. The breakdown had happened before. At times like these, hot words filled his ravenous mouth to celebrate, but between lips and voice, something always fled in the whisper of a winged thought. Mack's words would fail his mind, stumble and fall to dull platitudes and leave him mourning the loss. This had happened often through the years and he knew the loss was something he lacked, something of love. "My God, Grace, I've never. That was wonderful."

She answered him with a kiss and pulled his awkward mouth to her breast. As he began to kiss and caress her again she thought of her poor mother and tears squeezed from her tightly closed eyes. When her mind stopped whirling and her breathing calmed, she remembered her fruitless quest from earlier in the day. She recalled the inquiry that had been banished from her mind by Mack's horrible news of the new hit and run suspect. *Ace Collins. That awful man!* Maybe their combined investigations would help expose him for the beast he was. One thing for sure, her job as a reporter at the *Register* was over. She would *never* work in the same building with him again. "Mack, I found out something today also," she said and gently turned his face from her body. "Something may have happened between Mister Collins and Senator Harris Lillienthal. My impression might be wrong, but their relationship seems odd." Grace explained her Air Force idea, the photographs on the office wall and the frustrating phone call to ex-Senator Lillienthal.

"That's the way Lillienthal asked you the question, 'Does Ace know?', just like that?" Mack asked.

"Yes. Isn't that a strange question to ask a reporter?"

"Lillienthal's question shows he calls him, Ace, and that he evidently doesn't think your editor would approve of the question you asked him."

"Right. I wonder why not?"

"Who knows? Tomorrow we'll do some telephone work. Maybe working together we'll be able to find out more about Ace Collins and the 145th Fighter Wing in Con Thien, Viet Nam," Mack said. He lowered his head, pulled her close and resumed his leisurely exploration of her small, slim body.

She felt him harden against her thigh. Thought changed to need.

• • •

The gate opened with a thin squeal. Stubby, hairless fingers trembled with excitement as they lifted a bundle of dynamite and a half-full Clorox bottle that smelled of jazzed-up fuel oil. Vinnie had made the mixture himself to liven up the explosion, half high-octane gasoline-additive and half 30-weight motor oil. He'd found both ingredients in the gatehouse garage. The Clorox bottle would sit under the red sticks; he knew the high temperature of exploding dynamite would vaporize the fuel mixture and create a billowing cloud of fire. Fire was his scourge, but had always been his weapon of choice. And there would be no more mistakes like the last. No hospital for the woman-stealer; he would only have a small, shapeless body bag filled with red jelly, charred bones and teeth, taken straight to the morgue.

He nudged the gate closed and crawled up the driveway to the white pickup.

Serengeti Fancy's ears jerked up at the gate-squeal. She glanced at Great Alliance curled in a brown circle next to her. He slept on, lips quivering and one leg twitching to a dream-race. He was older and more experienced in the noisy world of men. She was still young and curious. This was a new noise to go along with all the other wonderful new things. She had almost decided to ignore the new sound when a stinging odor made her nose flinch. The smell was like the big shiny things over on the hard surface, but more intense. Then she smelled his pungent body odor. The red brindle shifted her head higher and sniffed for more of the interesting smells.

Vinnie had spent the late afternoon hours watching from his parked car down the street from the house. The redhead had come home an hour before sunset and parked her Swedish car on the street in front of the house. The investigator's white pickup had been parked in the gated driveway, but outside the opened door of the garage. As he waited for dark he'd wondered why they hadn't pulled the pickup into the garage and moved the woman's new Saab into the driveway. Probably too lazy, he thought and smiled because the truck-placement just made his final job that much easier - less distance for him to crawl. Just the two of them, he'd thought, probably drinking and getting themselves ready to screw. By watching the lights he'd guessed where the bedroom was and had waited for the light to go on and then off, signaling the woman and the woman-stealer had gone to bed. He considered blowing them up in bed, but decided the truck was more of a sure thing.

Vinnie had waited another hour before gathering up his deadly bundle.

The brindle greyhound blended almost perfectly with the dark, shadowy back yard. She rose quietly and walked toward the human shape crawling up the driveway. When she finally got close enough to try and lick the new human's face he had disappeared underneath the truck. Serengeti Fancy sniffed the strong-smelling human's shoes and settled down on her belly to wait.

A little fuel mixture had spilled as he slid under the truck. His fingers were slippery as he fumbled baling wire around the dynamite and the front axle. He checked the small, square radio receiver and the slender detonator. Everything felt right. Vinnie set the Clorox bottle where it would be hidden next to the left front tire and close under the dynamite. The job was nearly done; now for the final piece of his device. He wasn't sure of the battery-strength any more, so he placed the black remote-control box with the knobbed lever under the backside of the left front tire. This sort of scheme appealed to Vinnie's sense of humor. Like his fiery light bulbs, the target would send the kill signal. The burn-scarred man giggled and drooled a little on the oily asphalt. Next morning, when the truck began to roll backwards down the driveway, the tire would crush the box, close the circuit and send the signal eight inches to the waiting dynamite. Vinnie would enjoy the fireball from his car down the street. He controlled his giggles, pushed himself out from under the pickup truck and began to crawl back down the driveway.

The curious greyhound stood and padded softly to catch up with the creeping man. She moved up quietly beside him, leaned over the sweat-smelling head and gave the bald scalp a short, introductory lick.

Vinnie Romano didn't know about the greyhounds.

He thought he was alone in the yard - alone with death-visions and the wonderfully clever bundle of destruction. He felt air move and the hot touch of a phantom. Heat splashed his sensitive skin and a large shape blocked the night at the corner of his eye. He turned to a leering wolf-mouth full of long, bright teeth. Vinnie Romano's heart leaped. Seared lungs expelled their air. One arm flung itself to sacrifice while his other limbs pushed him away from the horrible apparition.

The out flung arm struck the curious dog in the neck.

Serengeti Fancy tumbled backwards, yelping alarm and landed near the sleeping dogs. They bounded up and yammered response to the shocked, frightened female. Soon all the normally quiet greyhounds in the dark yard were yelping and baying in a nervous chorus.

All except one; one greyhound rose very slowly to a low crouch.

Vinnie realized the apparition was just a frightened dog and lost most of his fear. He scrambled down the driveway to get away from the noisy dogs before the people came out. He knew, if no one actually *saw* him, the bomb could still go undiscovered. His clever plan would *still* work if he could get away unseen.

Great Alliance growled deep in his chest like distant thunder and the hard-muscled body shook with unaccustomed fury.

This odd-smelling stranger had disturbed his sleep, invaded his territory and frightened his kennel-mates. Rage filled docile sinews, filled the racer's heart with a new urge to pull down and tear. All the years of training and restraint fell away like loose skin. The grizzled jaw quivered. Black lips wrinkled back from long, curved fangs. In the dark yard with the baying pack, the frightened female and the dirty-smelling human, Great Alliance, the Champion, came unsheathed from tame reality to heed a dim urge from hunter ancestors. Rumble became gritted snarl. The great hound sprang forward. Muscles bunched and flexed and the injured leg was forgotten. He shifted and disappeared to a long shadow cutting the night like a wild dream.

The attacking greyhound hardly disturbed the air.

Vinnie reached the gate and felt for the latch. A breath of noise at his back made him pause - not a bark, or a clatter of humans, but the breath of a hard wind. Vinnie's hand had lifted the latch when the night took darker form and seventy-five pounds of canine fury landed on his bent back. Hot, quick fangs slashed his head and tried to find the artery in the slippery scars at the side of his thick neck. He screamed, tore at the savage mouth with oily fingers and fell through the small opening in the unlatched gate.

The dog dropped away, but leapt again and tore a gash in the back of the hairless head. Rip! Tear! Taste the scalding blood! Again! The third time he lunged, Great Alliance landed against the gate, slamming it shut behind his quarry. His jaws clacked together just behind the nape of the victim's neck. Missed again. The prey shrieked like a rabbit and fell forward, getting away. Great Alliance heard the man's running feet scrape and stumble down the dark street.

The savaging of Vinnie Romano had only taken seconds. He ran down the street expecting a scrape of claws, the husk of hot breath and fangs buried deep in his neck, but nothing followed. He slowed and tottered to a walk. Far enough away and free of pursuit, Vinnie began to think again, to look for his car. Blood-slippery fingers explored the gash in his scalp. He tried to ignore the slow ache, but understood pain was a small price for revenge. And he had succeeded.

They won't find the dynamite. The madonna stealer will die. Ah, madonna!

His mind slid crazily from hatred to love. Chickie's bedroom waited. There were only a few hours until dawn. Vinnie couldn't bear to miss his time with her in the gatehouse. Part of her was still up there. Except for the jumble of countless police inspections, her rooms were the way she'd left them. His mouth twisted as he viewed the pleasing mental images: her pillow still hollowed, high-heeled shoes forgotten near the closet, lipstick-smeared tissues on the dresser, blond hair in her brushes and rows of clothing that gusted her scent. He'd usually allowed himself the memory-haunted refuge only in the center of the night when it was too late for the police to conduct another search. During the days he had daydreamed revenge in his small cave and hunted for the investigator. Now, finally, he had succeeded.

Great Alliance whined disappointment through red smeared teeth. The tall greyhound didn't realize he could have easily jumped the five-foot fence. He was a champion runner, but he had never jumped a fence.

Suddenly the small yard, front and back, bloomed light. Darkness disappeared, doors clattered open. Mack appeared at the front. Louis Carfagno and Grace stumbled out the back into the midst of the yammering dogs.

"What happened, what the hell's all the racket?" Mack yelled as he walked to the gate and looked down the street. Nothing moved in the darkness beyond the rim of light. He touched Great Alliance's head with his left hand while holding the 45 down at his side. "What is it, boy?" Mack hoped the disturbance was Vinnie. He stood very still, trying to hear above the dog-noise. He sniffed the air. The high, sweet smell of fuel oil twisted in the night, veiling other smells, but Mack sensed a deeper odor under the tang of fuel. A stink hung in the air - like charred beans at the bottom of an iron pot - could it possibly be a person's smell?

He knelt level with Great Alliance's long snout and rumpled an ear. "Did you scare him away?" Mack asked. His eyes were drawn to a sparkle on the asphalt. Smears on the driveway reflected light. Oil? Kneeling next to the dog, he barely discerned oily handprints tracking under his pickup. He followed the marks, bent and saw the faint, pale shape of a Clorox bottle under the truck beside his front tire.

For a moment his mind accepted the homely familiarity. But why would trash have blown under his truck? *The smell of gas! The plastic bottle was upright! Vinnie!* His mind flared with sudden dread. *A bomb accelerator!* He straightened up. Fear dried his mouth and numbed his fingers as he waited for the white flash and death. Grace and Louis were still in the back yard, thirty feet away, soothing the dogs. "Listen to me, you two!" he called out in a nearly calm voice. "I think I found a bomb. Lie down on the ground and stay there until I say it's okay."

"What do you mean?" Grace asked. "Did you say, 'a *bomb*'?"

"Yes!" Mack hissed through fear and anger. "Vinnie was here. I think he planted a car bomb. Now lie down!"

Very cautiously he set the 45 in the truck bed, knelt beside the left front tire and reached under. Shadows from the porch light were deep black under the truck. His fingers gently dabbled through grease and over rough metal until they found paper-like tubes and loose, quivering wire. He froze when the wire trembled.

Where was the detonator? Was the blasting cap time-fused, straight electric, or wired to a radio-controlled circuit? Would the thing blow up in his face?

Then he saw the shiny black metal wedged under the curve of his tire, and the knobbed lever. The metal box was the type hobbyists use for radio-guided model cars and airplanes. Now Mack knew how Vinnie had set his trap and how he'd most likely blown up Clyde. "Grace!" he husked a stage whisper toward the back yard, "I need a flashlight." He saw her move toward him. "Wait! Go back. I'll meet you in the yard." Mack didn't touch the black box, couldn't be sure. He eased away from the truck very slowly and felt a thick, muscular haunch at his back. The big, male greyhound was standing with him, peering off into the night. Mack put his mouth close to the dog's long head, "Thank you, Big Al. You saved my life."

Great Alliance followed him to the back yard.

Grace came out and handed him a yellow plastic cylinder that looked like a child's toy. She held his arm as he began to turn away. "If you've found a bomb we should call the bomb squad, Mack, and let them disarm it." She blinked up at him, her face full of concern. "I don't want anything to happen to you."

Mack leaned and kissed her mouth, tasting sour sleep and a hint of perfume. "Me neither," he said. "But I can't call the cops. We've got a pack of greyhounds from a homicide scene and an AWOL racetrack employee hiding in the back yard. They'll charge me with something and hold me for questioning." He leaned close and allowed anger to roughen his voice. "Grace, listen. This bastard won't stop until he kills me and anyone else who happens to be nearby. I need some time to end this dangerous game before that maniac gets a chance to try again. Besides, I think I can handle the bomb myself. The bomb trigger looks like a remote-control device and Vinnie left the control box behind. Don't worry, I was a demolitions instructor in the Marines." He waved the flashlight and turned toward the truck.

"Mack!" she called.

He stopped and turned impatiently. "What do you want, Grace."

"How many years ago were you in the Marines?"

Mack smiled, shrugged and asked Louis to bring all the dogs inside while he disarmed the bomb. He'd seen the deep concern in her gray eyes and for a brief moment he felt almost lighthearted about handling detonators and dynamite.

Disarming bombs allows a human being to enter the rare world of the surreally insane, a world measured in instants of irretrievable time and spirals of fear where the mind quietly instructs the body to commit an act of suicidal madness. The trick is to cut a wire or pull a connector and then wait quietly for calm life or blind chaos. He had no choice. The bundle of dynamite was next to Grace's house and had to be disarmed. He'd disarmed explosives before as a Marine and a mercenary. Handling explosives was the highest, truest terror Mack had ever known. Mack hated the fear. He knew if he let the weakness take him away he would never be the same and always had to force himself to dabble in the insanity because, in the end, he had always been more anxious about the fear than the bomb.

He walked softly around his truck, turned on the flashlight and knelt down.

First things first, avoid stupid mistakes. Gripping the slippery metal in two fingers, he carefully removed the remote control box from under the curve of the tire and put the metal square into the truck bed next to the pistol so nothing could accidentally touch the knobbed lever. Then he scooted under the truck on his back to see the explosives. The flashlight peeked through grease and dirt to the cleanest thing under the truck, an obscene bundle of red tubes wired to the axle under the place where his legs would be when he was driving. Mack thought of Clyde and gritted his teeth.

The device was pretty crude: three sticks of dynamite and a small radio receiver connected by two wires to a thin silver tube - an electric blasting cap - buried half-way in the end of one dynamite stick. The idea was to send a radio signal over the right frequency and close a circuit in the receiver so that electricity darts down the wire to the shiny blasting-cap detonator which fires a hot charge of mercury fulminate into the waiting heart of the dynamite. Boom!

Simple and deadly, but was there a trick? Was the bomb booby-trapped?

Mack began to sweat, to envision the bright flash and unimaginable heat.

Don't think! But he couldn't stop his mind. He lay on his back and the ugly bundle of death hung just inches above his eyes. If the bomb went off he'd be a wet smear in a microsecond. And another thought stabbed. Could the dynamite explode if he didn't touch anything? He thought of remote control receivers. Those devices were usually pretty sensitive. Were there radio waves in Tucson...or other low frequency signals? Of course there were. The air in a big city night was full of low-frequency waves: cop cars, fire engines, ham operators, microwave ovens, garage-door openers, cellular phones. The air was laced with activity! And *any* stray radio signal could set the damn dynamite off. It was just a matter of time until the right sequence of electronic signals shot down the wires. Hurry! He tucked the flashlight under his chin, prayed he was right and yanked the blasting cap out of the dynamite.

Mack hissed and clenched his eyes against the terrible explosion

Nothing blew.

He disconnected wires from the radio receiver, unwrapped the baling wire from around the axle and removed the dynamite from under his truck.

Mack decided to keep the bomb. Thoughts of radio waves had given him the beginning of a plan. He slipped the electric blasting cap into the glove compartment of his pickup and put the dynamite, receiver and remote control box under the passenger-side front seat next to the bag of money. Better not have a fender-bender, he thought and shrugged. There were more immediate dangers.

Mack turned toward the lighted house, then paused and stood quietly a moment in the darkness to calm ricocheting nerves with reason. He obviously needed to find a jealous hit-man and stop him. But was that all this was?

Could this be a Mafia Don's answer to a broken contract? If so, how could Mack single-handedly take on the Mafia? And if the bomb ***was*** *Mafia business, why was Bruno Malatesta still using Vinnie Romano, the killer of his daughter?*

Nothing made sense.

But in the wash of relief his mind began to clear. Mack tried to visualize the minds capable of bombs and burnings and decided the situation boiled down to problem solving. Normal citizens solved problems in a social context with conversations, contracts, negotiations and finally lawsuits; they relied on rules, laws and courts. The mob relied on public ignorance and cold, unemotional force. The Mafia's way was neater, unless emotions and personal considerations got in the way and caused mistakes. Mack remembered the shot gunning of his truck in the desert. *That* was the routine Mafia way, a warning to demand respect. Mack sensed this particular car bomb was not Bruno Malatesta's idea. What clinched the matter in Mack's mind was when he remembered Bruno had negotiated a contract and Vinnie had twice tried to kill him before the contract was completed. Bruno was a businessman;

Vinnie was a jealous killer. When Mack publicly embraced Chickie on TV, the torch had apparently let jealousy interfere with his boss's business. Also, after Chickie was burned to death, Mack was positive Bruno Malatesta had cut all ties with his daughter's killer.... probably wanted the crazed pyro dead.

The investigator considered the alternatives and reached two conclusions: The bomb under his truck was *not* from a grief-stricken Don Bruno, and Bruno certainly wasn't hiding Vinnie. Vinnie was the immediate problem. Where was he? Simple elimination. Vinnie Romano was a stranger in the southwest. Where could a city-slicker hide in Tucson Arizona without Don Bruno's help?

Think! Imagine a psycho's mind.

The task was difficult. Mack was a man of action, of fists and guns who usually met an enemy face-to-face. He despised a monster who planted bombs and set fires and crept off to watch the agony. And this monster was careless: the explosion under Mack's truck could have easily killed Grace, but that obviously didn't matter to Vinnie Romano.

They watch the agony. They like to watch things. Vinnie used to watch Chickie sleep. He was obsessed. He would sit in her closet and... Ah!

CHAPTER THIRTEEN

A SMALL SECRET

"The Davis Monthan Air Force base information officer says he can find no listing of a 145th Fighter Wing or Squadron on active or reserve duty anywhere," Grace said. "He says the unit was probably disbanded after Viet Nam."

"Maybe we can find the 145th another way," Mack said.

"What do you mean?" Her voice was distracted, impatient.

He finished his third home-baked muffin and tossed down the last dregs of coffee before joining her on the couch next to the phone. "I haven't skip-traced any military personnel for years," he said. "I'm trying to remember where there is a military data-base that would have that kind of information and would be willing to share their records with civilians. Isn't there a central records depot in Atlanta?"

Grace was staring into space, listening to a dead line. Her muffin and coffee sat untouched on the coffee table. "I've already thought of that," she said, "but they would probably take forever. Listen, I found out who's organizing the Fighter Pilot's convention. Nice man. He said he'd have a friend call me with a list of the units represented at the convention. He said he'd be calling sometime today."

"Good beginning. You should be an investigator," Mack said with a wry grin.

"For your information, most good reporters *are* investigators," she asserted off-handedly before tapping another number on the phone key-pad.

Mack shook his head and thought of finding Vinnie Romano.

The afternoon was half over. They'd all slept late due to Romano's aborted bomb-attempt. Grace had called in sick to the newspaper and the morning had slipped by in streams of relieved conversation and worried speculation. Louis Carfagno wanted to get his fugitive greyhounds away from Tucson and Grace was determined to search her seemingly unscrupulous editor's background.

Mack smoldered with thoughts of the hunt.

Much earlier that morning he'd spent a thoughtful hour staring at the ceiling after everyone was back in bed. Calling the police had never really been an option. This was personal. Vinnie Romano had to pay for Chickie, Mitch and Clyde. Chickie had been much more than a friend for many years; Mitch Young had been a good citizen, unafraid to get involved in his community; Clyde Ralston had been a fine young reporter with a wonderful family and a bright future. Their deaths could not go unanswered. And Mack knew stopping Vinnie could not be the end of the matter. Repayment should include Don Bruno Malatesta who was responsible for bringing Vinnie to Arizona. He was, after all, the man who'd, directly or indirectly, ordered the deaths of Young and Ralston because they were hindering his money-laundering scheme. Vengeance should include the old man, but Don Bruno was protected by two retainers on an isolated ranch. How could Mack get close to the old man? He had ideas, but he couldn't do anything with Vinnie stalking him. He needed to stop the pyro before the sick bastard tried again and maybe killed him *and* Grace. "Grace," he said to the top of her head. "While you wait for your call, I'm going to check around and maybe talk with a few cops about Vinnie."

She looked up and smiled satisfied relief. "Good. I thought you would want to do your male *macho* thing and ride off to bloody vengeance. I couldn't have lived with that." She raised her face for a kiss. "Please come back before dark, I'm afraid that awful man will come back."

"No vengeance," he lied. "The police will handle Vinnie. I'm going to try and help them figure out where he's hiding."

She didn't like the sound of that. "But you *are* leaving it to the police, right?"

The phone rang. Mack left before he would have to do any more explaining. Grace had barely forgiven him for the shootings on the ranch even though he'd saved her life. The logic was puzzling. Mack wondered if the dogs being rescued had made the bloody mess in the desert more acceptable to her. But he had no time now to try and understand Grace Faber. He thought he knew where Vinnie was.

• • •

The big iron-strapped door to the gatehouse had been damaged. Deputies had not been gentle with the property of a Mafioso. The latch was sprung and the heavy wood was splintered as if from sledgehammer blows. Mack guessed the Sheriff's Department hadn't bothered with a warrant. The door opened to a cautious shove and swung closed with a thud. Mack held the 45 at the ready and stood very still in the darkness at the bottom of the stairs as his eyes become accustomed to the absence of daylight. Sharp, black angles in the stairwell were gradually powdered gray by sunshine from a window near the top. Upstairs a clock measured silence in brittle ticks and a tree-branch scored a roof-tile with a squeal. There were no dense sounds of people, but

Mack sensed a presence. The old gatehouse did not echo the lonely absence of an abandoned house. Was Vinnie here? The ghost of Chickie? Maybe the burn-scarred killer was upstairs listening and waiting. Mack thought of rushing up the stairs to confront him, but calmed himself.

Better to wait a moment and be sure.

Stale dust from old carpets mixed with the leached-lime smell of stone walls. A faint perfume sprinkled the heavier smells and reminded Mack of Chickie. He gripped the pistol, pointed it toward the top of the stairs and moved slowly up, hugging the wall, watching the light at the top for sudden shadows and listening for movement. He reached the top and waited a second. Caution wanted him to listen a while longer, but Mack had waited long enough. He took up slack in the trigger, crouched low and hurled himself, diving around the corner into her bedroom.

Unfamiliar shapes and shadows blurred. Mack rolled toward the bed and came up on one knee, arms extended, pistol rigid, eyes sighting down the barrel. The trigger was tight under his finger. Another ounce of pressure would do it! There! A body shape! No. Too high, too slender, it was a dress on a hanger. Mack's blood tingled with racing adrenalin. The closet door yawned. His eyes darted deep in the shadows, all senses wide to danger. Nothing. He was pumped, ready, but the room was empty. Vinnie wasn't here.

Mack felt foolish. He'd almost shot a dress hanging on the bathroom door. Reluctantly he stuck the 45 in his belt. Okay, he thought, Vinnie wasn't here now, but would he come here at night? If someone was living here part-time there had to be signs. First Mack checked the bathroom. Odd, the mirror had been broken. Vinnie? The tub was dry and faintly dusty, but the sink was clean and smooth. Mack realized a searching deputy washing his hands could have used the sink. The towels were neatly folded and dry. Bedroom next. Sheets were unmade and the pillow was still dented from her head on that night before he woke her to tell of the contract with her father. Finally, saving the most promising for last, he went to her closet.

Mack walked into the dim space among all her clothes, reached up and pulled the chain. Yellow light bathed the crowded space. He looked around at her rows and rows of clothes, smelled starch and soap and perfume. His eyes wandered a while and finally looked down at the closet rug. At his feet were four indentations in a square - the marks of the legs of her vanity stool. The dents were deep in the soft rug. He guessed the stool had been there only hours before.

Vinnie had been there recently, most likely early that morning. But where was he now? Probably in the desert. Mack considered the difficulties of searching the rugged foothills terrain. The area near the gatehouse was covered with cactus, waist-high scrub, thorny mesquite and criss-crossed with ravines and dry washes. There were probably animal burrows and small caves as well. He remembered the Sheriff's men had searched this area two or three times after the car-bombing of Clyde Ralston and had come up with nothing. Could he do any better?

Maybe he should just wait for the bastard. Or maybe....

He glanced up at the light bulb sticking down from the ceiling and pulled the chain to turn the light off. He unscrewed the bulb and stared at the warm glass a moment, thinking about Mitch Young and Chickie and how they had died under *their* light bulbs. He knew how Vinnie had killed them. Could he do such a thing? Mack decided giving the devil his due would be precisely appropriate.

First he needed the proper materials. Vinnie Romano had used gasoline in his nasty ambushes, but Mack would have to improvise quickly with what was at hand. In Chickie's dresser he found a large bottle of nail polish remover and read the label to make sure it contained acetone. Next he found a bottle of liquid soap, a small container of eye drops, complete with eyedropper and a tube of toothpaste with a big dollop of time-hardened paste sticking from the opening. He set these ingredients on the sink and took the light bulb down to the kitchen in the rear of the gatehouse. After checking carefully that Vinnie wasn't hidden in the garage or any of the other rooms, Mack turned on one burner of the gas stove and searched the kitchen drawers for a carving fork with a heavy handle. He needed one heavy enough so he could hold the handle while the fork-tines heated red hot.

First the smooth surface just blackened, but soon thin glass began to melt and pull back, bit by bit, like the lips of a tiny wound. After many re-heatings, but in less than a half hour, Mack had melted a small hole in the neck of the light bulb just above the metal screw-in part. He turned off the gas, replaced the fork in the drawer and took the glass bulb back upstairs. In the drinking glass he blended lots of acetone and a little liquid soap and eyedroppered them into the lightbulb until a third of the bulb was filled and the tip of the tungsten filament was emersed in fluid. Finally he smeared a gob of gummy toothpaste onto the burn-hole to re-seal the lightbulb for just enough time. As he carried the lethal surprise to the closet and sloshed the liquid around, he noticed how the pale, oily solution coated the inside of the glass like clear lacquer. Mack screwed the bulb back in the ceiling socket, washed and carefully dried the glass and put everything away.

Downstairs again, he pushed open the broken front door and hesitated, listening and watching to make sure no one was waiting - to make sure Vinnie hadn't come back. Silence was reassuring. A desert breeze cooled his face as he scanned the desert. Late afternoon sun lit thorny haloes on the cholla and tall saguaro cast long, crooked shadows in the dust. Mack was filled with foreboding. He considered what he'd just done and felt strangely ambivalent. Would he have felt better if he'd killed Vinnie in a blaze of gunfire in Chickie's bedroom? Of course. He pondered the implications, but decided they weren't something he should worry about. He knew some mens' crimes deserved worse punishment than boring prison or a quiet death-injection. What other people thought didn't matter. Guilt probed his conscience, but he told himself he didn't care, paused for another brief weakness and stepped into the light. He'd left the pickup on the shoulder of Speedway Boulevard a half-mile away with the hood up as though for engine trouble. As he hurried down the gravel lane to the main road Mack breathed in the twilight air and watched swallows hunt the lemony sky in wide, elliptic swoops.

• • •

She met him at the door, her face clouded with bad news.

"Mack, I located the 145th Fighter Wing," she began. Then she noticed his solemn expression. "What's wrong? Did you talk to the police? Did you figure out where he was hiding? Can we relax? Will they help us?" Her questions bubbled like boiling water.

Mack realized how frightened and confused she'd become and what a stranger she really was. He decided to put her at ease. "Yeah, I found him."

She was shocked and excited. "What happened? Have they arrested him?"

"They're going to arrest him tonight or tomorrow morning, I'm sure," he said softly and thought of Chickie Malatesta burning in his bathroom.

Grace knew something was wrong. She turned and walked to the kitchen. "If you've killed him, I don't think I can handle it," she said over her shoulder. "There's been enough killing in the last few weeks to last us a lifetime."

"No, I didn't kill him," he said as calmly as he could and followed her down the hall, smiling at the naive irony of her wording. He wanted to add the word, yet, and couldn't help putting emphasis on the word *kill*.

Grace sensed something terrible in the quiet denial. The man was protecting her from something, but at least he was confident about the arrest of the awful killer and they could all sleep a little easier tonight. There was so much she had to tell him: new discoveries and more ache and disillusionment. Since the Vinnie Romano problem seemed solved, she decided to ignore his evasions for now and tell him about her own deeply troubling find. She filled two glasses with tap water, gave him one and leaned against the counter to tell about her investigative triumph and tragedy. "I finally talked with a man who knew about the 145th fighter wing today," she said. "A unit historian who'd just arrived in town for this weekend's fighter pilot's convention called and put me in touch with a retired Air Force Colonel in Ohio who's writing a book about Viet Nam." Grace pointed a finger in the air and raised her voice, excited by her success in spite of the crisis. "Talk about luck, this Colonel has a phenomenal memory and has compiled lists of every air unit that ever served in Southeast Asia. He took a few minutes, looked up the unit for me and then, after reading his notes, remembered a guy named Crawford who was doing a history of the 145th Fighter Wing he'd met at a Gulf War Pride veteran's parade in Detroit five years ago. He even had the man's phone number in Lansing, Michigan." Grace nearly shouted the last word. She was proud of her accomplishment.

After twenty years as a cop and investigator, Mack understood her exhilaration. Most investigations are nothing more than time, persistence, legwork and hundreds of phone calls doggedly asking one question leading to another and another. He knew the exhilaration when you suddenly asked the right question to the right person. He was impressed by her work. "Crawford, huh? Great! What did he say about Ace?"

"So I called the number in Lansing." Grace wouldn't be rushed. "A man answered on the second ring. I told him who I was, and that I needed to do a background article on a veteran fighter pilot from the 145th named Ace Collins who was giving a speech in Tucson this weekend. The guy repeated the name, Collins, twice. He sounded suspicious, but after I talked a little about my story he became very cooperative. In fact he sounded like he *needed* to talk about Viet Nam. His name is Daniel Crawford and he sounded like an old man - too old to be a Viet Nam vet - and very bitter. I asked him about himself and he *hadn't* served in Viet Nam. Crawford is just a father turned historian who has a special interest in the 145th because his son, Yancey, had been with the 145th fighter wing in Viet Nam."

"His son?" Mack repeated. "That's great! Did you get to speak with his son? And why doesn't his son do the history...? Oh, you said, *had* been."

"Correct. Yancey Crawford *had* been a rear-seater in a phantom jet over Hanoi during operation Rolling Thunder," Grace said. "The unit apparently lost more than half its planes in one awful month of the war. Young Yancey was in one of the planes shot down."

"Helluva thing for a father to outlive his son," Mack muttered.

"Yes," Grace agreed. "The 145th was nearly wiped out. There was evidently a slaughterhouse over Hanoi in those terrible days. Mister Crawford sounds almost insane on the subject. He says those young pilots were given absurdly regulated missions into hotly contested airspace with very specific rules of engagement. They were sent in during the day over a ring of heavily fortified missile sites and anti-aircraft positions to strike certain pre-selected targets in the less populated areas of the city. They were *not* allowed to attack airfields, railroad terminals or flood-dikes and they could only launch missiles at radar installations if they were in their zone of attack." Grace finished her water, stared into Mack's eyes and shook her head. "Mister Crawford made Operation Rolling Thunder sound like a criminal conspiracy. According to him, we sent our young men into a death trap to score political points for some planned peace talks. He says the North Vietnamese knew *when* they were coming and *where* they would strike so they ambushed our young pilots with pre-targeted missiles and waiting squadrons of MIGs. And that's not all; he said the MIGs could take off, attack our planes and then run for the safety of their airfields. The rules of engagement only allowed our pilots to engage enemy fighters that were in the air over certain sectors of the city. Mack, the whole thing sounds insane!"

Mack nodded in sad agreement. "The war *was* insane. Viet Nam and Korea were wars the politicians fought to make policy statements, not to win."

"I was too young to protest the war in the seventies," Grace said. "But I remember how I hated the killing." Her gray eyes shifted to neutral. "It was the sad focal point of a generation. Most of my teachers and older friends opposed the war vehemently and their beliefs probably shaped my political views to this day."

Goddamn liberals, Mack thought. He believed the war protesters had made politicians too cautious, shackled the war effort and cost American lives. Like many veterans he hated war protestors with visceral passion. But Grace...? He suddenly wanted a beer. That was unusual. The last few weeks he'd cut his beer intake radically. Living with Grace Faber had been filling enough, but sometimes he needed the relief, the part-time amnesia. Like now. But he shoved the urge back, sipped his water and watched the slim redhead speculate on her past for a moment before abruptly reminding her of the present.

"What did this Crawford guy say about Ace Collins?"

Grace's mind snapped back and her eyes refocused. "Nothing, and I was getting darned discouraged. He said he had records for the fighter wing from 1969 until the unit was decommissioned in 1974. Crawford kept repeating there was nobody named Ace Collins listed on personnel rosters for the 145th Fighter Wing."

"That's probably easy to explain. Maybe there was a misspelling, or maybe you got the unit number wrong."

Grace shook her head impatiently. 'No, wait for me! Of course I'd thought of that. I was sure 145th Fighter wing was on the label of the framed picture in Ace Collin's office and when I asked Mister Crawford about any other Collinses, or names that sounded like Collins or Collier, or Rollins, he said of course there *was* a Mitchell Collins listed on the roster." Grace shrugged and blinked the frustration she had felt. "And I interrupted him, wondering why he'd held the name back. He said he hadn't mentioned Mitch Collins because he was absolutely positive Mitch wasn't making a speech at our Tucson pilot's convention. He said my source must have made a mistake about the unit number."

"Mitchell Collins, huh?" Mack repeated. "That *could* be your editor, couldn't it?. He might have changed his name to Ace after the war. Why did this Crawford guy think there was a mistake?"

Grace looked down and spoke to the linoleum floor. "No. He *knew* there was a mistake. He was positive Mitchell Collins couldn't be giving a speech in Tucson this weekend because Mitchell Collins was the other flier in Yancey Crawford's phantom. Crawford's father said half the squadron saw his son's plane explode in mid air after a direct hit from a Sam missile. There were no parachutes."

"Damn!" Mack grunted. "The right unit and a similar name is too close for coincidence. Could your boss have had the nerve to fake a war record on such slender facts? If he did, what made him think he could get away with such an impersonation? What made him think no one would find out?"

"Because most newspaper and political people don't bother to check these things that carefully," she said. "The same last name on the Air Force records was evidently enough. I've checked dozens of bios and never once thought of questioning something as bizarre as a duplicate name on a war record."

"Well he's been speaking at veteran's events for years with the uniform, the medals and all. Damn crazy thing, posing as a dead guy. He must have a pair of brass balls to carry out a charade like that in public for so many years. Either we've made a simple mistake, or your editor is the gutsiest fraud I've ever heard of."

"My editor?" she repeated with disgust. "After what we've found out, I think that's over. I'm finished with any newspaper that would harbor an Ace Collins. He will never be my boss again! But for many years he has been the boss of the people who are *supposed* to check on these things." Grace's anger roughened her voice to a growl. "And there *is* another person who should have known! And maybe he *did* find out. Maybe a certain retired Major General in the Air Force Reserve knows all about Ace Collins' so-called war record."

• • •

They thumped the Senator's huge, brass doorknocker that evening.

The sound boomed through long inner-spaces like a giant kettledrum.

Mack imagined a castle keep or the Hall of the Mountain King, but he knew the big noise was just high ceilings, heavy masonry and old Arizona money. They stood on a long, covered veranda under a brass carriage-light in front of a hand-carved, wooden door two feet taller than Mack. The Lillienthal home looked like a frontier fort. It was a sprawling, Territorial-style ranch house set on a small mesa at the base of the Catalina Mountains with a parapet roof and dark log-ends protruding near the top of the thick walls. The place was impressive, but felt neglected and somehow out of touch with the world.

No one had challenged them as they drove on the property through an open gate, up a long curved driveway over steeply rising terrain to come out on a five-acre expanse of desert surrounding the house. They'd remarked on the complete lack of security, but decided the Senator wasn't a Senator any more and had no more enemies. Or maybe his big home was security enough.

"Now remember, all we want is confirmation of our suspicions," Grace whispered. "Don't lose your temper and start questioning him like a suspect. Let me handle this. I'm more subtle than you and the editor is *my* boss, after all."

"Yeah, right," Mack said. "You're gonna be *real* calm and rational when you're discussing the asshole who almost certainly ran down your mother."

"I don't intend mentioning my mother," Grace said firmly. "That has nothing to do with this. We need to know if Senator Lillienthal can confirm that my editor is a fake war hero and, if so, why he chose to conceal that falsehood all these years."

Mack was about to mention political corruption when the door opened.

He had seen pictures, but the reality was at once breathtaking and saddening. The political icon had become an old, sick man. Harris Lillienthal was a political legend in the United States, an outspoken Western Senator with a reputation for handing out brutal truths in hard language. As head of a Republican ticket that lost in a landslide in the mid-sixties he had become well- known throughout the country. People loved him or hated him, but everyone respected his honesty. Famous for his jutted jaw, firm-lipped mouth and stern glower, his strong principles and fervent patriotism had anchored the dwindling right wing of the Republican Party through the troubled sixties and seventies. He had left the Senate in 1986. Now he was a retired statesman, Reserve Major General and wealthy landowner who had been showered with honors and acclaim by the press and his colleagues from both parties. A man of stature in the anti-hero culture of the late twentieth century was a rarity. Mack Robertson was convinced that, when Senator Harris Lillienthal retired the Republicans had lost their honor. In spite of Clyde Ralston's suspicions about the Lillienthal family's business dealings, Mack was hard-pressed to believe such a man would participate in so monumental a fraud as an Ace Collins combat pilot impersonation. Nor could he understand how such a man would allow his brother to do business with criminals like Bruno Malatesta.

Now the famous ex-Senator glared at him as though he was a Fuller Brush salesman or a Jehovah's Witness pamphleteer. Lillienthal had to be in his late seventies or early eighties, Mack thought, and was obviously in poor health. The old man hunched between high, bony shoulders over an aluminum walker. The craggy features were still there. Impossibly thin skin had sagged and softened like a well-used candle and red and blue veins webbed his high forehead and hawk-nose. The bright, defiant eyes flared hard and true in deep shadowed sockets.

As he stood speechless, Mack's nose gave him unbidden information. He recognized the sour stench of careless old bachelors, but there was a harsher undertone. He had smelled something similar before on other sick people: a low edge of rot steaming from diseased lungs and a raddled stomach. Mack guessed the old Senator was dying of cancer.

"What do you want?" Harris Lillienthal demanded abruptly. No smile. The hard-edged voice gurgled through thick barriers of phlegm and Mack stifled the urge to clear his throat.

Grace was equally impressed, but determined to confirm her suspicions about Ace Collins, no matter what. She sized up the old man and decided to assume a positive answer and take the direct approach that nearly always works on people who think they're in command of a situation. She remembered her confrontation with Detective Sergeant Sparks at the police station and how the statement of a fact seemed to work better than a question.

"We've discovered the truth about Ace Collins," she said quietly and firmly. "We wondered why people who are in a position to know the truth, like you, a retired Major General in the Air Force, have covered up this deception."

Senator Lillienthal was shocked. Thin, pale skin turned even whiter and the balding head sunk lower between wavering shoulders. He appeared to be on the edge of physical collapse. Mack moved to help, but the old man drew away from his hand. The deep-set eyes glared spirit that would not allow such weakness, or such familiarity. Strength in the eyes lifted the frail body and stiffened the gaunt shoulders. He tottered in the walker, but stood as tall as he could and sized the two people up - a big rumpled man and a pushy woman. He decided she was the one on the phone and the eyes opened wider with anger at such impudence. "Who are you?" he barked. "Get away from my door and off my property!"

"I am the reporter from the *Arizona Register* you hung up on yesterday," Grace responded calmly. "I decided to come directly to you and ask the question before I printed the results of my investigation and my speculations about you."

Harris Lillienthal was at a time in his life where niceties were unnecessary and where fear of anything but impending death was a dim memory. He had always known the truth would come out about that weak ruffian at the newspaper. In fact he'd often considered helping the matter along, but his younger brother, Robert, had invariably begged him to let sleeping dogs lie. Robert had reminded him that a friendly, subservient newspaper editor was a useful for business. For politics also, the old man admitted to himself. No matter, he thought. No real harm had been done, just an overstuffed fool acting out harmless fantasies. The Senator had never been a glad-hander or a friendly man, but now he was simply indifferent to other people and their opinions. Popular delusions weren't worth the bother any more.

"If that fool editor of yours won't stop you, then print your speculations and be damned to you." The phlegm-laden voice weakened and he gasped for breath.

Grace let anger fill her voice. She'd had enough of this wealthy, arrogant man who thought he was too powerful to be touched by scandal. She'd show him. "We also know Ace Collins was drinking and gambling heavily with your brother Robert and Don Bruno Malatesta in the Broken Arrow Ranch sky-box at the dog track." She pointed at the old man. "I believe a reporter named Clyde Ralston was killed because he was investigating *your* family's ties to organized crime, Emprise Corporation and Las Vegas money-laundering." She shook her finger in his face. "*And* I believe Ace Collins has covered up the real reason the reporter was killed because he knew *you* could ruin him by exposing his dishonorable masquerade as a war hero!" She stopped speaking and waited for a reaction.

"My family!" The old man tried to shout at the young woman, but the voice was strangled by anger and congestion. "We are an old and honorable Arizona family who has given much. We are a *pioneer* family. This is all dangerous nonsense! And you should remember it is *libelous* nonsense, young lady. I have heard these stories for years. My grandfather settled here over a hundred years ago and built a thriving market for farmers and ranchers settling the river valleys. My father was a successful businessman and entrepreneur, and my brother is also a successful businessman." He ran out of breath, sucked at the chill night air and gathered himself. "Rash young reporters like you speak of organized crime because some of our family friends and business partners happen to have Italian names. Be damned to you!" He began to turn away and reached a shaking hand to the door.

Grace knew he was going to close the door and there was nothing she could do. The ex-Senator still hadn't bothered to confirm Ace Collin's deception, or anything at all, she realized.

"Bruno Malatesta is a known member of the Chicago Mafia," Grace said, deciding to state it a different way. "His ties to Al Capone, Tony Accardo and Sam Giancana have been documented. He is *also* a partner in the Chicago and Vegas-based Emprise Corporation *and* owns the Broken Arrow Ranch with your brother. Come on, Senator," she taunted, "Don't you think *that* kind of connection matters?"

"I have known Bruno for many years," the old man said. "He is a fine man and a prominent businessman. I know nothing of the Mafia. Now go away and leave me alone." The aluminum walker creaked under his weight, sliding backwards on the tile floor. The heavy, wooden door began to close.

Grace knew she had failed.

Mack decided to get involved. The powerful old man had slapped them away like pesky flies. He figured they had nothing to lose, stepped forward and placed his foot in the door, jamming it partly open. He felt feeble resistance melt away.

"Hey you, move your foot! Get out of my house!" The worn voice behind the door was sturdier with outrage. "I'll have you arrested for trespassing and assault!"

"Mack, don't!" Grace cautioned. "Leave him alone. Maybe we're wrong about all this."

Her doubts further enraged Mack. For the second time in two months a reporter had caved. That first reporter was dead. Anger took over.

Being wrong never entered his mind. He *knew* they were right. His illusions had been shattered by the old man's calm acceptance of the allegations, and by his equally calm dismissal of them. Corruption fraud, deception and even assassination were being scoffed at and blamed on coincidence, social envy and ethnic bigotry. Libelous? That seemed to be a stock answer nowadays. All Mack's years of investigative experience told him they had hit on the truth and the old man was merely putting them off as he had put everyone off for so many arrogant years.

"You better listen to her, Senator Lillienthal," he said loudly and authoritatively like the cop he used to be. "This will all come out in court anyhow in the next few weeks. You have a national reputation for honesty and I always thought you were hot shit, but I guess I was wrong. Time to pay the piper, old man. Things have come unraveled. Your buddy, Ace Collins, ran down an old lady on Speedway Boulevard and left the scene. She died in a heap on the sidewalk, but he thought he'd gotten away clean. He didn't know a bystander got his license plate. There'll be a grand jury empanelled next week." He added the grand jury lie for the hell of it. Maybe the overstatement would cause the old man a few worries, cost him some sleep. You took your shots where you could. Mack felt a small resistance behind the door disappear. The Senator was listening or he'd gone to call the cops.

That's *all* they'd need.

"Mack, stop," Grace pleaded and tried to pull him away from the doorway, "And I really didn't want you to mention my mother."

"Listen to me, you old bastard!" Mack yelled. "You *could* come out of this with some honor still intact if you'd expose the cowardly son of a bitch before a grand jury and a very public hit and run trial hangs out *all* the dirty linen!"

There was no response. Silence hung empty behind the big door.

Mack was suddenly tired. He'd had enough of the whole terrible business. The institutions and people who were supposed to be the bulwarks of society against murder, mayhem and corruption had all failed. Maybe his do-it-yourself solution with Vinnie Romano wasn't so bad after all, and would become more common when people realized they were being robbed, swindled, murdered and finally lied to and misinformed by the very people they trusted.

Grace sensed his exhaustion, his resignation and became stronger. She pulled him away from the half-opened door and down the veranda steps. "Come on Mack," she said. "This old man doesn't care about my mother's death."

"Young lady, is that true...about your mother I mean?" the weak voice asked.

They turned. The door had opened. He wobbled in the slanted shadow like a bent old invalid.

"Yes, Senator," Grace said. "My mother was killed in a hit and run. The police think the driver was Ace Collins. They have a partial license plate. Don't you see? He's evidently always been a fraud, but now he's become a murderer."

Harris Lillienthal stood in silence a moment. Then his body stiffened as if in spasm. He husked a shuddering sigh from deep in his bones. "So the charade has finally come to this, the conceit of a secret," he murmured almost to himself. "Sometimes we are persuaded to make small choices that seem expedient at the time and years later the choice becomes the problem."

"This is a problem that needs to be solved now, Senator," Mack added.

"That is very easy for you to say, young man."

Mack was done. He turned to leave, would no longer bully the old man.

Grace had given up also. She was feeling tired and disgusted. Everywhere she turned, weak men watched each other's backs instead of doing what was right. "Goodby Senator." she murmured.

"The fighter pilot's dinner is day after tomorrow," the old man said quietly, almost to himself. "This time I *might* attend." His cadaverous head lifted, the eyes glittered in their shadowed holes.

"Maybe he'll go," Grace said as they walked to the truck.

"Yeah, right," Mack scoffed.

CHAPTER FOURTEEN

RETRIBUTION

Sunset was nearly over. Fading light was smudged gray like dirty bandages.

Fire-blackened metal caught Vinnie's eye in the last ghostly light seeping into the kitchen. He'd crept from his small cave earlier than normal to eat a can of soup from the gatehouse pantry. The can opener was in the drawer next to the sink. Odd. He was sure the burned fork had *not* been there before. He was sure he would have seen. But the fork showed *someone* had been in the gatehouse kitchen and that someone had been very quiet. Sheriff's men hadn't searched the place again. They were noisy with big cars and scratchy radios. He would've heard them. *Him!* Had to be him, the madonna stealer, visiting her rooms, searching for Vinnie, closing in. He had probably searched the gatehouse and pawed through her things. Would he come back? Maybe, but why was the charred fork here? Vinnie shrugged and realized he was too weak from hunger and pain to think or to delay any longer. The fork settled the matter. He decided to finish everything that night. He would leave at full dark. Then one final trip to the cave and down Speedway to change that nice, quiet neighborhood to bright searing destiny for them...and eternal peace for him.

He giggled softly, drooled soup down the front of his filthy shirt and set the half-full soup can aside. This would be earlier than usual, but he couldn't wait any longer. Vinnie needed to visit the darkness and be with his beloved one last time. Night had become his element. He swam in the darkness like a fish at the bottom of the sea or a fetus in the womb. Light meant mirrors, light meant reflections and a light in the gatehouse would have given him away many days ago. He swam up through the gloom, up the tower stairs to her bedroom and moved past her bed, trailing scarred fingers on cool sheets, probing his memory and once more experiencing her. Excitement began. Small movements filled his groin like a hive of insects. Maybe he was coming alive at last. Breathing quickened. He picked up the stool from in front of her vanity and took it to the darkness inside the darkness.

Vinnie forgot himself a while in the softness and perfume of the madonna.

Much later his mind slackened and he lost the storms of madness. Swirling clouds parted, the surface cleared. An image firmed as in the holy water font a few days before. Vinnie Romano saw what he had become. He saw a filthy wreck of soiled rags and scarred flesh crouched in a soft confusion of women's clothing - a pathetic stranger. What had happened to the sleek young man he knew? Visions of the past - the neighborhood, the corner on President Street near the social club, evening smells of tomato, basil, oregano, fluid words, mocking laughter, gesturing hands and shrugged shoulders - made him yearn for the comfortable world of another life. He saw the muscular body, the dark haughty eyes and slicked-back hair of the smooth-skinned Italian boy. Young Vinnie Romano rolled his shoulders, adjusted the collar of an expensive silk shirt and strutted past dark-haired beauties whispering behind their hands. *That* was who he was: a young man of honor with a gold money-clip and the world in his fist.

All that gone in a swirling brawl of flame.

Reality and madness returned to the small, dark closet. He was not a man, not a human being any more, but a foul ulcer in the soft welter of woman's clothing, a piece of refuse to be discarded like a scab at the healing. Enough. There would be no more torture. No more waking and sleeping. No more loneliness and need. And no more fooling around with receivers and wires. No mistakes this time. There were only three sticks of dynamite left in the cave, and one electric detonator, but he had no remote control to set off the detonator, no timing device. Up to now that would have been a problem, he'd have had to risk another visit to a model airplane store. But no more; he didn't need a remote. His car would be the detonator. He would set off the charge by crashing his big sedan through the wall of their bedroom. He would die with the madonna-stealer and his new woman. Vinnie smiled at the thought and immersed himself in her secret place, storing angry energy.

Finally he stood to leave her closet for the last time.

Like the soft touch of a lover's hand, the fold of a dress rested on his shoulder. A caress. Vinnie paused, turned, gathered the hanging dress in his hand and pressed the cloth to his face, inhaling her one more time. A sigh became a sob, tears and sweat stained soft fabric. Enough, he thought and turned again to leave. The light-chain tickled his forehead. Vinnie looked up to the black ceiling.

Why not? Why not one last look at all the memories?

He pulled the chain. A circuit closed. Electricity flowed down the short wire to the metal base of the light bulb and raced farther to heat the filament. A thin hair of tungsten flared to three-hundred-degree-incandescence in an instant. Acetone, oil and soap swelled to fiery napalm and exploded from the thin glass bulb. "POP!"

Blinding light filled his upturned eyes. Hot gas and liquid suffused the air and consumed all the oxygen in a millesecond.

Scar-shiny skin burned like candle-wax. A sticky blanket of fire flowed bright blue and yellow rivers down scarred skin and filthy clothes. Petals of flame dripped from his chin, his fingers, his elbows. Pain became his universe again. The roaring closet filled with screams. Fire hissed and flung its arms in celebration of the feast and the room filled with seething appetite. Filmy cloth tasted the heat and exploded in tatters of light; wood and plaster seared and bubbled to hot pulp and eventually the screams stopped.

• • •

Mack awoke to her angry voice.

"You lied to me!" she shouted and tossed the morning paper on the blanket. "I don't know how you did it, but Vinnie Romano died in a fire, just the way Mitch Young and that Malatesta woman did."

Mack blinked and cleared his mind as he picked up the newspaper.

ASSASSIN PRESUMED DEAD IN MYSTERIOUS FIRE

Police say Tucsonans can probably breathe a sigh of relief this morning. Latest reports from the Chief's office assert that Vinnie Romano, alleged murderer and car bomber, has died in a fire-gutted building on the far east side of Tucson. Because of an identification bracelet found at the scene, Police believe they have recovered the body of the man sought in the bombing death of Register reporter, Clyde Ralston. Sources close to the Coroner's investigation say identification of the charred body is not yet an absolute certainty, but will be verified by dental records being sent by Chicago police. The fire began in a bedroom and police are, as yet, unsure of its cause. Arson investigators say they have not found evidence of a purposefully set fire and observers speculate the victim must have been smoking in bed. The structure is an isolated out-building on the edge of a ranch owned by wealthy Tucson businessman, Bruno

Malatesta. A spokesman for Mister Malatesta states that no one has lived in the building since his daughter died six weeks ago.

If, in fact, the body is that of Romano, one of the most intensive manhunts in the history of Arizona law enforcement will end and the books will close on two terrible tragedies. "The fire only did the job a little sooner," is the terse sentiment of a highly-placed Sheriff's Department source who revealed to this reporter that members of a special task force were following certain leads which, in the next few weeks, would have led to the arrest of Romano for first degree murder.

Police say they will be able to close at least two homicide cases due to the Malatesta Ranch fire. Vinnie Romano was named as his killer by Clyde Ralston at the scene of the car bombing which eventually took the reporter's life and Romano was also identified as a person of interest in the hit and run death of long-time Tucson resident, Viola Faber, on east Speedway just over two months ago.

Mack finished reading the slick wrap-up with growing anger. He'd expected trite coverage of the hit-man's death, but the newspaper - and the police, he noticed - had tied everything in a neat bundle for the reader's breakfast. Just like television, nice and clean, no loose ends and a conclusion at the end of the hour. No mention of Emprise, dog track investigations or even the arson deaths of Mitch Young and Chickie. Vinnie's connection to the powerful man behind it all, Bruno Malatesta, was downplayed. Bernie Franks had apparently scared both newspaper *and* police. The police appeared to be using Mack's false identification of Vinnie at the scene of the hit and run to close *that* case. They'd avoided a lawsuit from *one* powerful man and also avoided embarrassing *another* powerful man who ran a newspaper. He realized they'd buried the bodies neat and clean - another Final Solution.

"Killing has become a habit with you!" She stood at the door like dark cloud, eyes alight with anger. "What a horrible way to kill a man; you burned him up in her house, didn't you?"

Mack decided not to bother with denials. "So what if I did," he said softly.

Grace was filled with anger, disgust and the shreds of a love that was still a warm, new glow. She was naked under the terry-cloth robe; they had made love the night before after returning from the Senator's house, and again that morning. And what fine lovemaking it had been! A sweet, slow lingering journey of sighs and moans that left her exhausted and smiling. She'd been almost sure - had felt the heart-melting excitement, the breathless anticipation she always thought would be a part of true love. For the first time since her mother's death, Grace had fallen asleep with a smile and had awakened to calm hunger. That morning she had risen from contented sleep in the gray light of false dawn to the need of him and the sound of the newspaper delivery truck slowing for the throw to her doorstep and then pulling away in a noisy grind of gears.

Before sliding out of bed to get the paper Grace had looked over to the other pillow and gazed lovingly at the new man in her life. She had leaned to kiss his sleeping mouth, reached to stroke him and gloried in her new hunger and growing confidence. He muttered in half sleep and smiled at her busy hand. She pulled the covers from his thighs and slowly, carefully lowered herself onto him. Scalding heat slid up inside her, all the way to her heart. She'd held him there for long minutes, barely moving back and forth, up and down, shifting, building the wonderful fire, building, and building until slow spasms began and she stared down into his eyes, ground her hips into him and groaned. He lunged against her and they were lost for a time in the heat. Grace had sat astride a long time while his body softened and their breathing calmed.

Nothing was said, only soft looks and smiles. She'd thought things were getting so much better.

All that was changed by the newspaper headline.

In unconscious reflex she pulled her robe together and retreated toward the door. She glared at him in anger and fear. "But why?" she shouted. "The police were on his trail. They would've arrested him and put him in prison, or an insane asylum where he belongs."

"The cops wouldn't have found him." He motioned at the article. "No matter what crap they're spouting there."

"But you've lowered yourself to his level now," she continued, her voice higher and her face reddening. "You've become a murderer now!"

Mack was tired, both physically and mentally, and although he'd expected her anger, he was very disappointed by her unbridled reaction. He was also feeling the dull, gray guilt settling again and lashed out, as much at himself as at the young woman - a damn reporter, he reminded himself. "You Goddamn liberals make me sick!" he shouted. "Always concerned with feeble concepts, but blind to causes and results." He slid his legs to the floor and looked for his underwear. "Don't you remember who that scum was? How he mutilated and killed Clyde? How he burned people?" Mack ran out of breath and gulped air before continuing. "Grace, don't you understand that madman was trying to kill me, to kill all of us? I did what I had to do."

Grace Faber suddenly calmed. His words had stabbed like harpoons, emptying heat and cooling angry passion. Now her words held only sorrow. "No, Mack, you did what you *wanted* to do!"

Mack knew any argument was too late, but reckless words filled his mouth before he could restrain them. "Listen, that son of a bitch burned and bombed innocent people. Don't you understand the human need for vengeance?" Mack didn't wait for an answer. "Well he damn sure won't be killing any one else now."

"You are not God." She was whispering now, her words curling around tears. "You don't have the right."

Mack tried for calm. "The police sure as hell weren't protecting us," he said as quietly as he could. "We *all* have the right to self-defense."

"The police say they were going to arrest him," she insisted.

"They were covering their asses." He scooped his underwear pants from the floor and slid them on." Have you forgotten they're covering-up for your mother's killer or that they pretend Bruno Malatesta is just a wealthy rancher?"

She answered him with white-lipped silence.

"You think the cops were doing their job?" he asked again. "Cops aren't *allowed* to do their job anymore. They mess with the wrong people they get sued or charged with a crime themselves." He shrugged in frustration at her stubborn silence. "Okay. Maybe I'm wrong; I'll call Karl right now and ask!"

Mack brushed past her and stormed down the hallway to the phone.

• • •

"Clearin' cases is what it's all about, ol' buddy," the police detective drawled. "Chief Hobbs is just tickled pink. He gets to clear three murders and a hit and run in one day without any evidence, testimony, messy trials, lawyers and all that justice crap."

Mack squeezed the phone and quelled his anger. There was no profit in yelling at his friend. "Karl, you know I lied about that hit and run eyewitness..."

"The less said about that the better," the policeman interrupted. "That stuff-shirt editor is gonna skate on the H and R. That is partly your fault, ol' buddy."

"I know," Mack admitted. "But will Bruno Malatesta get off too?"

"Damn straight. You got any evidence connecting him to the bombing of that reporter or the two arson deaths?"

"You know better than that, Karl, but what about Clyde's dying declaration of Mafia, Emprise and Romano? Doesn't that tie Don Bruno to the bombing?"

Mack heard the detective sigh into the other end of the phone.

Karl had heard the tale before and knew better than to let speculation, rumors and wish lists get in the way of hard evidence. In his many years of police work he had learned how quickly idealists burned out. He had seen how newspapers made and ruined careers and how news perceptions were more important than realities. But the hardest lesson for Karl to learn was that the public only wanted *certain* trash to be collected. "Mack, old son," he said. "The guy doesn't even have a traffic ticket on his record. His Mafia connections are thirty years old and we have only an educated guess that Vinnie Romano did any crimes on his orders." Karl paused. Mack heard a match strike. The whoosh of blown smoke roughened the next words. "Ol' buddy, as far as your Tucson police are concerned, Bruno Malatesta has been a fine, law-abidin', influential member of this community for over thirty years. He's a local businessman, a big political contributor and he's on a first-name basis with the Mayor, the County Attorney, all our Congressmen, both Senators and the Governor. Do you think anybody's gonna go after him because some black crime reporter says he's involved in somethin' complicated and dirty?"

"Black?" Mack repeated. "Where'd that come from? Do you think the fact Clyde was black had anything to do with his not being taken seriously?"

"His color damn sure didn't help with the good ol' boys who run this town."

"Well shit, Karl, that sucks! What happens next?"

"Not a damn thing, ol' buddy, this dance is over."

"Over?" Mack exploded. "Don't the police care about the murder of a reporter? Sure, the bomber's dead, but what about the man who gave the order?

"Mack, listen up! How the hell do you expect the police, or anybody else, to push for answers when the reporter's own newspaper doesn't seem to care?"

• • •

Grace stood in the hall with his suitcase. Her robe had gapped at the top and showed the soft separation of her breasts. She didn't notice.

Mack couldn't see anything else.

"It's all over," she said and handed him a shirt and his levis.

"Oh shit, Grace, what the hell does that mean," he reached for her.

"I can't handle the guilt any more," she said and pulled away, "guilt for our part in Clyde's death and guilt for the bodies strewn in your path. This horrible execution of Vinnie is the last straw. Death covers you like a shroud and you stink of all the blood. I can't let you touch me."

Mack didn't understand. He pulled his eyes away from her flesh and realigned his thoughts to disbelief and regret; after the passionate tenderness last night and that morning he'd thought they were falling in love. He covered his confusion by shrugging on the shirt and clumsily hopping into the levis. "But

Grace, the men I killed were trying to kill me. They deserved to die."

Grace stared through him and spoke in an intense monotone as though reciting a hard-studied lesson. "That is a judgement you are not allowed to make in our society. Losing my mother *and* my life's work to a heartless, arrogant fraud is bad enough, but I can't bear the killing, the endless cycle of violence that seems to follow you like a pursuing demon. For a while I tried to ignore my doubts, but I remembered what my mother used to say about people who constantly find themselves in certain situations. She was sure the phenomenon was not accidental. My mother was a non-practicing Jew, but a devotee of all sorts of unique Jewish folklore her mother had taught her when she was a young girl. She told me the old stories were important because they were the oral and written tradition of a whole race, the life experiences of countless people distilled down through the years. Mother said times change, but people are timeless. She believed in good and evil and she believed certain people were possessed by a being called a *Dybbuk*, a demon that enters the body of a living person and controls that person's behavior. Mack Robertson, I believe you are possessed by the spirit of death." She handed him his suitcase and stepped aside to let him out the door.

"Am I interruptin' somthin'?" Louis Carfagno stood at the door to the kitchen with his gray knit cap in his hand.

Grace was embarrassed. She clutched her robe and moved toward the old man. "No Louis...er, what can I do? Do you need something?"

"No, Ma'am, don't need nothin'." The bent old man put on his cap and gave it a tug. "We's leavin' today for the east coast. I done found me a used van in the want ads and the fella said he'd bring it over this mornin'"

"Leaving?" Grace repeated and then caught herself, "Oh yes, that's right. You mentioned it yesterday. I've been preoccupied and forgot."

Louis limped forward and held out his twisted hand first to Grace and then to Mack. "Been nice knowin' ya," he said.

Mack took the hand in both of his and held on. "Louis, I'll miss you," he said, realizing how desolate this one-more seperation made him feel. Alone again, death and driftings, even the new people in his life were moving away like sand- loose anchors. Incongruously, for the first time in his life, he felt the weight of his years. "I'll really miss you, and the dogs."

"Just wanted to thank you is all," Louis growled, emotion roughening his already raspy voice. "Both of you, for bein' there when you was needed. Ain't ever'body who'd put their keester on the line, so to speak, for a buncha run-down dogs and a cripple."

Mack followed the trainer out into the back yard to see the greyhounds he'd saved from the bullets that night. Grace's observation had hit very close. He'd considered the same thing many times, but could see no other way to confront aggression than with equal or greater aggression. He realized she was overly idealistic, but he was also certain in his private thoughts that, if everyone handled their problems his way, the world would be bloody chaos. He usually ignored his misgivings, but she had scored. She'd made him reconsider. Still, there *were* the dogs, he reminded himself - Great Alliance, Serengeti Fancy and the others. Mack needed to see the living, breathing results of *his* way of doing things. He needed to see the lives he'd saved.

In cool morning the Greyhounds were clumped in leggy brown and gray heaps in tree-dappled sunlight near the back fence and against the garage wall.

The humans stood and watched a moment.

The dogs had settled in well and were unaware of the impending change. Seven were in various stages of sleep, from the sprawled out, but head-up-eyes-drifting-closed-in-the-sun pose to the curled-in-a-circle oblivion of snores. The Faber yard was Greyhound heaven: food, friends and sunbathing. All were relaxed and unconscious of people except Great Alliance. He saw humans at the back stoop and sensed something was up. With self-conscious dignity he stood, yawned a jawbreaker, arched his back to a shuddering stretch and ambled over to stand a few feet away from Mack. The dog regarded the big man quietly, no smile, no panting, just close-mouthed, even regard. The Champion was available for a stroking hand, but did not want to appear anxious.

"He's waitin' for a proper greetin'," Louis whispered.

"Hi, old boy," Mack said and reached out a hand.

Great Alliance moved under the hand and nuzzled Mack's pant leg.

"Wish I could keep a hero like you," he murmured and scratched the tall dog between his ears. "But all I've got is that cramped old studio in the city. You wouldn't like it there."

Great Alliance closed his eyes and opened his mouth in tongue-lolling ecstasy from scratching fingers at that one spot he loved, but couldn't reach. He held still under the detective's hand, hoping the petting would last all day. But he knew the pleasure couldn't last much longer; the others were waking up.

Serengeti Fancy was the first to realize there was attention to be had. The slender, red brindle jumped up and bounded across twenty feet of back yard toward the humans in three swift leaps. She was fast, but her brakes were defective and she plowed into Louis with enough force to sit him down on the step. He laughed and grabbed her long head to deliver a mock scolding. Her kohl-rimmed eyes half closed in happiness between the old, rough hands.

"Just love that gentlin', don't ya, girl?" Louis crooned softly.

The other dogs heard and, in a flash the humans were engulfed in lean, muscular bodies, eager tongues and long, loopy tails flailing like whips.

Grace stood inside the door and felt the sorrow. Love was so easy and so hard. She watched the two men try to pet all the dogs. She watched Mack Robertson and smiled ruefully through a mist of tears. How could someone so gentle be so ruthless? She noticed how he petted the other dogs with his left hand, but kept his right on the head of the big male that had saved them all from the bomb. They were a pair, she thought, gentle and protective, but fierce and terrible. Grace considered the comparison, breathed a sigh and made a decision. "Louis," she said softly, "would it be possible for me to keep Great Alliance with me? He could have this whole yard and he would be keeping me company."

The old man was not surprised, had been expecting something like this, but sensed a deep chasm had opened between the tall detective and the redheaded woman. He wanted the greyhound to have a home, but wanted to help *them* also. "Waal, I dunno." He pulled off his cap and rubbed his head, thinking it over. "He's sure taken a shine to your man and there ain't no better dog-run, that's fer sure."

"Then it's okay?" Grace urged.

"If'n you promise me you'll keep him to yourselves, you two, and don't be givin' Great Alliance away to strangers who won't appreciate him."

Grace ignored the obvious implication. "Mister Carfagno, I will give him a good home."

"Oh, and there's somethin' else," the old man said quickly. "We can't be seperatin' him from Fancy. They been makin' a pair and Great Alliance has taken quite a fancy to Fancy." He chuckled. "Though he don't let on about it much."

Grace hesitated a moment, *two* big dogs, all at once? She'd never had a dog before. Her mother thought they were dirty and spread disease and her ex hadn't wanted to spend the money.

"Mates belong together," Louis added when he saw her pause. "Be a damn shame to separate them." He had figured this was going to happen. Had expected the offer when he saw the way the P. I. and Great Alliance had bonded from the first, and particularly after the hound had saved their lives. Also, there was the matter of the van. There wasn't going to be a van at all. The vehicle was a pickup with a camper. He and the six remaining dogs would be almost comfortable, but eight dogs would be stretchin' things a bit. He turned up the heat. "He saved your life once and prob'ly would again. Be a shame to take away his lady-love."

"Of course, I'll keep them both," Grace said. She was ashamed at her hesitation when she thought of what the Greyhound had saved them from. Grace moved off the back step and patted Serengeti Fancy and then Great Alliance - her new dogs. As she touched the big male on the head her eyes met Mack's level stare and she flinched from the pain she saw.

"Louis said he'd let the *two* of us have them," Mack reminded her.

Grace considered her dislike of the man she almost loved. *Couldn't be helped*, her mother would've said. Neither of the males could help what they were. Unfair. Life was so unfair, but there was no reason Grace Faber had to be. The rationalization came easy. "There's no reason you can't come and visit Great Alliance when you want to," she murmured. "I'll even give you a key to the gate."

As though on cue, an old battered pickup with a camper shell pulled in behind Mack's newer, more-battered pickup. Louis walked over and greeted a man he'd obviously spoken with on the phone. After some jocular negotiations, a deal was made and money paid. Louis loaded his few belongings, all the blankets he could borrow from Grace and the six remaining greyhounds into the back of the camper. Then he hugged Grace, solemnly shook Mack's hand, climbed into his new home, fussed a moment, ground the gears and drove off without another word.

Grace was becoming bewildered by the headlong finality. Her life was diminished; she felt smaller and shrinking. Pieces of her were disappearing like a film on fast-forward and the sudden change was frightening. But there were the new dogs, she remembered - pieces arriving and now more leaving. Grace stood in the driveway and watched Mack put down his suitcase, kneel and hug the big male. She heard him mutter endearments in the dog's ear and remembered when he'd said those things to her. "Well I guess that's it," she said to the back of his head.

He turned and looked up. "Guess so," he said and blinked his eyes in the fresh new sunlight beaming over her garage roof.

Was he crying? she wondered. Such a sensitive man to be... She didn't finish the thought.

He stood, picked up his suitcase and turned to the pickup.

Grace was devastated. She wanted to call him back. She was sure she would *never* be able to love him after what he had done, but her whole life was leaving her, week-by-week, bit-by-bit. She watched the roughly handsome man with the wrinkled clothes and the soot-stained suitcase walk to the shot-up truck and climb in, moving slowly and carefully like an old man. She wept silently for him, and herself. All gone now: in the space of two months she had lost her mother, a dear friend, the job that had filled her life since a divorce, and now a lover. Hot tears flowed, she tasted the salt, but didn't bother to wipe her cheeks. Who cared how she looked? Here she was, left with two dogs. She glanced at Great Alliance who was standing alert, ears up, wondering where his friend was going. Then she leaned and touched Serengeti Fancy's head. The red-gray brindle looked up at Grace and all the hope and trust in the world poured from dark almond eyes. Grace fondled the soft delicate droop of the dog's ear and read the tattooed numbers on the pink inner skin. How cruel their lives had been up to now, she thought. They *were* two wonderful dogs that needed her.

The way she had needed *him*, and her job, and her mother, she thought.

Mother. Dear, strict, loving mother. All those years, childhood, her first job, the first marriage and all the busy years of joy, accomplishment, sorrow and failure, mother had always been there to lend strength. She had never approved of whining and said crying never accomplished anything. "Get hold of yourself," she would say. "Stop feeling sorry for yourself and *do* something about it!"

Grace watched the white pickup pull away. He waved. She wiped her tears and decided to follow her mother's advice. She stared down the street at the space where the truck had been and examined the situation, the problem: her mother's death, the car-bombing and crass cover-up of motives and personalities involved. In the whole complex series of events everything led her back to one man.

After all was said and done, the basic problem had always been Ace Collins.

• • •

A newspaper editor was in the perfect position to hide corruption and eventually become part of the problem. Ace Collins, drunk, gambler and coward who'd left the scene of an accident, was probably not a purposeful criminal, but worse than that. Through his position as a supposedly disinterested watchdog, he had apparently allowed criminals and members of the elite country-club set to manipulate public works, embezzle tax money and take control of an unsuspecting city. And then he had allowed the murder of a reporter, one of his own! Another editor, one less flawed and corrupt, would *force* the police to get to the bottom of the bombing and uncover the reasons Clyde had been killed. Another editor would inform the public, enflame them with righteous anger and lead the charge to bring those responsible for ***ordering*** the murders to justice. Another editor would...

Grace pressed her lips together and sniffed back tears. All the what-ifs and all the soft memories were useless. First things first, she said to herself. You're a reporter! Do your job. Expose Ace Collins in a way he can't cover up. Maybe you *can* get your darn job back and maybe Clyde and Mother will finally be able to rest in peace. First she had to find a way.

It was time for action. But the editor was too powerful to simply accuse. He would certainly ignore her and accusations would fall like trees in the forest. The police were helpless. They could only do their job if backed by political will. Crimes had been committed and there *was* evidence, but they were told by the newspaper - society's biggest, most authoritative voice - that the criminal was dead and the crime was solved. But wait a moment, she thought. There *might* be something. The Fighter Pilots dinner was tonight. Senator Lillienthal said he might be there. He hadn't promised anything, but you never knew. There *could* be an unpleasant surprise for Ace Collins at the dinner. Grace Faber decided to arrange her own surprise and make sure whatever happened was news no one could ignore. She wondered how much a round-trip plane ticket from Lansing Michigan to Tucson, Arizona was going to cost. It was time to *do* something.

CHAPTER FIFTEEN

MAKING THE NEWS

The rug was still damp. A sour, acrid, burn-stench seeped from everything, but Cormac Robertson was home in his studio. His photos had survived, even though the glass was dingy and the frame-tops were covered in powdered ash. His things were *almost* the way he'd left them, except they were all filmed with dark smears and blots of black soot. Her clothing was still strewn about, mixed with his. He picked up her tee shirt and stared at it for a long time.

Horns honked, traffic skirmished outside. Mack stared at the cloth. After a while he shook his head and began to clean up.

Mack avoided the bathroom until he'd put his things away and made the bed with linen he'd bought on the way. Then he turned, walked in and faced the place. The electric fixture had been replaced. There was a new bulb. He didn't turn the light on. Paradoxically, smoke-smell was weaker where she'd died. As he stood imagining, his nose was filled with the dry alkali of new plaster and the sweet tang of fresh paint. Mack breathed the clean fumes and thought of the way she'd burned. Right here at his feet, but there was no mark, no stain, no sign of the horror.

Again, he saw that wonderful body wreathed in its terrible robe of flames. He could still hear her screams, feel her muscles surging under him, trying to escape the awful pain. Chickie Malatesta had been a friend and a lover. She hadn't been perfect, but nobody deserved to die like that. His eyes swam and he remembered Lord Byron had written about Friendship being Love without his wings. Nice touch, perfect for him and Chickie. Mack snuffled and swore at himself. He thought about a few beers to fill the void, but realized he'd gotten out of the day-drinking habit while living with Grace. He turned away from the memories to the desk. The phone answering machine was blinking away like a knowing little eye, reminding him there were still other people in the world.

He pushed the button.

A half hour later he'd written them all down - eighteen messages from the last three weeks, ten from friends and bill collectors, four from Karl Jenkins and four from Bruno Malatesta. Karl's messages were easy, he wanted to meet for drinks, talk about the case, but the last message was to tell him what a damn fool he was. Mack figured the message was after Karl had heard about Vinnie Romano's death.

The four messages from the Mafia boss were interspersed among the others. Don Bruno's calls seemed to cover at least two weeks of time in their content and diminishing passion. Most of the old man's extended message was short and cryptic because he was on an open phone-line, but the thin, sibilant voice reopened Mack's anger and made him swear and clench his fists. He thought again of Mitch and Clyde and Chickie, and the way they'd died.

Bruno Malatesta's words were laced with grief, but demanding and arrogant. "You never answer the phone. Are you there?" The scratchy tape aggravated the thready quality of the weak voice. "My daughter! She not in the hospital like you say and she get killed." His rage was obvious in the first message. "Hey, you better call me soon..." A series of coughs and sniffs interrupted. "...we gotta talk soon, you an' me." He left a phone number.

There were three more of like content. The last mentioned their contract.

La Condotta. Money, at a time like this? What a Goddamned monster! But Mack thought a moment more and realized the message made a kind of twisted sense. He could imagine the old man's mental state: unbearable grief, anger and frustration. The frustration of a man accustomed to nearly absolute power, but helpless to affect events so close to him, must be unbearable. "Tough shit, Bruno," the detective muttered through his anger. There was really nothing Bruno Malatesta could do to Mack Robertson with all the current publicity centered on him. He decided the Don was determined to punish him in any way he could. Bruno wanted his money back to fulfill a warped sense of honor and to ease the frustration a bit.

Five thousand wasn't much to Don Bruno, but was a small fortune to Mack. He'd spent a few hundred of the bag full of money on things like hospital costs, groceries for Grace, dog food for Louis and windshields and headlights for his truck, but most of the money was still in the airline bag behind his truck-seat.

In the truck with the dynamite and the shiny, black remote-control box.

Mack decided to meet with Bruno Malatesta and pay him what he was owed. He picked up the phone and called the number Don Bruno had left.

The old man answered the third ring. "Yeah, who's this?" he rasped. He sounded annoyed and tired, maybe expecting a business call.

"You wanted to talk about our contract?" Mack said.

"Oh. It's you," the voice became needle sharp. "You owe me big time."

"Yeah, well I'll pay you back. You don't have to worry." Mack tried for politeness and a hint of uncertainty. He didn't want the Don to be suspicious.

"You can never..." Bruno caught himself, remembered that in all his years of power and influence he was always in control and never showed his feelings to anyone. "Listen, you come out to my ranch and bring me my money."

Mack didn't want to go near that ranch. He was pretty sure he'd be safe for a while until things cooled down, but the ranch? But he could drive out there and disappear into the desert under those gloomy Rincons like yesterday's garbage. "No way, Don Bruno," he answered quickly. "We gotta meet some place public, out in the open where I can feel safe."

"I don't never go out in public."

"Look, that's the way any meeting's gotta be." Mack insisted. He wanted the meeting, but only on his terms. "For my safety, you understand."

"Haucch, hah!" The dry cough rattled over the line. "You think I'm a hoodlum or something? I ain't gonna hurt you." The old man paused, then the voice dulled again to a hard whisper. "But if that's the way you want, there is *one* place I go. You can meet me there."

"Where's that?"

"I go each Sunday to visit my daughter's grave. The grass still ain't grown and I leave her some flowers."

Perfect. A fitting place, Mack thought. "Sounds good," he said. "Sunday? What time?"

"Late in the afternoon, around five." The breathy words deepened a little in sadness, or rage. "When the day is chilly and the place is nearly empty."

Empty, huh? Oh well an empty graveyard was better than thirty miles in the desert. And Mack realized he hadn't visited her grave yet. "I'll be there with your money," he said. "Sunday at five o' clock next to Chickie's grave."

Bruno Malatesta hung up.

While Mack had been on the phone he'd been toying with the pile of mail that had accumulated during the past weeks. Nothing much, but when he tossed the bills and ads aside, he was left with one letter. The return address said *Arizona Register* and the envelope contained an engraved invitation to the Hotel Conquistador. This was the invitation to the Saturday Night Fighter Pilots Dinner he'd been promised by Ace Collins so many weeks ago.

Talk about fate. Saturday was tonight. Everything happens at once. Grace will be there for sure. Guess I'll have to go.

Later he went to the hardware store and bought a fresh, new nine-volt battery, one of those small, square ones the size of a box of matches. Best to do it while he was thinking about it. He knew the hardware store would be closed on Sunday.

• • •

The jacket was badly wrinkled and he must have smelled like wet ashes, but Mack had become accustomed to the smell and only planned to stand in back. The security man at the ballroom door wrinkled his nose and looked alarmed until Mack showed the invitation and leaned close. "I'm a fireman; just got off the job," he said and kept right on walking into the big room. He was late.

Hotel staff was beginning to clean up. People were turning their chairs from dish-laden tables to get a better view of the head-table spotlighted on the stage ten feet above the rest of the room. Important men in tuxedos and uniforms sat with their gowned women along one side of the long head-table with the speakers' lectern in the middle, all pretending they were calm and composed under the mass scrutiny of their fellow pilots. Mack spotted Ace Collins seated right next to the lectern in his Air Force Colonel's uniform. On the other side of the lectern he recognized the sparse sweep of white hair, blocky shoulders and square, ruddy face of Senator John McGraw. There was no sign of ex-Senator Lillienthal.

Mack sat down quickly in one of the chairs lined against the back wall near the door before someone asked for his Air Force or press credentials.

The hotel ballroom was crowded with tables full of expectant vets, some in uniform, but most of the men and women were in various degrees of formal attire. The dinner and speeches by dignitaries was the highlight of their yearly convention and they looked ready. Mack estimated thirty or forty big, round tables of mostly middle-aged couples had been crammed in the large room with just enough space between for waiters and serving stations. At first, Mack looked for someone he knew and examined a couple of good-looking women while trying to spot Grace. No luck, but the room was packed and he couldn't see everybody.

Some of the tables were full of younger couples, probably still on active or reserve duty, but the room was otherwise a sea of graying, receding hair, reddened puffy faces and expanding middles. Clusters of glasses and heaps of dishes showed there had been lots of booze consumed followed by a big meal and dessert. Smoke hazed the air in only one section of tables near the back, but Mack had been noticing for years how most people older than thirty and younger than sixty weren't smoking any more. Mack felt right at home with the happy veterans, but figured there was probably another Ace Collins speech coming. He was sure he was wasting his time since the ex-Senator wasn't there and, evidently, neither was Grace. Oh well, he had nothing better to do.

He decided he wanted a drink and motioned to a passing waiter.

The lights in the room dimmed, but the head table was still lit up.

Everyone's eye was drawn to the long white table with the tilted speaker's platform in the center. Someone tapped the microphone and asked for attention. The room became quiet. Ace Collins moved to the lectern. He stood proud and tall in his dress uniform, back straight, beribboned chest puffed slightly, and shuffled his papers before beginning to thank people and introduce the head table. His deep voice resonated through the large room and commanded attention. Mack thought he looked every inch a genuine military hero. The list ended after he introduced himself and peered out at the room expectantly. Dutiful applause spattered. He had not yet introduced the guest speaker and began, "a few brief remarks before I introduce our speaker." Apparently Ace Collins wasn't *really* there to give a speech, but was Master of Ceremonies. Typical. Mack was ready to leave, but the waiter brought him a bottle of beer and a glass and he decided to suffer a while.

Colonel Collins rambled through a series of references to past fighter pilot dinners and his role in them before launching into a righteous sermon on patriotism and about men who spend their youth in the service of their country. Mack noticed Ace's speech was ever so slightly slurred and wondered if the phony bastard always needed a few drinks to be able to moralize so convincingly.

The editor was flying high. One hand unconsciously wandered his broad chest, caressed the bits of colored cloth and metal that meant so much. Cool exhilaration raced through his veins. The familiar words slipped over his lips without his even having to think about them. This was his ninth Fighter Pilots dinner and he had grown to the occasion. He knew he was much more a hero than the balding, sweaty fools who eagerly hung on his every word and wished they were him. Ace Collins was at the top of his world, Editor of the largest newspaper in the state and military hero. He was flying. As the words flowed he warmed himself in the fires of exultation and anticipation of even greater heights.

Earlier, at the dinner table, Senator McGraw had leaned over and quietly reminded Ace he was on the Judiciary Committee and asked if his degree from Princeton was in Law. The hilarity of the question! It was an offering of a Federal Judgeship Ace was sure, *but what about confirmation hearings?* Alcohol sang a lullaby. Why worry? The Senator would protect his influential constituent from any *too* probing questions, wouldn't he? Everything was going so well. A new, lucrative sports arena was to be built and his creditors were satisfied. That nasty traffic matter had been settled and the horrible bombing had been put to rest. Things were getting back to normal. He even felt hot, old urges returning with the fervor of triumph. Maybe he would divorce his wife and find an endless series of frightened young things, eager to serve and pleasure.

Oh, to be entwined with this moment forever, he rejoiced.

His resonant, well-modulated voice sounded bold trumpets. Cool, dizzy thrills washed his veins. But only for five minutes more, he reminded himself and began to close his remarks with an unsubtle mention of his important position as an opinion leader in Tucson. "...and I too bear the burden of responsibilities which *all* leaders - like so many of the men in this room - must shoulder." He turned and smiled down at Senator John McGraw.

But something jarred the moment. There was a noise in the audience. Some one was interrupting and tearing his seamless cloth of words. He squinted into the darkness and tried to see what the disturbance was. There was a shouted question. A woman was standing and gesturing from a table up front near the stage. She was familiar. The Faber woman!

"Sir!" she shouted. "On the subject of responsibility, what about my mother's hit and run death? Has the County Attorney questioned you about that yet?"

Ace Collins reeled. Alcohol and ecstasy robbed him of an instant response. A space of silence opened. Conversation and comment buzzed. The audience recoiled in their chairs and stared at the brash young, redheaded woman.

"Answer the question, Sir," Grace Faber demanded. "The police have placed your license plate at the scene of my mother's hit and run. If you didn't run her down, why didn't you - the editor of the *Register* - at least stop and help her?"

Tables buzzed and hummed with shocked reaction, questions were muttered and dismissed. Interesting charges, but this was Ace's audience. They were *all* veterans together and this woman was obviously unbalanced, probably deranged.

Hoots of displeasure began, and loud calls for security.

Ace Collins gripped the podium and gathered himself. He was in control; he could handle this slender little scrap of female annoyance. "Ahem, ah...ladies and gentlemen, perhaps I should explain. We all should give this poor woman our sympathy," he said smoothly and gestured grandly to the room. "This woman is Grace Faber. You see, she is, or was, one of my reporters at the *Register.* Her mother was killed a few months ago and she has become quite beside herself with grief." He paused a moment and, as Grace opened her mouth to respond, he overrode her voice with his microphone-amplified explanation. 'She wasn't a very experienced reporter and has made rash accusations before. I have always made allowances, but Grace has not come to work lately and I have had to let her go. Her mother's death was a terrible tragedy, but she has made the situation worse by accusing people around her and ignoring her job. This is the sad result." Ace bowed a little to the angry woman and shook his head in regret.

Security guards closed in and gently, but firmly, assisted the slender ex-reporter away from her table and through the crowded room toward the door.

"Police have his license number," Grace shouted to the wall of faces. "Ask them. Ask them! Doesn't anybody care about my mother?"

Ace Collins grimaced and lowered his head in studied embarrassment.

"Doesn't anybody care?" Grace's jostled voice rang clearly from the darkness at the back of the room. "And the man's a phony war hero too!" Security guards had hustled her nearly to the door, but she wasn't going easily.

No one answered her. The room erupted in excited conversation.

The uniformed man at the podium allowed the buzz of conversation to continue for a moment, but quickly decided to divert the audience's attention elsewhere. "And now," he bellowed into the microphone, "it is my great honor to introduce." He paused, gestured for silence and repeated, "it is my great honor to introduce..."

"Take your Goddamned hands off her!" a gruff voice rattled through the buzz near the door. "She has the right to ask questions." Mack shoved the security guards away from Grace and put his arm around her.

"Mack, no!" she hissed up in his face. "What are you doing? Don't help me! I *mean* to be arrested and charged. I've called Daniel Crawford again. He'll testify for me in court. My getting arrested is the only way to force this out in the open."

Mack looked down at her, admired her courage, but pitied her blind, liberal faith in the system. "Hell, Grace!" he growled. "They won't let him testify. They'll smother you with lawyers and bleed you until you beg for your Goddamn life." Mack pulled her against his chest and glared at the hostile crowd like an angry bear.

There was a standoff for a moment. Security guards held back from the large, tough-looking man, but some of the slightly inebriated veterans were miffed at the interruption and decided to pitch in and help law and order.

Two men in tuxedos grabbed Mack and tried to pull him away from Grace.

He slugged one in the side of the head and slung the other man into a table. The big circular table tilted. Women shrieked. Dishes slid off and glasses smashed dully on the thick carpet. More people joined in, and the scuffle broadened to a noisy brawl. People began to get in each other's way, but a few got to Mack.

He dodged a roundhouse punch, ducked another and pulled Grace behind him toward the stage. Something smacked the back of his head with a liquid crunch, cold fluid ran down his neck, blood tickled high in his hair and then stung like fire. A fist connected. Light flared behind his eyes. Grace screamed something in his ear. He staggered, held onto the small redhead and almost lost consciousness.

Damn! This is becoming a disaster! In a moment there'll be ten guys sitting on my chest. Don't wanna fight. Wanna tell these damn fools about their Master of Ceremonies. Gotta do something dramatic... He pulled the 45 and cranked a round into the high, ornate ceiling. "Boom!" Sudden silence fell. A spatter of plaster hit a nearby table. "Wanted to get your undivided attention!" Mack shouted into the void. "You *all* are veterans and I'm a damn veteran, but that asshole up there," he pointed at the podium, "is not one of us. Ace Collins is not what he says he is!"

The roar of reaction was not what Mack had hoped. There were curses, cries of fear and alarm and someone shouted for the police.

A booming voice in a microphone instructed hotel management to call for a swat team. Lights came on. Mack blinked, shielded his eyes and grabbed Grace by the arm. He began to move down an aisle between the tables toward the stage.

Grace fought his grip. "Now look what you've done!" she screamed in his face. "We're gonna get shot by a swat team!"

And a mob of angry, but gun-wary, men was slowly closing in on them.

Mack decided he needed to say something else. Again, he raised the automatic toward the ceiling. Screams began to rise. The angry men dropped back, unsure of this maniac with a gun. People dove to the floor and scurried under tables, but in the middle of all the anger, fear and emotion, Mack noticed something odd, something apart from the chaos. A split-second picture appeared. The people at the head table hadn't moved, they sat at their places and observed the confusion below as though they were at the theater with the roles reversed. But Ace Collins had turned to the side, reached down beside the lectern and lifted a glass to his lips.

Perfect. Fifty feet. Simple silhouette, half the glass. Teach that sonovabitch. Mack aimed, took a breath and calmly shot the glass to wet dust. "Boom!"

Screams reached a piercing crescendo.

Ace Collins was numb. He held up his hand and stared at shiny bits of glass and moisture glittering on his skin. He was too drunk to be frightened.

"Now every Goddamn body freeze!" Mack shouted.

"Oh, God help me, no!" Grace Faber moaned. "Who have you shot now?"

"No, Robertson, *you* freeze," an excited voice insisted from the doorway. "Put the gun on the floor and put your hands in the air. Do it! Now!"

The policeman had been close, heard the disturbance and the shot. Off-duty cops were working parking lot security for the El Conquistador Hotel. A first-year rookie near the front door of the hotel had come running at the first gunshot. He recognized Mack Robertson, the Mafia-loving ex-cop. He'd heard squad-room stories about this guy. His finger took slack in the trigger. Fear tickled rage and excitement. The finger squeezed a little more.

Mack stooped and placed his gun on the floor. He knew he was lucky not to have been shot after blowing the editor's glass out of his hand. He saw the young policeman - the deadly intensity - figured the room full of people had saved him. He watched the young cop and remembered his unpopularity with the department. Mack moved very carefully. "*Now* we'll get arrested," he muttered and put his hands above his head. But the cop wasn't satisfied. Mack watched the young policeman's finger turn white on the trigger. The rookie's face was pinched with tension and fear. "Oh shit, maybe I'm not gonna be arrested." Mack said and motioned slightly with his raised hands. 'Calm down! Nobody's been hurt here."

No one moved. People waited breathlessly to see what would happen next.

Mack felt hundreds of eyes, heard small movements, but suddenly felt all alone in the big, crowded room. The crouching cop and the rumpled man were frozen together in a hole of silence. Neither knew what to do next.

"You *do* have a way about you, Mister Robertson," a calm voice rasped from the doorway. Ex-Senator Lillienthal clumped forward slowly, painfully on his aluminum walker and moved between the police officer and Cormac Robertson.

The young officer lifted his pistol toward the ceiling and moved sideways for a clear shot at Mack. "Stand back, sir!" he ordered.

"There's no need for the gun, son." The gaunt old man waved a careless hand in the air and then quickly regripped his walker. "This man doesn't want to hurt anyone. And I have something important to say." He gestured vaguely at the head table fifty feet away and moved forward slowly.

A sigh of release swept the room like a breeze over fallen leaves.

The ex-Senator didn't say who he was. He didn't have to. Everyone in the room recognized the jutted head, long jaw and fierce eyes of the most famous Arizonan since Cochise. All eyes were drawn as the legend fought to walk past Mack and the policeman and through the tables to the stage. The walker popped and creaked under his struggling efforts as he lifted the aluminum legs a few inches from the thick carpet and fell forward again to its support. The struggle was painful to watch, and magnificent.

The ex-Senator looked like death had already begun to claim him; pale bones were visible under his vein-webbed skin and wisps of hair clung like smoke to the sides of his large head. He'd put on his General's uniform jacket for the occasion. Five rows of decorations and ribbons, swayed to his movements and looked too heavy for the skeletal old man. He reached a shaking hand to Mack. "Put your hands down and give *me* a hand or I'll never make it," he said and grimaced with obvious pain. Mack put his arm around the man and supported his weight while Grace moved quickly to his other side. They struggled to hold him up, but the Senator was proud and independent, he wanted to be *helped*, not carried. They adjusted and soon established a lift-swing-pause cadence to their difficult progress. Halfway to the front of the ballroom the ex-Senator paused a moment, allowed his weight to fall into their supporting arms and raised his hand for attention. The uniform jacket slid back and revealed a bony, scabrous wrist dappled with pale, knotted blotches. Mack caught a sere whiff of death, turned his head away, gritted his teeth and held the frail man erect.

"There is something I must say!" Harris Lillienthal announced in a loud, but quavering voice. "I must be heard and I'm going up there to that microphone."

The pop and click of the walker measured their slow, deliberate progress.

The young cop watched the trio move toward the stage, shrugged and put his pistol away. He picked up Mack's 45 and stuck it in his belt. Fear and anger were forgotten. He was as fascinated with the swelling drama as everyone in the room.

As the ex-Senator, ex-cop and ex-reporter continued their slow, steady progress toward the stage, the disorder grouped itself and sorted out. People picked themselves up, helped each other, chairs were righted, glass and broken china was kicked out of the way, stains were blotted and finally drinks were refilled. But the voices still murmured quietly as though in a church.

Senator John McGraw jumped down from the stage and went to help Harris Lillienthal. "Senator, I'm delighted you're here," he said. "It's been a long time."

Ace Collins was shaken. The large, belligerent detective was a dangerous madman. And why was the old fool bringing him up to the stage? Unsettling, but his veins still pulsed with cool fire. He could handle anything. He checked his face for cuts and wiped himself with a napkin while trying to recapture the feelings of exhilaration. The ex-Senator was here to join the throngs of veterans and needed a strong arm, but the woman had been muzzled and the violence seemed to be over. He collapsed into his chair and grabbed his wife's drink. Everyone else at the head table simply sat where they were and waited. There was nothing else to do.

It seemed like hours to Mack and Grace, but a few minutes later, with the added aid of burly John McGraw, they reached the stage just beneath the lectern.

"Turned out to be quite a night," the old man commented loudly. "Someone hand me a microphone." He glanced at Grace. "I've checked your story, talked to Chief Hobbs. He thinks Collins is the hit and run culprit, but says they don't have enough to charge him." He lifted his famous jaw. "Time for me to speak out."

Senator McGraw motioned for the cordless microphone on the lectern.

Ace Collins' wife stood quickly and handed the mike down to the Senator. Then Mrs. Collins turned and eyed her husband as though daring him to object. She sensed something unpleasant was about to happen to Ace Collins.

Her husband wasn't listening. He'd finished her drink and slumped in his chair, apparently still recovering composure from the near-miss pistol shot. His eyes were glazed and he was lost in a cool dream somewhere deep inside.

The big ballroom went silent. Glasses clinked and liquid sloshed as people settled in their seats, recharged their drinks and prepared for the next act in this rough, but exciting show.

• • •

The ex-Senator held the microphone close to his mouth, braced himself between the walker and the front of the stage and took a deep shuddering breath. "My name is Harris Lillienthal." he began as if they didn't know who he was. "I'm a retired Major General in the United States Air Force and I should have done this long ago." He gasped from his efforts and Mack reached to support him, but the Senator shrugged him off and continued. "This would have been the right thing to do years ago, but I didn't have the guts. Hell, I didn't know I was dying years ago."

Gasps and exclamations rippled through the packed room. People farther back leaned forward and cupped their ears to hear the amplified, but unsteady voice of this famous man.

Mack watched him carefully. The admission of death seemed to ease his pain. He shrugged the uniform jacket higher and relaxed back into Mack's, Grace's and Senator McGraw's waiting arms, allowing them to support his slight weight. The flow of words began again, more forceful, with greater feeling and vehemence. "They were brave men who flew over Viet Nam in the last years of the war. Some of you here, like Senator McGraw, flew into that maelstrom and came back. Some did not come back. Twenty-six years ago on a terrible autumn day over Hanoi young Lieutenant Collins bravely flew his plane into a hell of fire and explosion." The old man paused and glanced down at his uniform jacket.

Veterans in the audience murmured approval and nodded to their wives, indicating the slouching Ace Collins with admiration.

'Our brave young pilots," Harris Lillienthal continued, "knew half of their number would be killed or injured, but they ignored the danger and flew into hell for their country." He turned in the supporting arms and gestured up toward the Master of Ceremonies slumped in his chair. "And Lieutenant Collins flew into hell with the rest..."

Ace Collins appeared to pay no attention to the old Senator's tribute. At first he'd been worried when the addled fool began to speak, but he listened to the tale of Lieutenant Collins' heroism and swelled with smug pride. He knew what was happening and wasn't worried any more. He'd planned the invention years ago, just out of journalism school. Fired with lust for renown, he'd needed the flair and dash he didn't possess to make the right press, business and political contacts. And he'd needed to feel good about himself too. The preparation had been easy for a newspaperman. No one cared about the war. Do a little research, find a war-decimated unit with the right name on the roster - someone from the mid-west with no wife and kids and no distinguished relatives. Gather facts, read about pilots and air combat and wait a few years until the war was an unpleasant memory in most people's minds. After time, he'd hung a few dummied-up pictures on the office wall, answered a question or two with coy admissions and soon he was a war hero. The game had been ridiculously easy, especially in a hick state like Arizona.

Nearly all had wanted to believe. He suspected a few had had suspicions after a while, but they'd kept their mouths shut because of his power, and because, once they'd swallowed the hook, there was nothing they could say without looking foolish. And besides what was the point? Who was he hurting?

Harris Lillienthal had been one of the doubters. Ace *always* knew and was careful to curry a doubter's favor. Now the beauty of his plan was bearing fruit. There was no way the ex-Senator could expose Ace Collins without exposing his *own* participation in the decade-long fraud. After all, people would ask, wouldn't a Major General in the Air Force have known all along if someone was an Air Force veteran or not? Lillienthal was a has-been. He would make a dramatic speech, but in the end, he would bow to a comrade in arms and protect a fellow member of the Arizona elite. Ace Collins sprawled back in a semi-drunken haze and sucked on the small cut he'd received when his glass exploded. He believed his coolness under fire would only expand the legend of Ace Collins.

The bemused editor didn't know the Senator had nothing to lose.

"But *Lieutenant Collins was* ***killed***!" Harris Lillienthal bellowed hoarsely. He surged up in the supporting arms and pointed a quivering finger at the Master of Ceremonies. "Lieutenant Mitchell Collins, holder of the Air Medal and the bronze star for gallantry, is ***dead*** these many years. *You*, Ace Collins, are an imposter!"

Air crystallized. Faces froze. Glasses paused in mid-lift. *What did he say?*

Ace Collins sat up and tried to clear his mind. This could ruin him. He had to regain the control lost to the redheaded woman and that crazed, homicidal detective. He stood and looked out at the faces of the veterans and their wives, *his* people. He opened his arms, gestured inclusively, smiled and nodded his head down toward the old man. "We *all* love the distinguished Senator," his rich voice projected over the crowd, not needing the microphone. "My newspaper, the *Arizona Register,* has always been his friend. I have been an admirer of his since my boyhood, but alas, age has evidently taken its toll. We know he is very sick and I suspect he has taken leave of his senses. This is a joke, right, Sir?" Ace glanced down at the old man, but didn't wait for an answer. "With all due respect, if this terrible misrepresentation were true, why would a United States Senator and a retired Air Force Major General wait all these years to voice his objections?"

Mack felt the Senator turn toward the roomful of veterans.

Harris Lillienthal was shaking with anger. Mouth against the microphone, his words resonated throughout the large room. "Just hear me out, you people." he said. "My grandfather left the narrow hatreds of Europe and came to the Arizona frontier more than a hundred years ago searching for a place of new beginnings, a place of re-birth." The old voice soared to new strength. "This wonderful country was built on the concept a man can be anything he has the will and the grit to achieve. When Ace Collins began at the *Register* he seemed a hard-charging, pro-business, no-nonsense newspaperman. He supported the Arizona delegation in Washington and we all liked what he had to say. Right from the first, I suspected he was stretching the truth about his war record and I checked on him." Here the Senator paused for a few deep breaths and gathered himself for the cleansing. "To my eternal shame, I did nothing," he continued in a lower, more subdued tone. "I privately disassociated myself from Ace, but publicly I did nothing. Imagine it if you will, and forgive me. I was trying to do my job in Washington. The editor of a powerful newspaper in my home state was in my guilty debt. For years we held the secret. For years I was able to control the information and criticism of the largest information center in the State of Arizona without lifting a finger or saying a word. All I had to do was refuse to take his calls and avoid him socially to remind him I was aware of his secret."

The voice stopped. Dull echoes died in the deep carpets. Time ceased to revolve. Everyone waited for more, but there was nothing left.

The old man slumped exhausted. Someone pushed a chair close and he was lowered into it. The microphone fell to the carpet. His uniform jacket rode up to his chin and he nearly disappeared in the stiff, blue cloth, head sunk to the side, legs loose and spraddled like a corpse.

"That is preposterous," Ace shouted. "You all know me. I'll bet there are some of you who flew along with the 145th when we raided Hanoi. This old man needs a hospital and we need to hear from my good friend Senator John McGraw." The editor looked over the sea of upturned faces and knew from their angry but skeptical faces the ex-Senator's denunciation had been a little too much for the vets and their wives to believe. He decided he'd won.

Conversation hummed through the tables. *The old ex-Senator* ***did*** *look very sick. Maybe he* ***has*** *lost his faculties. A* *high-profile person like Ace would never think he could get away with such a blatant hoax, would he?*

Ace overheard some of the comments and *knew* he'd won. There was no way these people, who were almost like family after the last ten years, would believe the incoherent ramblings of an old fool, no matter what he *once* had been. Ace Collins had won. He motioned Senator McGraw to rejoin him on the stage and gestured for the microphone.

"I'm terribly sorry for these interruptions," he shouted, "but allow me to..."

Grace picked up the fallen microphone and blew into it. The harsh sound racketed across the ballroom like the breath of God and stunned Ace Collins to silence. Her voice was low, but rumbled with electronic muscle. "There's a man coming to Tucson," she said. "His name is Daniel Crawford. His number in Lansing Michigan is 624-7741. He's the unit historian of the 145th Fighter Wing and *he* doesn't know an Ace Collins. He doesn't understand how the man who died in the flaming cockpit of a phantom jet along with *his* son could give a speech in Tucson, Arizona twenty six years later." She paused and looked up at the stage. "Mister Collins, you are a coward and a despicable con-artist." She turned again to the crowd. "Don't take my word. Call that number in Lansing and speak to Daniel Crawford, or wait until tomorrow afternoon. I spoke to Mister Crawford this morning; he's flying to Tucson tomorrow. I intend to interview him for the story I'm writing about the arrogance of power and the downfall of a fraud!"

That information changed the mood. Shots and fights had goaded the crowd. They weren't calm and reasonable any more, not ready to accept on faith any more. They'd built to a reckless, ragged edge. The name and numbers convinced them all the raw anger and passion they'd witnessed was real. Suddenly people believed her.

Senator McGraw climbed back up on the stage and approached Ace Collins with his fists clenched. "That woman is telling the truth, isn't she?" he asked.

The Master of Ceremonies stood tall in his uniform. He still looked the part of war hero and fighting editor, but his broad face had twisted to the pained pout of a child who's lost a game. Odd, he thought. All the bluster had failed. The facade began to crumble when that stupid woman walked in front of his car. The daughter had pursued him like an avenging demon and one clear assertion of truth had finally broken the structure. No one doubted the redhead. Ace knew it was over. "Senator help me," he pleaded. "I've always made sure the *Register* endorsed you."

The stocky McGraw grabbed the taller man by the uniform lapels and hauled him away from the lectern. "You don't deserve to be up here! In fact, first thing tomorrow, I'm going to ask the U.S. Attorney if he can charge you with impersonating an officer." He shoved Ace Collins off the stage.

• • •

Mack stood in the middle of the noisy crowd at the foot of the stage and smiled at all the drama. He imagined Clyde Ralston laughing and shaking his head somewhere. But then a thought interfered with his enjoyment.

Clyde shaking his head? Could this victory be less than it appeared?

What had they accomplished? Mack remembered Harris Lillienthal *hadn't* mentioned Clyde Ralston or the car-bombing investigation. The Senator *hadn't* mentioned his brother, the Mafia or Emprise. There was no reason to. Why should he air family problems while exposing a fraud? Had a powerful man just fed the public a victim so they wouldn't bother looking any farther? Mack realized he'd watched the ruling class cut their losses in a way the newspapers would want to play down. And Clyde always said, "If it ain't in the paper, it ain't news."

CHAPTER SIXTEEN

THE GRAVEYARD

High desert winters are usually cool and dry and jealous of their rain. Tucson averages 320 days of bright sun each year and monsoon rains come at the crescendo of summer when wet clouds waiting on the mountains finally rush down to wash the valleys. But some years in early December gentle moisture fills the cool air, soaks in slowly and feeds the desert. On those days, fog seeps from the earth like smoke from small, wet fires and sometimes morning snow paints the shadowed sides of ravines and puffs the tops of cactus. This was such a year and Sunday was such a day - snow and fog in the morning, drizzle all afternoon. The desert was full of moisture and the streets of Tucson flowed like slow, shallow rivers. It was a perfect day for cemeteries.

Mack stopped fifty feet away from the men and the dark blue Lincoln parked in one corner of Evergreen cemetery with the trunk open. He sat a moment and looked around. Rain spattered his truck windshield just enough to keep slow wipers busy. Hard to see clearly for any distance, but he could tell they were alone in this green island in the middle of the city.

Evergreen Cemetery was a lush, fifty-acre plantation of carefully separated stones. All types of monuments rested together in no obvious order of size or age, from large pretentious obelisks with names like fresh wounds in expensive, polished stone to crumbled, time-smeared blocks, tilted and dark. The landscaping was exquisite with crew-cut grass, neatly tended flower beds and shade trees clumped near curbed lanes that sliced the somber fields into neat one-acre squares. Along the edges of the expanse, tall, dark Italian Cyprus posed against the pewter sky and in the corners willows bent heavy with moisture.

There were three men, one kneeling on a newspaper holding a large ornate wreath of roses. The other two stood apart, but were focused on the first. Finally, one looked up, noticed him and spoke to the kneeling man.

Mack was a little nervous without his 45, but he didn't dare go down to the police station and ask for it. He opened the small, cloth overnight bag and made sure nothing was showing under the pile of money. Everything ready. *Rain and mist filled the air*. He wondered if moisture would hurt anything? Experience told him dampness would intensify an electrical connection like a hair-dryer in a bathtub. He slipped the remote-control box into his jacket pocket and decided he was safe enough without his gun for what he had to do. After *that* nothing would matter.

He got put of the truck, hefted the bag and walked toward her grave.

Bruno Malatesta met him halfway to the gravesite. Wearing a tan, expensive-looking, knee-length coat and a green, Alpine-style fedora tilted over his face, the scrawny old man looked almost fashionable in spite of the rain. Bruno motioned one of his men to take the bag. "Put it in the trunk," he said.

"Everything I owe you's in there," Mack said.

The Don didn't glance at the bag. "You know I oughtta kill you," he whispered and pulled his coat collar together against the chill.

Mack didn't give a shit what Bruno said. He watched the henchman put the cloth bag in the Lincoln's trunk and couldn't help flinching when the lid closed with a metallic thud. Then his eyes drifted to the tall gravestone and newly turned dirt. He remembered Chickie on that last day, going shopping with a girlfriend, so happy and sexy; his friend without the wings.

Mack's eyes clouded. He rested a while in memories before coming back to the hard, deadly present - to the graveyard in the cold December drizzle. He realized Bruno Malatesta had been speaking.

"... was the only child I had," the Don continued. The raspy whisper rose impatiently as though trying to win an argument. "You was supposed to protect her!" The old Mafioso held a clenched fist to his chest. "I loved her more than life. It should be me over there, instead of her."

Right.

"Listen, you old son of a bitch!" Mack exploded. "I wouldn't have her dead for anything, but *you* killed her! You brought that crazy bastard, Vinnie Romano, to Tucson. He left a pile of bodies on your orders. All his killing was your doing!"

Bruno's pale, thin face reddened. Anger boiled. Nobody talked to him like that. "You gonna..." but the threat died in a welter of mixed emotion. This was the *only* other person alive who had been close to his daughter. Maybe he had a right. Maybe this big, dumb jerk was the closest he would ever come to a son. Bruno didn't know what to do, to say, or how to treat this situation.

The grief had nearly killed Bruno Malatesta. Nothing in his long, brutal life had ever affected him so. He wondered if he was going soft with age, or if he really *had* loved another person more than himself. At times in the past weeks he'd pondered his own death and realized he had finally lost control. His life had escaped him and his daughter had escaped him. He spent hours now with his mind closed to his surroundings, immersed in pain. The business and the ranch were not enough and the drift of his life was completely intolerable. Controlling things was the way he'd used his - and others' - lives. He tried to reason, to think things out, and always came up with the same answer: he was a lonely old man who'd lost the one person in the world who really cared about him. That sounded about right - simple, selfish and in character. But the pain was nearly unbearable nonetheless.

Bruno decided to make this man understand. "Look, Vinnie was brought here to torch some stupid political headquarters and blow up a guy's car," he wiped moisture from his face with a gloved hand. Because he was lost in grief and self-pity, Bruno Malatesta began the longest explanation of his life. "Nobody was gonna die. Only some paper and a stinking car was supposed to burn. Maybe Vinnie could scare a reporter and keep an eye on that rummy editor of ours...."

Mack couldn't help himself. "Editor of *yours?*" he interrupted.

"Yeah, ours. We been using Collins for years. He's nothin' but a bum. He used to take trips to Greenbaum's place in Vegas. He lost a lot of money, beat up a few whores, ran up a big tab. We did some checking on his past, found out about his record. He was a bum." The small, old man took a deep breath as he considered the low-lifes he had to deal with. "Collins got so bad he couldn't control the drinking, hurt some young prostitute real bad and was up to his eyes in markers. We wouldn't let him come to Vegas any more, so he did his gambling at the local dog track. He complained, but tough shit. He was *ours* to the hilt. Collins. *Ace* Collins," Bruno sneered. A boozer and woman-beater." Then the whisper became a thin voice. "Lately, he got so bad we was worried he wouldn't hold up his end on a big-money deal comin' up, so Vinnie had to follow the weak prick to keep him in line."

"So *that's* why Vinnie was behind the hit and run," Mack muttered.

Bruno Malatesta shrugged and continued his explanation. "So I understood Vinnie was supposed to be weight, but not *too* heavy. Know what I mean?" He glanced up and met Mack's eyes. "But one night, when Vinnie and Joseph over there," he indicated the bodyguard who'd brought the money to Mack's studio, "was following my daughter, something bad musta happened." He looked hard at Mack. "I dunno what. Nobody'll tell me, but it musta drove Vinnie nuts."

Mack knew. That was the night with Chickie in the bar parking lot. Vinnie had watched the pickup rock on its springs and heard her howls of pleasure. That was the night of the shotgun warning. A few weeks later was Chickie's trial and the public kiss. No wonder the jealous bastard had come unglued. He held the old man's eyes and glared. "Nuts, huh? More like stupid to blow up a reporter."

Bruno Malatesta wondered if the P. I. was wearing a wire, but couldn't let the insult pass. "Stupid, huh?" he jabbed Mack's chest with a surprisingly hard finger. "Nobody's *stupid* enough to blow up a reporter. Like I said, I heard Vinnie was told to blow up the car as a warning and the guy got there too soon. Or maybe not," he shrugged. "Some guys say young Vinnie used to like to watch fires and hear people scream. So he might've been a little crazy. What can I say?"

"Clyde Ralston was a good reporter," Mack said through gritted teeth. "And he damn sure had your laundry operation at the dog track pegged."

Now Bruno Malatesta was *sure* the big guy was wired. He'd been wrong to let his feelings out. Never again. New anger lashed his grief, but old habits finally took control, "You come here to my daughter's grave and try to play games?" he whispered. "You got no respect. Anybody wants to talk about business they gotta talk to my lawyer, Bernie Frank. I got nothin' more to say to you." Bruno turned and motioned his men to get in the car. They walked to the big, dark-colored Lincoln. One held the door while Bruno got in the back seat and the big one Mack recognized got in the driver's seat and started the car.

Twenty, maybe thirty feet away; time to finish this thing.

Mack took the shiny black box with the little lever from his pocket and held it level. His thumb pressed against the knobbed lever. The small stick began to move. Mack wanted to enjoy the moment, paused and thought about retribution. One shove and the signal flashes through the air to the receiver, closes a connection and nine volts from the fresh, new battery zing up to a detonator buried in dynamite. One shove and the old man responsible for everything was dead.

One shove.

Rain misted on the black metal box. Clear beads danced together and formed droplets. Mack's eyes lifted in thought, reached through gray curtains and found her name cut in rain-dark stone. *Beatrice Malatesta.*

Everybody called her Chickie. His friend. Not many left. How had his life spun so low? And hadn't he already had this conversation with himself? If he blew Bruno to hell, he'd get arrested. The police would know, they'd hound him to a cell somewhere. There'd be courtrooms, trials, arrogant lawyers and disinterested judges. Prison meant death for an ex-cop with balls. Balls? Bombs and booby traps were for cowards. This was not the way. The thumb relaxed. He couldn't do it.

The Lincoln moved slowly up the lane toward him. Mack hefted the remote box and decided to tell the sick, sad old men what was in their trunk. He walked to meet the slow-moving car and motioned the driver to open his window.

The tinted glass slid down. "Whaddya want now?"

Mack held up the shiny box. "This is Vinnie's. There's three sticks of dynamite in your trunk."

The bodyguard didn't understand. "Vinnie's dynamite is in the trunk?"

Mack nodded and handed him the remote control box.

"Is this another game you're playing?" The thin voice seeped from the darkness of the back seat like acrid smoke.

"Yeah, Bruno I guess it's all a game," Mack said calmly. Then he had an odd thought. "Speaking of games, tell me why kill those wonderful greyhounds when they get hurt or can't win races? Why not put them out to pasture somewhere?"

"What?" The whisper quivered in the air. "Whaddyou mean, wonderful? They're just dogs. You been in the rain too long. We kill the worthless ones to save a coupla bucks. Joseph, shut the damn window!" The tinted glass began to close.

"You bastard!" Mack said. He shook his head and yelled at the old driver. "Look, there really is dynamite in the trunk... and a blasting cap! The three sticks Vinnie Romano tried to use on me last week are in the bag under the money. That's enough to blow you to hell and I wouldn't drive around Tucson in wet weather with explosives and an electric detonator in my trunk if I were you."

"What!" The soft voice rose to a yelp, "Goddamn, Joseph, this guy's crazy! Get that bag out of the trunk and check it!" Bruno believed him.

"Right, boss," The driver said and turned off the engine. "I'll get the bag out of the trunk." He opened the door and got out.

Mack shook his head and banished the worthless anger. He turned away from the Lincoln, spat disgustedly on the wet ground and wondered about the what ifs.

What if Clyde hadn't cared about those greyhounds being shot? And what if Viola Faber hadn't been hit by that car?

Out of the corner of his eye he saw the bodyguard lift a little, black, keyless-entry device hanging from his ignition-key chain. He was going to unlock the trunk with an electronic key! "No!" Mack yelled. "Don't do that!"

The trunk popped with a "thunk." Mack dove for the grass.

"WHAM!"

Silverware jiggled two miles away. Beer shivered in glasses at the bar down the street. The rear-end of the Lincoln bloomed fire that seared nearby willow leaves to wet, brown curls and the explosion rocked older gravestones in their dirt. The car bucked forward, lifted three feet into the suddenly boiling air and broke in the middle; everything inside bubbled to wet atoms and blasted over three acres of graveyard. A ball of soot-streaked flame rose like Satan's head over Evergreen Cemetery and burned the rain to steam. Moments later, black smoke punched a ten-story fist in the sodden Tucson sky.

Noise had numbed his eardrums. Heat flung hard waves from the burning, but Mack wasn't touched. He'd felt the blast move his prone body and flatten the damp jacket against his back, but that was all. The closed car and opened trunk had contained the blast and channeled it upwards.

Sirens called in the distance.

Mack lowered his head, smelled sweet, green grass and the sour steam of mulched earth. Sometimes it was enough to just be alive. He gloried in the chill rain on his neck and wondered how the cops would figure this one…or how Grace Faber would cover the story.

Made in the USA